WARNER ✷ FOREVER

# Bride of the Beast

*When passion
is fierce,
resistance
is futile.*

# SUE-ELLEN WELFONDER

author of *Knight in My Bed*

# DON'T MISS OTHER NOVELS BY
# SUE-ELLEN WELFONDER

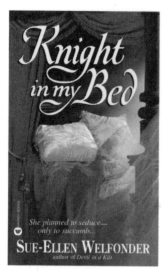

Available now wherever books are sold.

"Electrifying…provocative…lushly descriptive…a ripe and willing offering for romance readers who thrill over anything Scottish."

—RomanticFiction.com

# DEVIL IN A KILT

"A lovely gem of a book. Wonderful characters and a true sense of place make this a keeper. If you love Scottish tales, you'll love this one."

—Patricia Potter,
bestselling author of *The Heart Queen*

"A TOP PICK…Devil in a Kilt will catapult Sue-Ellen Welfonder onto 'must-read' lists. This dynamic debut has plenty of steamy sensuality, a dusting of mystery, and a touch of the paranormal."

—Kathe Robin, *Romantic Times*

"An engaging read. Very fast paced, with fascinating characters and several interesting plot twists….Devil in a Kilt is a keeper."

—Writers Club Romance Group on AOL

"As captivating as a spider's web, and the reader can't get free until the last word. It is easy to get involved in this tense, fast-moving adventure."

—*Rendezvous*

# Bride of
# the Beast

# Bride of
## the Beast

## SUE-ELLEN WELFONDER

**WARNER BOOKS**

An AOL Time Warner Company

WARNER BOOKS EDITION

Copyright © 2003 by Sue-Ellen Welfonder
All rights reserved. No part of this book may be reproduced in any form or by any electronic or mechanical means, including information storage and retrieval systems, without permission in writing from the publisher, except by a reviewer who may quote brief passages in a review.

*Cover design by Diane Luger*
*Cover illustration by John Ennis*
*Hand lettering by David Gatti*

Warner Books, Inc.
1271 Avenue of the Americas
New York, NY 10020

Visit our Web site at www.twbookmark.com

An AOL Time Warner Company

Printed in the United States of America

First Paperback Printing: January 2003

10 9 8 7 6 5 4 3 2 1

In loving memory of my father-in-law,
Gottfried Welfonder,
a man who bore a scar of his own and,
like Sir Marmaduke, carried it with dignity
and grace,
overcoming formidable odds to always stand tall.
He was a true gallant. A fine gentleman of the
old school, a hobby gardener and lover of books
who would have been so proud of me.
He lives on in my heart.

# Acknowledgment

Those who know me well are aware of my great love and passion for Scotland's hero king, Robert the Bruce. A great-hearted man who stood head and shoulders above other men, his bravery, valor, and compassion inspired love and devotion in those who followed him and grudging respect amongst those who did not. His flame burned so brightly its brilliance echoes through the centuries and still holds the power to enflame and capture the hearts of those who love Scotland. He certainly holds mine, and it is from one of his most shining moments, his great victory against the English at Bannockburn, that I took the inspiration for Sir Marmaduke Strongbow.

A true historical figure, Sir Marmaduke Tweng, was a notable English knight of the times, and known to be a man of honor. Unseated in the battle, he sought the Bruce, refusing to surrender his sword to any other. In respect and honor of Sir Marmaduke's chivalry, Robert Bruce invited him to his royal tent, entertaining him at his own table.

The real Sir Marmaduke was then released without ransom and allowed to return in peace to England. When I knew I wanted Duncan in *Devil in a*

*Kilt* to have a valiant English knight as his best friend, I remembered Robert Bruce and Sir Marmaduke. No other name for this character would do . . . and I hope both men would smile if they knew.

I want to thank the readers on my mailing list who fell in love with Sir Marmaduke in *Devil in a Kilt*. Their many requests for this special character to get a happy ending of his own is the reason this story came to be. This book is theirs as is my deep appreciation.

Heartfelt thanks go, too, to my wonderful agent and friend, Pattie Steele-Perkins, who loved Sir Marmaduke from the very beginning, and to my much-appreciated editor, Karen Kosztolnyik, for her great skill in helping me give him the best book I could. I am indebted to you both.

And, as always, to my handsome husband, Manfred, my own dragon slayer, for putting up with my late nights and harried dinners, and for making it possible for me to follow my dreams.

# Bride of
## the Beast

# Chapter One

## DUNLAIDIR CASTLE
## THE EASTERN COAST OF SCOTLAND, 1330

❖

"WHAT YOU NEED, my lady, is a champion."

Lady Caterine Keith stiffened her shoulders against her companion's well-meant counsel and continued to stare through the arch-topped windows of her tower bedchamber. Far below, the North Sea tossed and churned, its slate-gray swells capped with foamy white, its roiling surface a perfect reflection of her own inner turmoil.

A heavy curtain of silence fell between the two women until the crackle of the hearth fire and the hollow whistling of the brisk autumn wind reached almost deafening proportions.

Rain-laden gusts lashed at Dunlaidir's thick stone walls, rattling the window shutters with such fervor Caterine wouldn't have been surprised to see them ripped away and hurled into the sea.

A niggling sense of foreboding crept up her spine, its portent unsettling. A cloying premonition as cold and relentless as the dark waves battering the cliffs upon which Dunlaidir Castle so proudly perched.

Still, she said naught.

Her companion's suggestion didn't merit comment.

Undaunted by Caterine's silence, Lady Rhona gushed on. "I can see him before me: a mighty warrior who swings a

heavy sword, a belted knight of chivalric fame," she enthused, her young voice breathy with excitement.

Filled with flimsy fancies Caterine no longer believed in.
Mayhap had ne'er believed in.

Ne'er been *allowed* to believe in, much as her young
heart had once sought to cling to such foolish dreams.

"*My lady,*" Rhona implored, her tone striving to capture
Caterine's ear. "Think of it! A battleworthy knight able to
vanquish your foes with a mere glance. A brave man willing
to hew them to bits should you but ask. A great champi—

"I do not want a champion." Caterine swung around to
face her friend. "I desire naught but to be left alone."

"And I vow it is desire you need," the ever-romantic
Rhona blurted, then clapped a hand over her lips as a pink
tinge crept onto her cheeks.

Slipping behind Caterine, she yanked the shutters into
place, soundly closing out the rain and wind but plunging
the chamber into semi-darkness. "Of a mercy!" Rhona fretted, hurrying to light a brace of tallow candles. "I meant no
disrespect. 'Tis only you've never kno—"

"I know fair well what you meant," Caterine stated before the younger woman could babble on and embarrass
them both. Careful to keep her back straight, she sank onto
the cushioned seat built into the window embrasure.

It mattered scarce little that the slanting rain had dampened the finely embroidered pillows. She had more serious
issues to contend with than catching the ague.

"Your concern is appreciated but ill-placed." She leveled
a sidelong glance at Rhona. "I know much of men. Think
you having outlived two husbands has left me an innocent?"

"Of a certainty, nay, my lady." Rhona busied herself
lighting the remaining two candles. "No one is more aware
of your plight than I. Did I have aught but your best interests at heart, I would not urge you to send for a champion."

Caterine made an impatient gesture. "You speak of desire. I need a solution to my problems, to *Dunlaidir's* problems, not a man to warm my bed."

Leaning down, she scooped her tiny golden-brown dog, Leo, onto her lap. "I will not seek another man's attentions regardless for what purpose. Leo is the only male welcome in this chamber . . . as you are full aware."

"Leo cannot protect you from a man as powerful as Sir Hugh. The man is a dastard craven capable of great and vile knavery. Your only recourse is to ask your sister to send help."

"Think you one Highland warrior will deter a Sassunach earl with a garrison of mounted knights at his disposal?" Caterine drew Leo closer, taking comfort in the soft warmth of his little body. "Even a mighty MacKenzie would be hard-pressed to deter de la Hogue from gaining hold of Dunlaidir through marriage to me."

Rhona tilted her dark head to the side. "Then you must render such a union impossible by wedding your champion."

Indignation flared in Caterine's breast. "I do not *have* a champion. Nor will I impose on Linnet's good graces by asking her to send one. And were I so inclined, which I am not, binding myself to such a man is no more palatable than marriage to Sir Hugh."

"How do you know if you haven't met the man your sister will send?"

Caterine gave her friend a hard look. "I will not suffer a third husband, champion or otherwise."

Rather than answer her, Rhona began pacing the chamber, tapping her chin with a forefinger as she went. Caterine braced herself for the absurd prattle soon to erupt from the younger woman's pursed lips.

After years of companionship, she knew her friend well. Fingertapping always preceded outbursts of foolishness. Nonsensical ramblings that made sense to none save Rhona herself.

"I have the answer!" Rhona cried then, clapping her hands together. A triumphant smile lit her pretty face. "Simply pretend to wed the man your sister sends."

Caterine's brows shot heavenward. "*Pretend?*"

"Aye." Her friend beamed at her, obviously waiting for Caterine to comprehend the brilliance of such a scheme.

But Caterine comprehended naught.

Naught save her growing aggravation with Rhona's persistent beseeching.

Pushing to her feet, she carried Leo across the rush-strewn floor and set him upon his sheepskin bed near the hearth. "I fear you do not understand. I will not plead Linnet's aid nor will I enter into marriage again. Not even a false one," she said, meeting Rhona's exuberance with what she hoped sounded like firm resistance.

Firm and unbending.

Above all, unbending.

"But doing so is your best chance to rid yourself of Sir Hugh," Rhona wheedled. "Have you forgotten he vowed to obtain an order from his king forcing you to acquiesce lest you do not agree to the marriage by Michaelmas?" Rhona lifted her hands in supplication. "My lady, the feast of Michaelmas is long past."

"For truth?" Caterine plucked at an imagined speck of lint on her sleeve. "Since our stores have grown too meager to allow us to celebrate St. Michael's holy day, I hadn't noticed its passing. Nor do I care what Edward III declares I should do. Yet is this land held for young David of Scotland."

"Lady, please," Rhona entreated. "You have no other choice."

Stung to fury, Catherine clenched her hands to tight fists. Beyond the shuttered windows thunder sounded, the low rumblings echoing the churning bitterness deep inside her.

Rhona erred. She *did* have choices.

But, as so oft in her life, none appealed.

She'd e'er lived under a man's rule. Even now, newly widowed of an elderly but not unkind husband, a time when, at long last, she'd hoped to find some semblance of peace.

Peace and solitude.

Unbidden, Sir Hugh de la Hogue's thick-jowled face rose before her, his swinish eyes gleaming with satisfaction, the sound of his heavy breathing giving voice to his lecherous nature.

Caterine shuddered. The mere thought of the Sassunach's bejeweled fingers touching her made her skin crawl with distaste and sent bile rising thick in her throat.

"Lady, you've grown pale." Rhona's troubled voice shattered the loathsome image. "Shall I fetch the leech?"

"Nay, I am well," Catherine lied, flat-voiced.

Her dark eyes flooded with concern, Rhona rushed forward to grasp Caterine's hands. "Oh, lady, you must relent. The MacKenzie men are able and valiant. Your sister's husband is a fair man, he will send you the most stalwart warrior in his garrison."

Rhona released Caterine's hands and resumed her pacing. "Do you recall when he and your sister came for a visit some years ago? My faith, but the castle women were all aflutter did he but glance—"

"There is more to a man than the width of his shoulders and the charm of his smile," Caterine broke into her friend's prattle. "I will not deny my sister's husband is pleasing to the eye *and* possessed of a goodly character, but I warn you, Duncan MacKenzie is nowise a man by which to measure others. One such as he is a rare find. My sister is much blessed to have him."

For a scant moment, Rhona appeared duly chastised, but soon babbled on, her face aglow with renewed wonderment. "On my oath, more than his bonny looks impressed me. Ne'er will I forget how he unseated Dunlaidir's finest at the joust yet had the good grace to allow your late husband to best him."

Rhona aimed a keen-eyed stare at Caterine. "Aye, Laird MacKenzie is a just man. He will choose you a stout-armed warrior of great martial prowess, a man of honor to protect you."

*A man of honor.*

Caterine swallowed the sharp retort dancing dangerously near the tip of her tongue. She of all women had little reason to believe such a paragon existed. Though she'd seen many sides of the men who'd shared her life thus far, honor was one attribute most of them had sorely lacked.

Only her late husband had possessed a portion thereof.

A meager portion.

She folded her arms. "And you think this fabled and mighty Highlander, this man of honor, will lay aside his morals and agree to pose as my third husband?"

Rhona ceased her pacing and began tapping a finger against her lips. After a moment, the finger stilled and she smiled. "'Tis for honor's sake he will agree. What man of compassion, of worth, could refuse a gentlewoman in need?"

"Think you?"

"Of a surety." The tapping began again. "Especially if you inform the lady Linnet of the near ruination facing Dunlaidir. Once the severity of our situation is known, no man who abides by the code of chivalry would refuse you."

Saints cherish her, but Caterine didn't think so either.

*Then so be it* she almost said but a loud clap of thunder silenced her before she could form the words, stealing them as surely as if a swift hand had snatched them from her lips.

The thunder cracked again, a tremendous and resounding series of booms powerful enough to shake the floorboards and jar the window shutters.

The storm's black fury was a portent, she knew.

A sign the saints disapproved of the sacrilege Rhona would see her commit.

Or worse, an indication they agreed and frowned on her refusal to heed her friend's suggestion.

Something she would not, could not, do.

Caterine waited for the storm's rage to abate, then smoothed the folds of her woolen kirtle. Before she lost her resolve, her nerve, she drew back her shoulders and forced herself to speak the words she must.

"Lady Rhona, I respect your counsel and ken you are ever heedful of my welfare," she said, her voice surprisingly calm, "but I forbid you to breach this matter again. I will *not* send for a champion."

❧

A fortnight later, on the other side of Scotland, deep in the western Highlands, a lone warrior knight fought an invisible foe. Naught but the repeated swish of his great sword arcing through the chill predawn air marred the quietude.

Even Loch Duich, hidden from view over the list wall, gave itself silent, its dark surface no doubt smooth as finely fired glass for not so much as a ripple, not the gentlest lapping of waves on the pebbled shore could be heard.

The hour was well before prime, the time of day Sir Marmaduke Strongbow favored for practicing his martial skills. Soon, Eilean Creag Castle would come alive, the empty bailey would fill with a bustle of activity and his overlord's squires would trickle into the lists to join him, each one eager for him to prod and teach them.

Help them hone their own sword arms.

But for the moment, he stood alone.

Free to challenge his secret enemies, daring enough to face down the most formidable of them all: his own self and the self-created demons he carried within.

He paused and drew a deep breath, then swiped the back of his arm over his damp forehead. The plague take his cares. The saints knew he had much to be grateful for. Soon his own castle would be completed. Indeed, were he not a man who enjoyed his comforts, he'd move into Balkenzie now, this very day.

But he'd waited long years to raise his banner over a stronghold of his own, a few more months would not cost him overmuch. Then all would be ready and he would take possession of his new home.

A castle he and his liege, Duncan MacKenzie, had designed with great care.

A strategically ideal fortalice to guard the southern reaches of MacKenzie land.

A home perfect in every way save one.

Unlike his liege and closest friend, Marmaduke lacked a fair lady wife to grace his side. His would be a castle filled with men.

Quelling the bitterness that oft mocked him when alone, Marmaduke adjusted his grip on the leather-wrapped hilt of his sword and lunged anew at his unseen foes. Faster and faster, his blade rent the morn as he spun and dipped, thrust and withdrew, skillfully slicing his doubts and regrets to ribbons, banishing them one by one.

Until the morrow when he'd challenge them anew.

"*Sir . . .*" the soft voice behind him was little more than a whisper to his ears but a great roar to his warrior's instincts. Instantly lowering his sword, Marmaduke wheeled around to face the lady who'd addressed him.

"Fair lady, I am always pleased to see you, but you should know better than to approach a man's back when he wields a sword," he said, sheathing his steel. "Nor do I believe it is good for you to be out in the chill morning air."

"I am fit enough," Linnet MacKenzie countered, drawing her woolen cloak more securely about her before resting one hand upon her swollen middle. "I would speak with you alone, now before the others stir."

Sir Marmaduke peered intently at his liege lord's lady wife. Her lovely face appeared more pale than it should and lest the vision in his good eye was failing him, she bore faint purple shadows beneath her eyes.

Nor did he care for the rapid rise and fall of her chest. That she'd overtaxed herself in seeking him out was painfully obvious.

"Lady, you should be abed," he admonished, trying to sound firm but unable to be duly stern with her. "Does your husband know you are about?"

The two bright spots of pink that bloomed on her cheeks gave him his answer.

"I must speak with you," she said again and placed a cold hand on his forearm.

"Then let us adjourn into the chapel." Closing his fingers over her hand, Marmaduke led her toward Eilean Creag's small stone oratory. "It is closer than the great hall, and private." He gave her hand a gentle squeeze. "I would know you warm before I hear what troubles you."

He'd scarce ushered her inside when the oratory's heavy wooden door burst open behind them. With a resounding crash, it slammed against the whitewashed wall.

"Saints, Maria, and Joseph!" Duncan MacKenzie fumed, ignoring the sanctity of the holy place. Ill-humor swirling round him like a dark cloak, he made straight for his wife. "Have you taken leave of your senses, woman? 'Tis in your bed you should be. The entire household is searching for you."

Bracing fisted hands on his hips, he tossed a dark glance at Marmaduke. "Why am I not surprised to find her with you?"

"Becalm yourself, my friend," Sir Marmaduke urged, his smooth baritone voice unruffled by the other man's bluster. "No harm has befallen her."

"Were she your lady, I vow you would want to know her safe, too, Strongbow." Duncan ran a hand through his disheveled hair.

"I care for her as if she were my lady, as you know." Marmaduke placed his own hands on his hips. "Her well-being is of equal import to me. There is naught I would not do for her."

"My lords, please." Linnet leaned back against the recumbent stone effigy of a former MacKenzie warrior, one hand still resting upon her midsection. "I have told you naught will go wrong this time. I know it. My gift has shown me."

Duncan MacKenzie peered hard at her, his handsome features as set-faced as his stone-carved ancestor. After casting another dark look in Marmaduke's direction, he swung about and strode across the oratory.

Dropping to one knee, he busied himself lighting a small brazier in the corner near the altar. "Have you told him?" he asked his wife when he stood.

"Told me what?" Marmaduke quirked a brow.

"My lady would ask a favor of you." Duncan slanted a glance at Linnet. "A great favor."

Sir Marmaduke did not care for the way his friend spoke the last three words, nor the ghost of a half-smile suddenly twitching the corners of Duncan's mouth, but such reservations scarce mattered. He'd championed the lady Linnet since her arrival at Eilean Creag Castle five years ago, and she'd repaid his gallantry a thousandfold and then some.

In her presence, he could almost imagine himself rid of the scar that marred his once-handsome face and believe that, once more, his *looks* and not his well-practiced charm could turn female heads.

Indeed, he revered her greatly.

"No request Lady Linnet may ask of me is too great," Marmaduke vowed. Turning to her, he made her a slight bow. "How may I serve you, my lady?"

Rather than answer him, Linnet cast her gaze downward and began scuffing her toe against the stone flagging of the chapel floor.

Ignoring his friend's ill-concealed bemusement, Marmaduke lifted her chin, forcing her to look at him. "Name your desire and it is yours," he sought to encourage her.

She met his gaze but kept her silence. After a moment, she moistened her lips and said, "Now that I stand before you, I fear it is too much to ask."

Marmaduke shot a glance at Duncan then immediately wished he hadn't. His handsome friend now wore a bold smile.

A too bold smile.

Somewhere in Marmaduke's gut, a tiny shard of unease broke loose, a jagged-edged shard that jabbed his innards and grew more unpleasant by the moment.

The smile on Duncan MacKenzie's face grew as well and the gleam in the Highlander's eyes bode ill for Marmaduke.

He turned back to Linnet. "I cannot help you if you will not tell me what it is you wish me to do."

"I cannot," she whispered, shaking her head.

"And *you*?" He glanced at Duncan, alarmed to see that his friend's smile had now turned into a silly grin. "Will you divulge this great secret?"

"With pleasure," Duncan said, the mirth in his voice undeniable. "My lady wife's sister is in need of a champion."

Marmaduke lifted a brow. "I see naught amusing about a lady in need."

"Then you will go to her aid?" Linnet asked, the tremor of hope in her voice going straight to Marmaduke's heart.

Iron control hid the mounting tension swirling in Marmaduke's breast, the dull thudding of a heart filled with other plans than riding off to slay some unknown gentlewoman's dragons.

"Think you I am the man to champion her?" his valor asked before his heart could stay his tongue.

"We know of no one better suited," Duncan answered for his wife. "The lady Caterine is newly widowed and plagued by a persistent Sassunach earl who would press her to marry him. Her holding, Dunlaidir Castle in the east, is sorely failing. Without help she will lose both the peace she craves and the home she holds dear."

He laid his arm around Linnet's shoulders and drew her close. "Nor is it in our best interest in these troubled times to see as strategic a stronghold as Dunlaidir fall into English hands."

Marmaduke rubbed the back of his neck. "Why not send a contingent of able men to assist her? Many are the warriors you could choose from."

"Name one whose sword arm is mightier than yours." Duncan's fingers kneaded the woolen folds of his wife's cloak. "Who better than you, a Sassunach of noble blood, to challenge an English earl? You, with your martial skills and smooth tongue, are more suited to the task than a score of fighting Gaels."

Unconvinced, Marmaduke shook his head. "A full retinue would serve her better than a single man."

"Dunlaidir is possessed of a stout garrison. They only need direction. A firm hand and a clear-headed man to lead them. Nor can I spare more than a few men with Balkenzie nearing completion. Nay, Strongbow, the task falls to you." His smile gone, Duncan aimed a penetrating stare at Marmaduke. "Or would you deny my lady's sister of your skill?"

"You know I cannot. It is only—" Marmaduke broke off, near stumbling over his unusually thick tongue. He ran a finger under the neckline of his tunic. The chapel's somewhat stale, incense-laden air closed in on him with such pressure he almost gagged. "I'd planned to take occupancy of Balkenzie soon."

A lame excuse, to be sure, but he'd so hoped to hoist his own banner before Samhain.

"I'd hoped to see the castle well-garrisoned and secure, secure for *you*, before the onset of winter," Marmaduke said, his words casting down the gauntlet of his hesitation.

"And so you shall." Duncan's flashing smile reappeared. "Upon your return."

Marmaduke opened his mouth to rebuke the notion but Duncan silenced him with a raised hand. "You shall be snugly ensconced within your own keep's walls by Yuletide at latest," his liege declared. "Then we shall all gather at Balkenzie's hearth and drink to my lady's health."

"And to our bairn's," Linnet added, the conviction in her voice and the look in her eyes doing more to dismantle Marmaduke's resistance than all her husband's bold words combined.

As if he sensed his friend's crumbling will, Duncan clamped a firm hand on Marmaduke's shoulder. "It will not take long for a strong-armed warrior such as yourself to have done with one odious Englishman?"

Taking his hand off Marmaduke's shoulder, Duncan gave him a playful jab in the ribs. "A fat and ill-fit one, if we choose to believe the tongue-waggers."

Marmaduke swallowed hard.

Something was amiss.

And whatever it was, it slithered up his back, cool and smooth as a snake, to curl deftly around his neck and squeeze ever tighter the longer he watched the merry twinkle dancing in his friend's eyes.

Marmaduke frowned. "There is something you are not telling me."

Linnet glanced away and Duncan stretched his arms over his head, loudly cracking his knuckles. His fool grin widened. "As ever, I can hide naught from you," he said, his deep voice almost jovial. "I've long suspected you're as blessed with the sight as my fair lady wife."

Lounging against the cold stone form of his long-dead forebear, Duncan finally tossed down his own gauntlet. "Lady Caterine wishes you to pose as her husband. Only if word spreads she has wed a third time, does she believe she can rid herself of her current woes."

Marmaduke stared at his friends, too stunned to speak. None would deny he revered them well. Saints, he would gladly give his life for either of them. But what they proposed went beyond all lunacy.

Impossible, he should *pose* as any lady's husband no matter how great her plight.

No matter who her sister.

Never had he heard anything more preposterous.

"You ask too much," he found his voice at last. "I will offer the lady full use of my sword arm, and I shall guard her with my life so long as she requires my aid, but I will not enter into a blasphemous relationship with any woman."

He bit back a harsher refusal on seeing the hope fade from Linnet's eyes. "By the Rood, Duncan," he swore as softly as he could, "you should know I am not a man who would pretend to speak holy vows."

"Then don't," Duncan said, triumph riding heavy on his words. "Make the lady your bride in truth."

*Make the lady your bride in truth.*

His friend's parting comment lingered long after Duncan and his lady took their leave. Like the repetitive chants of a monk's litany, the taunt echoed, increasing in intensity until the words seemed to fill not just his mind but the close confines of the oratory as well.

*Make the lady your bride . . .*

By the saints, did his liege mean to mock him? Duncan MacKenzie knew better than most of the loneliness that plagued Marmaduke in the darkest hours of the night, was well aware of Marmaduke's most secret desire: to have a fine and goodly consort of his own once more.

And a sister of the lady Linnet could be naught but a pure and kindly gentlewoman.

Was there indeed more behind his friends' insistence that only he can champion the ill-plighted young widow?

A tiny smile tugged at the corner of Marmaduke's mouth

and a pleasant warmth the likes of which he hadn't felt in many years began to curl round his heart.

*Make her your bride . . .*

The words came as a song now.

A joyous one.

Hope beginning to burgeon deep within his soul, Sir Marmaduke went to the altar, sank to his knees, and bowed his head.

Sometime later, he knew not how long, a shaft of multicolored light fell through the chapel's one stained glass window to cast a rosy-gold glow upon his folded hands. The beam of light illuminated his signet ring, turning it to molten gold and making the large ruby gleam as if set afire.

Then, no sooner had the colored light appeared, did it vanish, extinguished as if a cloud had passed before the rising sun.

But Marmaduke had seen it rest upon his ring.

A portent from above.

Once more, Marmaduke murmured a prayer. One of thanksgiving and hope. When at last he rose, his decision was made.

As soon as he could muster what few men Duncan could spare him, he would journey across Scotland to aid a damsel in need, a lady he would offer not only his warring skills and protection, but marriage.

A true one.

If by God's good graces, she would have him.

# Chapter Two

❖

$\mathcal{C}$OLD RAIN POUNDED the outer stairs to Dunlaidir Castle's towering keep, drenching not only the steep stone steps but also the coarse woolen cloth of Lady Caterine's mantle. Preferring a soaking to the bone to moving aside and bidding entry to the Sassunach earl standing before her, she met his arrogance with the most impervious mien she could muster.

"You will forgive my lack of hospitality, Sir Hugh," she said, letting the iciness of her voice convey her true sentiments. "The hour of vespers is soon upon us and I fear our humble pottage of dried peas and water is not worthy of your exalted palate."

"Lady, a dry crust of bread would taste as savory as a haunch of well-roasted boar if consumed in your fair presence." Sir Hugh de la Hogue gave her a thin smile. "Would you cease your pointless attempts to resist me, I shall see you dine on naught but the finest of victuals for the rest of your days."

Giving heed to the urge to put distance between herself and Sir Hugh's thick-girthed, overblown self, Caterine stepped backward until she met the barrier of the hall's half-opened door.

With a cool grace she fought hard to maintain, she kept her head raised despite the rain coursing down her forehead.

"What I sup upon is no concern of yours," she countered her suitor's flowery speech. "With our cattle all but vanished these past months, I've grown quite fond of watery soups and seabird pasties."

"A pity your tenants have stooped so low as to steal from their own lady's herd." The earl made a great pretense of studying the rings adorning his small fingers. "Would you honor Edward's writ and pay obeisance to me as your new lord husband, I should deal swiftly with the thieving peasants."

"There are some who doubt our own people have aught to do with our dwindling fortunes." She leveled a contemptuous stare at de la Hogue. "A good night to you, sir. You will excu—"

Sir Hugh's arm shot out, his fingers curling in a tight grip around her elbow. "Very dear lady, I enjoin you not to wax too proud," he admonished, his features growing stony, the glint in his eyes, menacing.

He cast a meaningful glance at the walled courtyard below. His henchmen arrogantly sat their restive steeds, the horses' iron-shod hooves making hollow clacking noises on the rain-slick cobbles.

To a man, the mail-clad knights' appeared every bit as hostile as their lord, their hands hovering threateningly near the hilts of their swords in a silent but not to be mistaken show of might.

A warning only one as desperate as Lady Caterine would dare ignore.

His steely grip on her arm became a sickeningly slow and far too intimate caress. "It would cost you dear to vex me. Already I grow weary of standing in the rain. Do not provoke me further."

Caterine lifted her chin a notch higher. "Then pray do not delay your departure. I wish you Godspeed on the journey to the rainless refuge of your own hall."

She met his glare with equal arrogance, not even allowing herself the much-needed relief of blinking away the raindrops dripping onto her lashes and into her eyes.

More annoying still, her futile efforts to free her arm from the earl's grasp seemed to fuel his amusement.

And whet other interests.

Releasing her, he let his piercing gaze rake the length of her. His breath quickened, its foulness coming at her in fast little bursts while his generous paunch rose and fell with ever-increasing rapidity.

As if he could see beneath the scant protection of her well-worn garb, he gawked openly at her breasts and other secret places, blatantly ogling the way her drenched garments plastered themselves to what curves remained on her too-thin body.

Her skin crawled with distaste when his gaze fastened on the vee of her thighs. Nigh slack-mouthed, he brought his hand to the hilt of his sword. But unlike his dour-faced knights whose hands simply hovered near their weapons, Sir Hugh let his fingers toy with the leather-wrapped grip as if fondling a woman.

Or himself.

Caterine shuddered. Either image was too repulsive to ponder. Too reminiscent of other English hands doing other vile things, black memories best left buried beneath the weight of years.

A great heaving began in the depths of her stomach, roiling waves of aversion, flaming hot one instant and bitter cold the next, but she remained standing tall. Unyielding, and hopefully not showing the dread Sir Hugh and his minions ignited within her.

"You would be wise to remember I hold power of pit and gallows," he warned, at last returning his gaze to her face. "My authority extends over your dominions as well, Lady Caterine."

His fingers still plucking at the globular pommel adorning the hilt of his sword, he shot another swift glance at his men. "Word has come to me that some females in your family carry the mark of a witch-woman. I am not disposed to examine you and see for myself if you bear such a blemish. Yet." He paused for emphasis. "Should you displease me fur—"

Her restraint near to snapping, Caterine stepped forward, thrusting her face within inches of Sir Hugh's. "Would that I possessed such powers," she seethed, too riled to stay her tongue. "I-I'd turn you into a toad!"

"I was not aware you possessed such heated blood," the earl crooned, a look of high amusement on his face. "Mayhap I shall enjoy sating myself on you after all," he taunted, his tone dripping bravado. "I am a man of great appetite."

"I'd sooner face the pangs of purgatory than pleasure you," Caterine vowed, hoping he mistook the quaver in her voice for scorn rather than dread.

"My lady will never grace your bed, sirrah!" Rhona pushed through the door opening to glare at the earl. "'Tis spoken for, she is. A great Gaelic warrior will arrive any day to make her his bride. Her sister's husb—"

"*Rhona!*" Caterine whirled on her friend, the remaining shards of her fast-slipping dignity smashed by the unexpected blow of Rhona's fool pronouncement. "Be still—"

"I speak the God's own truth," Rhona cried, waving aside Caterine's objections. "My lady's sister is married to the MacKenzie of Kintail, the Black Stag, a much-feared warrior. He has negotiated a most agreeable marriage for my lady. She will wed the most accomplished knight in his garrison. A *champion*."

All amusement vanished from the earl's face. "Is this so?" He stared at Caterine, his expression a strange mixture of anger and incredulity. "Would you dare defy Edward of England's wishes? He has vowed to bestow your hand upon an Englishman—upon *me*. He desires Dunlaidir safe, in English hands. 'Tis his behest."

"Your king's desires are of scarce import to me, his behests even less. I hold no allegiance to an English sovereign." Caterine's distaste for all things English churned wildly inside her. "Nor will I wed a Sassunach," she said, her pulse racing faster with each spoken word. "Not you. Not *any* man of that tainted blood. I would sooner rot away of the pox before I'd allow Dunlaidir to fall into English hands."

"So you do mean to wed some Highland cateran?" Sir Hugh challenged her, his tone rife with autocratic vehemence. "Edward will be much displeased. *I* am displeased."

Caterine pressed her lips together. The blackguard could take what answer he might from her silence. She'd get her own answers, from Rhona, as soon as the odious earl and his grim-faced poltroons removed themselves from her holding.

Sir Hugh's heavy-lidded eyes narrowed to slits. "I do not believe you." His stare bored into her, relentlessly stripping away the last vestiges of pride she'd wrapped around herself in preparation of this latest confrontation with her foe.

"I do not think you'd accept another husband, Englishman or Gael." His knowing gaze pierced the darkest hiding places of her soul. All vestiges of his earlier attempts at chivalry gone, he derided her, "'Tis too dried up and peppertongued you are to give yourself to any man no matter his blood. Nay, I do not believe it."

"Be gone and may the pestilence take you!" Rhona dashed forward, near shoving the earl down the stairs. "Go now lest I fetch a blade and run you through myself!"

"Rho—" Caterine tried to call back her loyal companion, but her voice failed her, dying in a sputtering croak, her throat suddenly as dry as Sir Hugh had accused her manweary body of being.

As if he'd known exactly where to aim his hurtful words.

More shamed by his slurs than she cared to admit, she stood stiffly at the top of the stairs and watched her friend hasten Sir Hugh down the steps. At the bottom, he shook off Rhona's flailing arms and glared up at Caterine.

"Know this, I shall watch for the arrival of this Gaelic warlord," he vowed, his voice reeking of venom and spite. "*If* he arrives, I will be present at your nuptials for only then will I believe it."

Dashing the rain from his forehead, he glowered at her. "Should he not appear within a fortnight, I shall claim this holding, and you, for myself. Fourteen days, lady, and then my patience will come to an end."

Cold anger rolling off him, he stalked across the rain-shrouded courtyard to where his men awaited him, their solemn faces still set in hard, disapproving lines.

Caterine stood as if carved of stone, her hands clasped tightly before her, as Sir Hugh and his cavalcade rode out of the courtyard and across the narrow bridge of land spanning the deep chasm between Dunlaidir's promontory and the cliffs of the mainland, a formidable headland now all but invisible behind teeming sheets of rain and mist.

When the last clattering noises of their departure faded into nothingness and naught more could be seen of them, she relaxed her stance, finally allowing her shoulders to sag.

Only then did she push the wet strands of hair off her forehead and dash the cold moisture from her face. Only then did she allow herself to tremble. Her entire body shook, quivering uncontrollably like brown and dried leaves on an autumn-bare tree.

"Lady, come inside," Rhona soothed, once more at her side. She placed an arm around Caterine's shoulders and urged her toward the shelter of the waiting hall. "In fresh and dry clothes and with a belly full of hot soup, you'll feel better. You must not heed Sir Hugh's insults. He is furious because you've thwarted him."

"Aye," Caterine said, her voice flat. "And now it would appear you seek to thwart me. Or dare I hope your fool babble about Linnet sending a champion was just that . . . babble?"

"I never babble." Rhona flashed her a smile as they

stepped into the dimly lit great hall. "I may meddle now and then, but only for your own good," she added, pausing to secure the iron-studded door.

"And what meddling have you done?" Caterine probed, her blood thrumming with a new kind of agitation. "If you've ignored my wishes and sent for a champion, you've not only thwarted Sir Hugh, you've thwarted your own ill-considered plans as well."

"How so?" Rhona tilted her head to the side. "I may not have had the fullest right to send a courier to your sister, but once Duncan MacKenzie's man arrives, you will see the wisdom of having a brave master-at-arms to guard you."

"By pretending to marry me?" Caterine could scarce push the words past the gall in her throat.

Rhona gave her a look so guileless Caterine almost swallowed her ire.

Almost.

"Did you consider that with Sir Hugh in attendance it will be exceedingly difficult to hold a mock ceremony?"

Rhona's dark eyes rounded and her lips formed a little o. When she glanced at the blackened ceiling rafters and began tapping a finger against her chin, Caterine took leave of her, crossing the near-empty hall as swiftly as her rain-soaked clothes would allow.

She did not care to hear whatever new pearls of wisdom her companion cared to bestow on her. Truth tell, she already had a strong suspicion of what they'd be.

Rhona would smile, get that misty-eyed look on her face, and declare a true marriage to Linnet's chosen champion might prove to be the best solution to Caterine's woes.

Aye, such would be the words to tumble from her fanciful friend's too-loose lips.

Rhona would chatter on until she persuaded, or needled, Caterine into believing her. Trouble was, Caterine did not want to believe her.

Not this night.

Nor on the morrow.

And most especially not as long as a tiny and annoyingly persistent ember of hope nestled deep inside the hidden-most reaches of her lonely heart.

❧

Something was sorely amiss.

Nigglings of unease crept up and down Sir Marmaduke's spine as he surveyed the imposing curtain walls of the cliff-top fortalice that was the end of a long and harrowing journey.

Dunlaidir Castle sprawled high atop a massive rock formation jutting far into the North Sea, and attached to the mainland by a narrow ridge of land. Sheer cliffs fell straight to the sea on all sides making the stronghold near impenetrable . . . if only someone manned the empty gatehouse guarding the castle's sole means of access.

But naught more daunting than wheeling seabirds, a few hardy weeds, and a stiff sea wind, occupied Dunlaidir's most important defense.

No men-at-arms strode forward to question the approach of Sir Marmaduke and his four companions.

The gatehouse stood neglected, leaving the way into the stronghold's more vulnerable inner heart wide open.

Twisting in his saddle to face the four Scottish knights behind him, Marmaduke peered sharply at each man. Their faces reflected his own wariness, and their posture as they sat their sturdy Highland garrons bespoke keen alertness.

"Duncan claimed Dunlaidir possessed a stout garrison," Sir Lachlan, the youngest of the Gaelic warriors commented. "It would seem they are no more."

Marmaduke nodded at the recently dubbed knight, then cast another quick glance at the seemingly deserted gatehouse. In the distance, Dunlaidir's crenellated curtain walls rose proud against an iron-gray sky, yet not one sentry could be seen patrolling the impressive ramparts.

"All appears abandoned, yet I vow unseen eyes have observed our every move since we crossed onto Keith land this morn." He withdrew his great sword and rested the sharply honed blade almost casually across his thighs. "I do not believe those eyes belonged to the village folk who scuttled away the moment they caught sight of us."

As one, his companions nodded their heads in agreement. Sir Alec, the oldest and most battle-proved of the Gaels, spat on the rocky ground, then drew the back of his hand over his mouth. "An ill wind blows here," he said, unsheathing his own blade. "I don't like it."

The grim set of the other men's jaws assured Marmaduke they shared Alec's sentiments.

And his own.

A dark wind indeed lashed against the cliff-top stronghold, a formidable force of destruction threatening to plunge Dunlaidir's massive walls stone by stone into the cold waters of the sea if naught was done to stave the rampant air of decline so rife all around them.

Even the demesne's vast surrounds had seemed contaminated by an oppressive cloud of dereliction: the once far-reaching arable fields lay untilled and fallow, what few livestock they'd spotted had been small in number and ill-fed, the tumble-down cottars' dwellings forlorn and cold-looking . . . as empty as the cluster of stone cottages forming the village and now, the gatehouse and castle as well.

What few villeins they'd come upon had skulked out of sight, their haggard faces averted as if they feared they'd be cast to stone did they but glance at Marmaduke and his small contingent of MacKenzies.

Saints, the contamination swirled so thick Marmaduke could taste its foulness on his tongue.

Then the sharp yipping of a dog broke the silence. The sound came from afar, a welcome reprieve in a gray and chill world that presented itself more inhospitable than Marmaduke had dared imagine.

"It would seem at least one inhabitant of Dunlaidir has stirred himself to greet us," he said, prodding his mount toward the gatehouse and the narrow spit of land looming beyond.

"Come, ready yourselves to make the little fellow's acquaintance and, if the saints are with us, that of Lady Linnet's fair sister," he called over his shoulder as his companions fell in behind him. "May God have mercy on the perpetrators if aught has befallen her."

Without further ado, he rode beneath the raised portcullis, its steel-ended spikes benign and useless hoisted as they were and without a watchful guard to drop them in place should an enemy dare attempt to breach this first crucial defense.

But the only eyes to witness their passing were those of roosting gulls and a few fleet-footed rodents.

In the distance, the dog's barking issued anew, closer this time, and Marmaduke kneed his horse, impatient to close the remaining distance to Dunlaidir's impressive but unmanned curtain walls.

There, too, a second portcullis was locked into a fully useless position near the arched ceiling of yet another tunnel, this one carved into the very rock upon which the fortalice was built.

And here, too, no one barred the way. Nor did vile-reeking refuse or boiling oil come sailing down from above to impede their passage.

Nothing stopped them at all until they clattered into Dunlaidir's inner bailey and Marmaduke came face to face with the lady whose heart he meant to win.

The woman he so hoped would banish his long years of loneliness and put an end to countless nights spent sleeping in a cold and empty bed.

She stood not far from the outer stairs, a tiny golden-brown dog clutched in her arms, a look Marmaduke could only call serene resignation clouding what would surely be an angel's face if only she would smile.

His men drew up beside him, reining in their smaller garrons in well-rehearsed formation, two to his right, two to his left. Marmaduke took scant notice of them, so blinded was he by the vision before him.

The indrawn breaths of his companions left no doubt that they, too, were struck witless by the lady's stunning beauty and grace.

In truth, *two* lovely damsels stood before them, one tall and fair, the other pleasingly rounded and dark, but Marmaduke knew instinctively which one was his.

The fair one.

He knew it deep in his gut, and not simply because of the faint resemblance she bore to her sister.

It was the look of vulnerability in the depths of her dark blue eyes that skewered his heart and gave away her identity. The invisible burden of long-borne unhappiness, an unseen but palpable air of resignation weighing on shoulders she held so proud and straight.

His liege and his wife had spoken the truth. Here *was* a gentlewoman in dire need of a champion, and perhaps in more ways than they'd been aware.

And with a driving urgency Marmaduke hadn't felt in more years than he cared to count, he wanted to champion her, burned to chase the shadows from her face and replace them with the glow of happiness . . . of *love*.

His heart thumping against his mailed hauberk with the exuberance of a green and untried youth, Sir Marmaduke swung down from his saddle and strode purposely toward her. At his approach, she set the small dog upon the cobbles. The wee animal immediately bared his teeth and growled at Marmaduke, but scampered behind Lady Caterine's skirts as he drew near.

Recognizing the MacKenzie colors flung proudly over the approaching knight's shoulder, Caterine steeled herself against the man's formidable appearance and offered him her hand when he dropped to one knee before her.

Caterine's old nurse, Elspeth, the woman who'd raised her and her sisters, had e'er impressed them never to judge a man—or woman—by appearance alone.

What mattered was the goodness of one's soul, one's inner worth. The scar marring this champion's otherwise arresting face was surely the remnant of some noble deed or a battle worth fighting.

Even though she'd rather he hadn't come at all, she knew Linnet would never send her a man she could not trust, a man she could not rely on—even if his countenance might prove a bit difficult to gaze upon.

More than scarred, he appeared blind in one eye as well, but the expression in his good eye, a fine brown one, seemed a look of honest compassion and warmth. And, much to her surprise, the touch of his calloused hand as he lifted hers to his lips for a kiss, proved not entirely unpleasant.

Ne'er had a man touched her in such a courtly manner. For truth, he held her hand with so much tenderness, Caterine suspected he feared she might shatter beneath his fingers.

"Fair lady," he began, his *English-accented* voice instantly banishing the faint fluttery feeling his gallantry had stirred inside her. "Allow me to introduce myself," he addressed her in fluid Gaelic, perfect save the coloration of the Sassunach speech of his mother tongue.

"I am Sir Marmaduke Strongbow, soon of Balkenzie Castle in the west, come from your sister, the lady Linnet, to champion you."

"You are English." The words came out sharp and cold, colder than she'd intended.

At once, the knight released her hand and stood. He inclined his head. "Yes, my lady, I am of English blood, but my heart beats only for Scotland. You have no cause to fear me."

"I do not fear the English." Caterine gathered her skirts for a swift retreat. "I revile them," she said, then whipped around and sailed toward the stairs, her little dog, Leo, fast on her heels.

She mounted the steps two at a time, desperate to put the massive oaken door and the hall's thick walling between herself and the Sassunach knight her sister had had the ill-sense to send her.

Unfortunately, it was not as easy to run from the disturbing flare of raw and needy emotions his gallantry had breathed to life deep inside her.

*Chapter Three*

⚜

*H*OURS LATER, CATERINE sat in stiff-lipped silence at Dunlaidir's high table and tried hard to ignore her keen awareness of *him*. Even without looking directly at him, simply knowing him beneath her roof sent a strange warmth tingling through her.

Pretending indifference, she smoothed her fingers along the edge of the heavily scarred table. Torchlight fell across her late husband's elaborately carved great chair, calling conspicuous attention to the chair's emptiness.

And the gravity of her plight.

"Are you troubled by his scar?" Rhona's softly spoken words cut through the quiet.

With a start, Caterine snatched her hand from the deep knife scorings she'd been tracing with idle fingers. A silly occupation chosen solely to keep from sneaking covert glances at him.

She met her friend's probing gaze. "Think you I am so shallow?"

Rhona ran a slow finger around the rim of her wine chalice. "Nay, though the frozen-faced expression you've worn since he entered the hall gives me cause to wonder."

Annoyance, hot and tight, coiled in Caterine's breast. "You should know what it is about him that aggrieves me."

"*There is more to a man than the width of his shoulders and the charm of his smile.* Your own words, my lady," Rhona reminded her. "Mayhap there is also more to a man than his blood? He did come to champion you."

"He is English."

"He was sent by your sister."

Something snapped inside Caterine. "Then he holds Linnet in such thrall she's forgotten why I would never welcome an Englishman into my home."

Rhona's expression softened. "I doubt she's forgotten, though I wish you would." Reaching across the table, she pressed Caterine's hand. "This man is no craven. I cannot see him hurrahing over the land raping innocents and dirking men before their wives' eyes. Truth to tell, he seems quite gallant."

"An *English* gallant."

"You cannot blame him for the villainy of others, what was done to you years ago and by—"

"English soldiers, and more of them than I could count," Caterine finished for her, steeling her back against a deep-seated shame still as laming as the long-ago day she'd been so violated.

Half-turning in her chair, she pretended to study the nearby hearth fire. Anything but peer across the table and see sympathy in Rhona's eyes. Instead, she risked a glance at the broad-shouldered English knight. He sat at a table on the far side of the hall, quietly conversing with his men, holding their rapt attention with the same mastery his sheer presence dominated the vastness of Dunlaidir's great hall.

Vexation welled in Caterine's breast. Even seated, his bearing marked him as a confident man.

A leader of men.

A charmer of women.

Indeed, if not for the scar running from his left temple to the corner of his mouth, he would have been quite handsome. Marred or not, he made a striking figure and possessed an air of calm assurance she would have found most appealing were he not a Sassunach.

He looked her way then, almost imperceptibly inclining his head as if he knew she'd been perusing him. Knew, too, the conclusion she'd reached.

Her cheeks flaming, Caterine swung back to face Rhona. All traces of commiseration gone from her pretty face, the younger woman gave her a slow smile.

*A knowing smile.*

Caterine cleared her throat. "I did not mean to imply he is ungallant," she said, her voice hoarse with the admission.

It was the best she could do.

Rhona cast a slant-eyed glance at a glum-faced man slouched in the shadows near the hearth, "He is more courteous than some Scots nobles I shall not name," she vowed, low-voiced.

"Sir John has good reason to brood with de la Hogue and his minions housing in his keep," Caterine defended her late husband's friend. "We can be grateful we weren't visited by so ill a fate and it wasn't Dunlaidir Sir Hugh took possession of when he came north. God's curse on the dastard!"

"And I say a pox on any who frown into the soup you offer them," Rhona hissed, her unflagging loyalty coaxing an inward smile from Caterine's heart.

Outwardly, she kept her expression impassive. "Sir John has suffered much. He lost everything."

"Were it not for your hospitality, he would be sleeping in the heather." Rhona warmed to a favorite topic. "'Tis glad of a bed and dry roof he aught be, and not raise his brows at the food you set before him."

Tossing a glance at the English knight, she pressed her point. "*He* is quality. Did you see how tactfully he declined Eoghann's best attempts to seat him with us? You know he only refused because you made it obvious his presence anywhere near the dais end of the hall would displease you."

Caterine drew a long breath. She had noticed his chivalry

toward Dunlaidir's doughty seneschal, just as she'd noted the smooth gallantry he'd displayed when kissing her hand . . . and the way her heart had leapt at his touch. But the sour taste of her own bitterness weighted her tongue and kept her from making any such admissions.

Instead, she tore off a chunk of coarse dark bread—*peasants' bread*—but found herself tearing it to bits rather than eating it as she'd intended.

"Nor did he or his men rumple their noses at the salted herrings and cabbage soup Eoghann set before them," Rhona continued her litany of praise. "They surely received finer fare at Eilean Creag. I vow your sister's alms dish is better fil—"

"Cease, please." Caterine reached across the table and lifted Rhona's hand away from her chalice. "And stop running your finger around the rim of your glass. It's annoying."

As if to rile her even more, Rhona snatched the chalice, and, twisting around, lifted her glass at the English knight and his men. When they raised theirs in return, she flashed Caterine a triumphant smile.

"Aye, most gallant," she declared, plunking down her chalice with a grand flourish.

"He is English." The objection sounded peevish even to Caterine's own ears. "A Şassunach."

"A man." Rhona leaned forward. "One who went down on bended knee to offer his services to you. A Sassunach, aye, but with four stout-armed Gaels standing beside him. They do not seem to mind his English blood."

Smiling benignly, she trailed a finger along a particularly deep scar in the tabletop. "You should joy in such a brave man's attentions."

*I did,* Caterine's heart acceded.

His mere touch had warmed her in places she'd thought forever cold . . . until she'd heard his voice.

She stiffened, bracing herself against the disconcerting

sensation she was teetering on the edge of a bottomless chasm and about to lose her balance. "Not all at Dunlaidir are as enamored of our visitors as you and Eoghann," she said, tossing a pointed glance at the empty laird's chair.

The seat of honor usually occupied by her grown stepson, James Keith.

"Or have you seen James since their arrival?" Ire danced atop each word Caterine spoke. "He's abed. He said his leg pains him, but I suspect the real reason for his absence is because he, too, isn't pleased my sister sent a Sassunach to help us restore Dunlaidir's failing fortunes."

Irritation flashed across Rhona's face but she masked it with an artful shrug. "Would he exercise his leg more, he'd have no need to resent the arrival of those more able to defend his home than he."

"You are too hard on him. It is not his fault that he is lame."

"He is not lame, he was kicked by a horse." Rhona blew out an impatient breath. "Naught would ail him at all if he'd stop pitying himself."

Pausing, she cast a meaningful glance at the scar-faced champion. "*There* is one who manages quite well, and with a more daunting impairment than an aching leg."

Caterine, too, peered across the hall, irritation making her bold. She stared hard, her open gaze searching every inch of the man's strapping build, looking for faults and finding none. Worse, she couldn't deny the ease with which he conversed with Eoghann, one of the household's most loyal retainers.

Even more telling, the slump-shouldered seneschal stood straighter the longer he listened to whatever the Sassunach knight was saying to him. Bobbing his head in apparent agreement, Eoghann talked profusely and gestured about the darkened hall.

Like her sister and Rhona, the seneschal had clearly fallen under the man's spell.

A condition she would not fall prey to.

Rhona yanked on her sleeve. "Have you noticed the bulge of his arm muscles and the size of his shoulders? You could do worse, my lady," she purred. "Many are the maids who would crave his favor."

"Who would not notice his fine form?" Caterine snapped, annoyance loosening her tongue. "Or do you believe me as withered as Sir Hugh claims? Beyond taking note of a man so tall, so broad-shouldered?"

Rhona gave her a wounded look. "Ne'er would I call you—"

"I am neither wilted nor blind," Caterine cut off Rhona's prattle before the younger woman sent her into a fine fit of pique. "Acknowledging the flawlessness of his form is no different from admiring the fine lines of the great warhorses his accursed countrymen ride about on."

*Except no English destrier had ever set her heart a-flutter with one gallant hand kiss.*

Rhona reached across the table and poked her arm. "In the shadows of the hall, it's almost possible to imagine what he must've looked like before he was scarred."

"In mercy's name!" Caterine gave her friend a sharp look. "It matters naught to me what he looked like then or . . ." she trailed off to stare at the Sassunach's table.

He and his men now stood, and his companions had donned fur-lined cloaks. Two of them followed Eoghann toward the hall's vaulted entrance, disappearing with the seneschal into the cold night while the other two made for the turnpike stairs.

Stairs that led to the wall-walk.

They meant to patrol Dunlaidir's ramparts.

Caterine's breath caught at the unexpected lurching of her heart. An unaccustomed sense of being protected, *cared for,* cloaked her with all the warmth and comfort of a much-used and well-favored blanket.

An unfamiliar emotion, but powerful enough to wage fierce battle against her pique.

Too many were the months she'd gone to bed wary, half afraid to sleep lest she awaken to find de la Hogue's henchmen looming over her.

Or worse, the earl himself.

A sharp kick to her shin shattered the troubling image. "He—is—coming," Rhona mouthed the warning, barely finishing before the tall English knight stood before them.

"Ladies," he said in the fluid tongue of the Highlands, his voice deep and smooth.

Her own tongue too clumsy to form the simplest response, Catherine slid a glance toward the hearth, hoping support from Sir John, the only person at hand who loathed the English as soundly as she, but the sore-battered lord had slipped from the hall. The deep shadows where he'd stood loomed black and empty.

Wishing she could vanish as well, Caterine peered up at her sister's ill-chosen champion. "Good sir," she managed, her voice declaring her wariness despite the genial greeting.

Their eyes met and held, and a strange giddiness tripped through her. A curious breathlessness she'd never before experienced. Light from a nearby torch cast a sheen on his dark hair and glanced off the steel rings of his mail shirt, gilding them in such a way that his powerful arm and shoulder muscles appeared all the more pronounced.

Faith, but he unsettled her.

". . . ill suits you . . ." he was saying, but his proximity flustered her so thoroughly she caught but a snippet of what he'd said.

She blinked. "If what ill suits me?"

"If he speaks with you," Rhona answered for him.

Not heeding her friend, he gave Caterine a half-smile, and in the flattering play of light and shadow, that one brief smile clearly revealed that Sir Marmaduke Strongbow, late of England and soon of Balkenzie Castle in the west, had once been a very handsome man.

A very handsome man indeed.

"I said I regret if speaking with me ill suits you, but, nevertheless, we should do so," he said, his tone brisk, less warm than she remembered. "Now, before I join my men on the ramparts."

He studied her, and the intensity of his perusal gave Caterine the disturbing impression he peered into her very soul, saw all her deepest secrets.

Her dreams.

And laid them bare one by one.

Something . . . anger? frustration? . . . flashed across his face, but vanished before she could decide. "Lady, I assure you my intent in coming here was not to aggrieve you."

Heat surged up the back of Caterine's neck. "I know full well why you are here."

"But you did not expect a Sassunach."

*You did not expect a man whose visage would give you worse nightmares than those already plaguing you.*

"I did not expect any man," she said, surprising him. Pushing back from the table, she stood. "Aye, we must speak, but not here. I will accompany you to the ramparts."

Marmaduke didn't flinch when she ignored his proffered arm. "After you, my lady." He made her a stiff bow instead, carefully hiding how deeply her slight had stung him.

Calling on every shred of his hardihood, he followed her through the darkened hall, pausing only to retrieve his fur-lined cloak before ascending the curving stairs behind her. When they reached the top landing, he swirled his heavy mantle about her shoulders.

"It will be cold on the parapets," he said simply, his fingers brushing the smooth warmth of her nape, the silken weight of her braided hair cool against the back of his hands.

To his relief, neither of the two men he'd sent to patrol

the ramparts watched this segment of the wall-walk. Naught but the chill dark and countless winking stars greeted them.

The night sky, a frigid wind, and the steady thumping of his heart.

Going straight to the crenellated wall, Marmaduke rested his hands on one of the square-toothed merlons and gazed out at the sea. A crescent moon rode low on the horizon, its pale glow casting a thin ribbon of silver across the night-darkened water.

Gripping the cold stonework, he let the wind's stinging bite ease the tight knot of heat Caterine Keith's rejection had put at the base of his neck.

Steeling himself, he turned to face her. "Your sister sends you warm greetings and bade me to assure you she is well," he began, purposely omitting any mention of Linnet MacKenzie's tender state, as had been the lady's express wish. "She would like—"

"I doubt, sir, that you wished to speak to me about Linnet," Lady Caterine said, the agitation humming in her voice at stark contrast to the haunted look in her eyes.

A goddess of ice. Beautiful, proud, and mightily agitated.

She drew a deep breath, her annoyance palpable. "What I must tell *you* has naught to do with her either."

Marmaduke leaned back against the merlon and folded his arms. "Then speak your heart. I am listening."

"My heart, sir, has even less to do with it." She looked sharply at him, escaping tendrils of her hair dancing on the night wind. "See you, there has been an error. My sister was duped. I did not send for you. My companion did. Lady Rhona. My dearest friend and worst enemy."

"Your worst enemy?" Marmaduke lifted a brow, noted the tiny lines at the corners of her eyes, the shadows beneath them. "I think not, my lady. I doubt she deceived you with ill intent."

"She stirs mischief without thinking of the consequences."

Heeding an irresistible urge to be near her, Marmaduke pushed away from the merlon and went to stand before her. "And are the consequences so unpalatable? For truth, I have been here but a few hours and can already see you are in grave need."

She cleared her throat. "I did not want a champion, nor am I desirous of a . . . man."

"And now your friend has plunged you onto a forcing-ground where you must suffer both."

She nodded, a flash of anger sparking in her beautiful eyes. But she said nothing. She simply stared at him, her chin lifted in clear objection to everything he was and had hoped to do for her.

*With her.*

Hoping the dark hid the muscle jerking in his jaw, Marmaduke fought the overpowering urge to lower his mouth to hers and silence her objections with a kiss.

A fierce and claiming one.

"Lady Caterine, 'tis well I know I am not a man to turn heads and steal hearts," he said at last, the words coming from the devils that rode his back and not his own true self.

A self still handsome and unmarred.

"But scarred or nay, English or not, error or otherwise, your sister asked me to champion you and I shall," his true self said. "I gave the lady Linnet my word. Denying her would be as impossible as not drawing breath."

"Aye, impossible," Caterine agreed, the sheer futility of her situation as annoying as the inscrutable look on her unwanted champion's face. She peered at him, willing him to say the words she'd hoped to hear when she informed him he'd come in error.

Summoned in a wild scheme spun by her meddlesome friend.

But rather than announce his swift departure, he watched her with an unbelievably vexing air of imperturbability and baldly informed her he intended to champion her whether she wanted him to or not.

Worse, thanks to Rhona's underhanded machinations, she had little course but to accept his help.

His leaving would only hurl her into more troubling waters.

"Lady, I desired to speak to you privily because I must inform you there is one request your sister made upon me which I cannot fulfill," he said then, his rich-timbred voice mellifluous as a bard's.

Spoiled only by its trace of Englishry.

Caterine arched a brow, taking refuge from the lure of his oddly soothing voice in a studied veneer of indifference. "And what request of Linnet's might that be?"

"My shoulders are good and wide, Lady Caterine. Well able to bear any burdens troubling you," he said, more disturbed by her chilly reception than he cared to admit. "Any and all burdens save one. I will not pose as your husband."

An indefinable expression crossed her face, and before it could blossom into something he'd rather not see, Marmaduke clasped his hands behind his back and began pacing the narrow breadth of the wall-walk, his gaze fixed on the far horizon.

Anywhere but on her face.

Anything but risk seeing her horror when he proposed a true marriage.

"Four well-blooded warriors came with me," he said, hoping only he heard the slight quaver in his voice. "We bring you full use of our sword arms and our steadfast protection."

He stopped before her then, clenching his hands against the unsettling notion he was about to make himself look a fool. "And I, Lady Caterine," he rushed on before his nerve took flight, "I would offer myself to you. Not as a pretend husband, but as a true one."

She gasped. A tiny, breathy sound, barely audible above

the wind. Not that she needed words to convey her revulsion. Her whole demeanor, her wide-eyed stare, screamed her displeasure louder than any winter gales that could race in from the sea.

"No." The terse rejection ripped a deep chasm between the man he'd once been and his dreams of ever being that old self again.

"And why not?" the sons of Beelzebub made him ask.

To his astonishment, a tiny wry smile curved her lips. "Not for the reason you suspect, I assure you." She lifted her hand to his face, tracing his scar with a touch light as air.

Marmaduke stiffened. No woman had ever touched his scars. Not the slashing one that marred his once-handsome face, nor the countless welts criss-crossing his back.

No woman until now and the gentleness of that one fair touch near melted his heart.

She withdrew her hand, a look of confusion flashing across her face as if she, too, had felt something. But the look passed so quickly it may never have been there at all.

"Your scar does not bother me," she said, her bluntness taking him off guard. "I find your looks . . . arresting," she added, surprising him even more.

She drew a deep breath. "My situation has changed since Rhona took it upon herself to plead my sister's aid. It is indeed a true husband I now require, not simply a man willing to play the role," she said, her pronouncement sending hope thundering through Marmaduke.

"But I cannot accept you as that man." The plain-spoken words dashed his newly revived spirits as thoroughly as if she'd plunged him over the rampart wall and into the sea.

"Still, I wish you to know my feelings have naught to do with your face." She smoothed a fingertip along his scar once more, the gentle touch torturing him this time. "Nor is it anything you have said or done, not you personally. 'Tis your English blood alone. That, sir, is a taint I cannot overcome. My sister should have known better."

For the first time in Marmaduke's life, words failed him. Her frank avowal careened through him, mocking him and taking staunch sides with his demons.

And stealing his ability to do aught but stare at her.

"Lest I lose my courage," she plunged ahead, clearly unaware of the raw anguish twisting inside him, "I would beg one favor of you."

"Name your desire and it shall be done." The chivalrous words came of their own volition, spoken as if by a stranger, though the voice was undeniably his.

She peered at him, a profoundly earnest look in her deep blue eyes. "As my sister surely told you, Sir Hugh de la Hogue, who has been plaguing me for months, has vowed he will soon take me, and this holding, by force."

"de la Hogue?" Marmaduke's gut clenched at the mere mention of the abased churl's name.

"You know him?" The simple words seemed to etch worry lines onto her face.

"I have met him, yes," Marmaduke admitted, the pulsing knot at his throat sending tendrils of heat into his shoulders and up his neck. "In the early years of my knighthood—at the English Court. A more debauched dastard never walked this earth, may the devil roast his hide."

"He is the reason I must ask your help. Not so much for myself, but to protect James, my stepson," Caterine said, mentioning the young man Marmaduke had heard of but not yet seen.

The heir to Dunlaidir.

"Should Sir Hugh make good his threats, he would have done with James before the nuptial vows passed my lips. And with James dead, his two-thirds of Dunlaidir revert to me . . . to Sir Hugh if I am forced to wed him."

*And the black-hearted whoreson would have your life as quickly.* Marmaduke kept his suspicions to himself, but from the look on Lady Caterine's face, she knew this danger without him giving voice to it.

"You needn't fear de la Hogue, my lady." Marmaduke held her gaze, his own cares, his disappointments, forgotten. "He will regret the day he drew his first breath if he dare so much as look at you. On that, I give you my solemn oath."

Averting her gaze, she stared into the darkness, the brisk sea wind whipping his cloak about her legs. "Thank you," she said, her pride doing visible battle with her need of him.

Marmaduke struggled with his own battered pride. "I came here to help you, but if it is a husband you seek and you will not wed me, then what it is you would have me do?"

"Your men," she said, looking back at him. "I beseech you to persuade one of them to marry me. A marriage in name only . . . to protect Dunlaidir and my stepson."

Marmaduke frowned at the rekindled hope rising in his breast upon hearing her words.

"Fair lady, I must disappoint you." He hated the way her face fell, loathed himself for seeing his own good fortune in the crushing of hers.

She looked down. "They are already wed," she said, correctly guessing the reason for his denial.

"All save Lachlan, the youngest. And even he is spoken for. The lad left behind a much-loved maid who eagerly awaits his return."

She closed her eyes for a moment. "Then there remains only you."

Marmaduke nodded, his throat too thick to speak.

"Then so be it," she said, the moon's pale light falling full on her face and leaving no doubt about her distaste for the notion. "But a marriage in name only."

Easing his cloak from her shoulders, she handed it to him, then slipped through the half-opened door before he could stop her.

Or warn her he meant to win her heart.

He took a step forward, but already she was gone, swallowed up by the darkness of the stairwell, leaving him alone.

Alone with the cold night and the heavy weight of his mantle, still warm from her body heat, indelibly branded with her scent.

For a long while, Marmaduke remained where he stood and looked out at the sea, the cloak clutched in his arms. The moon was higher now and, may God forgive him for taking advantage of her plight, so were his spirits.

Lifting a calloused hand to his face, he retraced the path of her fingers. Saints, he'd almost swear his scar yet tingled from her touch.

He knew his heart was still affected.

A marriage in name only.

Marmaduke blew out a long breath. He wanted more, so much more. He wanted to love again . . . and to be loved.

But a marriage in any form was better than none at all. It was a start . . . a beginning.

More than he'd dared hope for a scant hour before.

Once more, his fingers strayed along his scar, moved gingerly over the ever-tender lid of his bad left eye.

A dark oath welled up inside him, but he willed it away. Now was not the time for pity. And in truth, his scars were paltry compared to the deep ones Lady Caterine carried inside.

His were on the outside for all to see, while hers were hidden within.

Unseen and grave, but by no means permanent like his.

Hers could be erased.

Banished with time, care, and the abiding love of a man willing to give her his heart.

And able to conquer hers.

Squaring his mail-clad shoulders, Marmaduke made a pact with the silent night. "I will vanquish her scars and win her love," he vowed, the distant stars and the impervious sea his only witnesses.

"And none shall stop me," he said to the darkness in his heart as much as to the blackness surrounding him.

*Not even her own sweet, proud self.*

*Chapter Four*

❦

$\mathcal{I}$N THE GLOOM of earliest morn, nothing stirred in Dunlaidir's cobbled bailey save thick tendrils of mist curling along the ground and drifting between the stronghold's deserted outbuildings like a phalanx of spectral sentries.

Naught disturbed the breaking day save the hiss and zing of Marmaduke's sword arcing through the silence. A furious onslaught aimed at the demons e'er lurking along the darkest edge of his soul.

Vile miscreations endlessly eager to mock him with every disappointment, failure, or loss he'd ever had to bear.

The whoosh of his slashing blade echoed and re-echoed in the empty bailey, a fierce battle cry against a fate that had been anything but kind.

His unseen tormentors besieged at last, the fire in his gut quenched for another day, Marmaduke lowered his steel and drew a deep breath of the tang-kissed air.

Chill damp air, brisk and invigorating.

Flavored with hard-won peace.

Blessed quietude marred only by the fog-muffled roar of the sea, his own heavy breathing, and the faint rustlings of someone slinking about behind him.

Swinging around, he caught a fleet movement in the shadows even as a long-bladed dagger sped toward him.

With a swift agility few could match, he hurled himself to the side just as the blade whistled past his shoulder and skittered to a halt not two feet from where he'd stood a moment before.

His sword at the ready, he ran toward the sounds of a scuffle, chaos erupting all around him. Shouts rang out from above as young Sir Lachlan and Dunlaidir's seneschal tore down the outer stairs in hot pursuit of a third man now racing toward the farthest seaward wall.

Fast gaining on him, they chased the intruder, drawing swords as they ran. Marmaduke pursued a dark-cloaked figure using the confusion to flee along the bailey wall.

"Halt you!" he called, closing on the man. "Cast down your blade and show yourself."

The figure stopped but crouched deeper into the murk rather than come forward. "I have no blade," he rapped out, anger crackling in his voice. "I've been disarmed."

Only then did Marmaduke see the discarded broadsword, its gleaming length bright against the damp cobbles. His gaze on the cloaked figure, he kicked the sword aside. "Your name," he demanded, approaching the other. "Speak lest I force you."

At the answering silence, Marmaduke hoisted the interloper a good foot off the ground, pinning him roughly against the wall. "Who—are—you?" he bit out, emphasizing each word with a jab of his sword tip into soft flesh beneath the man's chin. "Speak, whelp, or make ready to greet your Maker."

"Christ God, release me," the man wheezed, indignation blazing in his dark eyes. "I am James, lord of this holding."

Marmaduke loosened his hold but didn't release the other man. Much as he wanted to. The swordless knave reeked fouler than an overripe cesspit.

"For truth?" Marmaduke's brow arched heavenward. " 'Tis a rare young lord who smells so rank." Careful not to breathe too deeply, he used the tip of his blade to ease back the woolen cowl hiding the man's face.

Freed of the concealing hood, a much younger man than he'd expected shook back a thick mane of dark hair. A mere stripling, scarcely blooded to be sure, the wretch glared at Marmaduke from a face that would've been noble-looking indeed were it not so twisted in anger.

"So you are James." The bristling lad could be no other. "The elusive young master of the castle."

Easing him to the ground, Marmaduke lowered his sword. He clamped a comradely hand on James Keith's shoulder. "Saints, lad, where do you sleep or can it be you never bathe?"

"'Tis not my stench I wear." Panting, James wrenched free of Marmaduke's grip. "The foulness clung to the miscreant who tried to kill you. I saw him and another man emerge from one of the latrines and gave chase."

"Two men?"

James nodded. "They took off in different directions. I sent Sir John after one and I caught up with the other, your assailant, just as he sent his blade flying."

Marmaduke jerked his head toward the discarded sword. "And how did you lose your blade?"

A dark scowl drew the young man's brows together. He blew out an agitated breath. "We struggled. He knocked my sword out of my hand. I . . ." Trailing off, he cast a rankled glance across the bailey to where Lachlan and Eoghann engaged the intruder.

With apparent ease, they were backing him into the curtain wall. Clearly, the offal-encrusted assailant posed no challenge to Lachlan and the surprisingly well-skilled seneschal.

Equally clear was James's shame at being bested.

Marmaduke returned his attention to the troubled-faced lordling. "Mind you, had your watchfulness not alerted the keep, who knows what damage yon blackguard may have wrought."

"I but displayed my ineptness." Jerking around, James limped away, his humiliation slinking after him, as plain to see as the exaggerated way he dragged one leg.

Marmaduke started after him but froze in place when a sharp, pain-filled cry rent the air. Dunlaidir's luckless heir forgotten, he spun around, his anger cresting at the scene unfolding atop the far seaward wall.

Eoghann grappled with the intruder, the furious clang of clashing steel giving bold voice to the ferocity of their struggle. Lachlan lay sagged against the base of the wall, a dark stain spreading across the left side of his tunic, his sword still clutched in his hand.

With an enraged roar, Marmaduke pounded across the bailey. In one fluid movement, he vaulted up behind his would-be assassin, eager to give the varlet a fine taste of his metal. The whoreson whirled on him, swinging his blade in a vicious arc meant to kill.

Marmaduke countered the blow with ease, deflecting his attacker's sword with such sheer force the man lurched wildly to the side. His eyes wide in stunned disbelief, he toppled through the unprotected notch between two of the wall's merlons.

A keening scream, silenced almost before it'd begun, bore a blood-curdling testament to his fate.

Breathing hard, Marmaduke cast down his steel and peered over the wall. The man's body sprawled spread-eagled across the jagged rocks far below, already slipping into the hungry sea.

His boat, a hide-covered coracle little bigger than a cockleshell, bobbed on the waves.

Marmaduke dragged his arm over his brow. "He must've scaled the cliff, then climbed up a latrine chute to gain entry."

"Black-hearted son of a sow!" Eoghann raged beside

him, his breathing labored. "'Tis a well-deserved end he met, smeared with dung. I never trusted that one, a queersome fellow he was."

Marmaduke glanced at the seneschal. "You knew him?"

"Aye. Cadoc was his name and he hailed from Wales." Eoghann's eyes glittered with contempt. "A knight errant he called himself. A misbegotten cur, I say."

"Of a certainty," Marmaduke agreed, frowning on the dark expanse of the sea. "Did he offer his services here?"

"That was the way of it." Eoghann spat over the wall. "Swore homage to old Lord Keith, but no sooner did my master fall ill, did the scoundrel up and vanish. Like the rest of them, to a man."

Eoghann's fury poured out in a passionate flood. "Forsworn bastards. Selling their souls for a few obols and a promise of land. Keith land. Or so that devil Sir Hugh planned, thinking to wrest Dunlaidir into his own foul clutches."

Marmaduke's jaw hardened. "The man is a disgrace to his gentle blood. I swear to you he will not lay claim to a single stone of this holding."

"His villainy in these parts is beyond telling," Eoghann said, sheathing his sword. "He is worse than a ravening wolf."

"He will soon have cause to regret his misdeeds." Hot anger coursing through him, Marmaduke leapt from the wall. He dropped to one knee beside Lachlan. "So, my friend, let us see what's been done to you."

As carefully as he could, Marmaduke eased Lachlan's blood-soaked jerkin away from the still-bleeding wound, relief washing over him, swift and sweet, upon glimpsing the cleanness of the cut.

"God's mercy, it is only a flesh wound," he said, forcing a twinkle to his good eye. He tousled the younger man's hair. "I'm afraid you will live to survive many more such skirmishes."

Lachlan pushed up on his elbows. "It pains me but a little," he said, the tint of white around his lips giving lie to his brave words.

"Hurting or no, you will spend a few days resting until you've fully recovered," Marmaduke said, his voice a shade more gruff than usual.

"Aye, laddie, and it shouldn't prove a hardship to stay abed with our fair ladies seeing to your comfort," Eoghann prophesied, dropping down beside them. "Our good Lady Caterine has the touch of an angel."

She looked like an angel, too.

An earthbound one, sent down to tempt him past all restraint.

Smothering a curse at the way his pulse leapt at the mere sight of her, Marmaduke watched her approach, his smitten heart thundering as she crossed the bailey with Alec, the oldest and most battle-torn of his men.

Alec's long-strided gait had her hurrying to keep pace and her haste sent the voluminous folds of her mantle billowing out behind her. The cloak's soft dove color blended so well with the gray of the morn, she appeared to be walking on air.

Indeed, with curtains of mist swirling about her and her unbound hair flowing to her hips in a shimmering cascade of palest gold, she could pass for a mythical Celtic goddess.

An ethereal being too beautiful for this world.

Too lovely by far for him.

Marmaduke bit back an oath, acutely conscious of the fearsome sight he must make with his hair wild and his clothes sweat-soaked and stained with Lachlan's blood.

Not to mention his face.

Always his face.

❧

"I cannot see their faces through the fog, can you tell who is hurt?" Caterine glanced at the grim-cast man striding beside her. "Is it him? The Sassunach?" The words escaped her before she realized she'd even formed them.

"Strongbow?" The Highlander's voice held unmistakable pride. "Nay, it will not be him. He never takes a scratch. The saints look out for him because he's already taken his share of battle scars." He winked at her. "And he's that good."

Aye, good. The knowledge came from nowhere and everywhere, lighting on her conscience only long enough to send a tremor rippling through her.

An odd tingling, not at all unpleasant and very much like the delicate shivers that had so surprised her when she'd touched his face on the ramparts.

"Is aught amiss, my lady?" The big man gave her a questioning look. "Shall I escort you back inside?"

"Nay." Caterine shook her head. They'd almost reached the seaward wall. "I would see who's been injured."

Inexplicable relief surged through her when the Sassunach proved as unscathed as the Highlander predicted he'd be. Linnet's champion knelt beside the youngest of his men, his face turned away from her, the ghost of a breeze ruffling his dark hair.

"Lady," he said, without looking at her.

"Good sir," she returned, near choking on the two words, for the tingling sensation had given way to an unaccustomed tightness in her throat and chest.

He shot a glance at her rough-hewn escort. "Any word of the second varlet?"

Alec shook his head. "We searched every inch of the keep, every passage and cranny, all the outbuildings," he said, shrugging burly shoulders. "There's some that say the young lord must've imagined a second man. I swear to you, if there was one, he must've left the same way he came for he's nowhere to be found."

"We'll search again, nevertheless," Sir Marmaduke said, peering at his man's face for a long moment before he tore a strip of cloth from the bottom of his tunic and pressed the wadded linen to Lachlan's wound.

Caterine shifted her weight, grateful he hadn't fixed her with such an intense perusal, hadn't seen her eyes widen at the sight of him.

Faith, he may well have knelt before her naked!

So indecently did his hose and dampened tunic cling to his hard-muscled frame.

Every rock-hewn plane.

Every bulging muscle.

As if to make greater folly of her discomfiture, the breeze gusted suddenly, lifting the side panel of his tunic to give her a bold glimpse at yet another of his bulging muscles.

A most masculine one.

She drew a quick breath, the sharp intake of air prompting him to glance at her. "'Tis a clean enough wound," he said, clearly mistaking the reason for her gasp. "My young friend will survive this day and many yet to come."

Caterine nodded, her heart hammering in her breast. His nearness, and the sheer male power he exuded, wove a spell around her, consuming her very senses so fully she required all her strength to wrench her gaze from his.

Turning her attention to the injured knight, she lowered herself to the ground beside him . . . and forced a quiet calm she didn't feel. She reached for his hand, banishing the cold from his fingers with the warmth of her palms.

"Noble sir," she breathed, wishing *he* wasn't staring at her. She needed to take her mind off his disturbing English self and the curious way he unsettled her.

"Noble sir," she began again, focusing her attention on the pale-faced young knight, "would that Dunlaidir yet housed a full garrison. I would command them to scour the land and demand reparation for the ill-done welcome you've received to my home."

As she'd hoped, Lachlan pushed to sit up straighter and color began seeping back into his face. "Think nothing of it, my lady," he said, the strength in his voice pleasing her. "I have seen worse blood-letting."

He slid a sidelong glance at the Sassunach. "Before we return to Kintail, we will raise men and means enough to spare you future embroilments with such rabble as we saw this morn."

"And I thank you for your chivalry." Caterine smoothed the sweat-dampened hair off his forehead. "Your valor shall be long remembered."

*He* cleared his throat. "'Tis full kind of you to have come, lady, but we must see Sir Lachlan inside now."

The rich timbre of his deep voice wooed her, deftly banishing the morning's terrors and wrapping her in golden warmth . . . until her ears discerned the faint coloration of his birth-land.

And hearing it soundly routed the breathless wonder whirling inside her ever since she'd spied his broad-shouldered self, unscathed and whole.

All male and glorious.

"We'll need wide strips of clean linen," he was saying, his voice irritating her now. Its Englishness offending her. "The most potent wine in your stores, valerian if you ha—"

"I ken what we'll need." She glanced sharply at him, appalled by her snippy tone, but unable to keep the edge from her tongue. "I've run this household and others for many a year."

Something inscrutable crossed his face but vanished in the time it took her to blink. She peered at him, trying to decipher the fleeting expression but he'd schooled his features into an unreadable mask.

No emotion showed at all save the concern for his friend reflecting in the brown depths of his good eye.

To her horror, though, other eyes stared at her over his shoulder.

Leering eyes.

Lust-filled English eyes and pawing hands.

Brutal hands tearing at her gown, ripping to shreds more than the linen of her kirtle and the tender flesh between her thighs.

She saw not the man who'd come to champion her, but many men. Barbarous marauders who'd not just defiled her body, but had crushed her soul.

And slain her first husband before her very eyes.

Blessedly, a barely audible wince and a slight tremor in Lachlan's cold hand vanquished her secret foes. "Who did this?" she asked, looking across him to Eoghann.

"A seditious Welsh dog named Cadoc," Sir Marmaduke supplied, ignoring the pang of annoyance that she'd asked the seneschal and not him.

"Cadoc?" Her eyes widened.

"Aye, and it cost him dear." Eoghann spat, a fierce scowl darkening his weather-lined face. "He lost his life for want of English coin and the saints know what else was promised him."

"Sir Hugh." Caterine slid a glance at Marmaduke. "He will be in a rage since your arrival," she said, contempt icing her words but not quite hiding her fear of a malefactor powerful enough to breach Dunlaidir's walls.

Marmaduke fought back a curse that would've curled Duncan MacKenzie's toes. "No one will gain entry again," he said, pressing another handful of bunched cloth against Lachlan's side. "Not even in the unsavory manner this blackguard did. I will personally install an iron grid over the latrine chute opening."

She blushed. "My stepson told us how he entered. Not that we wouldn't have known after sme—*ah*—seeing James. Rhona is preparing a bath for him now." She looked at Lachlan. "One for you, too, my lord."

Lachlan blanched.

Alec glanced heavenward and pinched his nose. "Dinna think to decline the lady's offer of a bath, laddie," he jested. "Your need of one is great."

*"His* need?" Eoghann pushed to his feet and held his own sweat-drenched tunic out from his chest. "I warrant we all have need of a good soaking."

"I shall have extra water heated," Caterine said, standing. Her blue gaze lighted on each man save him. "Baths will be readied for each of you."

She turned to Lachlan, a half-smile curving her lips. "Once your wound is treated and sewn, you may rest in my late husband's solar," she said, holding up a hand when the young knight sought to demur. "Sir, you were injured within the walls of my home, do not deny me the honor of looking after you. It is my will and pleasure to do so."

"Come, my lady, I'll see you inside." Eoghann joined her. "I don't trust those fool idlers in the kitchen to boil water lest I'm there to watch o'er them."

The moment they moved away, Alec gave Lachlan a bold wink. "I daresay it will be well worth losing a few drams of blood if it means having the lady and her friend bathe you, eh?"

Leaning forward, he wiggled his ears. "'Tis a lucky knave you are, laddie. I'd not mind two pairs o' soft hands a-washing my old bones."

"I am none too keen on a bath, sir." Lachlan flushed bright pink.

Marmaduke's blood heated, too, but not in embarrassment.

*He'd not mind two pairs of soft hands washing him,* Alec had jested.

One pair would serve Marmaduke quite nicely.

The self-same hands whose light-as-air touch had filled him with such wonderment when she'd traced her fingertips along his scar.

What bliss would he know were she to smooth those hands over the scars on his back? What rapture would be his were she to caress his aching muscles?

Most especially the one surging to bold life beneath his braies.

"I can wash myself," Lachlan protested yet again.

"Ladies always tend injured men of the castle garrison," Marmaduke reminded him. "And esteemed guests."

Before the others could glimpse just how much the lady stirred him, he leaned down and lifted Lachlan into his arms. "There is naught untoward in letting them bathe and care for you."

Lachlan didn't appear convinced. "'Tis the way of things, I know, but . . ."

"To refuse would be an insult," Marmaduke said, his tone closing the matter.

Without further ado, he carried his friend across the bailey, gladful of the morning's cooling mist on his heated flesh. More grateful still, of the long years he'd spent learning to shield his emotions.

# Chapter Five

✦

INSOLENT, FULL OF folly and disrespect.

Too fond by far of men of steel.

Swayed by smoldering gazes, her mind turned by fanciful dreams of strong men hewn of blood and fire.

Caterine stood in the comforting circle of warmth thrown out by the great arched fireplace in Dunlaidir's kitchen, a near-full pail of heated water clutched in her hands, a round dozen accusations burning the tip of her tongue.

And each one vied to be the first to fly at her meddlesome companion for bringing her to this pass.

Unfortunately, an equally damning charge, one aimed at her own fool heart, kept her lips pressed firmly together.

Of late, her own dreams echoed with the allure of mail-clad men.

One mail-clad man in particular.

Outrageous imaginings that burgeoned into splendiferous bloom the instant she closed her eyes to sleep. Disturbing wanderings of the mind ever ready to pierce the cloak of indifference she attempted to wear by day.

She slanted a look at Rhona. Blissfully unaware of Caterine's simmering agitation, her friend busied herself spreading thick woven matting around the bases of three wooden bathing tubs.

James, already submerged to his shoulders in one of them, followed her every move, his dark eyes carefully hooded to shield his adoration.

A condition Caterine suspected she alone was aware of.

"This should do it," Eoghann's gravelly voice drew her attention. He filled a small bucket with hot water from an iron cauldron suspended over the cook fire, then poured the bucket's steaming contents into her larger pail.

Newly bathed himself, but with cold water drawn from the cistern just beyond the kitchen wall, the seneschal returned the scooping bucket to its hook above the hearth. "The good sirs will have baths worthy of any great lord's hall," he said, a note of pride in his voice.

"And you, dear sir, aught not have to serve as a common bathman." Ire pricked her conscience at seeing the loyal retainer thus demoted.

"Nor should you be doing the work of a kitchen lad, my lady." The deep voice, so English yet irresistibly compelling, laid fast claim to the torch-lit kitchen and all within its smoke-stained walls.

Caterine whirled around, hot water spilling onto the floor. He stood in the open doorway, the stone-walled passage to the keep looming dark behind him. Fire glow from the wall torches gilded the length of him, emphasizing the wide set of his shoulders and his great height.

With his injured friend cradled in his arms, he looked more the lord of the castle than her late husband ever had, even in his best years.

A wave of heat washed over Caterine, an inner blaze that had nothing to do with the room's smoky warmth.

She'd half-dreaded, half-desired this moment ever since the need to offer heated baths arose, yet now her heart lodged firmly in her throat and despite her best efforts, she couldn't squeeze the simplest greeting past it.

"Set down the pail," he said, and she obeyed, any refusal

she may have attempted made futile by the sheer intensity of his gaze.

Stayed by his piercing perusal and the obvious care with which he held his friend.

A depth of concern even one who loathed the English couldn't deny, though acknowledging its portent, that he possessed a good heart, held ramifications she didn't care to consider.

Fisting her hands against her attraction to him, she squared her shoulders and lifted her chin.

Even Leo appeared awed. The instant the English knight came forward, the little dog scurried away to a dark corner where he scooted beneath a chair to growl at his latest foe from a safe distance.

"God's eyes, man, put me down." Lachlan squirmed in the Sassunach's arms. "By the Mass, I've but a wee scratch and you coddle me as if I've lost a limb!"

"Moderate your words, my friend," Sir Marmaduke said, the camaraderie in his tone cushioning the reprimand. "Or would you have the ladies think you are of the same cloth as the beggarly varlet who cut you?"

He eased the strapping young knight onto one of the backless benches set against the wall as if he weighed no more than a sack of goose feathers.

His friend comfortably settled, if scowling at the unwanted attention, he crossed the kitchen with long, purposeful strides, reaching Caterine's side before she could so much as blink.

Without a word, he took her hands. Turning them, he trailed the backs of his fingers over her reddened palms.

"May the saints smite me here and now would I dare allow your hands to grow as calloused as a simple scullion's," he vowed, a slight pulsing in his jaw revealing an inner tension held masterfully in check.

An equally tense silence descended, a palpable quiet so

heavy Caterine could almost hear her heart knocking against her ribs.

"I've told her the same myself," Eoghann's genial voice broke the spell. He glanced at Caterine's tub-bound stepson. "Isn't that the truth of it?"

James nodded. "We still have servitors enough to see to such tasks would she allow them to do so."

A wide grin spreading across his lined face, the seneschal bobbed his head. "See?" He beamed at the English knight. "It gladdens my ears to hear you tell her so. She won't listen to us. Mayhap she'll heed you."

"I shall do my utmost to convince her," Sir Marmaduke said, the warmth of his hands on hers near scattering her wits and sending dangerously delicious tingles shooting up her arms.

"The arrow has yet to be loosed that can persuade me to fall prey to honeyed words," she found her tongue at last, aided by the ill-timed surfacing of other Sassunach voices.

Harsh male voices ordering her to do their will lest they suffer more sorrow on her than the mere taking of their pleasure.

Distant terrors, resurrected by the Englishness of the man who meant to champion her.

With a speed borne of her shame, she yanked her hands from his grasp, snatched the water pail and dumped its contents into the nearest bathing tub.

She let the empty bucket slip from her fingers and met Sir Marmaduke's unperturbed countenance with a long hard stare. For good measure, she tossed an equally hot glare at the seneschal.

"Bardic prose and courtly verse are the purest folly," she fomented, spurred on by a parade of leering faces rising cruelly from the depths of her soul. "I ceased listening to such gushing at a tender age and will not be persuaded to do so again."

She paused for emphasis. "Most especially not from English lips."

To her mortification, a flare of sympathy, or mayhap regret, flashed across Sir Marmaduke's scarred face. Coolly ignoring her outburst, he simply lifted a brow.

"Dare I suggest, my lady, that perchance the men who sought to impress you with fair words did not possess deep enough hearts to put enough of their own into winning yours?"

His words, smooth and rich, embraced her, beguiling her with startling ease and pouring warmth and light into corners of her soul that had never known a shred of gallantry.

She opened her mouth to say something, anything, but he'd already moved to stand before James's washtub, his withdrawal leaving her oddly bereft.

It was as if all the light in the kitchen had followed him, leaving her to stand alone in the dark. Even the warmth of the cook fire seemed to have cooled.

Waving a careless hand at Eoghann when he peered oddly at her, she stared after the Sassunach, uncomfortably drawn by the surprising rush of pleasure his silvered words had spent her, sharply conscious of the tantalizing tingles still rippling across her palms and up and down her arms.

*He* seemed wholly immune to the turmoil he'd unleashed in her. His features perfectly controlled, he addressed her stepson. "Sir Alec and several others are making a renewed search of the castle and grounds. If a second intruder yet lurks here, they will find him."

James's fingers ceased lathering his hair. "I was mistaken," he said, casting a sullen-eyed glance at Rhona rather than meet Marmaduke's gaze. "There was only one."

Paying scant heed to their exchange, Caterine stared down at the toppled pail. Water trickled over its rim to form a growing stain on the stone floor.

A stain as dark as the one stamped so indelibly on her heart.

A heart she could not give to an Englishman.

Much as she might be persuaded to want to.

*I am a man of boundless patience.*

She tensed in surprise. The words, his words, had sounded as clearly as if he'd murmured them in her ear. Yet he still stood across the room, calmly conversing with her stepson.

Not sharing private revelations meant for none but her to hear.

*Rest easy, my lady. I respect and revere women. Never would I force you to do aught against your will.*

The words came again. Less substantial than an angel's sigh, but oh-so-sweet, they slid past her ear to caress a part of her no man had ever before touched.

Imagined words.

"I promise you, it is naught but your own heart's desire I would see done."

Not imagined.

Simply low-voiced and smooth.

*Seductive.*

And irrevocably English.

Despite herself, Caterine basked in the warmth of his assurances. Imagined or nay, they touched off yearnings she'd held back too long. She looked up, fully expecting to see his all-knowing gaze fixed on her, but he merely turned away from James's washtub with a half-shrug.

"*As pleases you, my lady,*" she thought she heard him say, but already he'd returned to his friend's side. He stood with his broad back to her, whatever emotions might plague him, well hidden from view.

Eoghann walked away as well, mumbling to himself about chores needing his immediate attention.

"Yon water grows cold and our guests await their ease," Rhona's voice seemed to come from a great distance.

Caterine nodded absently, her attention riveted on the tall

knight across the room. He was unbuckling his sword belt and the simple act seemed so blatantly . . . *intimate.*

A strange prickling sensation sprang to life deep in the lowest part of her belly. A warm pulsing that grew and spread the longer she watched his hands work at the low-slung belt's buckle.

He caught her staring and tilted his head, calmly watching her watch him. "You do not expect us to bathe in our soiled clothes?" he asked, and the heavy leather belt came free.

When he reached for the hem of his dark-stained tunic, Caterine's nerve shattered. She swung around, near colliding with the fly-catcher, a honey-dipped rope hanging from the ceiling.

Embarrassed by her clumsiness, she swatted the dangling nuisance out of her way and stared pointedly into the cook fire. Its flames crackled loudly, wholly unaware of the mad whirling of her senses. Tongues of red and gold licking innocently at the fat logs piled on the blackened hearthstone.

Her heart began a dull thudding.

The look he'd fixed on her had been anything but innocent.

The *clunk* of his belt dropping on the floor, an explicit challenge.

The sound of his tunic being drawn over his head, an affront that sent thrilling streaks of pleasure jabbing into a deep-seated core of pure female need she hadn't been aware she possessed until this very moment.

Stretching her hands to the fire, she used the pretense of warming them to keep her back to him and the two empty bathing tubs looming so close behind her.

One of them soon to be occupied by him, *naked.*

Her cheeks flamed at the notion, her entire body heating up.

Another sword belt hit the floor, followed by the soft rustlings of a second tunic being stripped off.

Lachlan's belt and tunic.

Or Lachlan's belt and *his* hose, for the soft rustling sounds could just as well have been Sir Marmaduke rolling down his leggings.

"'Twas only my young friend's shirt," his richly timbred voice solved the mystery.

And proved to Caterine he could indeed read her thoughts.

Beside her, Rhona held her own hands toward the flames. "It ill becomes you to appear so inhospitable, my lady."

"Inhospitable?" Caterine shrugged out of her cloak. "Would I have poured the last of our precious lavender and thyme oils into their bath water or lined the tubs with fine linen did I not wish to be hospitable?"

Rhona shrugged. "You have not exactly encouraged them to revel in the warmth of your welcome."

Agitation rising in her breast, Caterine tossed her mantle onto a nearby table. "Were I as unwelcoming as you claim, would I have hung our best drying cloths near the fire so they may dry their bodies with warmed toweling?"

"There are more ways to warm a man than by offering him heated bath linens."

*Tell me how,* a silent voice pleaded from the most secret corner of Caterine's heart.

As if she'd heard, Rhona's gaze lighted on James. "Watch how I bathe him. You would be wise to tender your champion the same care."

"I have bathed enough men—" Caterine began, breaking off when her friend walked away. "Wait! 'Tis I who always assist James. . . ."

Left alone, the ancient laws of hospitality bore down on Caterine's shoulders, a crushing weight, sacred and not to be ignored.

The intimacies she must spend on the English knight danced across her conscience, as real as if she'd already dipped her hands into his bath water and, even now, smoothed them over his wet skin.

In truth, he merely lounged against the far wall, watching her in disconcerting silence, branding her with the heat of his stare. Raw masculinity poured off him in such extremes that simply being in the same room with him made every inch of her thrum with crackling anticipation.

Caterine turned aside to smooth her trembling hands on her skirts.

*I have naught to fear . . . I have seen scores of bare-bottomed men.*

*The backs and the fronts of them.* She mouthed the words, a silent litany, her palms growing more damp with each beat of her heart.

She had no cause for alarm.

Many were the knights and nobles she'd granted such attentions.

"'Tis but a custom, my lady," came his voice again. Deep, smooth, and much nearer. "A mere courtesy, the execution of which means nothing."

Caterine swallowed hard at his lie. He erred. The execution of this particular courtesy would cost her much.

And not in the way he'd believe were she to voice her hesitation.

Her acquiescence sealed, she locked her gaze on his. He stood not four paces away, one arm slung about his friend's bare shoulders, his own broad chest equally clothes-free.

And so perfect, her knees went liquid at the sight.

His hard-muscled magnificence, every taut well-defined plane, stole her breath and sent a floodtide of stunned surprise spiraling through her.

Wave upon wave of something so intense, so thoroughly different from anything she'd experienced, she could only stare.

A dusting of crisp dark hair arrowed down the sculpted tautness of his abdomen to disappear beneath the rolled waistband of his braies. The light woolen cloth, still damp from his rigors in the bailey, hugged his muscular thighs and clung to his maleness in such a brazen manner, nary a secret remained about the grandness of his virility.

Finding her voice at last, Caterine . . . gasped.

*He* smiled.

A slow and lazy half-smile of such bone-melting potency the wonder of it reached clear inside her soul to the secret place her gasp had come from.

The place she hid her dreams.

*He* hid nothing.

And nothing could stop the waves of tight-pitched anticipation rippling through her the longer she stared.

"Heavenly saints," she breathed at last, her throat going unbearably dry.

"They had nary a hand in it, I assure you," he said, a bitter edge marring the beauty of his voice.

And slicing through the mysterious bond his oh-so-seductive gallantry had been weaving of her long-slumbering desires.

Hopes and dreams so deeply buried, she'd forgotten she'd ever spun them.

Lifting a hand to his face, he trailed long fingers down the scar slashing across his left cheekbone. "Dear lady, the good saints had their backs turned the day I was thus blighted, but they watch over me now, I assure you."

She looked away, heat flooding her cheeks.

"And as they guard me, so shall I guard you." He skimmed his knuckles down the curve of her cheek. "Your person, your home, and your sensibilities."

"My sensibilities?"

He nodded. "The bathing ceremony is a much appreciated custom amongst men of breeding, but I am not an old done man incapable of tending my own needs."

*There is naught old and done about me,* his heart proclaimed, demanding her ear.

"Nor am I injured," he said, tempted beyond all reason by the sensual promise of her lips. "I can bathe myself."

"I am sorry." She had the good grace to blush, and her high discomfiture turned her eyes a deeper shade of blue.

So dark a blue, he released her at once lest he drown in their sapphire depths.

She touched his arm and his breath caught at the simple contact. "You truly do not mind?"

"And if I did?"

She hesitated but a moment. "Then I would oblige you."

"But not willingly."

"Willing, aye," she said, surprising him. "But not happily."

A pang of bitterness shot through him at her frankness. "Then we shall wait."

"Wait?" She blinked. "Wait for what?"

Marmaduke allowed himself a wry smile. "Until you attend my bath because it is your will to do so."

"My will?"

"So I have said." He smoothed a few wispy strands of pale gold hair off her forehead. "Your will and your desire."

Her brows arched, but before she could say a word, he laid claim to the only washtub yet unoccupied. Without further ceremony, and certainly without shame, he undid the cord to his braies and shoved them to his ankles.

Something fierce and hot leapt inside him. A bold need that made him stand thus a shade longer than was chivalrous. The sheerest moment only, but long enough for her to note the one part of himself he knew to be unflawed and impressive.

Only then did he kick aside his discarded drawers and ease himself into the large wooden tub.

Heated water swirled around him as he settled onto the low bathing stool, the bath's scented warmth lapping at his shoulders and sending him the comfort he'd rather find in her soothing embrace.

Her will and her desire. Anything less was unacceptable. Resting his head against the linen-covered edge of the wash-tub, he let out a great tension-freeing sigh.

He was a patient man.

He would make her want him.

*Love him.*

Unlike the fools who'd sought to woo her before and failed, he possessed a deep enough heart to succeed.

Fending off the dark nigglings of doubt springing to life at his bold assumptions, Marmaduke drew his hand down over his face and closed his eyes.

Then he laid calm siege to his doubts, routing his demons one by one before they could tell him otherwise.

⚜

About the same time, in a far and dark corner of Dunlaidir, two heavily cloaked figures huddled in the dank chill of a long-empty storeroom.

A damp undercroft in one of the castle's most neglected towers, once used to house all manner of goods but now filled with little save dust and cobwebs.

Murky light fell through two narrow air slits, faintly illuminating the scowling face of one of the two figures. "Your regrets come over-late," the figure said, taking up a position at the storeroom's heavy oak door.

"If you are caught escaping, and dare utter my name, I shall see every man, woman, and child who bear a drop of your blood, put to the sword." The speaker thrust out a warning finger. "You have my solemn oath on it."

The other, a thick-set man of squat stature and reeking like a cess-pit, grimaced. "You have fullest right to be wroth," he offered, "but the attempt was ill-starred from the onset. How could we know the young lordling would choose that moment to visit the jakes?"

"If you would stay in my peace, and your lord's, then I council you not to fail again."

The stocky man patted his sword-hilt. "On my life, I swear I won't."

"Your life, aye. That is as sure as a buzzard rides the up-draughts," the other said, and cracked the door just enough to peer out into the fog-hung morning.

Turning back to the dung-crusted figure, he continued, "Word is that he brought a special dispensation from the Bishop of Aberdeen allowing them to wed with all haste. See to it he never gains the chance."

The squat man shuffled his feet on the hard-packed earthen floor. "'Tis said the saints watch o'er him, keeping him from bodily ills."

The other gave a snort of contempt. "He is cunning, naught else. And wise enough to know your liege will be aware of his moves. He will make a careful circuit of the walls when the day of his nuptials dawns. No doubt of the village as well, if Sir Hugh and his men fail to appear."

"But how are we to dispatch him if we aren't there?"

The figure by the door let out a long, slow breath. "You will be there. But not in full knightly regalia as he will expect."

Opening the door just wide enough for the other to slip through, the dark-cloaked figure swelled with the scent of victory. "Tell Sir Hugh to send his best men to hide behind every bush and tree. I will assure the one-eyed whoreson passes close enough to be cut down."

The other opened his mouth, but before he could speak, the figure by the door gave him a rough shove, hurling him into the bailey's damp gloom.

"Go now," the figure called after the hurrying man. "My salutations to your lord."

# *Chapter Six*

❧

*M*UST I REPEAT myself times without number?" James Keith grasped the armrests of the laird's chair and glowered at those unfortunate enough to be within sighting range. "You badgered me before my bath, now I've scarce washed the dung from my limbs and you'd harry me anew."

Anger glittering in his eyes, he slammed the flat of his hand onto the high table's scarred surface. "I've been bested once this morn, would you see me beaten down by a hail of questions as well?"

Dunlaidir's few remaining men-at-arms, so sparse in number they scarce filled the nearest trestle tables, exchanged significant glances but said nothing. Marmaduke's own men, urged by the young lordling to join him at the dais end of the hall, stared at their trenchers or reached for their tankards.

Sharp discomfiture hung in the air, palpable and thick as the smell of wood-smoke and soured ale. Two of the Keith men feigned coughing spells. Others shifted in their seats, clearly ill at ease.

"For the last time, there was only one," James ground out, anger rolling off him in black waves.

Sir Marmaduke watched him from the shadows near the bottom steps of the turnpike stairs. Carefully keeping his mien one of quiet calm, he folded his arms and leaned one mail-clad shoulder against the tapestry-hung wall.

The stripling's ire didn't surprise him, but his avoidance of meeting the others' eyes, made Marmaduke's pulse quicken with alertness.

A sharply honed warrior's instinct, ignited because James only averted his gaze when stating he'd seen but one intruder and not two as he'd originally claimed.

"'Tis plaguey sad when the new lord shies away from discussing matters of such grave import," groused a stern-featured man-at-arms at one of the trestle tables.

"New lord . . . *faugh!*" someone else scoffed. "The whelp would sooner offer up his own bed to the English than draw steel on 'em!"

"It would require more than mere steel to parry a man as cunning as Hugh de la Hogue." Sir John, a tired-looking noble of middle years, glanced over his shoulder at the carping men-at-arms. "He gives no quarter to any who dare to challenge him. God the Father himself would be hard-pressed to help those Sir Hugh chooses to ruin."

He slid James a dark look. "If the dastard so desired, he'd slight this holding with a fury so ravenous naught but a few scattered stones would remain."

"That's why it's so sad we have such a weak-hearted poltroon as new lord!" a riled voice rose from one of the other tables.

All color drained from James's face. When his jaw began working in agitation, but no words came forth, Marmaduke raked a hand through his still-damp hair. Stifling a curse, he started forward at the same time Caterine pushed to her feet.

Her back straight, her pride glowing as brightly as the gleaming gold braids coiled over her ears, she stared accusingly at the Dunlaidir men. "Is it not a greater sadness that we need the sword arms of a braw English knight and his men to stave off the havoc and disaster you dread, my lords?"

Her words froze Marmaduke's feet.

Had she truly called him braw?

His heart surged, all manner of interpretation galloping through him as he stepped from the shadows.

"Where is loyalty and honor when more than half of our garrison abandon us to face every peril alone?" As yet unaware of his approach, Caterine Keith challenged the men who'd shamed her stepson. "Where were you when James chased after the intruder? His daring, good sirs, was not the act of a weakling."

Some of the men-at-arms lowered their heads, appearing duly chagrined; others drew their brows together in further annoyance and continued to grumble amongst themselves.

Sir John frowned, telling lines etched deep into his haggard features. Lost in his own thoughts, he absently slipped bits of cheese to the dogs scrounging in the rushes beneath the high table.

The tiniest dog, Lady Caterine's pet, ceased his scavenging to bare his teeth at Marmaduke. Ignoring the wee beastie's snarls, he stepped up to the table and placed a hand on Caterine's shoulder.

She glanced at him, her deep blue eyes still sparking with agitation, but to his relief, she made no move to pull away.

"Disloyal retainers do not stay on when they could dine off silver plate elsewhere," Marmaduke said, speaking to her, but nodding to her men. "Good men remain through all weathers, as these here have clearly chosen to do." As he'd hoped, his words wiped a fair portion of the ill-humor from their faces.

"'Tis looking after the horses, we were," one of them called out, his grieved tone declaring his still-simmering annoyance. "Some of us thought we saw lights flickering in the stables. We are too few to be everywhere, milady."

"He has the rights of it," another agreed. "We ne'er thought some craven ruffian would come climbing out of the jakes!"

Nods and hearty blusters echoed the voiced sentiments, but the tension gradually dissipated. Satisfied, Marmaduke looked back at Lady Caterine.

His breath caught at her radiance. She was staring past him, looking at the garrison men. Flickering torchlight silhouetted her profile, gilding the elegant lines of her face and the proud lift of her chin.

Her dignity stirred him, but the vulnerability evident in the flush high on her cheeks moved him more. Something rare and potent slid through him, seizing fast hold of his very soul.

He watched her, his heart pounding slow and hard. The smoky hall and all in it seemed to merge with the shadows until only she remained, clear and bright as a sunlit day.

The disgruntled Keith men, his amused-looking ones, and even the rows of tables and benches, everything faded save his keen awareness of her.

She stood tall and proud, the fireglow caressing her, the shifting light and shadow revealing the sleek lines of her body, teasing him with the pleasing fullness of her breasts, and tempting him with a subtle sensuality any man of depth would burn to awaken.

And Marmaduke possessed more depth than most.

Desire slammed through him and his body tightened, responding to her with gripping need. A yearning far more powerful than the well-rounded wenches he'd favored in recent years had e'er stirred in him.

The saints knew he'd avoided slender coupling partners, hadn't craved the supple curves of a lithe-limbed woman in years. Not since—

Frowning, he curled his hands against the image rising in his mind . . . and the sharp lust heating his blood. A throbbing ache much deeper than mere physical want.

"Aye, and 'tis full loyal we are," a loud voice rang out, dashing cold water on his need and soundly dispelling memories better left unstirred.

"Not all can be turned by coin or cowed by that son of Beelzebub!" another agreed.

Others joined in and the disruption poured a river of relief through Marmaduke, swiftly restoring his wits and re-sealing his most tender wound.

The one that bore his late wife's name.

Drawing a great breath, he gave his *new* lady's shoulder a light squeeze. And knew profound satisfaction when she leaned into his hand, welcoming his touch.

"Such stalwarts are worth two of every knave who left," he told her, his voice a shade huskier than usual. "Do not fret their loss. Sometimes it is wise to concede a battle if in doing so, we achieve later victory in the war."

James pinned him with a glare. "Did you come here to champion us with your brawn, sir, or is your purpose to impress us with your bottomless fount of wisdom?"

Caterine's brows shot upward at her stepson's rudeness. Her champion tensed, but except for the slight jerking of a muscle in his jaw, his face remained amazingly calm.

"A man worth his salt makes equal use of both," he said, his deep voice as smooth and unruffled as his expression.

"And you would intimate I have neither?" James's face darkened.

"James, please—" Caterine began, but steely fingers pressed down on her shoulder. Heeding the unspoken warning, she held her tongue as James pushed to his feet.

"Nay, sir, do not trouble yourself to answer," he bristled, drawing up before Marmaduke. "I already ken the answer."

Snapping his brows together in a mask of fury, he stormed from the table, his hobbling gait more pronounced than ever. But to Caterine's astonishment, it was his *good* leg he dragged behind him.

Sir Marmaduke's grip tightened when she tried to wrench free. "Leave him be," he said, accurately guessing her desire to follow her stepson. "Only after he's faced his dragons and laid them to rest, will he be able to rise high enough above himself to win yon men's admiration."

"And I suppose you are well-practiced at winning men's esteem?"

A ghost of a smile touched his lips. "So some might claim."

"He wins the ladies, too," Sir Alec boasted, plunking down his ale mug. The crusty Highlander dragged his sleeve over his mouth. "Steals their hearts afore they ken what hit 'em, he does."

"Their hearts and all else they toss after him," another embellished with a bold wink. Others chorused agreement, her men joining in the ribaldry as well, until the remaining shreds of dissent evaporated amidst a flood of ever bawdier jesting.

". . . he's so bi—er—*well-blessed* none of the ladies will even glance at the rest of us after he's—"

"By the Mass, Ross, hold your tongue," Marmaduke's commanding voice carried clear to the inky dark corners of the hall.

His man, a ruddy-faced Highlander, shrugged burly shoulders but appeared anything but abashed. "A spellcaster, he is!" he called out, slapping his thigh for emphasis. "Charmed Arabella, charms 'em all."

The more vocal amongst those present roared their approval and a swell of chortles tripped down the length of the high table and beyond.

Visibly paling, he released her shoulder at once. "'Fore God, that's enough!" The massed power pouring off him silenced his men as much as the heat of his words.

Bracing his hands on his hips, he raked the lot of them with a fearsome stare. "I charge you to remember there are ladies present," he said, the very walls seeming to draw pause and listen. "Think well before you spout such foolery again, my friends."

"Beg pardon, milady," a bearded Highlander said, half-rising off his bench. "'Tis a hard-bitten lot we are, not always fit for a fine lady's hall."

Generously proffered agreement poured forth from the others as well, but Caterine scarce heard the well-meant atonements nor her own murmured acceptance, for other words echoed in her heart.

Some sent heat inching up the back of her neck; others pinched deep into a hitherto unknown streak of feminine pique running straight through her core.

*Big,* the ruddy-faced MacKenzie had meant to boast.

Well-blessed, he'd amended.

Caterine's face flamed. The English knight was both, as she'd seen.

With startling clarity, the Highlander's words summoned the unhindered view she'd had of his naked maleness in the moments before he'd settled into his bath.

A most splendid array of manhood.

And he'd been fully at ease.

Caterine's heart flip-flopped and her mouth went dry. Something deep inside her contracted to a tight and hollow ache. The recalled image, even in its relaxed state, weighted her belly with a pulsing warmth. Imagining him at need, fully aroused, filled her with a greedy, gnawing hunger she'd never believed existed until now.

"Do not heed their buffoonery, my lady. They forget themselves at times," he spoke at last, the smoothness of his voice warming her soul as surely as remembering his male perfection fired her body.

Caterine drew a shaky breath, the image of his nakedness still emblazoned on her senses. She blinked, awakening as if from a haze. *He* was peering oddly at her.

Everyone in the hall peered oddly at her.

Someone sniggered.

It was a low titter, but enough to shatter the strange intensity charging the very air between them.

Conversation resumed at the tables. Everyday sounds of hungry men partaking of what humble offerings Dunlaidir could place before them. The sheer accustomedness of the noise made bald mockery of how quickly her own personal sense of normalcy had changed since the English knight's arrival.

Acutely aware of him, Caterine lifted a hand to her

shoulder. Though he'd released her, the tingling warmth where his fingers had pressed against her yet lingered.

As if privy to her thoughts, he smoothed the back of his fingers down the curve of her cheek and the tingles spread, tumbling down her back in a startling cascade of pleasure spilling clear to her toes.

"You mustn't let my men unsettle you," he said, lifting away his hand.

*You* unsettle me! she wanted to shout, but the hint of an amused gleam in his good eye gave her halt.

And made her bold.

Daring enough to challenge the sensations he'd awakened in her.

She wet her lips. "Is it foolery, my lord?"

"Is what foolery, my lady?" The barely there gleam became a full-fledged twinkle.

She stared at him, gladful that Eoghann had just plunked down a platter of roasted seabird. The rich smell of the savory gannet meat staved off curious glances.

Emboldened, she stepped a bit closer to him. Just near enough to test the persuasive mastery streaming out from every muscled inch of him.

"Are you a spell-caster?" She tilted her head to one side, her gaze as direct as her words. "A charmer of women as your men claim?"

His lips curving in the faintest smile, he caught her hand and began massaging her palm with the calloused pad of his thumb. "I would rather leave that for you to decide," he said, releasing her. "Mayhap one day soon you will favor me with your assessment."

Too stunned by the delicious prickling sensation dancing across her palm, Caterine blinked at him, too flustered to remember what else she'd wanted to ask him.

Before she could even catch her breath, he seized her hand once more and placed a searingly tender kiss on the inside of her wrist.

At her quick intake of breath, the skin around his eyes crinkled in amusement and his smile deepened to reveal a set of utterly appealing dimples. Two vertical creases running from mid-cheek to just below the corners of his mouth, and as charming as his scar was daunting.

But they vanished as quickly as they'd appeared. Without a further word, he turned and strode off into the shadows.

Only then did she remember what else she'd wanted to know.

*Arabella.*

The woman his men said he'd charmed.

"Who is Arabella?" her lips formed the silent question.

Three whispered words to taunt her.

A name to temper the fluttery excitement his touch and his dimples had left behind.

*Who is Arabella?* This time her heart asked.

And more importantly, why was she so desperate to know?

⚜

*A braw English knight.*

The words swirled around him as he passed through the darkened hall. Sweet praise to cajole him, a simply stated comment bursting with wondrous possibilities and brimming with hope.

The same kind of giddy elation a drowning man must feel when tossed a rope.

Braw, she'd said.

Marmaduke's heart swelled.

No maid had called him thus since he'd been blighted by his scar.

Slowing his steps, he considered abandoning his desire to seek out her ill-humored stepson and attempt to cure the young man's aches. An irresistible urge seized him to return to the high table, fetch his new lady, haul her into his arms, and see to tending his own woes.

And hers.

But while her words beckoned, the expression she'd worn after he'd kissed her wrist lent renewed speed to his feet. Wonder and bewilderment had filled her sapphire eyes and the memory of both rode hard on his shoulders.

Her wonder urged him to tear away the cool restraint she kept wrapped around herself and awaken her womanhood with as many soul-stealing kisses as it cost him.

The bewilderment signaled the need to woo her gently.

Caterine Keith's passion would require finesse, skill, and infinite patience.

So he strode on, searching the shadows for James and calling on every shred of his iron will to ignore the parade of conflicting desires trailing in his wake.

Her dog, the snarling beastie, followed him as well, snapping at his heels until he whirled around and gave the mite a ferocious look of his own.

The wee creature froze, his snapping jaws halted as surely as if Marmaduke had emptied a bucket of ice water on him. For a heartbeat, the little dog peered up at him, stunned surprise brimming in his round eyes before he tore off across the rushes, his short legs pumping faster than if a pack of rabid hell-hounds chased after him.

Soundly repelled by one fierce look.

A fearsome scowl from the ravaged face of a man once rumored to be amongst the most handsome of England's chivalry.

Marmaduke almost laughed and would have, did his accursed vanity not choose that moment to plunge cold shards of bitterness into his heart.

> *. . . forget so soon*
> *How you and I, the world away,*
> *Once lay and watched the moon?*

The song, its familiar words a poignant memorial to a long-past time, sliced into him with all the vengeance of a marauder's arcing sword.

He spun around, his gaze searching the farthest end of the hall whence the haunting verse seemed to come. He spotted her immediately, despite the darkness of the deep window embrasure where she sat, softly plucking a lute and singing . . . as she'd done so many nights during their too-brief marriage.

*Arabella.*

Her slim body wrapped in the furred bed-robe he'd gifted her with a mere sennight before her death, her glossy raven hair hanging free, his long-buried wife strummed her lute and sang for him.

> *Can you forget the day,*
> *The day that we—? But I'm a fool,*
> *Alas, my love, that day is faded and gone.*

Blood pumping wildly through his veins, Marmaduke made straight for her, uncomfortably disturbed by the way his heart exchanged Arabella's free-flowing black tresses for satiny locks of gleaming gold.

Even his ears betrayed him for they strained to catch softer, more honeyed notes than the throaty, smoky-sounding tones drifting from the shadowy corner.

Telling too, his burning desire to see her look up and gaze at him from sapphire eyes. But the first eyes to meet his when he reached the little alcove were dark.

Dark and masculine.

James shot him a sour glance, then scooted around on the window embrasure's cushioned seat, turning his back on Marmaduke to stare out on the great sweep of the iron-gray sea.

On the facing windowseat, Lady Rhona set aside her lute. "Sir," she greeted Marmaduke, her smile as cordial as James's rigid back was cold.

"Lady." Marmaduke inclined his head, still too flummoxed by what could only have been a cruel trick of the light to offer more than a perfunctory greeting.

Not lissome at all, nor as beautiful as Arabella had been, his lady's companion adjusted the furred skins tucked around her plump thighs and hips. "Your man, Sir Lachlan, rests comfortably in the late Lord Keith's solar," she said. "We squeezed a bit of sea lettuce juice into his wine to help him sleep. I will redress his wound later."

"Have a care lest you coddle him." James twisted back around to glare reproach at her. "He has but a flesh wound."

"That as it may be, there are times all men have need of being cosseted." She leveled a look of clear censure at him. "As there are times such pampering is wholly misplaced."

James stared at her, tight-lipped. He didn't so much as glance at Marmaduke, not that he cared. The skin on the back of his neck still prickled too coldly for him to pay heed to the charged undercurrents bouncing back and forth between his lady's friend and Dunlaidir's blazing-eyed heir.

More disturbing by far was the queer glimpse he'd had of long-ago days best forgotten.

Swallowing the bitterness rising in his throat, he studied Rhona, seeking to decipher what beyond Arabella's favorite love sonnet had summoned such painful echoes of another time.

A queersome instance, for naught on his lady's friend resembled his late wife save the same dark coloring.

"'Tis good you've come, my lord," she addressed him, her high color and James Keith's scowling countenance hinting they'd been engaging in more than lute playing and songs before he'd disturbed them.

"My lady has long had need of a champion," she added, casting a quick glance at James. "I knew her sister's husband would send a daring man in mail and sword-belt. A warrior unafraid—"

"By all the rogue saints!" James leapt to his feet. "Would you try a man to the limits of his patience? Bold, strapping man of steel!" he railed, snatching up the lute as if he meant to break it in two. "Must a man be hung with metal to win your favor?"

He shook the lute at her. "Fool that I am, I thought you meant to bethrall me with your singing, your kis—" Tossing the instrument onto the windowseat, he broke off his tirade to whirl away from her.

The lady Rhona stood, too, one hand clutching the lute, the other extended to James, but he stormed off before she could touch him, his stride purposeful and strong.

Beautifully smooth.

And wholly without a limp.

Marmaduke glanced sharply at Rhona and the joyous smile spreading across her face warmed his heart.

His lady's friend was astute indeed.

If her machinations to summon him hadn't proved it, her ploy just now had. Her boldness also proved where her heart lay, and Marmaduke's own sentimental heart smiled at the revelation.

James Keith would need a wench with backbone at his side when Marmaduke and his men returned to Balkenzie.

With a breathy little sigh, Rhona sank back onto the windowseat. She looked out at the sea, but she hadn't turned away swiftly enough for him to miss the glimmer of moisture swimming in her eyes.

He watched her for a long moment, some of the darkness inside him ebbing. For the first time since his arrival at Dunlaidir, a true shimmer of hope burgeoned in his heart.

If he could convince Caterine her stepson, and Dunlaidir, would be in sound hands after their departure, his chances of persuading her to accompany him should vastly improve.

"Lady, you possess greater insight than many men I know," he said, meaning every word. "Were you not a woman, I would knight you here and now in admiration for your wisdom. James is fortunate to have your devotion."

"He is not lame," she said, glancing at him. "His right leg

was sorely hurt when a horse kicked him, but I suspect he scarce remembers which leg took the blow. The injury is long healed."

She paused to smooth the furred skins across her knees. "Regrettably, he is convinced otherwise. Perhaps you can persuade him to believe differently?"

"Such is my intent," he promised, a plan already forming in his mind.

"You will succeed, my lord," Rhona predicted, glad-eyed. "Both with James and my lady."

Marmaduke raised her hand and kissed it. "Fair lady, I shall hold you to your word."

"Then go and see you to it." She smiled at him, then turned back to the window, giving him leave to do just that.

Moving away, Marmaduke scanned the dimly lit hall. He spotted James bearing down on the great iron-studded door to the outer stairs.

And, once again, he walked with an exaggerated limp.

Marmaduke caught up to him just as he reached to open the door. "Have you a smithy?" he asked, closing his hand around the younger man's arm.

His brows shooting upward, James stared at him as if he'd sprouted horns. "A smithy?"

"A blacksmith. A master ironworker."

James tossed back his hair with a jerk of his head. "I am not a dullwit," he seethed, struggling to free his arm. "I ken what a smithy is, and, nay, we do not have one. Not any longer."

Marmaduke released him, but blocked the door by leaning his back against its heavy oak panels. "Then we shall make do on our own," he said, crossing his ankles, his tone deliberately jovial. "We can reward our exertions with a refreshing plunge in the cold waters of the sea."

"The sea?"

Marmaduke nodded. "After we visit the forge."

"We?" James's brows arched a notch higher. "I am not an underling to be ordered about."

Full aware all eyes in the hall watched their exchange, Marmaduke flicked an invisible speck of lint off his steel-clad arm. His tone as casual as he could make it, he said, "I said we, my friend. Ne'er would I breach the laws of hospitality by issuing orders to my host."

Satisfied when a bit of the fire went out of the younger man's eyes, Marmaduke pushed away from the door. "A well-meant suggestion, mayhap, but never a command."

Visible tension still thrumming through him, James glanced toward the shadowy window embrasure where Lady Rhona still sat. "There is no point in visiting the forge. It holds naught but rusting iron and dust-covered bellows. Our smith abandoned us months ago. As for bathing in the sea, I-I . . . do not swim."

True alarm had glimmered in James's eyes when he said he didn't swim, so Marmaduke focused on the task at hand.

Securing the latrine chutes and bolstering James's confidence.

"Four strong arms should compensate for one disloyal smithy," he said.

James shoved a hand through his hair. "I will take you to the forge, but do not expect assistance from me. As you saw this morn, I am not much good to anyone."

"You will only be of no avail if you persist in dallying about with your lady rather than coming with me." Marmaduke reached out and gave James's upper arm a fair squeeze. "You have brawn enough for what we must do."

From the high table, Caterine watched their exchange with increasing amazement. Rather than protest when the Sassunach tested his muscle, a faint flush crept onto her stepson's cheeks and he stood a wee bit straighter.

And, for once, he did so without losing his balance.

The two men walked toward the hall's entrance vestibule together and Caterine would've sworn she'd caught the hint of a smile on James's face as he snatched his cloak off a bench near the door.

*He* waited while James adjusted the fall of his mantle before he fetched and donned his own. Then, in a gesture that smacked of comradely ease, he slung an arm around the younger man's shoulders as they exited the hall, her champion's stride powerful and self-assured, her stepson's less confident but nowise as hesitant as his usual limping gait.

Caterine's heart warmed.

Ne'er had she thought to see James walk with a spring in his step again.

Slowly sipping her wine, she stared into the shadows of the entrance vestibule long after they'd closed the great oaken door behind them.

More and more, her sister's chosen champion was proving himself a man truly worthy of the title.

But even as her heart softened toward him, her mind wrestled with other concerns.

Grave ones of a most serious import.

Such as when exactly she'd ceased referring to him as the Sassunach champion and started thinking of him as simply *her* champion.

❧

Other eyes watched their departure as well.

Brooding, hate-filled eyes hiding in the shadows near the bottom of the outer stairs.

The observer's brow arched with disdain when they passed.

Soon the English interloper would ride a swift and cold wind straight to the bowels of hell, hastened there by a well-aimed English arrow.

That irony curling the watcher's lips, the dark-cloaked figure slipped deeper into the dank chill of the white mist still blanketing much of the bailey.

# Chapter Seven

✦

"'TIS AS I told you," James said, a short while later. He peered into the dank interior of the long-deserted forge. "There is naught of use here."

Ignoring him, Marmaduke retrieved a wobbly three-legged stool from the shadows and used it to prop open the door. The once bustling workshop needed airing.

Dunlaidir's forge wasn't merely neglected, it smelled.

Of damp charcoal and rusting iron, of sea brine and mold.

And worse things he didn't care to identify.

A gust of brisk salt-laden air swept past him, blasting through the opened door to lift choking clouds of dust and ash off the hard-packed earthen floor.

"Let us be out of here." James wrinkled his nose in distaste, the flare of purpose he'd displayed in the hall rapidly fading. He crossed his arms. "I will not go in there."

Marmaduke quirked a grim smile at him. "Would you concede defeat before the battle is fought?"

"Only those battles too pointless to pursue," James said, scarce loud enough to be heard. "Like walking straight or *me* challenging two swords—"

"Two swordsmen?" Marmaduke voiced what he'd already guessed. "And why did you change your story? Why claim there was but one?"

James compressed his lips and turned away.

Beneath the other's silence, Marmaduke heard James's roiling frustration, louder and more penetrating than the screeching seabirds wheeling overhead.

Going to him, Marmaduke clamped a hand on his shoulder. "Together, we can bring the curs to heel," he said. "But only if you will trust me."

The younger man's brow creased, but when he gazed heavenward and blew out a long breath, Marmaduke knew he'd won this round. "Well?" he tried again, taking his hand from James's shoulder. "Why did you lie?"

"Because when I spoke the truth, the others laughed and declared I'd embellished the incident by insisting there were two when in truth I couldn't bear admitting I'd been bested by a single swordsman."

"So you let them believe what they wanted so they'd leave you be?"

James nodded.

"Mayhap that is as well, and we shall allow them to think that folly is the truth a while longer," Marmaduke said, glancing at the screaming gulls riding the air currents high above the forge.

"You believe me?" The incredulity in James's eyes spoke worlds.

"That I do," Marmaduke said, resting his hand almost casually on his sword-hilt. "But the saints know I wish I didn't," he added, his deep voice suddenly threaded with steel.

The amazement vanished from James's face. "Pardon my confusion, sir, but how can you profess to believe me yet council silence about the second intruder?"

"If indeed he was an intruder. The man may have been invited, or assisted on his way out," Marmaduke said, carefully picking his words. "Mayhap both."

"That's madness." James shook his head. "I cannot believe it."

Marmaduke shrugged his mail-clad shoulders. "Several

thorough searches were made, yet no trace of this elusive interloper could be found. Flesh and blood men do not vanish into thin air, my friend."

"And you believe someone in my household aided his escape?"

"I would give you my oath on it," Marmaduke returned. "Therefore it is prudent not to let anyone save, perhaps, the lady Caterine, know we are aware of any possible in-house treachery."

James stared at him, slack-jawed, but Marmaduke turned away before the younger man could further question him.

He knew much of in-house scheming and its dangers.

He carried the mark of such perfidiousness on his face and tasted the bile of its memory in the cold bitterness rising to choke him.

With a broad sweep of his arm, he cast aside a swaying curtain of cobwebs and stepped into the chill damp of the forge. "We can speak of this later," he said, glancing over his shoulder at James. "For now, we need a few sound pieces of grating to seal the garderobe chute."

"You speak as if such a task were simple." James hovered on the threshold.

"Naught in life is simple," Marmaduke said, halting beside a dirt-encrusted stone trough, once filled with cooling water, now demoted to a receptacle for all manner of refuse. "But each mastered challenge makes the living more worthwhile."

James took several hesitant steps into the forge, once more favoring his leg. "Think you?"

"Nay, I know so."

Bending, Marmaduke retrieved a grimy leather pouch off the floor near the long-cold smelting furnace. He upended the satchel and shook it hard. When nothing but dust emerged, he leveled a hard look at his companion.

James Keith reminded him more of himself at a younger age than he cared to admit.

"Come here," he said, something fiercely elemental twisting inside him at the anger and doubt he knew plagued the Dunlaidir heir.

Potent enemies, both.

And capable of laming the young man in a far worse way than some long-ago horse kick.

Fending off his own demons, Marmaduke held out the leather pouch. "'Tis fair dark in here," he said. "You have two good eyes. I have but one. Our purpose is better served if you search the corners, while I gather what I can from the area near the door where the light is stronger."

"I—" James started, then snapped shut his mouth and came forward to snatch the satchel from Marmaduke's outstretched hand.

Mumbling to himself, he began stuffing odd lengths of wire, once used to craft links for mail, and rust-caked tools, into the leather sack.

Near the entrance, Marmaduke held up a good-sized drawplate and pretended to examine its many holes of varying sizes. The large sheet of metal was ideal to seal off the cliffside latrine chute. In truth, though, he paid little heed to the absent smith's prized tool for making wire, preferring to study James out of the corner of his good eye.

Though still grumbling beneath his breath, he moved about easily enough, displaying only a trace of his usual awkward gait.

Just as Marmaduke had hoped.

Seeing the younger man too preoccupied to remember to limp, warmed Marmaduke's heart and encouraged his conviction that he'd been sent across Scotland for more reasons than simply lending his warring skills and his name to a lady in need.

At the thought of her, other parts of him began to warm as well, so he smoothed his fingers over the cold metal of the drawplate, testing its strength, and letting its chill staunch the flow of heated blood to his loins.

His lips twitched in irony.

What his own most-times unflagging resolve couldn't wholly achieve, keeping his baser urges at bay, the onerous task before him accomplished with ease.

The distasteful undertaking would steal the itch from any man's tarse. And if it didn't, he'd simply make good his vow to bathe in the sea.

Trouble was, he desired his new lady with more than a persistent pull in his groin. He wanted her with his entire being.

Body, heart, and soul.

And neither his iron will nor the shock of the North Sea's icy waters was a mighty enough elixir to assuage a need that burned so deep.

❧

Still unnerved from the potency of the kiss her champion had placed on the inside of her wrist, and from the persistent way the name Arabella continued to nibble at her pique, Caterine mounted the circular tower stairs to her bedchamber.

Iron-bracketed wall torches set at convenient intervals in the stairwell hissed and sputtered, their uneasy flickering mirroring her jangled nerves. At the landing, her little dog, Leo, abandoned her to streak down the shadow-cast passage, then hurl himself against her closed bedchamber door.

By the time she caught up with him, he stood with his forelegs propped against the door's oaken panels, his tail wagging furiously.

*Rhona.*

Caterine's meddlesome companion had to be inside her bedchamber. No one else elicited such an enthusiastic response from Leo. Bracing herself, for she'd hoped to enjoy a few moments of solitude before looking in on Sir Lachlan, she opened the door.

Leo gave a yelp of joy and dashed inside.

Caterine gasped.

Her friend *was* in the room, but rather than Rhona's pretty face, it was her companion's well-rounded bottom that greeted her.

Bent near double, Rhona had opened the iron-bound strongbox at the base of Caterine's curtained bed and appeared to be rummaging through its contents.

"Rhona!" Caterine closed the short distance between them. "Whatever are you about there?"

Straightening immediately, Rhona whirled around, almost tripping over Leo, who ran gleeful circles around her, barking his excitement. "Merciful heavens, but you startled me!" Her eyes wide, she stared at Caterine, a large wooden bowl clutched in her hands.

A wooden bowl with a round, cloth-covered lump inside it.

*The Laird's Stone.*

A near perfectly round stone of dark gray granite speckled with crystal quartz.

A magical stone said to weep copiously, its tears filling the wooden bowl, each time a master of Dunlaidir died . . . and again, this time for joy, when a new lord took his place.

Or so the legend claimed.

Caterine had never seen the phenomena.

"What are you doing with that?" she prompted when Rhona continued to stare at her, gog-eyed and blushing.

She reached for the bowl, but Rhona cradled it protectively against her middle. "I wanted to see if the stone had wept for James yet," she said, back-stepping toward the bank of arch-topped windows behind her.

"For truth, when will you admit that nonsense is naught but stuff and bother?" Caterine blew out a breath of sheer frustration. "A fool legend spun by some long-dead taleweaver to fill cold and dark winter nights."

"I saw it shed tears when Laird Keith passed." Rhona set

the cloth-covered bowl on the cushioned seat of the window embrasure and folded her arms. "You saw the water in the bowl, too. Everyone did."

"After you fetched the silly thing!" Caterine snapped, fast losing patience. "Mayhap you poured water over the stone."

"Hah! Think you I would stoop to such trickery?"

"And whose deception do we have to thank that an *English* champion now dwells within these walls? A Sassunach I am soon to wed . . . in large part because of your trickery."

Rhona's brow knit. "I thought you were coming to favor him?"

Glancing away lest her friend read too much into the heat Caterine could feel blooming on her cheeks, she sought haven from her whirling emotions in the familiar expanse of sea and sky stretching beyond the tall windows.

The well-cherished view calmed her as soundly as the chill salt air streaming through the opened windows cooled her burning cheeks.

"Whether I favor him or nay, the Laird's Stone and its legend has no more credence than any other bard's tale," she said, her gaze on the wind-whipped sea. "Sir Marmaduke Strongbow is and shall remain an Englishman."

*And I am not woman enough to follow the yearnings of my heart . . . the ghosts of too many other Englishmen stand in the way.*

Squaring her shoulders, Caterine turned back to face her friend. "Tradition, fanciful or nay, deems a new laird's worthiness must be recognized by the stone before it will weep." Her gaze locked on Rhona's. "Even if the legend were true, think you truly the stone would welcome James as new lord with *him* beneath our roof?"

She waved a silencing hand when Rhona started to protest. "I do not believe such folly, but you do. So how can you expect the stone to honor James as Dunlaidir's new master when one so brave and bold—"

"So you are coming to care for him."

"I am not . . ." Caterine trailed off when Rhona's mouth crooked in a knowing smile. Crossing her arms, Caterine fixed her with an unblinking stare.

"You *do* favor him."

"He . . . *intrigues* me," Caterine admitted, not willing to concede more. Taking the younger woman by the elbow, she escorted her across the rush-strewn floor and out of the chamber. Only when she closed and barred the door behind her, did she release the breath she'd been holding.

Across the room, the wooden bowl and its cloth-covered contents beckoned, but at the moment, she'd rather plunge her hand into a pit of hissing vipers than peek beneath the harmless-looking cloth.

Should, after all these years, the Laird's Stone choose this moment to perform for her, its tears heralding Sir Marmaduke Strongbow as Dunlaidir's new master might prove more of a shock than she could shoulder.

For Rhona knew her well.

She favored him indeed.

And that knowledge disturbed her almost as much as her reasons for not wanting to.

⚜

"By *rope*?" James gaped at the sturdy length of knotted rope disappearing over Dunlaidir's seaward wall. "A horde of flaming firedrakes wouldn't send me down that cliff on a rope. The drop is sheer with nary a ledge to rest upon."

Sir Ross stopped tying knots in a second rope long enough to toss him an amused glance. "Dinna tell me you'd prefer the latrine chute?"

The other men chuckled. Even the most-times dour Sir John joined in their mirth. "It would be a fast ride down," he agreed, peering over the wall. "That I warrant."

James remained silent, his mouth pressed into a tight-lipped line.

"Aye, a swift descent to be sure . . . if a bit smelly," another of the MacKenzie men, Sir Alec, blustered, the good-natured gleam in his eyes evidence to all save James, that he meant the words in harmless jest.

"Enough." Marmaduke swept them with a comradely but warning glance.

"No ill will meant, young sire." Alec gave James a friendly thwack on the arm. "Our blood yet runs high from this morn, is all."

"And the day is not yet spent. Jocular banter will not see the latrine chute sealed." Marmaduke glanced at the line of dark storm clouds crouching above the horizon before turning to Ross. "Have you finished with the second rope?"

"Aye," the Highlander affirmed and yanked hard on the rope. "It bears enough knots for its purpose and is strong enough to support an ox if need be."

Marmaduke tossed a glance through one of the crenel openings at the jagged rocks, below. Chill seawind whipped his hair and whistled past his ears, but he welcomed its salt-laden bite.

The intruders' round-hulled coracle still bobbed atop the swells and great plumes of sea spray shot high up the cliff face. Of his assailant's corpse, was nary a trace. Only the tiny boat, the roar of the surf, and the dangling rope.

Turning away from the wall, he unbuckled his sword belt and handed it to Sir John. The fourth MacKenzie warrior, Sir Gowan, helped him shrug out of his mailed shirt. Once free of his undertunic as well, he slanted a sidelong glance at James.

The young lord peered over the wall. "You do not expect me to go down that rope?" A dull red flush began inching up his neck. "I . . . I cannot swim."

"And no one is asking you to," Marmaduke assured him, stretching his arms over his head and flexing his fingers.

"The second rope is to lower the satchel and drawplate. I will use the other to climb down the cliff. You and Ross need only hold the ropes."

"Him hold one of the ropes? Best say your prayers if it's yours." The gruff voice came from the back of the circle of men gathered near and was quickly followed by a merry round of sniggers and snorts.

The Keith men.

". . . a-taking your life in your hands, Strongbow, or rather, leaving it in his hands," another called out, his booming voice echoing off the thick stone of the seawall.

Quelling their buffoonery with a black look, Marmaduke knelt on the cobbles to secure the satchel and the drawplate to the knot-free end of the second rope.

"Have a care holding this," he said to Ross, then tossed the rope and its weighty cargo over the wall. "I do not wish to attempt this twice."

Saints, his innards twisted at the very thought.

They clenched even more at the possibility James Keith might not have the stamina to support his weight.

But he'd take his chances on both counts.

The expectant expressions on the faces of Dunlaidir's household knights left him little choice.

Thus committed, he returned to where the first rope disappeared over the edge of the same embrasure opening his assailant had fallen through earlier.

The man's death scream echoed in his mind the instant his fingers closed around the knotted rope.

"Do not disappointment me," he said, thrusting the end of the rope into James's hands. "I am not yet ready to exit this world."

Then, before his own niggling doubts about James's capabilities could stop him, he swung himself over the wall. Fierce gusts of sea wind seized him at once, ceaseless blasts of brine-laden air that bit into his bare back and whipped his hair across his face, making the perilous descent even more difficult.

He kept his gaze on the vertical rock face in front of him. Glistening wet and dark, the very stone reeked of the sea and a fouler, more rank odor that could only have to do with the purpose of his descent.

As he neared the bottom, great plumes of whitish foam shot upward, encircling him in a shimmering, luminescent cloud that misted his skin and lent cooling relief to his straining arm and thigh muscles.

At last his feet met the jumble of rocks at the cliff's base, but a thick coating of darkish slime and slippery clumps of long-tendrilled seagrass made the simple feat of standing an earnest challenge.

Frigid waves slammed into the backs of his knees, posing a further test to his balancing skills. The satchel and drawplate rested nearby and the garderobe chute loomed not five feet above the rocks, protected from the sea's endless pounding by a cave-like niche carved deep into the face of the cliff.

Securely tied to one of the larger rocks, the coracle rose and fell with the sea's turbulent rhythm. Eager to be done, Marmaduke thrust his dirk into the hide-covered hull. He made several long gashes, then cut the tethers, freeing the little boat to sink beneath the waves.

Straightening, he made his way to the cliff face. Someone long before him had cut deep into the rock, widening what must've been a natural fissure. An alcove of sorts, shielded from the most vicious lashings of the wind but filled with heavy, stagnant air.

Long-corroded shards of twisted iron protruded from the opening's edges, bearing testament that a grate of some sorts had once guarded this foul-reeking route out of, or into, the bowels of Dunlaidir.

Revulsion and a keen awareness of the pressing need to

be done before the heavens cracked open, lent speed to his handiwork.

Blessedly, the drawplate proved a perfect fit.

No further murder-minded miscreants would use the chute to breach Dunlaidir's walls.

At least not until he knew his lady safely on the other side of Scotland, happily ensconced in his own soon-to-be-claimed, better guarded, and eminently more comfortable Balkenzie.

But closer than Balkenzie and, at the moment, of far greater import, the storm that had appeared so far out to sea neared at an alarming pace. The air around him crackled, prickling his skin and lifting the hairs on his arms.

Arms no longer slick with mere sweat and salt spray, but streaked with grime.

His hands were worse.

Swallowing hard, Marmaduke stared at the tossing waves. Cold and wild, there was no question they'd be invigorating as well as cleansing.

And he had promised himself a dip in the sea.

Above him, James leaned through one of the crenel openings, watching him. His baited expression left no doubt that he waited to see if Marmaduke would make good his boasting.

He'd lose already-gained ground with James should he abstain. His decision made, and before his good sense prevailed, he dived off the narrow ledge of rocks.

The icy water embraced him, its shock near stopping his heart. A strong undertow threatened to whisk him out to sea, but before the current could pull him deeper, another more powerful cross-current caught him in the side, rolling him over and over before slinging him against a wall of submerged rock.

His head and shoulders broke the surface close enough to the base of the cliff for him to grab hold of one of the rocks and swing himself over its edge to safety.

His lungs screamed for air, his entire right side burned as if afire, and the sting of the saltwater near stole the vision from his good eye, but he'd kept his word.

For a long moment, he didn't move and simply let the water course down his limbs. He took several deep, restorative gulps of air, filling his lungs before he squeezed the water from his hair, then ran both hands down his face.

Clean hands.

Clean arms.

A body freed of every last speck of foul matter, his manhood so thoroughly chilled even the tempting image of his lady unclothed and willing wasn't potent enough to stir him.

*For the moment.*

The corners of his mouth lifted in a wry little smile.

It was time to face another challenge.

One requiring an infinitely greater act of faith than diving into the sea.

He was about to discover if James Keith was man enough to help him scale the cliff.

And to rule as Dunlaidir's master once he and his lady were gone.

# Chapter Eight

✦

$\mathcal{A}$ BRACE OF candles, tall ones of purest beeswax, and a bronze oil lamp suspended from the ceiling on a chain, illuminated the late Niall Keith's private solar. Caterine sat on a stool next to the chamber's curtained bed, scarcely breathing, and trying hard to quell the disquieting sensation that someone, *something,* watched her from the shadows.

Shifting pools of blue-black filled the corners, well beyond reach of the wavering candle glow and the cresset lamp's low-burning flame.

Dark and eerie, of a certainty, but not a trysting place for spirits.

Feeling somewhat better, she drew a deep, backbone-steeling breath and unclenched her hands. Her edginess was as foolhardy as Rhona believing in stones that cried.

The room held naught more daunting than dust and stale air.

Originally intended as a true solar, her late husband had preferred to sleep within its mural-painted walls, leaving her to her own quarters, a much more welcoming room, if colder with its windows opening directly onto the sea.

The haven of her bedchamber called to her now, but she tamped down the urge to return there and, instead, reached down to stroke Leo's back. The little dog lay curled atop her feet, his warm weight a comfort in the oppressive silence.

A heavy quiet broken only by the patter of rain beating on the windows and Sir Lachlan's occasional snores. The injured Highlander slept in the freshly dressed bed, lulled to a deep slumber by the potency of Caterine's specially prepared painkilling elixir.

Once, he'd opened bleary eyes and smiled at her, mumbling a few unintelligible words before falling swiftly back to sleep. If the saints smiled on her, he'd awaken again. His genial company would be a glad respite from the uneasy memories welling inside her since crossing the solar's threshold.

Reaching out, she smoothed the bedcovers for the wounded knight. His steady breathing and lack of fever foretold a rapid recovery, and little else mattered.

Least of all Niall's ghost peering at her from the shadow-cast corners.

Mocking her for having ne'er been able to rouse him.

Caterine's brow knitted.

Niall hadn't been an ogre. He'd not even sought her affections after the first year of their marriage. And not once had he chided her for her inability to properly stir him.

He had understood how her initiation to womanhood had robbed her of all desire to explore her femininity.

Patient even in those first twelve months, her late husband often let her withdraw to the sanctum of her own chamber, tactfully claiming her next visit to his bed would prove fruitful.

But they never had and he'd eventually ceased sending for her.

And now, with a new marriage looming on the horizon, the very walls of Niall's old solar seemed steeped with his presence.

Disquieted, Caterine shifted on the tapestry-covered stool. She'd brought the stool from her own chamber, not wishing to sit in the cumbersome chair of richly carved oak Niall had reclined in to watch her disrobe during those early attempts at what he referred to as conjugal pleasure.

Determined to vanquish him, she scooped Leo onto her lap, snuggling him close against her, her gaze on the three arch-topped windows set into the opposite wall.

Unlike her own chamber, the solar boasted windows of glass. Small, round panes set in lead and of an indiscernible opaque color. Difficult to see through, but a luxury nevertheless.

As were the thickly strewn furred skins covering the cold stone of the floor. An extravagance Niall had allowed himself, and one that kept the room much warmer than hers.

So why couldn't she banish the chillbumps from her arms?

Even the pulsing heat emanating from the hearth's low-burning peat fire failed to warm her.

Fighting the urge to chatter her teeth, Caterine glanced at the Highlander. He'd rolled onto his side and flung one well-muscled arm over his face. But still, he slept.

Relieved, she turned back to the windows. Gloaming neared and the light, what little there was of it on such a storm-swept afternoon, had changed, lending a rare, luminescent quality to the milky window glass.

The skin of her nape prickled, for the color of the panes came very close to the pale gray of her late husband's eyes.

Eyes that peered at her from the rain-streaked glass!

Hundreds of pairs of Niall's eyes.

Her heart slammed against her ribs and a cry rose in her throat, lodging there when the image shifted and the silver rivulets of rain became tears, the hundreds of staring eyes, her own.

A loud crack of thunder shook the room, rattling the fragile glass panes and sending Leo bolting from her lap to seek refuge under the great four-poster bed.

The thunder's still-echoing rumbles banished the disturbing image as well.

Once again, the three tall windows appeared as they always had, with naught save a fine layer of dust and a sad build-up of grime to distinguish them.

A great shudder ripped through her, streaking clear to her toes. Amazingly, the young Highlander slept on, blissfully unaware of the storm raging outside, blessedly ignorant of the one warring within Caterine's own breast.

Only Leo sensed her ill-ease. He peered at her from beneath the bed, his round eyes quizzical and tinged with sympathy she didn't want. Not even from dear sweet Leo.

She alone crafted her nightmares, and she alone would besiege them.

To prove it, she twisted around and stared hard at Niall's oaken great chair. If aught in the chamber wished to taunt her, it would be his monstrosity of a chair.

But the empty chair stood mute.

Harmless.

A hulking mass of dark wood in the farthest corner, well-hidden by shadow.

No image of an aging husband reclined in the chair, his gaze anxious and hopeful, manifested to torment her.

Her pulse slowing somewhat, she started to turn away, but the cresset lamp's flickering light flared bright before she could. Caterine stared, spellbound, as the lamp's soft glow spread into the murky corner to mesh with the echoes of days and nights long past, and sprang to bold life in the massive oak chair.

But it was not Niall's sprawled form her imagination conjured.

It was *his.*

Her champion's.

And wearing his fur-lined great cloak with naught beneath!

He'd flung one powerfully muscled leg over the side of

the chair and held a magnificently jeweled chalice to his
lips. His cloak gaped slightly, its heavy folds draped open
just enough to give her a tantalizing glimpse of his hard-
trained body in all its masculine glory.

For it was the glory part of him the gaping mantle revealed.

Fine, manly splendor fully aroused.

And every bit as imposing as his jesting men had im-
plied.

Caterine gulped, her heart thudding.

Looking more real, more full-bodied and whole, than a
dream image aught do, the Sassunach took a slow sip of
wine, then lifted his chalice in silent toast to someone she
couldn't see. His expression held a wealth of some emotion
she couldn't define for she'd ne'er seen such a look on a
man's face.

A look her heart recognized even if she didn't.

A look of infinite adoration.

*Of love,* shining, pure, and true.

Something she'd doubted existed and might be tempted
to believe was possible . . . were she looking at a flesh and
blood man and not peering deep into the darkest corners of
her own soul.

There, where her hidden desires resided.

A fierce yearning consumed her, a need so intense she
ached with wanting. Her throat tightened painfully even
while the rest of her seemed to soften and grow warm.

But another great peal of thunder and a silvery flash of
lightning shattered this image, too, and then, as if the raging
elements meant to mock her, the storm seemed to hold its
breath, going so silent she could almost hear the fierce
pounding of her own heart.

That, and a low rumbling too near to be lingering echoes
of thunder.

Not rumbling . . . growls.

And by the time the realization dawned, Leo's snarls

erupted into a series of sharp little dog barks. Hackles raised, he burst from beneath the bed to charge the door, reaching it just as it swung open to reveal *him*.

In a flash of golden-brown fur, his jaws snapping, Leo pounced on Sir Marmaduke's ankles. His shrill barks reached an ear-splitting level only to stop abruptly when the tall English knight turned a stern look on him.

With a yelp, Leo streaked back beneath the massive bed. Still shaken, Caterine would've yelped and run for cover, too, but her limbs proved too leaden to move and her throat seemed stuffed with wool.

Lachlan gave a low moan and tossed on the bed, the distraction allowing her time to gather her wits. She cleared her throat. "W-what are you doing here?" she asked her champion.

"In this chamber or beneath your roof?"

He came forward with confident strides, his broad-shouldered presence overwhelming in the close confines of the solar.

Caterine swallowed, her heart skittering out of beat.

Candle shine glinted off the thick mane of his dark hair and spilled across the hard-muscled expanse of his tunic-clad chest. but the flickering light didn't illuminate his face, and with his features half obscured by shadow, traces of the handsome man he'd once been were hauntingly apparent.

Caterine pushed to her feet, amazed her legs supported her. Faith, but her knees trembled. Nay, they *knocked*. "I . . ." she trailed off, a heated blush flaming her cheeks.

"I know what you meant." Placing his hands on her shoulders, he cast a glance into the dark recess of the curtained bed. "I came to see how Lachlan fares. I'd heard he rests comfortably, but wanted to see for myself."

"Oh." Caterine blinked.

Ne'er had she felt more a fool.

But, of course, he'd come to look in on his man.

Then she caught the twinkle of humor in his good eye.

He caught her hand to his lips. "And I came to see you," he said, releasing her.

A veritable cascade of pleasurable sensation swept through her.

To hide her discomfiture, she flicked her hand at a nearby tray of half-eaten buttered bannocks and roasted sea-tangle, a palatable seaweed, the stalks of which made a fine savory dish. "My stepson brought me a respite earlier," she said, wincing inwardly when he arched a skeptical brow at the meager offerings.

"Humble but filling fare," she said, with a proud tilt to her chin. "James tells me you shall be with us but a short time," she added, seized by an uncontrollable urge to give voice to something that had plagued her ever since James revealed what he'd gleaned from the MacKenzie warriors.

Sir Marmaduke's brows snapped together. "It would seem young James needs instruction in stringing words together as sorely as he needs to practice wielding a sword."

"He spoke falsely?" The intensity of her relief surprised her. "You are not planning to leave?"

He looked past her to the bed. His man still slept. "I will not lie to you," he said after a moment, and folded his arms. "Your stepson spoke the truth, though I suspect he did so rather clumsily."

Caterine's relief spun away, as short-lived as the popping sparks that shot up occasionally from the smoldering peat fire. Her plans, Dunlaidir's safe-being, *everything,* whirled around her and crashed at her feet, bursting into a thousand fractured pieces.

He meant to leave.

To give her his name, then depart.

A name alone wouldn't repel Hugh de la Hogue, not without the man and the sword arm attached to it.

"You agreed to champion me, to lend us your warring skills," she finally said, her pride thick on her tongue.

"Indeed I did," he acceded. "To lend them to this strong-hold."

A sinking suspicion wrapped itself around her, its weight bearing down on her shoulders like a too-heavy cloak. "I see," she said, glancing away to stare at the windows. Blackness now pressed against them, and the flickering candles reflected off the glass panes. "Your skills and those of your men are but on loan."

Marmaduke swallowed an oath as dark as the young night descending outside the narrow windows. "That is a rather bald way to put it, my lady," he said, resisting an equally strong urge to throttle her stepson.

She looked back at him, her deep blue eyes bright in the mellow lighting. "Then how would you declare it?"

Glancing at the door he'd purposely left ajar, Marmaduke searched for words, for once at a loss. His much-acclaimed silver tongue failed him, deftly stilled by the top swells of his lady's breasts peeking at him above her gown's low-cut neckline.

The *arisaid* she'd draped around her shoulders had slipped, revealing just enough creamy flesh to challenge urges he'd rather keep in check . . . for now.

More distracted than he cared to be, he captured her chin with his thumb and forefinger. "Lending you our strength does not mean we shall leave on the morrow," he said. "I rode far to champion you and am well apprised of the villainy of your foe, as are my men. We shall not depart until this stronghold can sit secure on its own. That I swear to you."

She looked down and began nudging her toe against the edge of one of the furred skins on the floor. The gesture reminded him sharply of the way her sister had scuffed her toe against the stone chapel floor at Eilean Creag the morning she'd sought him out with her absurd plea.

A brief but thoroughly pleasing warmth sluiced through

Marmaduke. Toe scuffing was something Linnet MacKenzie did whenever something truly plagued her.

Something important.

A habit that always went straight to Marmaduke's heart.

Releasing Caterine's chin, he clasped his hands behind his back and resisted the urge to smile. "What troubles you, fair lady?"

The toe-nudging ceased instantly.

She looked up at him, sober-faced. "It is not for myself that I—" she broke off to clear her throat. "You came here aware of our plight, yet you see fulfilling your role by giving me your name and then abandoning us to remain as unprotected as before?"

"Did you not hear me promise this holding shall have sufficient strength to stand solid against any threat before we go?" He caught and held her gaze. "I do not break my word."

She appeared to mull that over, the slight crease between her brows making her look anything but convinced. "James cannot stand on his own and the remaining men in our garrison are too few to speak of. Our tenants and those villeins who haven't fled, are demoralized. Full weary from having to scratch out a living without our support."

Turning away, she pulled the woolen *arisaid* back up around her shoulders. "We do not even have stores enough to adequately feed those within our walls, much less aid the villagers who've depended on us in the past."

One corner of Marmaduke's mouth lifted in a lopsided smile. Unclasping his hands, he flexed his fingers. Such cares could be easily rectified. He'd faced greater challenges over the years, and mastered each one.

Mastered most, his demons amended.

Ignoring them, he gently turned her to face him.

"Those problems can and shall be dealt with," he assured her, letting his hands rest lightly on her shoulders. "Every last one of them. As I've vowed to give you the protection of my name, I give you my solemn oath on—"

"If you can accomplish such feats, which I can scarce believe," she cut in, doubt coloring her words, "then my bearing your name seems of little consequence."

She paused to reach down and stroke her little dog. The wee beastie had crept from his hiding place and now pressed himself against her legs. "Nay, sir, your name alone will not aid me," she said, straightening. "Most especially after you're gone."

"What you presume was never my intent," Marmaduke said, keenly aware of the dog's unblinking gaze.

"Nay?"

Marmaduke shook his head. "May the saints strike me down were it so."

"But you admit you mean to leave. James mentioned as soon as Yuletide—" He silenced her by placing the tips of two fingers ever-so-lightly against her temptingly soft lips.

"My intent was and remains the exact opposite of what you believe," he said, giving her his special smile.

One he'd practiced carefully in recent years.

The one he knew brought out his dimples.

"James heard correctly," he said, touching her cheek. "I would savor naught more than to be home by Yuletide . . . with you at my side. And not simply as the woman bearing my name but as my own true bride."

"Your true bride?"

"Of a certainty," he said, and her heartbeat quickened. "In every sense of the word."

⚜

". . . have done with him in every way I can think of," one of Dunlaidir's household knights bristled about the same time in the great hall. "The debased varlet doesn't deserve to live," he added, hammering the blunt end of his

knife on the table in bold emphasis of each angrily spat
word.

"Let him dangle him till the wind whistles through his
bones is what we aught do!" someone else broke in from one
of the other long tables, his fury almost palpable in the
smoke-hazed air.

"Hanging's too good for de la Hogue," a third vowed,
winning loud agreement from the others.

Though bone-chilling damp pervaded the hall's vastness,
strong spirits and stronger words heated the blood of the
men gathered at the bench-lined trestle tables.

At the end of the one nearest the low-arched entry to the
turnpike stairs, an aged black-frocked priest, Father Tomas,
kept a placid face, appearing more intent on smearing
mashed sea-tangle on a buttered bannock half than paying
heed to the escalating grumbles and curses.

His buttering efforts completed, he turned to the man at
his right, the Highlander, Sir Gowan. "God be praised you
are here," he said. "With your help, mayhap the travails Sir
Hugh has suffered upon the people hereabouts will soon be
naught but an ill memory."

"Hah!" Farther down the table, Sir John snorted with
telling eloquence. He waggled a finger at the old priest.
"That dastard won't be easily suppressed. He hasn't earned
his black reputation for naught. He glories in ruination and
has enough metal-clad henchmen to see us all in our
graves."

"All the more reason it should gladden us to have the
MacKenzie men at our sides," Father Tomas said, turning
his attention back to his bannocks.

An awkward silence fell, stretching uncomfortably until
Sir Ross half-rose off the bench, his ale mug held aloft. "A
toast!" his deep voice boomed. "To ridding this land of Sir
Hugh and his ilk, and to Strongbow and his new lady!"

Hearty acclamation rang out, voices rising and falling
with toasts of their own, all accompanied by the pounding of

fists on the long tables and the echoing thunder of stamping feet.

"By God's good graces, may this union be more propitious for him than the last!" Gowan shouted, waving his ale cup in the air.

"Sir Priest!" another voice rose above the ruckus. "When shall the happy twain be joined?"

The din wound down as all gazes sought the aged holy man. "In a sennight," Father Tomas answered around a bite of bannock. "Seven days."

The furor erupted anew with well-meant cheers, and a few bawdy jests.

And then the mood swung angry again.

". . . make a sound reckoning with him!"

". . . headsman with a blunt ax!"

". . . his quarters suspended in chains!"

And when the shouting reached a fever pitch, all brows dark with scorn and tempers high, a lone figure rose and quit the hall.

At the door to the outer stairs, he turned to survey the dissent behind him . . . and smiled.

Thanks to the ranting poltroons and their babble, he finally had viable news to share.

Viable, *valuable,* news.

Feeling much pleased, he swirled his cloak about his shoulders and stepped out into the cold, wet night.

# Chapter Nine

❦

*IN EVERY SENSE of the word.*

Tight bands of heat snaked around Caterine's chest as excitement stirred to life deep inside her.

"I cannot go with you," she blurted, purposely avoiding the most unsettling part of the Sassunach's declaration of her being his true bride. Her senses spinning, she grappled for excuses. "I am needed here. This demesne is . . ."

Something about the way he looked at her made her trail off. Wholly captivated by the strange thrall he'd cast over her, she stood silent as he lifted his hand to her face.

Holding her gaze, he smoothed his thumb along the edge of her jaw. "This demesne is in sore need of a masterful hand," he finished for her, his deep voice flowing into and over her. Smooth, warm, and utterly compelling. "James could hold it well if you would allow him to cease hiding behind your skirts."

"James—" His thumb slid oh-so-lightly over her lower lip and her objections evaporated, pushed aside by a sigh.

A great heaving one she could no sooner deny than the rapid thundering of her heart.

"Your stepson is not the only reason I would urge you to leave with me." He looked deep into her eyes, effortlessly holding her gaze. "Think you I am without needs, my lady?

Do you truly believe I could wed you and not wish to make you mine?"

Caterine swallowed. "S-such an arrangement was never intended," she stammered, tantalized by the sheer intimacy of standing so close to him, entranced by the way his mere words seemed to embrace her.

A spell-caster indeed, his nearness enfolded her in a charmed circle of burgeoning desires bold enough to make her half believe his touch might erase the darkness in her heart.

Challenge her worst fears . . . and win.

Watching her closely, he rubbed his chin and the candle glow caught on his signet ring's cabochon ruby. The large gemstone flashed red fire at her, instantly evoking the jeweled chalice he'd lifted in toast in her conjured image of him sitting in Niall's chair.

Heat shot up Caterine's neck.

She forced herself to hold his gaze, tried her best to ignore the winking ruby. "A true marriage was no one's purpose in scheming to get you here."

He arched a brow. "Think you?"

Caterine nodded.

"Sometimes others know us better than we know ourselves, my lady."

"Linnet and her husband know me well enough not to have pledged me to . . . to an Englishman."

"Indeed?" He slid his knuckles ever-so-gently down her cheek. "'Twas they who suggested I make you my bride in truth."

Caterine gasped. "Then you have charmed my sister."

"Nay, the good Lady Linnet charmed me," he said. "Had I known one of her sisters would hold such appeal for me, I swear to you, I would have come to win your heart years ago."

"As you won Arabella's?" The question sprang off her tongue before she realized she'd formed the words.

Embarrassed, she tried to glance away, but he crooked his fingers beneath her chin, his firm grip leaving her little choice but to stare back at him.

His face had gone a shade paler, and the line of his jaw appeared to have hardened a bit, but his expression didn't bear any of the anger she'd expected.

"Indeed I would like to woo you as I did Arabella," he said, his voice a notch deeper than usual, "and to speak to you of your sister as well . . . to tell you why I revere her."

He glanced at the door. It still stood ajar. "But first, I would have private words with you."

"Private words?" she echoed, her senses still careening with the intensity of his nearness, the name Arabella spinning a tight little knot of disquiet somewhere beneath her ribs.

"Perhaps I should say words spoken in private." He strode to the door, clearly confident she'd follow him.

And she did, much to his relief.

Closing his ears to the ethereal whispers breathed to life by her mention of Arabella's name, Marmaduke stepped into the torchlit passageway, glad to close the solar door on memories of summers gone and bliss-filled nights long past.

His new lady's scent swirled around him, its crisp, clean lightness chasing away the dark of another, long-faded fragrance, and sweeping through him with all the wonder of a bright new day.

A new life, he hoped.

She peered at him, questions filling her sapphire eyes, the smooth cream of her cheeks touched with just a hint of rose. "Will you tell me about her?" she probed, the words scarce audible above the wind whistling past the corridor's shuttered windows. "Who she was?"

Marmaduke nodded, too thick-throated to speak, the iron bands around his heart both tightening their grasp and snapping free.

Tugged in two directions.

One beautiful and dark, but cold as the sea battering Dunlaidir's cliffs; the other equally lovely but awash with all the golden light and warmth of a sunburst.

*Vibrantly alive,* and calling to him louder than the fast-fading echoes of another time.

Another woman's love.

"Aye, I will tell you of her," he forced the words, "but not in this corridor."

"Then, where?" She tilted her golden head to the side and her *arisaid* parted just enough to tempt him with another sweet glimpse of the top swells of her breasts, luscious enough to rub the silver clean off his tongue.

"Have you a squint?" he heard himself ask, the fool-sounding question tumbling from his lips before he could better articulate his concerns.

He almost grimaced, and would have, were it not for his scar. She already peered queerly at him, her brows arched in confusion.

Allowing a scowl to twist his features into an even more unappealing visage would only distress her further.

She blinked. "A squint?"

"A laird's lug," he clarified, using the more familiar Highland term. "A secret place where we can speak without prying eyes and straining ears."

*A safe trysting place where I might unburden my soul and where the dimness will flatter my ravaged face.*

*And keep my ghosts at bay.*

"There is one," she answered after a moment's hesitation. "It's built into the wall by the minstrels' gallery and reached by a hidden stairwell."

"Then let us go there." Marmaduke made to turn, but she stayed him with a surprisingly firm grip to his arm.

But rather than explain herself, she moistened her lips. Letting go of his arm as if touching him had singed her, she clasped her hands before her and peered at him from beneath down-drawn brows.

Relying on a wellspring of patience that could vex some beyond endurance, Marmaduke leaned one shoulder against the wall and crossed his ankles and arms.

Then he waited.

"I am well aware times are perilous," she said, her voice a little breathless. "But I do not see the need to seek out that wee cranny to speak privily."

"I would go there all the same," Marmaduke said, pushing away from the wall.

She frowned.

The toe of her slipper edged from beneath her skirts to nudge at the stone flagging of the passage floor.

Marmaduke re-folded his arms.

Her cheeks colored a deeper shade of pink. "The door to the hidden passage is in my bedchamber's ante-room," she said, at last giving price to her true reason for not wanting to take him there.

"It matters not," he said, trying to keep the corners of his mouth from turning up at the advantage her revelation gave him.

*Most especially since, as of this night, he intended to sleep in that ante-room.*

*And in a sennight, nearer still.*

"But—"

Marmaduke shook his head, his steely resolve cutting off her protest as soundly as if he'd snatched the words from her lips.

"Come," he said, raising his voice above the rattle of the shutters. "You may trust that I would not seek the cramped confines of a squint to bandy words with you did I not believe the measure to be necessary."

Placing his own trust in his ability to win her confidence, he overlooked the doubt in her eyes, an unflattering hesitancy he preferred to ignore, and held out his hand.

"Come," he repeated.

Slowly she took two steps forward, then slipped her hand

into his. A powerful emotion curled round his heart at the feel of her slender fingers lacing with his own, and his senses snapped to sharp-edged awareness.

"Ach! Here is a wonder." The lady Rhona's cheery voice scattered his dust-coated dreams.

His lady's companion came toward them, a basket of dried sphagnum moss clutched under one arm, and an earthen mazer of some sharp-smelling unguent in her free hand.

"My faith!" She gave them a look of contrived astonishment. "Is it not a mite cold and draughty to be standing about, here in the middle of the passage?"

She eyed their still-clasped hands. "Mayhap you should take yourselves off someplace more . . . private?"

"There is nary a corner of Dunlaidir that isn't private these days." Caterine's fingers tensed in his hand. "Lest you happen to be about," she added, leveling a bald look at her friend. "You, my lady, appear to be everywhere."

Her eyes widening, Rhona affected an injured look. "Then I shall repair myself to poor Sir Lachlan's bedside and see to my duties."

With feigned subservience, she wheeled around and reached for the door latch. Somehow, the edge of her basket bumped against Marmaduke's right side and he winced, drawing in a sharp breath as his ribs, still aching from his tangle with the submerged sea rocks, throbbed and burned.

Pressing his lips together, he waited for the pulsing waves of hot discomfort to recede. The saints knew he'd suffered worse in his time.

Without doubt, his lady's plump friend had jabbed her basket into him a-purpose, cleverly maneuvering herself so she could rake her makeshift weapon along his bruised ribs.

But why?

He knew women too well not to recognize a ploy.

"Faith and mercy!" Rhona cried then, her brows arcing upward. "James told me you'd hurt your side repairing the latrine chute, and now I've gone and made it worse. How clumsy I am."

Looking over-pleased with herself, she thrust her small bowl of foul-smelling unguent into Caterine's free hand. "'Tis crushed St. John's wort and betony," she said. "Naught is better for treating wounds."

Her gaze lighted briefly on Marmaduke's middle. "Mayhap the unguent will lend a spot of comfort to milord's bruised ribs?"

Before his lady could reply, Rhona slipped inside the solar, shutting the door soundly behind her.

"Come you, I would see that squint now," Marmaduke said as quickly, and hoped the shadows hid his elation.

He glanced at the wooden bowl of healing salve clutched in his lady's hand. Thanks to her friend's mischief, she now had little choice but to smooth the unguent onto his abraded flesh.

The corners of his mouth fought to widen into a wolfish grin, but Marmaduke resisted the urge and thanked the saints instead.

"Let us begone from here," he urged again. "I would be most obliged if you will apply your friend's unguent to my ribs."

"In the laird's lug?" She looked up at him, her gaze skeptical.

Marmaduke nodded.

The snug comfort of such a confined space suddenly boasted an appeal of a much different nature than merely shielding them from unwanted listeners.

"And will you?" he indicated his proffered arm.

She hesitated the breadth of a heartbeat, then linked her arm with his. "Aye, sirrah, I will," she agreed with a slight tremor in her voice.

Her simple acceptance of the task sent warmth coursing through Marmaduke.

"Then lead on, my lady," he said.

As they moved down the darkened corridor, Marmaduke breathed another silent prayer of appreciation for this small victory.

He hadn't yet won the battle, but with a spot of unexpected help, he'd successfully laid the groundwork for besieging his lady's heart.

❧

Sir Marmaduke Strongbow passed through the sanctum of her bedchamber with all the lordly overbearing of the master of the keep, but also with a long-strided confidence that spoke to her most feminine core, beguiling her with its seductive potency.

Without even glancing at the great curtained bed, its covers already turned back invitingly for the coming night's rest, he entered the chamber's tiny ante-room.

"Behind the chest and the tapestry?" he asked, his brow quirking in amusement as his gaze latched onto the secret door's hiding place.

Caterine nodded.

Words weren't necessary.

The ante-room's walls were bare save a small assortment of cloaks hanging from pegs, a few sputtering torchlights, and two very narrow windows facing straight out onto the night.

Heart in her throat, her pulse louder in her ears than the howling wind, she watched him shove the large iron-bound strongbox out of the way, then lift down the heavy Flemish tapestry to reveal a low round-headed door cut into the thickness of the wall.

The door's rusted hinges screamed protest when he opened it, and a whoosh of stale air sailed into the little ante-room, the musty smell a clear challenge to any daring enough to breach the dark threshold and mount the curving stair beyond.

"Can we not speak here?" Setting Rhona's healing unguent atop the chest, Caterine rubbed her arms against the chill damp streaming in through the unshuttered window slits.

Better to freeze than suffocate on age-old dust and mold.

Rather than answer her, Marmaduke took one of the resin torches from its bracket on the wall, and, holding it aloft, indicated the worn stone steps circling upward into the darkness. "My sorrow that such a measure is needed," he said, his gaze compelling her to follow him.

For here was a man whose commanding presence held such power, a stone carving would melt at his feet.

*A female stone carving.*

Caterine hitched up her skirts and ascended the winding stairs behind him. He'd already thrust the torch into an iron holder on the wall when she emerged into the closeness of the laird's lug and its flickering light cast wildly dancing shadows all about them, lending a surreal atmosphere to the tiny chamber.

Little more than a widening in the thickness of the wall, the laird's lug offered two spy holes. One gave a fair view of the great hall directly below, while the other allowed those who so desired to peer straight into the minstrels, gallery just beyond the farthest wall.

The cramped space made the English knight seem taller, his broad shoulders wider, and the poor lighting erased his scar and shadowed his bad eye, leaving only the proud, masculine lines of a nobly formed, strikingly handsome face.

One he no doubt wanted to show her but could never have done by the light of day or in the great hall with scores of torches set a-blaze.

But he showed her now, and what she saw was a face that won hearts.

*Arabella's heart.*

Suddenly needing air, Caterine moved to the spy hole that looked down onto the hall. She stood on her toes to draw in great gulps of the less offensive air pouring in through the small opening.

Air seasoned with the tang of wood-smoke and roasting meats rather than the stifling scent of old stone and closed places.

Far below, men clustered at the trestle tables, noisily partaking of the evening meal. They argued, for their raised voices carried, the deeper ones echoing off the little spy chamber's walls and low ceiling.

But Caterine scarce heard their bickering.

She only heard another woman's name.

She swung round to face him. "You will think me devilish bold, sir, but I am not a woman prone to courtly airs," she said with as much dignity as she could muster. "I have little patience with such foolery and prefer plain speaking. Thus, I must say, for whatever purpose you dragged me up here, I shall make ill company lest you tell me who—"

"Who Arabella was?"

*"Was?"*

"Aye, was, for she lives no more." Stepping closer, he cradled her face between his hands, a wealth of loss and empty years mirrored in the depths of his good eye. "Arabella MacKenzie was my liege laird's sister, and she was my wife."

Caterine gulped back the cold shame swelling in her throat. Guilt because his answer both sorrowed and relieved her. "Will you tell me of her?" she asked, wincing inwardly when a shade of discomfort crossed his face.

Ill-ease swept over her, too, for the intimacy of the laird's lug and the warmth of his large hands on her face stirred disturbing emotions deep inside her, and left her more open, more vulnerable, than she'd ever been.

He slid his hands behind her neck and began caressing the sensitive skin of her nape. Caterine sighed, her shame falling away, washed free by the bliss of his touch, banished by the tingling warmth his gently massaging fingers sent spilling through her.

"She was a proud and passionate woman," he began, the words overlaid with a dark, hollow tone as if wrenched from the very depths of his soul. "She died because she overheard a plot to murder her brother. The perpetrators were my liege's own lady wife and his half-brother, the harlot's lover. They poisoned Arabella to still her tongue."

Caterine gasped. "Were they punished?" she asked in a tight little voice, her conscience smiting her for encouraging him. The pain on his face shattered the casing of her heart with more effectiveness than any silvered words.

"They are both dead," he said after a long moment, "and I have no doubt they've had to account for their wickedness before a greater judge than man."

Staring past her, he heaved a great sigh. "The strife they caused has long been laid to rest and is best forgotten, my lady. Life goes on and it is the privilege of the living to make the best we can of each new day."

"You speak like a holy man."

"I am no monk, that I assure you," he said, a definite trace of amusement in his voice.

"Nor am I a fool." He let his fingers light briefly on the scar slashing across his cheek. "As you see, I was left with a living reminder of the dark deeds done that day, but I learned well from the errors I made—"

"That is when you were scarred?"

He nodded. "My own foolhardiness bested me as much as my opponent's mastery with a sword," he said, and blew out a breath of clear frustration. "So outraged was I, that I ignored the most elemental rule of swordplay and let my emotions make me careless. The mistake cost me dear."

"I am sorry."

Caterine stared at him in the muted light, seeing not the Englishman, but simply *a man*.

One who'd lost much.

"What has gone before cannot be undone, " he said, his tone indicating he meant more than his own ill-starred past. "Nor are all hurtful experiences entirely bad if we learn and grow from them. The burdens I've carried have made me a wiser, more cautious man."

He paused, waiting as a particularly boisterous clamor from the hall below swelled into the laird's lug, then slowly ebbed away. "I will not allow you to fall prey to the same underhanded machinations that cost Arabella her life."

"That is why you wished to speak to me here? To caution me that you fear a turncoat moves amongst us?"

"I do not fear it, I am certain of it," he said. "James was indeed fallen upon by two intruders, though I would bid you to keep the knowledge to yourself. Someone in your household aided the second interloper in his escape."

He stepped back from her, and the sudden withdrawal of his warmth, his strength, left her almost shivering.

Clasping his hands behind his back, he began pacing the spy chamber's scant length. "I've sealed the cliff-side latrine chute, thus rendering that access useless, but such precautions are of little avail if someone within your walls would throw wide the gate for your enemies."

"Then what precautions would you suggest?"

"Your priest will proclaim the third banns for our nuptials in a few days and he tells me we can be wed in a sennight." Hesitating, he peered hard at her. "Until the day, and as of this night, I shall bed down in your ante-room."

"But—"

"We have both been married before. No one will raise a brow if they believe we wish to become better acquainted before you wear my ring."

Caterine's gaze dropped to his ruby signet ring. Just looking at it, and knowing its significance, sent a slow-pulsing warmth curling through the lowest part of her belly.

"I do not wish to wear your ring. The marriage is to be in name only," she said. "A pretense."

"A pretense only works if it is believed."

"You cannot sleep in my ante-room."

He folded his arms. "Only until we speak our vows."

Relief, and a wee tinge of regret, sluiced through Caterine.

But not for long.

Her eyes flew wide. "What do you mean *only until*?"

"Exactly that," he allowed, feigning a look of mock innocence some secret part of her found . . . endearing.

"Once we are wed, I shall sleep where all good husbands are wont to sleep," he informed her. "In my lady wife's bed."

⚜

In a different tower chamber, one located at the very end of yet another of Dunlaidir's winding passageways, James Keith sprawled in a chair before his hearth fire nursing his aching leg and his fouler mood.

Across the room, his great four-poster bed loomed empty and cold, a silent sentinel to his dark musings and his inability to fill its splendor with aught but his own fool self and his more foolish dreams.

Expelling a sigh, he pushed to his feet and limped to the windows. The most magnificent in all of Dunlaidir, the bank of tall, traceried windows followed the curvature of the chamber wall, offering sweeping views not only of the endless expanse of the sea, but also of the rugged cliffs on which the stronghold stood.

Night-blackened now, their shutters flung wide to embrace the wet chill and racing wind, the opened windows looked out on an impenetrable curtain of darkness.

A perfect reflection of James's own self.

And his prospects as master of this massive pile of stone perched on the very edge of the sea.

*The Laird's Stone hadn't yet wept for him,* Rhona had told

him earlier . . . as she'd reminded him every night since his father's passing.

*But it would,* she'd hasten to assure him.

As if the mere assertion would make it so.

James raked a hand through his hair and filled his lungs with the cold salt air. If only he could fill his heart with the valor that should have been bred in the bones of one such as he, then mayhap the stone would indeed acknowledge him.

But daring and skill couldn't be absorbed as easily as chill briny air, nor could iron-fisted fathers be pleased by less than the ablest of sons.

And the Laird's Stone wouldn't cry for a failure.

Bracing one hand against the molded edge of the nearest window, James tried to ignore the throbbing in his leg. But he could no sooner vanquish the knifing pain than he could block out the roar of the sea crashing against the rocks below.

Or stop his ears from straining to catch a lighter sound, one he waited for each night: Rhona's footfalls as she neared his door with a ewer of wine.

A nightly ritual.

An innocent game he suspected she concocted to make him feel like the lord he wasn't.

*The laird's due,* she called it. Something she claimed he needed before retiring . . . his wine cup replenished!

Scowling, he almost hurled the empty chalice out the opened window. Instead, his fingers clenched around its cold stem until his temper receded. He didn't need spirits to aid his slumber.

He needed . . . Rhona.

Her open arms and willing kisses.

Not the libations she dispensed so sweetly each night.

Nay, not *sweetly.*

Provocatively.

For, of late, she often appeared at his door with the neckline of her gown dipping so low, he'd swear she purposely altered them . . . or, at the very least, loosened their ties.

And all so he'd be sure to catch a glimpse of her dusky nipples!

A glimpse and nothing more.

A bounty offered but not served.

A sweetmeat presented solely to bedevil him.

Frowning darker than the night, James turned away from the windows and returned to his chair. He settled onto its cold oaken seat with a *harrumph* angry and bold enough to suit the most jaded laird-watchers.

Then he cradled his empty wine cup in the palm of one hand and waited for the light footfalls and quick tap-tapping on his door that would herald another torturously sweet glimpse of the lush wares of the maid he hoped to make his own.

And for the coming dawn and his first lesson in lordly sword wielding.

Instruction in the fine art of being a brave Scottish laird.

A lesson offered and taught by an English knight!

The irony of it stung his pride but also gave him hope.

Hope enough to chisel a bit of the scowl off his face and inspire him to thank the saints for his sweet-nippled lady and her meddling ways.

# Chapter Ten

❧

"I WILL MAKE you a bargain, my lady." Sir Marmaduke examined the red-gleaming facets of his signet ring's sizable ruby, feigning greater interest in the gemstone than in the look on Lady Caterine's upturned face.

She wore an expression unflattering enough to thoroughly negate the dubious measure of advantage he'd hoped to gain from the spy chamber's muted lighting.

Indeed, she peered at him as if kissing a round score of lepers held more appeal than him sleeping in her bedchamber's ante-room.

Stiffening his spine, he braved her unblinking stare on his firm conviction that the slight narrowing of her sapphire eyes had more to do with her own stubborn pride than any true aversion to his announced intentions.

"I do not like to bargain," she said at last.

"Then a promise."

"What manner of a promise?" Her wary gaze latched onto his ring.

A perfect focus for what he meant to say.

"Lady, I am not a callow youth," he began, squaring his shoulders. "I am a man, and fully equipped with all the usual accoutrements, I assure you. I will not promise you a chaste marriage bed for that would be a falsehood before the words left my tongue."

He raised her hand to his lips. "But I swear I shall never touch you intimately lest you will that I do so."

Her eyes flew wide. "Meaning you shall touch me in *non*-intimate ways? At will? As it suits you?"

"Nay, my lady, my desire is to suit *your* will."

"Mayhap I do not wish to be . . . suited?"

"Then, once you are mine, I shall be the more hard-pressed to convince you otherwise." He released her hand. "And to please you."

Something—temper, disbelief, or perhaps even a spark of interest—flared in her eyes. "And you believe you can?"

"Convince you or please you?"

She moistened her lips, her cheeks turning scarlet. "Both."

"Of a certainty, I shall endeavor to accomplish both." He made the words a frank statement. "Especially the pleasing part."

Touching his ring to the tip of her nose, he added, "As you shall please me."

*Faugh! She would sooner diddle the devil,* his demons roared with malicious levity.

Fortunately, their insolence only sharpened his determination, and spurred him to defy the niggling doubts they'd flung at him by pursuing a bolder avenue to his objective.

Such as having her massage the healing ointment onto his flesh.

Now.

He glanced about the shadowy laird's lug for the little bowl, remembering too late that she'd left the sharp-smelling unguent in the ante-room.

For an interminable moment, silence yawned between them, its heavy pall coating the air. The night must have lengthened, for thick quiet rose from the great hall as well.

Dunlaidir's occupants, their hunger sated and their thirst

quenched, had either sought out their guard posts or laid themselves to rest.

Save two.

And one of the two peered at him with as much doubt peeking out from the blue pools of her luminous eyes as he himself kept stashed under lock and key in the deepest pit of his soul.

"You think I shall please you?" The hushed words came so soft Marmaduke scarce believed he'd heard them.

But he had, and they melted his heart.

"I know you shall. Never doubt it." The rich timbre of his voice as well as the portent of his words enfolded her in a wondrously languid warmth.

Made her feel . . . wanted.

And almost free of shame.

Watching her with an intensely focused expression, he traced his fingers along her cheekbone, then eased his hand around the back of her neck. His caress, light as a summer breeze, sent tingling ripples of sensation fanning through her.

Sensations she'd only known long-ago inklings of, but never the full glory . . . till now.

He looked down at her, his gaze disturbingly knowing, its intensity wooing her senses as surely as his touch stirred pleasurable flutters low in her belly.

Closing her eyes, she reveled in his warmth and the bracing scents clinging to him: the fresh tang of the wind-whipped sea and salty breezes, leather and clean, polished steel.

A hint of wood-smoke, the spicy musk of his maleness, and the magic of starry nights and moonbeams.

*Starry nights and moonbeams?*

Caterine's eyes snapped open.

She bit her lower lip . . . and tried not to inhale.

He smiled.

Then he took away his hand and stepped back, his withdrawal leaving her breathless.

Stunned, more than a little confused, and yearning for more of the brief glimpse of magic he'd shown her.

She lifted her own hand to her nape and skimmed her fingertips over the place where he'd touched her.

The skin there still tingled.

And her heart hadn't yet ceased knocking wildly against her ribs.

"Will you apply the unguent now, Caterine?" His voice came deeper, a note huskier than before. "Mayhap below, before the fire in your chamber?"

She nodded, not trusting herself to speak.

Not that her thick tongue would've formed a coherent word had she tried.

*He* suffered no such affliction.

With all the mastery of a well-practiced spell-caster, his words and his touch worked their magic. Little by little, he tore loose the locks and restraints shielding her from his charm, ripping down her defenses and casting every last shred of her resistance to the four winds.

His Englishness remained the one thing he couldn't undo, but, much to her surprise, even that blemish didn't seem so glaringly annoying . . . at the moment.

So long as he looked at her as he was doing now.

She waited as he turned away to lift the resin torch from its bracket on the wall. Her chest tight with prickling anticipation, she followed him down the winding stairs and through the little ante-room, pausing only long enough to snatch the bowl of healing salve before tagging after him into her bedchamber.

He made straight for the hearth, his bold claiming of her private quarters and the undeniable ease with which he moved through them, sending showers of tremors spiraling through her. Just watching him breathed pulsing life into all her dormant hopes and dreams, long-lost bundles of wishes winking at her from the farthest horizons of her heart.

Unbidden, the layer of years peeled away, falling aside as if time no longer existed, leaving only the fanciful girl she'd once been and the woman she was fast becoming.

A woman entranced, and very close to entering the untrodden realm of her own beckoning femininity.

Content to simply look at him, Caterine lingered in the threshold to her chamber, allowing herself a few moments to savor the wonder of him . . . before other memories could intrude, their hold on her sealing the door to her soul.

A door he'd cracked with brilliant ease.

Unthinkable, if ever he flung it wide.

"You said my sister charmed you," she blurted, those other memories pushing hard on the door. "I do not believe you. You are the enchanter, the one who ensnares, pulling others into your web of smooth words and moonspun magic."

He cast a skeptical glance at the closed shutters stretching the length of the opposite wall. Nary a glimmer of moonlight fell through the wooden slats.

Even the deep alcove of the window embrasure with its two facing seats swam in darkness.

Looking back at her, he cocked a single brow.

The simple gesture spoke volumes.

"There is no moon this night," he said anyway. "Only a storm."

"I am full aware of both those facts." Caterine pulled her *arisaid* more securely around her shoulders. "Especially the storm."

"I see that you are," he intoned. Not meaning a whit of the wind and rain blasting through the night. "I, too, have noted it," he added.

And meant the storm inside her.

As had she.

His gaze lighted on the bowl of unguent clutched tight in

her hand. Caterine swallowed, already wishing she hadn't agreed to smear the salve on his ribs.

The very thought undid her.

She drew a shaky breath . . . and stared at him, wholly unable to move.

A bone-chilling damp pervaded the chamber, but she burned with the heat of a thousand flaming torches. Someone, most likely the e'er faithful Eoghann, had stoked the hearth fire, but its token warmth couldn't match the fire raging in her belly.

Nor could its welcoming glow and smoky-sweet scent entice her to take a single step forward.

For truth, the hapless clump of smoldering peat hissed and spit in its grate, seeming to warn her to keep her distance lest she find her defenses paltry proof against Marmaduke Strongbow's pervasive allure.

An amazingly powerful appeal had seized firm hold of her the instant he stepped to the edge of the fire's glow and began unbuckling his sword belt.

"I said I would tell you how your sister charmed me," he said, placing the belt and his brand atop a nearby table.

"Would you believe I could not even smile before she began plying me with potent healing concoctions to relax my damaged facial muscles?"

Caterine blinked. Thinking of her sister made the corners of her own lips curve upward. "Linnet was always good with herbs and healing."

"She healed hearts, too. Especially my liege's." He paused to strip off his tunic. "Saints, we thought he no longer possessed one, but she proved us wrong. She swept into our lives, spilling light and laughter in her wake, and charming us all."

Charmed as well, Caterine's feet took a few tentative steps toward him.

Holding his hands to the fire, he flexed his fingers. "Your sister slayed many dragons at Eilean Creag."

He glanced at her. "I would slay your dragons, my lady," he vowed. "If you will let me."

Caterine froze. Too transfixed by the hard-muscled expanse of his chest—and the honeyed promise in his words—to think, much less continue her stilted progress across the rush-strewn floor.

She drew a deep breath. "Have I not expressed my gratitude for your help in ridding us of Sir Hugh's tyranny?"

"I did not mean de la Hogue." His words confirmed what she suspected. "'Tis the dragons gnawing at you from within that I referred to."

To Caterine's surprise, she suddenly found herself standing frightfully close to him.

Drawn by her fascination with the muscular contours of his body, the intriguing dusting of crisp, dark hair disappearing beneath the waistband of his hose, and the magical pull of his mellifluous voice.

"You truly couldn't smile?" She blurted the first thing that popped into her mind.

Anything to steer the conversation away from her dragons and the sea of self-doubt they swam in.

"I could do little but grimace, so tight was the skin around my scar," he answered, one finger worrying the pale seam marring the left side of his face. "Nor did I have much cause to smile in those days."

Caterine's gaze lighted on his mouth. "You are smiling now."

A twinkle lit his good eye. "So I am," he said. "Times change, and I find I have much to be pleased about these days."

"Linnet may have enchanted you, my lord, but I vow you beguiled her as well."

*As you are now beguiling me.* The truth of the notion surprised her almost as much as discovering her fingers dipping into the healing unguent.

Dipping most eagerly.

Looking quite pleased with himself, he said, "So you've concluded I am indeed a charmer?"

"I think you cast some sort of glamour over Linnet." It was as close to the truth as she cared to venture. "Especially if you smiled at her like that."

With the self-same bone-melting smile that now drew her unguent-smeared fingers inexorably to the bruised flesh of his ribs.

They hovered there, just above his skin.

Too shy to touch him; too captivated to retreat.

He gave a short laugh. "Lady, I admire your sister greatly, but I never once looked at her as I am now looking at you." He glanced at her hovering fingers. "And never have I craved a woman's touch more than I desire yours this moment."

Caterine swallowed.

Not a dainty, lady-like attempt to recover her composure, but a bold, hopefully not too audible . . . *gulp*.

With great effort, she tore her gaze from the taut-muscled plane of his abdomen and her trembling, ointment-coated fingertips. She looked up at him to discover he no longer smiled, but peered at her as if he could see into each and every corner of her soul.

Holding her gaze, he curled his fingers around her wrists and guided her hands the rest of the way to his midsection. He used his own hands to keep hers pressed lightly against his flesh, moving her fingers in slow, comfort-dispensing circles over his sore ribs and his stomach.

He also took great care to assure that her fingertips slid over each sculpted ridge of muscle he could boast of.

Her soft gasp amply rewarded his efforts.

Marmaduke smiled.

His heart sang, for her quick indrawn breath could not be mistaken for anything but what it was: a clear sign of outright female appreciation.

A reaction he knew well for there was naught lacking about his muscles, or his manhood.

His prowess could match the best of men.

Oft were the nights he could choose amongst a fawning swarm of comely maids, each one eager to lift her skirts and discover if the rumors about his mastery at pleasing a willing wench proved true.

And never yet had one left his bed disappointed.

Only he had remained unfulfilled, his ease taken, but his soul more needy of sustenance than before.

The kind of nourishment such light-skirts, usually serving maids ablaze to sample a nobleman's tarse, couldn't spend him if he stood on his hands for a fortnight pleading for it.

His lady drew a sharp breath, obviously realizing he'd released her wrists and that her fingers, no longer spreading the salve over his ribs, now explored the dark hairs curling just above his waistband.

"Oh!" She jerked her hands from his abdomen and met his amused gaze, two bright spots of color staining her cheeks.

"Very dear lady, surely you have touched a man's body before?"

"N-not like that." She made a fluttery little motion with her hands and her *arisaid* slipped off her shoulders. Digging her hands into its folds, she clung to the woolen wrap as if it were a shield.

But she didn't gather its folds around her shoulders again.

Meeting his gaze full on, she said, "I have ne'er toyed with a man's body hair, sirrah."

Marmaduke almost choked on her frankness. Her candidness shot straight to his loins, and he could no sooner ignore the insistent pull there than keep himself from enjoying the creamy expanse of flesh now exposed above her gown's plunging neckline.

"Saints, you are indeed a woman of plain speech," he managed, his voice two shades gruffer than he would have liked.

She glanced toward the windows where the full fury of the storm now battered the closed shutters. The night's damp chill warred with the peat fire's gentle warmth and challenged the sputtering flames of the wall torches.

The cold air seeping into the chamber, or preferably something else, assaulted her nipples as well, rousing them to hardened peaks that thrust proudly against the linen of her bodice.

They beckoned to him, their enticements so close to the top edge of her gown a mere flick of his fingers would release them.

Marmaduke swallowed thickly and wished the front flap of his tunic still covered his groin . . . and the undeniable evidence of his arousal.

"Did you mind touching me thus?" he asked suddenly, deciding to speak as directly as she.

"It was not wholly unpleasant," she said, her voice barely audible above the lashing rain.

Not wholly unpleasant?

The tip of her tongue darting out to moisten her lips indicated otherwise.

Marmaduke fought back a disgruntled *harrumpf.*

"I found it most pleasant indeed." He drew himself to his full height. "Pleasurable enough to ask you to do it again."

Her brows shot upward. "Toy with your body hair?"

The bold wording grabbed fast to his maleness and squeezed.

A firm, rousing squeeze.

"Rub more of the salve on my body," Marmaduke ground out, amazed his voice didn't crack.

"And," he added, the unquenched throbbing in his nether parts urging him to press his good fortune, "you may toy with . . . whatever catches your favor."

*Most especially the sizable specimen of man-flesh she will find if you peel down your hose for her,* the devil whispered in his ear.

Marmaduke cleared his throat. "Lady, the good saints themselves would weep if they knew the great comfort your hands afforded me just now." He spread his arms wide and nodded to the little bowl sitting so innocently on the nearby table. "Will you not continue until all the healing unguent has been used?"

Her white-knuckled grip still holding fast to her *arisaid,* his soon-to-be-bride appeared to consider his plea and his form, for her deep blue gaze flitted over the hard-slabbed muscles of his shoulders and chest.

Letting go of the wrap at last, she pleased him immensely by scooping up a fat dollop of the ointment. "Aye," she agreed, "it would be a shame to waste the salve."

"A shame indeed."

Pleasing him even more, her attention dropped to his stomach and lingered almost expectantly near the waistband of his hose as if she wished he'd strip off that impediment to her perusal as easily as he'd discarded his tunic.

The very thought sent a fresh surge of blood pumping through his loins, filling him in a manner the thin wool of his hose could not hope to disguise.

Yet she looked on, seemingly fascinated by the taut muscles of his abdomen, her fingers spreading the cold salve in ever-wider circles over his abraded flesh.

And all the while, his manhood swelled and lengthened beneath the ever-more-uncomfortable confinement of his braies.

At last she lowered her gaze, no longer peering at his midsection but at *him* . . . at the very essence of his masculinity.

A roguish beast no longer his own.

Her fingers stilled immediately. "Merciful heaven."

*'Tis heaven indeed when properly tended,* his demons roared with mirth.

Her eyes widening, she gasped again, an earthier, blood-firing gasp this time. The kind he'd not expected to hear from Caterine Keith's sweet lips for it was more the breathy sort of heavy-lidded moan man-eager bawds give forth at the sight of a ready-to-pleasure-them piece of well-aroused manhood.

Not the gasp of a well-born lady raised on monkish preachments against the pleasures of the flesh.

But then, Caterine Keith was not just any lady.

She was a plain-speaking one.

"Your men spoke the truth," she said, proving it anew. "You are over-large."

Too flummoxed to speak, Marmaduke inhaled a great fortifying breath and expelled it as quickly, for his body had gone so tight his lungs could scarce expand.

"And you are well-versed in judging such . . . endowments?" he jerked out with a breathless wheeze.

He regretted the words the instant they left his tongue, for that tarnished vehicle of thoughtlessness had misspoken them, lending an appalling veneer of censure to a meaningless snippet he'd meant in jest.

Surprisingly unabashed, she tilted her head slightly and narrowed her eyes to peer even harder at him.

Blessedly, at his face.

She only looked at him, though.

Not that she needed words to tell him how she'd come by such knowledge.

That sad truth, was writ all over her face . . . and not from bathing visiting knights and tending the wounded.

His ardor soundly deflated, Marmaduke resisted the urge to grimace as darkly as the frowning crags of granite on which her castle stood.

Saints forbid, she'd think his displeasure targeted her and not a past that hadn't been kind.

Steeling himself against his own ghosts, he drew a deep demon-banishing breath.

"Lady, you asked about Arabella," he said, the calm of his tone at stark contrast to the knot in his gut. "I shall tell you of her, and how I came to renounce my own blood."

She lifted a brow, her frank gaze declaring her willingness to listen, her resumption of her sweet ministrations, sealing his fate.

Saints, he would spin her the *Song of Roland* in its entirety if only she would continue to gentle her fingers over his flesh in such a bewitching manner.

"My tale is not a chivalrous one." He had to warn her. "'Fore God, it is quite ugly. Will you still hear it?"

"I am most intrigued to hear of your wife," she said, her hands drifting to his shoulders, kneading the muscles there. "And how you came to pledge fealty to my sister's husband."

"Then so be it."

Though each word would cost him, Marmaduke knew a satisfaction deeper than the solace of her gifted fingers, for while her face still appeared a shade too pale, a blue spark of interest now replaced the dimness that had cloaked her beautiful eyes just moments ago.

Girding himself, he stared at the burning peat until its cheery reddish glow grew and surged, eventually becoming angry licking flames consuming the simple wattle-and-daub homes of the innocent.

Innocents who happened to dwell on the wrong side of a border.

Bile rose in his throat and he almost swung away, breaking the spell of the past—and the magic of her hands—but then, to his amazement, a second pair of hands joined hers. Gentle and cool as Highland mist at dawn, they smoothed over him, helping her ease the knots in his shoulders . . . and his tongue.

A familiar touch, giving him free to tell her tale as well.

Releasing him to care for another.

A great shudder tore down his spine, and then he began. "Many years ago, the summer I earned my spurs, I soon learned that shining symbol of knighthood was all I shared with my peers. That, and mayhap a too-generous dose of pride."

One pair of the caressing hands, the warm ones, stilled a beat. "'Tis known English knights are proud."

"Indeed. Proud of rank and heritage, the privileges vested to them, and their hope of amassing enough *honors* to dine off gold and silver plate."

He paused to shut his good eye for a moment, to block out the nightmare long enough to draw a deep, soul-cleansing breath.

Expelling it, he continued, "My values conflicted with theirs. I honored virtue, loyalty, and the high reputation I believed synonymous with being one of England's finest. But on my first foray into Scotland I learned that, for most, being a *Flower of English Chivalry* meant having a license to embark on a career of outrages."

"Outrages?"

Something in her tone made Marmaduke glance sharply at her.

And hate what he saw mirrored on her lovely face.

Caterine of Dunlaidir knew exactly the kind of outrages he'd meant.

"You sought to halt these . . . spoliations?" she said in her forthright manner.

Proving his assumptions yet again.

Marmaduke nodded. "I refused to take part in such brigandage, especially the ruination of innocent women, some of them little more than children. It seemed my peers' chivalry toward the fairer sex did not extend across the border . . . or the classes."

"And you thought differently?"

Cold fingers traced his scar.

*Loving fingers.*

Ethereal ones meant to encourage when he may have faltered.

"I took up my sword against my own men. Men I now think of as black-hearted sons of Satan for the wickedness they displayed that day. I would have cut down every last one of them, but these were amongst the best fighting men in the Realm and I was one facing many."

"What happened?" she asked softly, the compassion in her voice melding the two pairs of tender hands into one.

And with Arabella's *blessing* came the strength to confront his other ghosts.

The English ones.

Ripping open old wounds forced him to relive every biting lash of the whip that had scored his back.

"Do you not wish to speak of it?"

Marmaduke blinked. "Nay, I do not mind, for it is how I came to meet my late wife, and I do believe good comes of all our trials and hardships even if we must sometimes search far and long to see the truth of it."

And despite that truth, a bitter taste filled his mouth. Even after so many years, he could still feel the corded flails shredding his flesh.

The worst pain of all had been knowing that English hands wielded the whip, for each time their lashes had cut into his back, another of his youthful ideals had withered and died.

Until none remained at all.

Even his burning love of his homeland had been wrested from him that day.

"I was stripped and beaten," he finally told her, sparing her ears the vilest of the grisly deeds they'd visited upon him. "Flogged and left for dead by my own men."

"Duncan MacKenzie found you?"

"His father," Marmaduke amended. "That good man took me to his hall where his womenfolk nursed me to health.

Every man, woman, and child beneath his roof welcomed me into their midst and refused to let me die. They tended my wounds, inside and out, and it's been my greatest honor to serve them ever since."

Glancing away, he stared at the slow-burning peat fire, once more seeing other flames . . . friendly ones this time. As were the faces evoked by the recollection of the massive hearth in Eilean Creag's great hall.

Then a strong gust of sea wind rattled the window shutters and the flames and the faces faded.

The memories remained.

Caterine trailed her fingertips along his collarbone, down his sides and then away. "Arabella was one of the women who tended you?"

"Nay, she was but a slip of a girl at the time." The images that had once made him throw back his head with laughter, now flooded him with pain. "She was ruled by her passions even then . . . a spitfire and hellion. She made faces at me and called me names some knights I'm acquainted with wouldn't know the meaning of."

"But she grew into a beautiful woman and stole your heart."

"That she did, my lady." Marmaduke couldn't lie. "And for all her devilry when I first arrived at Eilean Creag, not a night of our marriage passed that she didn't massage my blighted back."

"Do you think she'd mind if I lent you such comfort now?" The words came so soft they could've been a rustling of the wind.

*No, she'd be pleased.*

This time the words *did* carry on the damp breeze.

The hairs on the back of Marmaduke's neck lifted and he started to answer, but already his new lady had taken gentle hold of his arms and was turning him around.

Turning him so she could see his back.

A bone-crushing dread took hold of him as well . . . the

fear she'd cry out in horror, wholly repulsed. Or worse, that she'd pity him, and such a reaction would lance him deeper.

Marmaduke held his breath.

She pulled him now, urging him steadily away from the peat fire's meager glow and closer to the nearest wall torch.

The one that burned the brightest.

"The old wounds pain me no more," he said, strangle-voiced. Already feeling the warmth from the blazing torch . . . full aware its hissing flames well-illuminated the maze of raised welts criss-crossing every inch of his bare back. "There is no need for you—"

"God in heaven!" His new lady's outrage allayed his dread in one fell swoop.

And swelled his heart.

Not a tone of revulsion colored her outburst.

Nor the slightest tinge of pity.

Only indignation.

Then she was upon him, smoothing her bliss-sending fingers over the travesty that was his back. "Your men did this to you?" she breathed, the horror in her voice clearly addressing his malefactors and not the state of his flesh. "Your own peers?"

"Lords and barons of the land or belted knights, each one."

"May their debased souls roast on the hottest hob in hell."

Marmaduke wheeled around, undone by her ire. "Saints cherish you," he said, and rested his hands on her shoulders. "My back . . . *I* do not repulse you?"

Shaking her head, she traced the tip of one finger down the scar slashing across his face. "I told you once, sir, your scars mean naught to me. Each one is a badge of honor and any who does not see them thus is a fool."

Marmaduke's hopes soared, but they crashed to the rush-coated floor when her brow knitted in a manner sure to bode ill.

For him, and most especially for his dreams.

Disengaging herself from his light hold on her shoulders, she moved to the table and filled two pewter cups with wine. She handed him one. "You are much to my liking," she said in that matter-of-fact tone he'd so admired till now. "And you have seen I do not speak fair words meant to deceive."

She paused to take a sip of wine. "But whether I am fond of you or nay," she continued, and Marmaduke's heart plummeted deeper with each spoken word, "I must say you honestly that I cannot accompany you when you leave."

*As we told you she wouldn't,* his personal minions of Beelzebub boasted with glee.

Ignoring them, Marmaduke counted his blessings.

She'd forgotten to object to his sleeping in her ante-room.

❧

And many hours later, in the splendid solitude of that self-same little chamber, Sir Marmaduke Strongbow stood before one of the ante-room's two narrow window slits and held council with the moon.

The distant orb, cold and aloof, sailed from behind a cloud. A lone one, wispy and thin, for the night's winds had finally chased away the storm.

As he would whisk away his new lady's reservations.

One by one until each dragon was slain and laid to rest.

Much like the cloudless heavens, his own night's peace gained at last, Marmaduke turned away from the little window and sought his rough pallet on the ante-room floor.

To sleep and rest his weary bones.

And dream of better days to come.

# *Chapter Eleven*

❧

$\mathscr{S}$IR MARMADUKE STIRRED to wakefulness well before dawn.

A light pitter of rain, a ferocious stiff neck, and his lady's soft breath warm on his bare shoulder, greeted him.

When she planted wet, tickling kisses along his upper arm, he smiled and opened his good eye . . . to stare straight into two round and unblinking brown ones.

"By the Rood!" He leapt to his feet, instantly awake.

Leo yelped as loudly, any friendly overtures he may have been trying to initiate, forgotten. The little dog streaked from the ante-room before Marmaduke could even scowl at him.

So he frowned into the semi-darkness instead and yanked on his braies. His hose, tunic and boots were donned as quickly, his sword belt girded on with unparalleled haste.

And all the while, he pretended not to notice Leo's offended glare boring holes in him from Lady Caterine's bed. The sneaky bugger even had the cheek to curl himself most proprietarily against her bared thigh.

Marmaduke raked his hands through his hair and tried equally hard to overlook the lush tangle of golden curls beckoning from just above the sleek expanse of naked thigh, a wealth of temptation revealed by the careless whim of the mussed bedcoverings.

A sweet enticement almost but not quite hidden by shadow.

A visual delight that caught him off guard and propelled him right out the door before he forgot his desire to woo her gently and heeded his baser needs there and now.

Praise the saints, she'd slept through the ruckus.

Had she awakened and peered at him from sleepy blue eyes, her lips full and rosy-sweet, the luxuriant thatch of her intimate curls so innocently on display, he may well have spent his seed before he could have bid her a good morrow.

His loins uncomfortably tight, he set off down the passageway, making for the stairs to the great hall. Once below, he went straight to the laver set into the back wall of an alcove near the entrance vestibule.

Blessed relief was almost his.

Stepping up to the stone basin, he thrust his hands into the freezing water and splashed a goodly amount on his face.

Then, his features carefully schooled lest some stealthy varlet be watching him, he scanned the hall.

All slept.

To his relief, the chorus of assorted snores, wheezes, and other indefinable noises rising up from the men still slumbering on their makeshift pallets attested to the collective depth of their oblivion.

Allowing himself a pained smile, Marmaduke pulled his hose away from his body and trickled ice-cold water onto his fully charged manhood.

Purging deliverance came swift and sweet.

Thus relieved, he readjusted his hose and continued on his way, the fearsome look on his face a formidable warning to anyone fool enough to admit having seen him minister to himself in such an absurd manner.

And if James Keith so much as lifted a brow over the damp stain on the front flap of his tunic, he'd renege his assurances they'd parry with blunted swords and insist on instructing the hapless lordling with *real* blades.

The razor sharp variety capable of splitting a hair!

A dark oath and the clatter of steel skittering across stone alerted him of James's presence in the undercroft the moment he reached the bottom of the dank stairwell that curled down to Dunlaidir's lowest level.

Cold and sparsely-lit by a smattering of pitch-pine torches and what gray light could leak through a handful of arrow slits, the groin-vaulted basement provided a secure storeroom for the stronghold's most valuable provisions while its semi-underground location and thick walls offered a more private arena for James to learn the fine art of lairding than the open bailey where Marmaduke preferred to train.

Careful not to venture near a teetering pile of arrows and crossbow bolts, he paused in the less hazardous shadow cast by a wall of stacked wine barrels. Unaware he'd entered the undercroft, James snatched up his blunted blade and, frowning darkly, thrust and lunged at a side of hanging salt beef.

Lunged most miserably, but not because of any lack of balance. Nay, his legs and his well-muscled arms seemed in good working order.

'Twas the anger in his pinched features that ruined what could have been a perfect parry.

"Would you truly hope to live by the sword, you'd best bury your temper before you unsheathe your blade," Marmaduke said, striding forward.

James halted in midlunge and nearly toppled to the stone-flagged floor. "I was—"

"—on the best path to having an arm lopped off," Marmaduke finished for him, unbuckling his sword belt and placing it atop a creel of rolled oxhides.

Stretching his arms above his head, he cracked his knuckles, then helped himself to a blunted practice sword propped against one of the thick pillars supporting the vaulted ceiling.

He stood still a few moments, testing the blade's feel.

"Such passion as blazes in your eyes is better spent in a fair maid's arms than on the field." Turning slightly to the side, he feigned interest in the well not far from where they stood. "There, in the heat of earnest battle, you will only retain your limbs if you keep your wits."

The words scarce spoken, he whirled on James, his blade slicing the air with a speed that would have left an onlooker reeling with dizziness. In the blink of an eye, James's sword clanged to the floor and the blunted end of Marmaduke's pressed firmly beneath the younger man's chin.

"That was your first lesson, my friend. A cool head . . . or no head. The choice is yours."

James bristled. "God and his saints as my witness, did I not wish to learn, I would not be here."

"I am glad to hear it." Lowering his blade, Marmaduke used its tip to motion to the fallen sword. "Shall we begin?"

"I thought we had," James huffed and swiped up his weapon.

"A mere exchange of pleasantries until we've worked the ire out of you. Now heed the look on my face and imitate it."

"There isn't a look on your face," James rapped out. "It's blank."

"Exactly." Marmaduke backed up a few paces and took up a fighting stance. "You'd best master looking disinterested now, because on the morrow you shall have an audience . . . a comely dark-haired wench whose fair presence will help you learn to ignore distractions."

James blanched. "You wouldn't."

Marmaduke cocked a brow. "She'll agree, too. I am certain of it."

Pressing his lips together, James stared at the ceiling.

"All that stands between you and bettering yourself as a swordsman is proper motivation," Marmaduke pointed out.

"The desire to win the lady Rhona's admiration will spur your drive to improve your skills."

"You ken I favor her." James shot him an accusatory glance. Leaning on his practice sword, his chest heaved as if they'd already parried a few rounds. "I will not have her here to—"

"Cool your blood or I shall fetch her now."

"She will see my clumsiness."

"She will see your triumph," Marmaduke corrected. "If you so will it."

James expelled a gusty breath. Then, to Marmaduke's immense pleasure, a closed look settled over the younger man's handsome face and he lifted his sword. A slight tic working just beneath his left eye remained the only outward indication of any simmering agitation.

Sensing James was as prepared as he'd ever be, Marmaduke beckoned to him.

"Have at me," he encouraged, his own sword at the ready. "Pretend you are at a great tourney, your lady is watching from the lodges and has just tossed you a ribbon from her hair . . . imagine that her eyes twinkle with the promise of later delights."

"You are cruel."

"I have been called worse." Marmaduke recalled the myriad unflattering terms his liege had heaped on him over the years. Never spoken in earnest, to be sure, but definitely more unsavory than cruel.

"Concentrate on those delights," he added, deciding his young friend needed a bit more goading. "The lascivious ones."

The ploy worked.

The hard-won look of indifference on James's face vanished instantly. He came forward without any further hesitation, countering Marmaduke's tireless sword-thrusts with surprising skill.

Until low-voiced bickering from the stairwell caught his

attention and Marmaduke backed him against the well house.

"You would be dead now were I a true foe." Marmaduke cast aside the blunt-tipped practice sword and dragged the back of his hand over his sweat-grimed brow.

Panting, James ignored him, his full attention riveted on the shadow-cast opening of the stairwell.

The voices neared, still at strife. One a man's deep grumble, the other a woman's.

And she was clearly winning the verbal sparing.

"The salt beef is full o' worms," the man argued, his exasperation echoing off the undercroft's thick walls.

"There must be *something*," Lady Rhona's unmistakable voice insisted. "We cannot have a wedding without a marriage feast."

And then the twain burst into view. A look of keen interest sparked on Rhona's pretty face. "I thought I heard swordplay, but when it ceased so abruptly, I consigned the disturbance to the castle ghosts."

"Ghosts," Eoghann groused. "The only wraiths hereabouts—if there are any—would be too weak from hunger to go about clashing swords."

"Then we shall have to assure every table at the wedding feast groans beneath enough sumptuous fare to fill the bellies of *all* Dunlaidir's residents." She beamed at the seneschal. "Past and present."

Her smile put a furious scowl on James's face.

Until Marmaduke stamped on his foot and whispered, "A look of bored detachment will serve you better."

"The same detachment you wear when looking at my stepmother when you think yourself unobserved?" James muttered out the side of his mouth, his gaze still fastened on the object of his affection.

Marmaduke bit back a smile and cuffed him on the arm. "Had that been a sword thrust, you would've pierced my heart," he murmured for James's ears alone. "Mind that precision when next we train and you shall soon earn your gold spurs."

Rhona stepped up to them, the seneschal close on her heels. She smiled at James. "'Tis been a while since we've seen you wield a blade."

"Mayhap I've decided to amend that oversight," he said, pushing away from the well. In his haste, he stumbled and the practice sword slipped from his hand.

He froze, his gaze going straight to the blade's blunted tip.

A squire's learning tool, not a man's.

Marmaduke's heart twisted at the younger man's blunder. With lightning speed, he used his foot to flip the sword into his hand. Rhona noting the blade's impotence would only cause James further shame.

As quickly as he'd seized it, Marmaduke tossed the sword, rounded tip and all, into a dark corner where it landed with a metallic *thwank* on a pile of haphazardly-stacked crossbows.

He cleared his throat. "I desired a sparring partner and as Lord of Dunlaidir, James hospitably volunteered his services," he lied.

"Lady," he addressed Rhona, "I appreciate your sentiments about a lavish marriage feast, and I would surely enjoy one, but from what I see of your provisions, such an expenditure is not feasible."

Eoghann swelled his chest. "That's what I've been telling her. No victuals, no feast." He snorted derisively. "Lest we serve braised mist harvested from the fog e're rolling in off the sea. Of that, we have plenty."

At his words, a new kind of prickling seized Marmaduke, the kind of nigglings he cherished . . . the birth of an idea.

The beginnings of a plan.

Three sides of salt beef hung from the ceiling. Ancient-looking, they appeared to be the only source of meat in all the undercroft's fastness.

Save a few scrawny seabird carcasses, yet to be plucked and dressed.

"You once had an impressive herd of cattle." Marmaduke slanted a glance at James. "My liege raved about them for days after his last visit. He swore he'd never eaten finer beef."

"Aye, the best beef to be had within a three-days ride is what was said," James owned. "Now, with our cattle grazing the fields de la Hogue usurped from Sir John, we have scarce enough stores to satisfy the grateful belly of a single wandering friar."

Resting his hip on the edge of the well, the young lord seemed to age years. "In my father's time, this holding was a major strength in this part of Scotland," he said, somber-voiced. "Then Sir Hugh smashed his iron fist on us, not taking our walls but ravaging our land and lifting our cattle."

"Put the fear of God into the burghers, too," Eoghann supplied, gall etching hard lines into his craggy face.

"A black-hearted blighter if ever there was one," James agreed.

Only Marmaduke withheld comment, his attention on the creel of oxhides.

At last he knew what must be done.

"You wish to host a marriage feast," he said to Rhona. "I humbly accept. But," he added, glancing at Eoghann, "we shall celebrate two wedding feasts."

Behind him, James made an odd choking sound. "Two?"

"One feast following the nuptials, serving up whatever is on hand," he explained. "The second a few nights later and garnished with the best beef to be had within a three-days ride."

"You are full mad." A look of sheer incredulity stole over James's face.

"Nay, I am hoping my wedding night will prove a dark and moonless one," Marmaduke corrected. "The first marriage feast will be our smokescreen."

"*Smokescreen*?" That from Eoghann.

Marmaduke nodded. "A ruse to allow a few of us to slip onto Sir John's old lands and win back your cattle."

"I still do not understand," James puzzled.

"I do," Eoghann owned. "I can't believe I didn't think of it."

James looked confused.

"Don't you see?" A gleam came into the seneschal's eyes. "Who would expect a man to launch a cattle raid on his wedding night?"

"Oh." Comprehension began to steal across James's face. "And what about the night of the second marriage feast?"

"That, my friend, remains to be seen," Marmaduke lied for the second time that morning.

He knew exactly what would transpire.

⚜

Shellfish and seaware.

Food for the poor.

And soon to be the mainstay offerings at a marriage feast she'd only this day learned would take place.

The second celebration presented even more absurdities, but of a wholly different nature.

All manner of disquieting prospects parading through her mind, Caterine tossed another handful of wet, dripping sea tangle into one of the dozen or so creels scattered along the narrow shoreline where Dunlaidir's cliffs met the sea.

Inhaling deeply of the salt-laden air, she pressed cold-numbed fingers against the small of her aching back and wished herself anywhere but here . . . on the one tiny sliver of beach accessible to the stronghold's residents.

Reached by a precarious path carved centuries ago into the living stone of the mainland's cliff-face, its tidal pools and shallows, protected by the deep curve of a hidden bay, provided rich harvesting ground for a variety of seaweed and other gifts of the briny deep.

Blessed sustenance she and the most trusted members of the household had been gathering for hours.

And the gloaming would soon be upon them, a day spent in toil and labor.

And the hatching of covert plans.

Closing her eyes, Caterine turned her face into the chill, blustery wind and contemplated the wisdom of grown men sneaking about disguised as oxen.

A fool notion to her, a brilliant strategy to those who meant to act it out.

Especially her champion, who'd sprung the idea on them, claming the late King Robert Bruce had once used the same trickery—the tossing of oxhides o'er one's crouched body, then using the stealth of darkness to merge with a herd and thus near a watching garrison undetected.

Caterine scoffed at the very idea. *She* had never heard of Scotland's hero king sneaking anywhere.

And if he had, he'd certainly not done so camouflaged as a . . . a *cow*!

"There are distinct advantages to this day's ungentle chores," a familiar voice whispered in her ear.

Caterine's eyes flew wide.

A blast of massed trumpets couldn't have startled her more.

She stared hard at her companion. "I know that look on you," she said. "You were collecting limpets from the rock pool on the other side of the strand. What *advantages* drove you over here to startle me out of my wits?"

"You wound me." Rhona whipped a bulging sack of the conical shells from behind her back. "This is the sixth one I've filled. As for the advantages . . ."

She cast a sidelong glance at the straining muscles of Sir Alec's bared back as he hefted a full creel of glistening dulse onto his shoulder for the climb up the cliff stairs.

"My lady, have you e'er seen so much prime male flesh in one place?" she wanted to know.

Caterine glanced toward the water where the MacKenzie men and a few of Dunlaidir's best waded through the shallows, their seaweed-filled nets floating behind them.

To a man, they'd discarded their tunics. Some had even removed their hose, opting to brave the cold waters in naught but their braies.

They may well have been naked.

Every last one of them, including *him*.

"Aye, I've noticed." Caterine saw no need to be coy.

She'd also noted which man's clinging underhose revealed the largest and heaviest-looking bulge.

And the sight of it filled the lowest part of her belly with a warm, pulsing *tingle*.

She sent a glance down the beach to where an equally shirtless James worked the rock pool. "Think you James would approve of your ogling?"

Rhona shrugged. "There is no harm in looking. I suspect James Keith would lose all interest in me if he thought I couldn't appreciate a man's well-fleshed pleasure tools. Especially when they're displayed so—"

"*Pleasure tools*?" Caterine near choked on the term.

"'Tis how I think of them, but there are other ways of calling them."

"How can you occupy yourself with such foolery when you ken full well why we are here?" Caterine glanced at the men with the nets.

No better than her friend, Caterine's attention sought and rested where it shouldn't.

There was something sublimely arousing about the way the thin cloth of the men's braies hugged that part of them. The damp linen molded itself so perfectly to their flesh, not just the length of their shafts and the swell of their ballocks could be determined but also the abundance of the thick hair sheltering their maleness.

At once, a weighty tension began pulsing deep in Caterine's belly, becoming even more insistent when her gaze settled on the thus-displayed male parts of the man who raged heads above the others: her champion's.

"He would pleasure you well, my lady," her friend declared, low-voiced.

"I do not want to be pleasured," Caterine denied, appalled by how stale the statement tasted.

*How false.*

Her entire body ached to know pleasure.

Rhona tossed her bag of limpets onto a growing pile of limpet-filled sacks. "I take my pleasure where and when I can find it," she said, then strode down the beach toward James and the waiting rock pool.

*Even then, she was ruled by her passions.*

Unbidden, Sir Marmaduke's description of his first wife popped into Caterine's mind.

Taunted her, was more like it.

Caterine's chest tightened with discomfiture. Like Arabella, she suspected her companion, too, was a woman of passion.

*She* was not.

Not that she didn't know what passion was . . . she did.

Especially since *his* arrival.

She'd just never reached out and grabbed hold of it.

But maybe she should.

Her decision made, she scooped up another dripping handful of sea tangle and dropped it into the waiting creel. She'd buried two husbands—the first dying of cold English steel when he was but a few years older than James is now. The second died of old age—and she wasn't getting any younger.

No one would fault her if she took advantage of her attraction to the Sassunach . . . and let him teach her what it meant to be a woman ruled by passion.

So long as she kept her heart out of such intimate explorations, she wouldn't fault herself either.

# *Chapter Twelve*

✦

$\mathcal{M}$ANY HOURS LATER, in the most silent depths of the night, Caterine stole from her bed and into the ante-room. *He* hadn't yet sought the rough pallet he'd made for himself on the tiny chamber's rush-strewn floor, and the saints knew where he held himself.

Most likely he walked the ramparts.

Or mayhap he'd found succor in the arms of a fetching kitchen wench eager to air her skirts for one of his rare dimpled smiles and a few fair words.

More piqued by that possibility than she cared to admit, Caterine frowned at the innocuous pallet.

Lumpy and straw-filled, it loomed empty but held the imprint of his braw self as surely as if he reposed on it in all his well-hewn glory.

Seized by the odd tightening of her chest that seemed to plague her each time he came to mind, she hastened from the ante-room only to have to acknowledge his all-encompassing presence pervaded the whole of her quarters.

Not just the small portion he'd claimed for his own.

Even the curtained confines of her great four-poster bed couldn't spend her sanctuary for it was there the strangely palpable feel of him proved the most pervasive.

Which was why she'd fled its cold depths in the first place.

And dared to do so as bare-bottomed as she slept.

Surprised by her daring, heat inched up her neck even as the fresh night wind pouring through the opened shutters kissed her flesh with chillbumps.

Not at all unaccustomed to men seeing her undressed, having been robbed of all maidenly timidity at a tender age, the thought she'd risked having *him* awaken and view her thus, set off alarm bells of the most serious nature.

And sent rivulets of trickling excitement spilling through her.

Acutely aware of the throbbing tension building low by her thighs, she snatched her discarded camise off the strongbox at the foot of her bed, and pulled it swiftly over her head.

Not that its thin linen could shield her from the keen-edged anticipation eddying inside her.

Ripples of sensation put there by the damning knowledge that, soon, she would stand naked before him and, despite the reservations of her heart, her body, long starved of any form of tactile pleasure, would joy in it.

Revel in encouraging him to assuage an ache she no longer cared to deny.

Her senses reeling, she stood before the strongbox, desiring to watch the remainder of the night drift by from one of the his-and-her seats carved into the sides of the chamber's largest window embrasure, but found herself unable to move.

The iron-bound chest exerted an irresistible thrall, soundly staying her feet and demanding her attention.

Beckoning to her.

Or rather, the cloth-covered clump of granite inside the chest, beckoned.

*The Laird's Stone.*

Her blood pounding in her ears, she stared hard at the innocent-looking strongbox. Legend claimed the Laird's Stone measured a man's prowess and chivalric courage when recognizing a new Master of Dunlaidir. So shouldn't the Sassunach's bold claiming of her quarters, the sheer proximity of his stalwart self, influence the stone's allegiance?

Inspire it to weep?

If indeed it could.

Before she could stop herself, she dropped to her knees, fumbled with the cold iron of the lock, and raised the chest's lid.

Not that she believed in such nonsense.

But on the wee chance the tales did bear substance, the stone's tears would mean Sir Marmaduke would remain at Dunlaidir as its master, his indubitable strength assuring the good of them all, his physical presence slaking the burgeoning needs he'd awakened in her.

*Bodily* needs she could indulge without regret.

Casting a fleeting glance toward the purposely unbarred door, she strained her ears for approaching footsteps, but the only sound she caught was the crackle of the hearth fire and the dull thudding of her own heart.

The great stronghold lay silent, its stout walls and those within, at peace.

Even Leo slumbered. The little dog lay curled on his bed, as unaware of her turmoil as the black wind racing past her windows.

Caterine expelled a relieved breath.

No one would witness her folly.

Then she gathered her courage and lifted the Laird's Stone from the strongbox.

Ignoring the little voices that called her a fool, she pushed to her feet and carried the heavy wooden bowl to the nearest cresset lamp. Caught in the night breeze, the bronze lamp swayed on its chain, but its flame burned true . . . and cast a healthy enough glow for her to examine the stone.

*If she dared.*

"Oh Mary Mother," she muttered, angry at herself for

hauling out the fool piece of granite, angrier still at her hesitancy to peer at it.

Then, with enough passion in her blood to make the boldest heart proud, she stiffened her spine and yanked the cloth off the stone.

It was dry.

Bone dry, with nary a droplet of moisture glistening on its quartz-speckled surface or misting the smooth grain of its wooden bowl.

Stunned by the merciless punch of her disappointment, Caterine stared at the much-revered Laird's Stone, and wanted to weep herself.

For being a fool.

And most especially, for imagining, even for a moment, that a cold lump of stone might cry.

❦

At the same small hour, but two levels lower, the cold stone walls of the Keith family chapel offered an involuntary trysting place for Sir Marmaduke and a few select men.

*His own.*

The four MacKenzie Highlanders of Kintail.

And the aging Father Tomas, present out of necessity and respect.

Each man stood full aware of the furtive nature of their meeting as they huddled together near the rood screen. They conversed in low tones, staunchly ignoring the bone-deep cold seeping through the soles of their shoes and chilling the tops of their ears.

Resisting an urge to stamp his feet against the bite of the frigid air, Marmaduke rubbed his hands together and stared up at the wheel-shaped *Corona lucis* suspended high above their heads, his gaze drawn by its score of burning tapers.

The fine wax candles cast weird shadows on the men's

earnest faces and sent shifting patterns of pale light weaving across the oratory's mural-painted walls.

Nothing else moved in the stillness, an eerie, otherworldly atmosphere rife with the heavy weight of age and the cloying scents of dust, old stone, and stale incense.

"It is because de la Hogue will know our every move that I would take such a risk," he spoke then, returning his attention to the worried-looking priest.

The aged holy man hadn't stopped fretting since Marmaduke divulged his intentions to marry in the parish church rather than within the safety of Dunlaidir's curtain walls.

And to do so with every able-bodied man in the burgh not only in attendance, but armed with the surplus mail and weapons now gathering dust in the stronghold's undercroft.

"My good fellows, nothing is so certain as that Sir Hugh will make some move the day of the wedding." He cast a sidelong glance at the hand-wringing priest. "Father Tomas tells us the knave has vowed to be present. Whether he is or nay, there is no doubt his men will infiltrate the crowd."

"Then why provoke an altercation by using the village kirk?"

All eyes turned on Sir Lachlan. Still a mite pale from his wounding, the young knight leaned against a stone pillar and appeared as perplexed over Marmaduke's strategy as Father Tomas.

Forgetting the sanctity of their meeting place, Sir Alec snorted. "If you had a bit more experience at warfare, you'd ken why," he said, drawing a self-important breath.

"I am not a newly-born cockerel," Lachlan tossed back, the knuckles of his fisted hands gleaming white in the candlelight. "I've seen my share of battle."

"Highland skirmishes." A good-natured wink took the sting out of Sir Ross's observation . . . and the heat out of Lachlan's eyes.

"As I mind it," Alec hurtled on, "a village wedding will

lead those miscreants right into our hands, which is exactly where we want 'em. One false move, and we've got the bastards."

The other men nodded agreement.

Only the aging priest appeared uncertain.

Snatching a tall brass candlestick off a side altar, Sir Gowan raised its wax taper before his bearded face. "All we need is one," he said, tossing a glance at Lachlan. "We'll loosen the varlet's tongue with a bit o' Highland persuasion until he spills who in this household is de la Hogue's man."

"Have a care lest you set yourself afire." Marmaduke took the flaming taper from Gowan's hand and returned it to the side altar. "We'll need every man we can muster."

He gave the gruff Highlander a pointed look. "Including you."

Father Tomas lifted nervous hands, his worry-filled gaze flitting from man to man. "You believe Sir Hugh will launch a full-fledged attack?"

"Scarce that," Marmaduke sought to ease the graybeard's trepidation. "Sending a mounted host to fall upon a wedding party is too bold a measure even for a scoundrel of Sir Hugh's ilk."

"That's not wha—"

Marmaduke silenced Lachlan with a withering glare.

"I knew de la Hogue passing well at the English Court," he went on, speaking to the priest, but keeping a wary eye on Lachlan. "He executes his villainy with stealth and intrigue, and shuns the honor of pitched battle."

Walking over to the free-standing baptismal basin half-hidden in a murk-filled corner near the chapel door, Marmaduke trailed his fingers over the cold stone of the intricately carved font cover . . . and silently prayed the old priest would swallow the half-truth.

Few knew better than he of the treachery one such as de la Hogue was capable of. The dastard's dark deeds were known the length and breadth of England.

Which was why he wanted the burghers armed.

And why he deemed that particular risk the lesser of the two evils.

"You said his very spittle could burn holes in the ground, so why—*oophf*!"

Marmaduke whirled around in time to see Alec jab two fingers into the small of Lachlan's back. Drawing an exasperated breath of the chapel's fusty air, he clasped his hands behind his own back and returned to the others.

He cleared his throat. "Sir Priest, you claim the burghers are frightened but not disloyal. Will they stand against Sir Hugh if properly armed and guaranteed our protection—and sanctuary within these walls, if they choose to seek it?"

For an interminable moment, Father Tomas looked as if he expected to be dragged off to his doom, but then he nodded his cowl-covered head. "Aye, they would," he affirmed. "I am certain of it. They are sore tired of Sir Hugh's brigandage."

"Then so be it." Marmaduke's steely tone challenged his men to object.

"We are to supply peasants with armor and weaponry?" Alec dared.

"We are to win their trust and rebuild their confidence," Marmaduke rephrased the sentiment. "By doing so, we strengthen this holding."

Skeptical glances met his pronouncement.

"And if they turn those weapons on us?" That from a dubious-sounding Gowan.

Marmaduke planted his hands on his hips and simply stared back at the bearded Highland knight.

The look on his face said enough.

His men let loose a few mumbled imprecations and exchanged a grudging look or two, but no one voiced further protest.

Not directly.

And that, too, was enough.

Satisfied, he relaxed his shoulders, let some of the tension ease out of him. "The wedding is but a few days away," he said, turning to Father Tomas. "You, Sir Priest, shall inform the burghers they will receive mailed shirts and whatever surplus weaponry we can spare. The day of nuptials, they are to crowd the roads and church, but disguise the hauberks beneath their normal wear and carry their weapons as unobtrusively as possible."

Alec made a derisive *harrumph,* earning himself an elbow in the ribs from Ross.

That disturbance quelled, Marmaduke gave his attention back to the holy man. "Assure them Dunlaidir is once again in strong hands and shall remain so. Once Sir Hugh has been dealt with, repairs to their homes and fields will be seen to without hesitation."

"Outfitting ruffian rabble with steel, tending their fields—"

"Give them these assurances on my knightly word," Marmaduke deepened his voice to prevail over Gowan's grousing. "Let it be known any villager yet fearful may seek shelter within these walls until they feel safe enough to return to their homes."

"You speak braw words, English." Sir Ross spoke at last, and sounded so much like Duncan MacKenzie, Marmaduke almost pivoted on his heel to see if that great lout stood behind him.

Marmaduke smiled, but bittersweet, for, of a sudden, a powerful urge to see his old friend overcame him.

A burning desire to be *home* again.

Home at *Balkenzie.*

And to be there with his new bride beside him.

Blinking back the unexpected emotion stinging his good eye, he threw back his shoulders and faced his men.

"You will transport the hauberks and arms," he said, appalled at the thickness still swelling his throat. "In the interest of secrecy, you'll work nights, preferably between

Matins and first light, hiding the goods in a secure place until Father Tomas has met with the burghers."

"And when do we begin this noble undertaking?" Gowan again.

Some inner devil, but not his usual ones, made Marmaduke glance at the chapel's tall lancet windows. Blackest night pressed against them, stealing the color from their multi-hued panes . . . and cloaking the world beyond in shielding darkness.

A perfect night for stealth.

Alec followed his gaze. "Nay, Strongbow, you cannot mean this night?"

Marmaduke almost laughed at the stricken expression on the other man's face. Instead, he gave him a friendly clap on the arm. "You are more quick-witted than I'd thought."

His tone almost jovial, he added, "I shall reward the lot of you a thousandfold and then some when we return home."

Rolled eyes and ill-humored mutters greeted his offer, but one by one, his men took their leave and Marmaduke knew they'd have much accomplished before the sun breached the horizon.

"God go with you," the old priest murmured into their wake, not quite able to keep the catch out of his voice. When their footfalls faded, he turned grateful eyes on Marmaduke.

"You are a good man," he said. "The burghers won't fail you."

"Nor shall we fail them, that I promise you." Marmaduke reached for Father Tomas's hand and gave it a reassuring squeeze.

Then, without further ceremony, he, too, exited the chapel, but unlike his men who'd descended into Dunlaidir's bowels, he climbed a winding turret stair to his lady's chamber, a wry smile lifting the corners of his mouth.

A *good man,* the priest had called him.

Not this night.

Nay, far from it.

This night, he intended to be bad.

Very bad indeed.

❧

To Marmaduke's great consternation, the only eyes to greet him from the shadowy recess of his lady's bed proved round and accusatory. Definitely not the sapphire ones he'd hoped to encounter, their blue depths heavy-lidded and drowsed with sleep.

Nor did the low rumbles coming from deep in Leo's chest ring anywhere near as sweet as the soft gasp of surprise he'd expected to hear upon easing back the bed curtains.

Soon, very soon, though, she'd enchant him with soft, *sated* sighs.

Of that he'd make certain.

But first he had to find her . . . and preferably without the aid of her wee shadow.

"Profound apologies, little man, but I do not crave your unswerving regard whilst I seek to win your lady's favor." Leaning forward, he returned Leo's bristly glare with a fierce glower of his own.

"If you are wise, you will go back to sleep and dream of four-legged bits of fluff and leave your fair mistress to me," he added, closing the bed curtains on the tiny creature's bared teeth and menacing snarls.

The glare or his sage words must've worked, for thick silence issued from behind the drawn curtains.

Thick silence and the muffled rustlings of the wee beastie making himself comfortable again.

The ghost of a smile tugging at the corners of his lips, Marmaduke turned his back on the great four-poster and his soon-to-be-slumbering nemesis.

Naught but the chill air stood between him and his first

true attempt to introduce his bride-to-be to the mysteries and enchantment of the love he hoped to share with her.

Even his demons had been routed for the night, soundly banished by his abysmal desire not to let anything hinder him in wresting at least one sweet sigh of pleasure from his lady's tender lips.

His vision now accustomed to the dimness of the sparsely lit chamber, his gaze probed the shadows . . . and quickly found her, her place of refuge in the draughty window embrasure revealed when the hiss and crackle of the nearby cresset lamp's guttering wicks drew his attention.

The bronze lamp swung on its chain, its sputtering flames casting odd patterns onto the walls of the little alcove. She huddled on the cushioned seat, a furred skin tucked around her legs, her *arisaid* gathered loosely about her shoulders, the whole of her bathed in the pale silver glow of a sickle moon.

Blessedly, she faced the night-darkened sea, her back conveniently turned his way . . . the self-same back she'd favored several times during their toil on the strand earlier that day.

A back he knew must still ache from exertion.

*The excuse he needed to touch her.*

His smile returned, this time with a decidedly wicked slant.

Drawn by a powerful urge to put all the years of empty nights behind him—and assault a few of her dragons as well—he crossed the rushes until he stood a scant heartbeat behind her.

Scarce daring to breathe, so loudly did his blood pound with need, it took him a full minute to recognize the roar in his ears not as his own, but as the muted thunder coming through the opened window . . . the rhythmic crash of the waves breaking against the rocks far below.

Not even considering his overtures might be met with scorn, Marmaduke flexed his fingers and heaved a great breath to strengthen the hope in his heart.

Then, feeling much the benighted heathen out to achieve

his goals by any means, fair or foul, he placed his hands on her shoulders.

He kneaded the tension there, much affected by the moonlit wonder of her, wildly distracted by the warm silk of her braids brushing the backs of his fingers.

She stirred at once, gifting him with the soft sigh he'd hoped for as he'd made the winding climb to her chamber, delighting him further by twisting around to give him a sleepy smile.

"Thank you," she said simply, and lifted her braids out of the way, leaving his fingers aching to reclaim them, then surprising him even more by shrugging her *arisaid* off her shoulders.

His sharp intake of breath at her unmistakable willingness to accept his proffered ministrations—*his touch*—didn't surprise Caterine.

He couldn't know she'd been aware of his presence since the moment he'd cracked the door of her chamber and stepped inside, couldn't know she'd been waiting for his arrival.

Or that she'd caught his whispered words to Leo.

Truth tell, once he'd entered, she'd sat still as stone, burning inside, and silently pleading him to join her in the window embrasure and . . . place his hands on her.

Sitting up straighter on the cushioned seat, she leaned her head forward to free more of her neck and shoulders to the magic of his bliss-sending fingers.

"You are surprised I enjoy your touch." The softly spoken words were a statement.

Another of her frankly stated truths.

But one that streaked right through him to land squarely in his groin.

"I am pleased," he said, opting to be as candid, amazed he could push the words past his teeth, so fierce was the heated tightening in his loins.

So great the swelling of his heart.

"I knew your back—" He broke off the instant the word passed his lips.

'Twas her shoulders he kneaded through the soft linen of her camise, not her back, and some weird magic lying thick in the silver-kissed air made him half-believe even thinking his wishes this night might spur the oddest results.

And voicing them, more dire consequences yet.

Like her asking him to glide his hands lower down her body and massage her aching back as well.

Trouble was, the raging need straining thick and hard against his hose couldn't withstand such a temptation.

His exalted prowess and stamina, roundly defeated by the supple curve of a single camise-encased back.

"My back aches more than my shoulders," she said.

Even before she reached up to circle her hands around his wrists and lift them from her shoulders, Marmaduke knew what she was about to do.

Holding his breath, he squared his own shoulders against the challenge he was about to face, stared past her out the tall, arch-topped windows, and waited.

Far out to sea, high above the horizon, a horned moon sailed from behind a cloud, its wan light spilling little more than a thin thread of silver across the night-black waters, but somehow managing to illuminate each unveiled inch of creamy skin she revealed to him.

And, thanks be to the advantage of his great height, that blissful view encompassed the naked globes of her lush breasts . . . including their deliciously thrusting nipples!

"Saints, Maria, and Joseph," Marmaduke breathed, borrowing Duncan MacKenzie's pet oath, well past caring if she knew she'd set him on his ear by peeling down her undergown clear to her waist.

"I've surprised you again," she said, looking up at him over her bared shoulder, her blue gaze as guileless as the newborn day, her full breasts, moon-washed and glorious.

Aching to be caressed.

Her hardened nipples demanded to be administered to in ways that would make the devil beg forgiveness.

"Are you not cold?" Marmaduke cringed at the stilted sound of his voice. A eunuch could have addressed her more smoothly!

"Are you?"

*Nay, I am afire with wanting you,* his fully-charged shaft tossed back at her.

"I am anything but cold as I believe you must know," he said, matching his words to the directness she preferred.

He even let his gaze drop to purposely linger on her nipples. "But I am puzzled."

She lifted her chin and Marmaduke would've sworn he caught a flare of . . . *disappointment?* . . . flash across her beautiful face when he lifted his gaze from her bared breasts.

"I simply want you to touch me. To massage the knots from my back." She turned her face to the sea again. "It will feel better without my camise obstructing your fingers."

Marmaduke narrowed his good eye at the back of her fair head, his desire to win her charms, and her love, with careful and leisurely deliberation, hard at war with the beast she'd called forth with her boldness.

"You are full blunt," he said at last, his voice tight with the cost of his restraint.

"I told you, I am a woman of plain words," she reminded him. "I am also practical."

She leaned forward then, and a swath of moonglow spread slowly down the length of her naked spine.

"Please," she urged, the breathiness of her tone near as bewitching as the satiny skin awaiting his attentions. "My back aches and your touch is . . . soothing."

Marmaduke swallowed.

His hands obliged her.

Smoothing, stroking, kneading.

Spending her every ounce of pleasuring his roving fingers could supply, and driving himself to the brink of madness.

"Think you I can do this and not desire to touch the breasts you've bared as well?" *That* part of him borrowed his tongue. "Be warned, lady, I am not an inexperienced stripling to be tease—"

"Nor is it my wont to provoke you. I do not mind if you touch my breasts," she said, and his tarse lengthened another full, aching inch.

Marmaduke stood silent, unable to speak.

Or move.

His hands stilled on the small of her back, his entire body tighter than a full score of tautly drawn Welsh bowstrings.

Twisting her head around, she peered up at him again. "You want to know why I do not mind." She read him as clearly as if he wore his thoughts emblazoned across his forehead.

"I do not mind," she went on, her sapphire gaze as earnest as her tone, "because it felt good when you gazed upon them just now."

Marmaduke's shaft swelled to such a painful degree he almost embarrassed himself.

A lesser man would have.

"You enjoyed having me glimpse them?" He could scarce push the words past the dryness in his throat.

She nodded, her lovely face shadow-cast in the moonlight. "I have not known much physical pleasure. I would like to address that deficiency," she said, the words coming out in a rush.

As if, despite her frankness, she sought to have done with them before they damned her.

Marmaduke inclined his head, his hands moving again, but kneading less and caressing more. Sweeping in ever more intimate circles up and down the length of her spine, his fingers itching to curl round her ribcage and brush against the side swells of those lush, heavy breasts.

Dying to slip beneath the bunched folds of her undergown and comb through the thick tangle of golden curls he knew awaited him betwixt her shapely thighs.

A luscious nest of intoxicating sweetness he ached to explore in great depth and leisure.

A ragged groan rose in his throat, but he swallowed it whole. He needed his every breath to form the question searing the tip of his tongue.

"You wish to know pleasure? *Carnal pleasure?*" The words came as mere rasps, scarcely audible, but hanging so heavily in the air between them, not even the brisk night wind could sweep away their portent.

She scooted around to face him, the front of her fully exposed, her magnificent breasts, wondrous bare and as unashamedly displayed as if she'd merely extended a hand in casual greeting.

"Aye, sirrah, I wish to experience such things, and in all variety of nuances," she said, the admission—and the view—sending veritable sheets of molten fire sluicing through him. "*Desire,* as the lady Rhona once informed me I am sorely in need of."

"She told you that?"

She nodded again and the movement caused her full breasts to sway a bit. "She suggested such the very day she told me I'd best send for a champion."

"And you did."

"*She* did."

This time Marmaduke nodded. "And now you have one."

"Aye, I do. A champion, a soon-to-be husband, a . . . man."

Marmaduke bobbed his fool head again, his senses too befuddled from studying the tightly ruched areolas, the hard, elongated peaks of her nipples to draw breath, much less speak coherently.

"I have decided I am as much in need of the third as the first two," she explained, leaning back on her hands so her breasts thrust slightly upward and forward, so their stiff peaks looked him straight in the eye.

*Her* eyes gleamed bold as Bathsheba's. "For good or ill,

I am not a shy woman," she said, taking his hands, lacing her fingers with his.

"My body has been seen and . . . *used* . . . by too many for me to hide behind pretenses of false modesty. Now, I find I would indeed enjoy exploring the fleshly delights the bawds sing of when they think all ladies have left the hall."

She guided his hands toward her breasts, holding them prisoner mere inches from her hardened nipples.

So close, he could feel the heat streaming out from them.

"Will you send me such pleasure?"

Marmaduke scarce heard her, so thick was the haze of his arousal, so achingly sweet, the powerful verging of his need.

"Can you indulge me? Will you do so knowing I wish to keep all emotion out of any . . . *physical intimacies* . . . we practice?"

That he heard.

But his protest died in his throat, overrun by a moan when she brought his hands even closer to the tips of her breasts.

Clearly mistaking the pitiful sound for his acquiescence, she touched his fingertips to her nipples.

"Jesu God," the oath burst past his lips the same instant his passion broke.

"Then you agree?" Her matter-of-fact voice pierced the fog swirling round him.

Marmaduke nodded, unable to deny her aught in that moment.

Even such a fool proposal as she'd just shielded.

One he had no intention of keeping.

But now, *this* moment, he had greater concerns on his troubled mind.

Such as how to keep her from noticing the tell-tale stain dampening his hose and the front flap of his tunic.

For he, Sir Marmaduke Strongbow, champion of fair ladies and slayer of dragons, had just joined the ranks of lesser men.

*Chapter Thirteen*

❖

*E*NCHANTER OF WOMEN.

A charmer of untold skill and finesse.

Capable of seducing the virtue from a self-sacrificing virgin saint . . . or so his men claimed.

So why had he pulled his hands from her grasp—away from her straining nipples—and dropped to his knees on the rush-strewn floor?

Kneeling before her, his dark head slightly inclined, he looked anything but a man well-apprised of the fine art of winning female hearts.

He appeared soundly defeated.

Worse, he looked . . . *pained.*

Caterine worried the soft folds of the *arisaid* bunched on her lap, instinctively seeking its comfort, silently willing him to raise his bowed head and look at her.

To touch her again.

And rekindle the tight whirling of heated pleasure that had spun through her the instant his fingers had lighted on her breasts. She'd only just begun to near its edges when he'd pulled away, his unexpected reaction hurling a flood-tide of embarrassment through her.

Had he done so because she'd bared herself?

The notion curled sharp-ended talons of mortification

around her pride, cruelly dashing every last remnant of the exhilarating tremors called to life by his touch. Tingle by tingle, they fizzled into a congealed pool of cold perplexity somewhere in the very pit of her belly.

Caterine stared at him, one half of her admiring the way his thick hair gleamed in the moonlight, the other half cringing inwardly when her gaze lighted on his tightly clenched hands.

At the sight of those white-knuckled fists, the weight of her harlotry pressed heavy on her shoulders. That she'd joyed in such wantonness, pressed heavier still.

Steeling her spine, she drew back her shoulders against her shame and lifted her chin a defiant degree. He certainly wasn't shy about her seeing his nakedness . . . he'd stood calmly before her, fully unclothed beside the bathing tub the morning he'd repaired the latrine chute.

And he'd been full aware of her measuring gaze. If anything, a flash of pride had shown on his face.

So why shouldn't she revel in the thrill of having him gaze on hers?

Her stomach knotting at the madness taking possession of her, she stretched her hand across the cold air between them and boldly slid her fingers through the thick mass of his shoulder length hair.

"Have I shocked you, my lord?" She put her vexation to words, the soft whisper scarce louder than a sigh, but rife with her pique. "Has my . . . *daring* offended you?"

His head snapped up, the muscle working in his granite-hewn jaw boldly proclaiming she'd done that and more.

"In the name of all the saints and apostles," he pushed out, more to himself than to her. "Is that what you think?"

His deep voice held nary a note of censure, but purest agitation stood etched in every line of his face, and the barely repressed irritation spoke more eloquently than any words of denial.

As did the tense set of his broad shoulders.

"Well?" He regarded her with that calm, all-seeing intensity of his.

Not that he needed to glare the truth out of her.

Her ire burned to sling every ounce of it against his hard-muscled chest.

Moistening her lips, she nodded. "If you truly want to know, you look as if you've not only taken ill, but also as vexed as if you've just been informed you were to be denied all the sacraments."

A look of incredulity flashed across his face.

Caterine held his astonished stare. "Aye, doomed ever-lasting," she embellished, warming to her topic. "As if you'd . . . died."

"Some do call it the *little death*," she thought she heard him mutter.

"And now?" That, she knew she heard.

He leaned forward. So close his warmth teased her naked breasts. "How do I look now, my lady?"

*Like you want me,* her body cried, responding as his pained expression ebbed into one of . . . concentrated passion.

The all-consuming, smoldering kind.

"You look . . . intrigued," she said, for once choosing a less bald turn of phrase.

For truth, he looked as if he might lean just a few inches closer and rain wondrous kisses across her breasts, and the mere idea kindled a spooling, languid warmth inside her.

"Intrigued?" He arched a brow. "I would say pleased," he said, his gaze caressing her. "Very pleased indeed, for your boldness is a joyous gift."

She blinked. "A gift?"

He nodded. "A far more precious one than you know," he murmured, a new huskiness in his voice.

A fiercely intent look on his face, he touched the large ruby of his signet ring first to one of her nipples, then to the other, leaving it there. "A gift I shall return to you many times over, my love."

Caterine's eyes widened at the endearment, but the stone's cold surface pressed so firmly against the sensitized peak, proved too wildly arousing for her to object.

She opened her mouth to try, but before she could, he pushed to his feet and closed the shutters, blocking out the chill wind but also the strange magic of the silver-washed night.

Turning back to her, he swept her into his arms, cradling her, the crumpled *arisaid,* and even the furred bed cover, high against the hard wall of his chest.

"'Fore God, lady, there is much I would give you and I'd like to speak to you about some of those gifts now, but first I would know you warm," he said. "Your teeth are chattering."

And if he'd had to endure the bounty of her naked breasts winking at him in the moonlight another instant without taking her, truly taking her, his ballocks would've drawn so tight he might well have maimed himself for life.

So he contented himself by whispering a single kiss against her temple, then strode across the darkened bedchamber, not releasing her until he reached the circle of pulsing warmth still emanating from the dying embers in the hearth.

"Don't move," he said, sliding her down the length of him, just for the pure enjoyment of doing so.

Lowering himself on one knee before the hearth, he tossed a few clumps of peat onto the grate, then used an iron poker to rekindle the fire until new flames, smoky and sweet, began to take the edge off the sharp chill.

Satisfied, he straightened, still careful to keep her shawl in front of him as he passed by her to fetch his fur-lined cloak from the ante-room. The newly stoked fire crackled happily by the time he returned, as did a new blaze sparking in the depths of her sapphire eyes.

Clutching the furred bed coverlet tightly about her, she met his gaze, the provocative angle of her pretty head a fair indication that whatever fool notion plagued her bode serious ill for him.

"You rise too quickly in your assumptions if you believe I desire gifts, my lord," she said, promptly confirming his assessment. "Of a certainty, I shall enjoy exploring *fleshly pleasures* with you, as we've discussed, but accepting any other form of gift implies an intimacy I cannot give you."

The lie of her words rode the slight quavering in her voice, and gave Marmaduke the fortitude to calmly drape his cloak, fur side up, over a heavy oaken chair near the hearth.

He settled himself into its sturdy embrace as casually as he could, then stretched out his long legs and crossed them at the ankles. "Then come, my lady, and let me at least warm you," he said, opening his arms. "I would tell you of my home in Kintail, of Balkenzie."

"This can be your home."

Undaunted, Marmaduke gave her one of his special smiles.

The one he'd needed years of painstaking practice to master.

To learn to form around his scar.

He upped its potency by letting a devilishly careless gleam enter his good eye.

A casualness at high odds with the tense pounding of his heart.

He meant to do so much more than *tell* her of Balkenzie.

He hoped to make her want to live there.

"Come," he tried again, extending his hand. "We shall speak of naught more intimate than the thickness of Balkenzie's walls, its proud location on the southernmost shore of Loch Duich, or how pleased I am to have many of its windows fitted with fine panes of polished horn."

She watched him from down-drawn brows, the wildly

fluttering pulse at the base of her neck revealing he'd chosen the wrong words to soothe her.

"I wish you to remain here," she said, placing her hand in his. "You are needed here, as am I."

Marmaduke's brow furrowed.

He wished he could lie.

Instead he heaved a great sigh and drew her onto his lap. "My use here is but for a brief span of time," he said, settling her so her back rested against his chest, then smoothing the ends of his fur-lined cloak across her legs. "Your purpose here, my lady, is long expired and does more ill than good."

She twisted around to level a pointed look at him, the movement causing the furred bed coverlet to slip off her shoulders. "I am lady here, I—"

"You *were* lady here," he reminded her, and tried not to notice the coverlet had dipped low enough to expose the top halves of her breasts.

They swayed a bit with her agitation. Just enough to give him a fleeting glimpse of her nipples. Now relaxed, the surprisingly large circles of her areolas struck raw need straight into his groin.

"God's eyes, woman," he swore, unable to stop himself from peering beneath the gaping coverlet, watching in riveted fascination as the oh-so-rousing rounds of pinkish-brown flesh contracted into two hardened peaks.

In a gesture that would have pleased the lust-abhorring St. Jerome himself, Marmaduke adjusted the coverlet so it once more concealed her lushness, then eased her against his chest again, this time careful to snake one arm as unobtrusively as possible across the slender stretch of her waist.

He cleared his throat, determined to have his say, over-large areolas and thrusting nipple peaks, or nay.

"As I was saying," he began, cradling her head against his shoulder so she couldn't shoot blue fire at him again, "you *were* lady here."

"Meaning?" The ice in her voice worked just as well.

"Meaning, so long as you remain here, you will be as a shadow on the turret stairs. A palpable presence at the high table even when you are not physically there," he tried to explain. "Your strength will hover behind James, casting a pall over all he says or does so long as you reside within these walls."

"You only seek to lure me away," she accused, stiffening in his arms.

"I seek what is best for you." He spoke the truth as he saw it. "You, and your stepson."

"And what you want for yourself."

"Aye, what I wish for myself as well," he admitted, moving his fingers over hers to rub the chill from them. "Mind you well, fair one, in every man's beginning is his end and oft times we reach it far too soon."

He paused to gently kiss her brow. "Often, those we'd hoped would make the journey with us, are stricken along the way or take another road, leaving us alone."

"And what does that have to do with me?" she asked in a small voice that clearly declared she already knew.

"I have many empty years behind me . . . lonely years," he said, each word costing him in its naked honesty. "And now I've the rest of the journey ahead of me, a proud stronghold awaiting my return, and, aye, a heart that yearns to love again."

She said nothing, but her fingers, warm now, laced with his . . . and gave him hope.

"I would love you, Caterine, if you will let me." He skimmed the knuckles of his free hand down her cheek, his heart turning over when he discovered warm moisture there. "At the very least," he added, his voice thick, "I would enjoy your companionship and value your skill and grace as Lady of Balkenzie."

She released a long breath.

Marmaduke simply held her, and waited until the rising

wind stopped rattling the shutters and the placidly burning peat fire ceased sending loud-popping showers of sparks into the air.

"Do you know what will happen to James if I leave?" Caterine spoke first, and the night fell silent again.

She glanced up at him, a powerful longing near undoing her. A crushing urge to cast aside her concerns and lose herself in the comfort of his words.

His embrace.

He was looking away from her, toward the window embrasure, the scarred side of his face in shadow, soft fire glow illuminating the unmarred side, the flickering light calling cruel attention to the strikingly handsome man he'd once been.

Her heart twisted at what he'd lost, and so much more than mere good looks. Caterine blinked back the sudden heat stinging her eyes and drew a deep, cleansing breath of the earthy-sweet peat smoke. She forced herself to dwell on other storms and shadows, the ones that darkened her own heart.

Storms she couldn't let break, shadows she didn't want shrouding the lives of those she loved.

Or might come to love.

"Do you know wha—" she began again, but he pressed two fingers against her lips, silencing her.

"James will outgrow your shadow," he said, his word choice making her wonder if he could indeed see into her soul, the conviction in his voice almost but not quite convincing her.

"Your stepson has an untrodden path to follow, a difficult one, true, but not insurmountable."

"Sir Hugh—" she tried to speak past his fingers.

"—will be dealt with, I assure you."

He slid his thumb across her cheek, smoothing away the dampness, and her heart flip-flopped at the tenderness of the gesture, his gentle touch quelling her objections more thoroughly than any silencing fingers.

She brought her hand up to cradle the scarred side of his face, her breath catching at the emotion banking inside her. But other emotions whirled through her, too.

Wholly different ones, called forth by those she held most dear.

Dunlaidir's gruff seneschal, Eoghann, his bony shoulders having carried a weighty burden far too long. Sir John, her late husband's friend, and a man whose own heart had been crushed by Sir Hugh. Even the lady Rhona, for all her meddlesome ways.

But most of all, James.

With the exception of her brothers, all of whom she hadn't seen in years, her stepson was the only male to have e'er truly cared for her.

His kindness alone had made her early years at Dunlaidir bearable . . . had helped her patch together a semblance of her tattered pride and feel worthy again.

Despite the stains tarnishing her very soul.

She couldn't leave him now, not when he needed her most.

"I believe you have lived away from the English too long, Marmaduke Strongbow," she said, finally managing to speak past the tightness in her throat.

She traced her fingertips along the crease of his scar, hoping the caress would gentle the bitterness of her words. "Your people are as sand kernels on the strand," she began. "Dispatching Sir Hugh will bring but a breathing space of relief, for no sooner will he have been rooted out, but another will come to replace him."

Her champion did not speak, but his silence affirmed his acknowledgment of the truth.

"That, my good sir, is why I bid you to stay. James will ne'er be strong enough to stand against such might." She glanced into the hearth fire, not wanting him to see the moisture dampening her eyes. "Already, the garrison respects you. If you leave, they will lose heart again and we will be defeated before the first blow has even struck."

"You err," he murmured against her crown.

She shook her head, her gaze still averted.

"Aye, you err gravely," he said again, louder this time. "And you just voiced the most glaring reason I must leave. My very honor demands it."

Caterine looked at him, no longer caring if he saw her distress. "Dear sir, I see only reasons for you to remain."

Winding one of her braids around his hand, he caressed its links with his thumb . . . much as he'd smoothed the same over her cheek moments before.

"Then you are not looking deeply enough to see the other reasons." Releasing her hair, he slipped a finger under her chin and lifted her face. "Or you are seeing only what you want to see . . . a weakling unable to stand on his own."

"That is not true."

He quirked a brow at her.

"It is true indeed. James is not a weakling," he said. "He is merely troubled, and I'd mind you the distinction is a great one. He is a fast and able learner, as he's proven to myself, and to Lachlan, who trains with him often."

"You are leading him down a path to nowhere with all your training . . . the men here will not follow him." Caterine met his gaze full on, her unwavering stare daring him to challenge her logic. "They look to you."

He sighed then, and pulled her closer, snuggling her spoon-fashion against the hard contours of his body. "Do you not see they will continue to do so if I stay? Your garrison will only accept James once he's proven himself worthy and he cannot do so as long as we stand in his way."

"We?"

He had the audacity to nod.

Caterine stiffened and would've jerked out of his arms

were his hands not moving in such soothing circles up and down her back.

Purposely lulling her, trying to win her agreement.

"Aye, we, " he whispered into her hair. "You, for coddling him. Me, because—"

"Because you wield a heavy sword," she snapped, her temper revolting against being *lulled*.

"As can James," came his unruffled reply. "With practice. And if you let him."

"L-let him?" she stammered, indignation hobbling her tongue. "There is naught I would not do for—"

"It gladdens my heart to hear it." The circling hands stilled for a moment. "For when we truly love someone, my lady, sometimes we must also care enough to let go of them."

He began kneading her shoulders then, much as he'd done earlier, and, as before, cascades of warm, pleasurable tingles slid through her at his touch.

His magical touch.

Caterine sighed, her eyelids suddenly growing incredibly heavy.

"Sleep, sweeting," he murmured. His wondrous hands loosened her muscles—and her cares—one by one, easing her into a dreamlike state where the air was soft, misty, and warm.

Where the arms cradling her proved more inviting than all the pillows mounded high upon her bed.

The rhythmic rise and fall of his warrior's chest, his steady breathing, and even his soft snores, spent her more comfort than she'd ever known.

*Snores?*

Her eyes snapped open.

Watery, gray light leaked through the shutter slats heralding the approach of a new day.

The cold embers in the hearth seemed to mock her . . .

and gave irrefutable evidence she'd spent the night in Sir Marmaduke Strongbow's arms.

And slept well there.

As had Leo.

The little dog lay curled against the Sassunach's feet . . . and appeared utterly content.

A *harrumph* rose in her throat, but lodged there with the damning realization that she felt no less at ease waking wrapped in her champion's warmth.

*Sometimes we must care enough to let go.*

His words came out of nowhere, or perhaps they'd lingered through the night, floating in the darkness . . . waiting.

Hovering on the threshold of some magical place the night had tried to take her, in the hopes of capturing her with the rising sun?

*Care enough to let go.*

Could she?

Let go of all she knew and loved . . . and the darkness inside her?

Could her champion slay her hidden foes as easily as he meant to rid her of more tangible menaces?

As she lay snuggled against him in the darkness, Caterine stared into the deep, gray silence of the new day and wondered.

⚜

*The laird's due.*

To most, fortress, title, and powers.

To James Keith, an empty ewer of soured wine, an equally drained chalice, and a raging ache in his temples.

His laird's *duty,* pacing the broad sweep of his bedchamber's curving bank of windows and keeping his gaze trained on the narrow spit of land connecting Dunlaidir's walled compound with the rugged cliffs of the mainland in a cold vigil he'd kept all through the night as his burning eyes attested.

A poltroon's assignment.

A fool's errand as unpalatable as guzzling an infusion of devil's dung.

An indignity made bearable solely by Lady Rhona's bonny presence.

Her generously proffered agreement to spend the night at his side, not in his bed where he'd like to have her, but patrolling the tall windows with him, watching the Highlanders and old Father Tomas trudge back and forth across the precarious causeway, bringing stuffs and weaponry to the villagers, then returning for more.

Wasted hours spent perusing mist and darkness.

Peering through wind-borne sleet.

Imbibing stale wine.

"Master of Dunlaidir," he scoffed, throwing Rhona a dark glance. "Useful for naught but the far-reaching view out my fool windows."

She grabbed his arm at that, halting his endless pacing, tempering his ire with an arched brow. "You will concede they need your keen eyesight as well?"

"I concede that is what they claimed." He yanked his arm from her grasp. "Trying to console me is closer to the truth."

"The truth," she said, stepping closer to trail one finger down his arm, "is no one within these walls has eyes as good as yours."

"Or a better view."

"I think the view is rather fine," she gave back, her tone annoyingly amiable, her steady gaze making plain she meant anything but the broad vista of sea and headlands they'd been staring holes in since the wee hours.

"By all the saints," James swore, the corners of his mouth turning upward despite himself. "I warrant you could make a rock smile."

"I'd be content to see one cry," she said, her own smile fading for a moment.

"And *seeing* is what we're supposed to be doing," James said, the rueful note in her voice spurring him to stand straighter, to at least appear more lairdly.

He placed his hand on the small of her back and guided her toward the tall windows. "Come, let us continue to make use of this *eyrie* of mine," he added, drawing her close.

He was glad enough to window-watch the remainder of the night if only she would continue to press her soft, sweet self against him as she did this moment.

"There, do you see them?" He pointed to the cliff-side path leading out from the village. "They are almost at the gatehouse."

He'd scarce said the words before the Highlanders emerged onto the narrow causeway. Hulking shapes, they moved through the darkness, their great brands slung over their shoulders, their mailed shirts gleaming dully in the gray light, a veritable arsenal of dirks and other wicked-looking paraphernalia of war thrust beneath their belts and in their boots.

Several burdenless packhorses plodded behind them, their slow gait and hanging heads telling evidence of the long night's toil.

His brows drawn together in a frown, James strained his eyes to peer even deeper into the darkness to discern if they were followed or spied upon by an interloper.

Just as he endeavored to spy on whoever the miscreant might turn out to be: if indeed such a forsworn craven existed.

But naught skulked through the blustery night save the Sassunach's own men, and now, with the merest hint of a lighter gray edging the horizon, they'd no doubt made their last haul for the night and were eager to slip back into the warmth of the hall and seek the comfort of their makeshift billets.

Until the next night when they'd make the trek anew.

As he would stand vigil once more.

Partaking of his nightly *laird's due.*

And, if Rhona graced him with her company again, striving to feel more lairdly than the day before.

❖

Sir Marmaduke stood at one of the two narrow window slits in the little ante-room and stared out across a pewter-colored sea of glass and wished the hours of the strange, magical night hadn't passed so quickly.

Holding his lady as she'd slept had been a bliss beyond all telling.

But now the cold gray of a new morn crept ever deeper into the shuttered bedchamber behind him, its damp chill stealing the wonders of the night, negating them before they could take seed and grow.

The time of reckoning was upon him, the first being the highly suspicious puddle in the very middle of his pallet. The wetness had winked at him the instant he'd slipped into the ante-room just moments ago.

Nay, *limped,* not slipped, for allowing his lady's puddle-piddling pet to spend the night sprawled across his ankles had put his feet to sleep.

And not just one, but both of them.

Marmaduke rumpled his nose at the wet spot.

The little dog had a skewed way of showing gratitude, and he yearned to glare his displeasure at the wee creature, but he had more pressing matters to attend, and he'd best be about them before *she* awakened and caught him at it.

Some things weren't meant for a woman's fair eyes.

Especially when the woman in question was the one a man sought to impress.

Thus motivated, Marmaduke tried to pretend he didn't feel as if a thousand needle-footed insects marched over the soles of his feet, and knelt beside the large leather satchel he kept near his pallet.

A pouch that held a few of his most prized possessions.

His mouth pressed into a grim line, he rummaged through its contents until he found what he sought: a bronze mirror of great beauty and antiquity he'd once recovered from the oozing mud bank of a Highland peat bog, and a plumpish earthen jar of Linnet MacKenzie's special ragwort salve.

*She* called the bright yellow ointment a beauty treatment.

He liked to think of it as an anti-scar unguent.

By any name, after long years of daily use, the highly effective healing preparation had diminished the most frightful effects of his scarring, relaxing his facial muscles enough for him to re-learn the wholly underestimated art of being able to smile.

Though he'd never regain the handsomeness he'd once been so proud of, thanks to the miraculous workings of the lady Linnet's salve, he no longer looked as if he'd been cross-bred with a toad.

Marmaduke curled his fingers around the little jar, his gratitude heavy in his heart.

He never went anywhere without an ample supply, and not a day passed that he didn't rub a dollop of the precious wonder cream onto his blighted face.

This morn he'd splurge and use two dollops.

Bracing himself for the sight that never failed to smite him, he pushed to his feet and carried his treasures to the nearest window slit.

One hand curled tight about the mirror's intricately worked triple-looped handle, he angled its polished surface to catch what watery light spilled through the narrow window, then began massaging a generous portion of the ragwort salve onto his scar.

In two days he'd marry again, and he needed all the miracles he could get, for the same muscles that allowed him to smile, also enabled him to kiss well.

And he meant to kiss his lady very, very well at the nuptial ceremony.

He'd already won a goodly portion of her trust, even access to her sweet body.

But he wanted more.

He wanted her heart.

And a curl-her-toes-and-steal-her-breath wedding kiss seemed a good way to begin laying siege to the one thing she'd vowed she couldn't give him . . . her affections.

Her love.

The saints knew she already had his.

With great care, his jaw set with hard determination, Marmaduke massaged the glistening salve into his skin until every trace had been absorbed. Then he inhaled deeply of the briny new morn.

Two days.

Two more chances to reap the greatest benefit of Linnet MacKenzie's beautifying ointment.

And then his assault would begin in bitter earnest.

With soul-stealing, knee-melting kisses.

With relentless, irrepressible care.

# *Chapter Fourteen*

❦

*T*WO DAYS LATER, on the other side of Scotland, a glittering coat of frost iced the stout walls of Clan MacKenzie's island stronghold, Eilean Creag. A keening wind, cold and black, tore with all its force across the crenellated battlements and whipped the surrounding waters of Loch Duich into a churning, white-capped frenzy.

But inside the castle's massive walling, in the smoky warmth of its dimly lit great hall, nothing stirred to greet the approach of another day.

Nary an errant draught dared ruffle the rush-strewn floor . . . or disturb the couple sleeping soundly in the bulky timbered bed claiming a place of honor on the raised dais at the far end of the cavernous hall.

Even the snores of the many MacKenzies slumbering 'round the hulking bed were *muted* snores. Those who valued their necks didn't snore at all.

Or toss and turn in their sleep.

Duncan MacKenzie, the dread Black Stag of Kintail, had issued strict orders: his lady wife's rest was not to be disturbed.

Nor was she allowed to leave the bed.

That she'd repeatedly done so, ignoring her husband's wishes and all good sense, was the reason he'd dismantled their bed, carted it belowstairs, then reassembled it in all its four-posted glory in full view of every man, woman, and child within Eilean Creag's walls.

And every last one of them had been ordered to keep an eye on her.

But this morn's dawning brought a fearsome determination to Linnet MacKenzie's waking heart.

A powerful urge to climb the turret stairs, brave the icy winds blasting across the ramparts, and greet the new day with special fondness and joy.

She would, too, if the great swell of her stomach hadn't robbed her of her usual strength . . . and if her most ardent nocturnal watcher hadn't plied his usual tricks by keeping one impressively muscled thigh slung possessively over her legs and an equally well-crafted arm clamped around her girth.

Careful not to disturb the handsome brute, Linnet slid a sidelong glance at her slumbering husband and weighed the dangers of slipping from his well-meant clutches.

"Do not even think to attempt it," Duncan MacKenzie warned, not even cracking his eyes.

But he did tighten his hold on her.

"Today is the day," his flame-haired wife responded, an odd breathiness in her voice, a sentimental thickness only she and a certain ugly-faced lout of an Englishman could achieve.

And the sound of it, coupled with the cryptic words, banished any last dredges of sleep he might have hoped to cling to, instantly replacing them with cold, stark wakefulness.

"The day for what?" Pushing up on his elbows, he peered at her from narrowed eyes, his heart, his whole being, lurching with ill-ease simply from the look of her.

Faint torchlight leaking through the half-opened bed curtains spilled across her pale face, revealing gold-flecked eyes swimming with moist luminosity, and worse . . . a slight trembling in her lower lip.

"The babe?!" Duncan launched himself to his feet, heedless of his naked state, uncaring of the public place their bed now stood.

"Saints, Maria, and Joseph!" he roared, shoving his hands through his hair.

"Crucifix! 'Tis too soon!" he bellowed, a wounded beast, dread like none he'd ever known sluicing through him in great, cold waves. "Mother of God, preserve—"

"Of a mercy, husband, becalm yourself." Shaking her head, Linnet smiled.

A reassuring smile meant for him . . . and every MacKenzie who now gaped at them, grog-eyed from sleep, the same terror stamped on their startled faces as on her husband's handsome one.

"Everyone is staring," she said, clutching the bedcovers to her tender breasts. "You've roused them all with your blustering, and to no purpose. The babe will not come for some weeks yet."

"And it is awake they aught be!" Whirling around, he planted fisted hands against his hips and glowered at any who dared to meet his stare.

Glared at the lot of them until their sniggers reminded him of his unclothed condition.

Until the portent of his lady wife's words sifted past the thick cords of alarm twisting 'round his innards, tying his guts in knots and bows.

*The babe will not come for weeks.*

Cool bliss on his fired nerves.

Soothing balm to allay his fear of losing her . . . and their bairn.

The first she'd managed to carry this long.

Heaving a great sigh, Duncan raked every fool gawker in his hall with a formidable stare. "This bed is here for one purpose only," he called out, his deep voice rising to the vaulted ceiling. "*You* are gathered round it for the same reason: to alert me if my lady attempts to leave it . . . or stop her folly if I am away."

He cast a dark look over his shoulder.

At her.

He'd deal with her repeated endeavors to defy him later, *after* the safe delivery of the healthy bairn she insisted they'd be blessed with.

His bug-eyed men would taste his wrath now. "Lest you wish to wear sackcloth and dine on naught but soot and ash the rest of your days, hunker back down on your pallets or where'er else you choose to rest your heads and ignore what transpires in or near this bed . . . lest my lady seeks to escape its confines."

Folding his arms, he waited until their grumbles, grunts, and rustlings found an end, then turned back to confront his misty-eyed wife.

If the babe wasn't the reason for her mawkish expression, he had a good idea who was.

The only other person with as big a heart—as *soft* a heart—as Linnet herself.

Lowering himself onto the edge of the bed, he took her hand in his . . . and hid his dismay at the clammy feel of her fingers behind a long huffed-out breath.

"What is with the great lout?" he asked, concern for his friend almost as laming as his fear for her and the babe had been. "Have you had a vision? Is he in danger?"

Linnet shook her head again, the smile welling in her heart swelling her tongue as well.

Her husband frowned—a daunting sight to any who knew him less well than she. "Your sister, then?" He smoothed the hair back from her brow, the tender gesture belying his fearsome expression. "Is she in danger?"

"Only of losing her heart," Linnet spoke at last, her joy at the knowledge almost overwhelming her. "*He* has already lost his," she added, a fat tear leaking from the corner of one eye.

Her husband glanced to the side.

When he looked back at her, an unusual brightness misted his own eyes. "They are happy?" he asked, his deep voice low and gruff. "Your gift has shown you?"

"Aye, my gift, but also my heart," she said, pressing the back of her free hand against his beloved cheek.

Capturing it, Duncan placed a warm kiss on her palm. "That one-eyed bastard truly loves again?" he persisted as if he found the possibility highly improbable.

The raw edge to his words gave bold voice to how much the prospect pleased him.

"And she loves him?"

Suddenly tired, Linnet pulled her hands from his grasp and leaned back against the pillows. Lacing her fingers protectively over her stomach, she gave him a wan little smile.

"I doubt she knows it yet, but, aye, she does."

A roguish smile spread across Duncan's face. "Saints, but I am ready to see that English whoreson again," he vowed. "I shall bedevil him from here to the gates of purgatory and back for being so bull-headed when we first urged him to go to your sister's aid."

A cantankerous snort came from somewhere in the shadows. "And when will we get to see the lovesick fool again?"

Linnet's smile widened upon recognizing the voice.

Her husband's dark brows snapped together as he combed the smoke-hazed gloom, searching the dimness for Fergus, Eilean Creag's aged seneschal, and the only soul in all of Kintail who'd dare break his edict of silence.

The grizzle-headed old goat thrust his bristly chin forward the instant Duncan's stare found him. "I grow weary of his frippery and gewgaws a-crowding my hall," the gray-beard complained, excusing his daring with a nod toward the teetering piles of Sir Marmaduke's possessions stacked just inside the hall's arched entry.

A veritable mountain of household goods, weaponry, and, as Fergus had claimed, fanciful baubles and trinkets only one as romantically inclined as the chivalrous Sir Marmaduke Strongbow would appreciate.

A wealth of goods Duncan and his men had been transporting across Loch Duich, to Marmaduke's as-yet-unoccupied Balkenzie, by the boatload, for weeks now.

And still they hadn't made a dent in the Sassunach knight's accumulated belongings.

" 'Tis time he returns and life gets back to normal in these parts," Fergus grumbled, then flounced onto his side on the makeshift pallet he shared with his equally aged wife, the bony arm he flung over his head clearly signaling he'd lose no more words on the subject.

And if there'd been any doubt, his particularly distinctive snores—high-pitched wheezy ones—soon heralded the irrefutable end to his disruptions.

"So, sweeting," Duncan murmured, turning back to his wife, "when will we get to see that lumbering oaf again? Is his return upon us? Is that what you meant when you said '*today is the day*'?"

"Nay," Linnet answered in a tremulous voice, her sweet lips trembling again. "I do not know when they will return. You should ken by now that I cannot scry at will."

Pausing, she sent a quick glance to the mounds of goods crowding the opposite end of the hall. "But I pray it will be in time for Yuletide at Balkenzie as we are hoping."

"Then what day is today?"

"Their wedding day," she said, and Duncan didn't doubt her for an instant. "Today is the day they will marry."

⚜

*Her wedding day.*

Caterine paused on the top landing of the outer stairs and stared down at the milling throng crowding Dunlaidir's bailey. The unaccustomed activity stirred an odd warmth in her heart . . . and plunged her headlong onto a proving ground that hovered somewhere between exhilaration and ill-ease.

"They came, my lady," Rhona enthused beside her, *her* elation barely contained. "They came just as he said they would."

Too moved to speak, Caterine reached for her friend's hand and squeezed tight.

The burghers had indeed come, just as her soon-to-be-husband had predicted, and from what she could tell, they'd brought all their friends and family with them.

Her emotions welling to a dangerous degree, she strained her eyes to peer through the billowing sheets of thick white mist drifting across the cobbled bailey.

A sea of familiar faces returned her gaze.

*Beaming* faces full of pride and . . . hope.

Beloved faces she hadn't seen in many long months, but that now stared up at her from the bottom of the stairs. Or shouted well-wishes from as far away as the distant gatehouse.

Clinging to Rhona's hand, Caterine drew a deep breath of the frosty air and struggled to find her voice.

"Are there truly so many?" she finally pushed past the hot lump swelling her throat.

"More than the stars in the night sky," Rhona answered, a suspicious catch in her own voice. "For truth, I vow they line the causeway to the mainland as well, *and* clog the cliffside path to the village . . . if my eyes aren't teasing me.

"And," she went on, tilting her head to the side, one finger tapping furiously against her chin, "if my ears aren't playing tricks as well, isn't that the kirk bell?"

It was.

Muffled and faint, but its every chime striking loud and beckoning chords in Caterine's heart.

Its pealing, and her companion's exuberance, carried her off the proving ground, but handed her into the risky arms of exhilaration.

And hope.

Though, were she wholly honest, the exhilaration had been winning the field ever since *he'd* ridden into the courtyard, dropped on bended knee, and pressed a gallant kiss to her hand.

The hope had come later, but grew stronger by the day.

"Come, my lady," Rhona urged then, tugging her down the stairs even as she spoke. "It is time."

*Aye, it is, and many blessings to you. . . .*

The voice, feminine, dark and sultry, rose above the revels of the crowd, soft as the drifting mist, but as distinct as if the words had been whispered directly in Caterine's ear.

She whirled around to ask Rhona if she'd heard the voice, too, but James had already seized her friend's arm and was now escorting her toward a waiting palfrey.

And not a one of the boisterous shouts of the villagers matched the soft, almost melancholy, note of the woman whose blessing had just hushed past her ear.

A chill that had nothing to do with the frosty, cloud-cast afternoon streaked down her back, but Caterine lifted her chin against the mystery, drew her cloak against the cold, and let Eoghann help her onto her mount.

Suddenly eager to reach the little cliff-top church and the brave champion who awaited her there, she'd no sooner gathered her reins before a furtive movement near the seaward wall caught her eye.

A lone woman stood there, hauntingly beautiful, dark as Rhona, but tall and willowy.

Strangely silent.

And cloaked more by the swirling mist than the cowled robes she wore. As Caterine stared, the woman lifted her hand in salutation, then drew the back of her fingers across her cheek, just below her shadowed eyes.

*As if to wipe away tears.*

The skin on the back of her nape prickling, Caterine tried to wheel her mount toward the woman, to go to her, but in that same moment, Eoghann thwacked her mare on the rump and James called out the command to ride forward.

Her efforts thwarted, Caterine and her little party clattered beneath the raised portcullis of the innermost gatehouse. But before her mount could carry her too deeply into the darkness of the tunnel-like pend, she twisted around to look back.

The woman was gone.

Nothing moved near the seaward wall save curtains of shifting mist.

Then the crowd surged forward, pushing into the pend behind them, each celebrant caught up in the excitement of the day, just as the strange woman's words were caught up in the wind.

A cold, dark wind that followed her through the yawning tunnel as surely as the cheering burghers.

*Love him well, Lady Caterine,* the voice implored.

*I bid you love him well.*

❧

Looking far too confident for one so blighted, Sir Marmaduke Strongbow waited for his bride beneath the arched entry porch of the village church, and drew the simmering wrath of a dark-cloaked figure standing but a few paces away.

Every bit as hard-bitten as the Highlanders gathered round the tall Sassunach, the silent watcher fought back a sneer of disdain at their protective stances.

Their weapon-hung brawn and steel-eyed bravura.

As if his man would strike now, with the cold she-bitch and her entourage nearly upon them. He almost gave a derisive snort, but wisely disguised it as a cough.

For some reason he couldn't fathom, his liege still wanted the woman. Nor would he wish a melee to erupt amongst the villagers, who, for whatever dubious reasons, chose this day to spend their obeisance to the castlefolk.

The cloaked figure glowered at the lot of them.

Simpering fools to a man, but his lord needed their backs and would take out the loss of a set of toiling hands on his back.

His gaze returned to the Sassunach.

God's blood, but the bastard could stand proud.

Gall bubbled and roiled in the cloaked figure's belly, but he ignored the discomfort. The Sassunach's comeuppance would claim him soon, after the nuptial ceremony. And neither his skill with a blade nor his fierce-eyed Highlanders would save him.

Most especially not the gawking simpletons lining the road.

Drawing the hood of his mantle closer about his face, as much to shield his ears from the incessant pealing of the kirk bell as to hide his black frown, the man turned his attention to the bridal party's approach.

But in truth, his gaze moved carefully down the rows of burghers flanking the village road.

He searched the crowd for a single man.

But as if the very saints had taken sides and weren't on his, thick sea-mist rose in great clouds over the cliffs to drift inland, creeping over roofs and between the densely clustered stone cot-houses.

Undulating curtains of fog sent from above to cloak the jostling onlookers in a giant white shroud.

A near impenetrable one that hampered his ability to locate the face he sought . . . and soundly darkened his mood.

As did the piercing glare he knew was aimed his way from the distant hillock where Sir Hugh de la Hogue and his men watched the proceedings from a goodly distance.

A safe distance, for de la Hogue had no desire to soil his hands this day.

The sorry task had been left to *him*.

And he'd passed it on to a graceless craven who seemed to have vanished in the crowd.

Giving up all pretense of playing the amused courtier to

a wedding of two people he abhorred, the cloaked figure indulged himself in the huff of contempt he'd been holding back, and slipped away from his position near the church steps to meld with the masses.

His nose wrinkling in distaste, he suffered the indignity of rubbing elbows with the lower classes . . . and went in search of Sir Marmaduke Strongbow's assassin.

✤

"Shall we disperse them?" Sir Alec ranged himself closer to the edge of the church steps.

Tearing his attention from the approaching bridal party, Sir Marmaduke followed his friend's gaze to a distant ridge where de la Hogue and his contingent of mounted miscreants aimed fierce glowers at the men of Kintail.

Their stares, more felt than seen because of the swirling fog, bored holes straight through Marmaduke's fur-lined cloak, the resplendence of his deep blue surcoat, *and* the steel mesh of the hauberk he wore beneath it.

Hand on his sword-hilt, he shot another quick glance at his lady. Nearing the middle of the village, she held herself tall in the saddle, the lift of her chin bearing evidence she'd noticed their uninvited guest . . . and possessed the backbone to ignore him.

His chest swelling with pride, Marmaduke let his gaze cling to her, and gloried in every detail of her appearance. The shimmering folds of her sister's wedding veil—just one of the special gifts Linnet had sent along for her. The luster of the braids curled over her ears, their gleaming perfection teasing him through the transparency of the head veil.

Reminding him of the darker gold of her *other* hair.

At once, heat to rival the devil's own furnace blasted into his loins.

"Bleeding saints of Christ!" The invective burst past his lips, louder than he'd intended.

Marmaduke scowled toward the distant hillock.

The very idea of de la Hogue having even courted the idea of making Caterine his, doused the fire her comeliness had sent licking through his loins.

"We have keen-eyed archers near that hill," Gowan said beside him, clearly mistaking the reason for Marmaduke's momentary loss of composure. "A few well-placed bow shots—"

"Nay."

"*Nay?*"

Marmaduke turned to his friend. "The dastard seeks but to provoke us," he said, dipping into a well of patience the Highlanders sorely lacked. "Allowing him to do so, would be to bow our knees to him."

A look of incredulity washed over Gowan's bearded countenance. "Since when do you shy from a good blood-letting?"

"Mayhap since I do not wish my lady to witness a massacre on her wedding day."

"Mayhap since falling in love has turned you into a mushpot, I'll own," Gowan muttered, and Marmaduke didn't bother to contradict him.

He *had* fallen in love.

Cuffing his friend on the arm, he said, "Mayhap since I refuse to let some swollen-headed blackguard foul my own pleasure in this moment."

Gowan swung round to the other MacKenzies. "I knew he loved her," he guffawed, slapping the nearest Highlander, Sir Ross, on the back.

Good-natured ribbing ensued, the tension, for the moment, diffused.

Letting them to their ribaldry, Marmaduke curled his fingers around the signet ring pressing into his palm and scanned the crush of burghers pouring into the little churchyard.

Interspersed among them were heavily armed men from the Keith garrison, those who'd been there upon his arrival at Dunlaidir, and a few village men newly elevated into their ranks.

Unlike the burghers, who deftly concealed the habiliments of war recently distributed to them, these men wore their metal boldly and were well-skilled in its use.

Other stalwarts skirted the village, unseen and silent, these men accomplished in darker methods of warfare.

A ruffianly lot, but loyal.

And willing to ply their unsavory trade without blinking an eye if need be.

Only Marmaduke's own men shifted and fidgeted, their jesting already giving way to more serious pursuits. Their brows once more darkening with Highland edginess, they cast repeated glances at the distant hillock.

"All are in readiness." Sir Ross claimed Marmaduke's ear. "One word and—"

"Not this day." The clipped words left no room for further appeals.

With a grim nod, Marmaduke indicated the perspiring Father Tomas. The holy man hovered just inside the church door, praying and wringing his age-spotted hands.

At the sight, some of the bluster ebbed out of the Highlanders and Marmaduke released a long breath. "There are times I am almost grateful for the coolness of my English blood," he said, more to himself than his men.

"The cur will be brought to heel soon enough, but lest he come closer, I mind it's wiser—for now—to let him see this marriage is a true one," he added, lifting up his voice so the black-frocked priest was sure to hear. "We can draw steel on him later . . . when innocents won't be caught in the fray."

An audible sigh of relief came from the candle-lit interior of the somber little church.

Grumbles of discontent issued from his men.

But both the relief and the grumbles soon gave way to the joyous roar that went up from the crowd when at last the bridal party rode into the churchyard and Lady Caterine Keith reined in before her groom.

# Chapter Fifteen

❧

"In the name of the Father, the Son, and the Holy Ghost," Sir Marmaduke said, slipping his signet ring successively onto the thumb, fore, and middle finger of his bride's left hand.

Awed by the raw emotion surging through him, he drew a ragged breath, holding it for the sheerest moment—an eternity to let his demons rage and howl—but not a one of them raised their ugly heads. Nothing stirred inside him save the fierce pounding of his heart.

For once, his devils showed mercy and gave him peace.

Then, on the cold and windy porch of the little stone church and before they could change their minds, he released his relief on the breath he'd been holding and uttered the words that made Caterine Keith his wife.

"With this ring I thee wed," he said, and eased the ruby heirloom onto her finger.

Surprised at the thickness in her new husband's voice, Caterine held the too-large ring in place with her thumb, and wondered at the unexpected rush of emotion closing her own throat.

Something fine and sweet burst to splendid flowering deep inside her, and she stood perfectly still, savoring it, as he reached for her head veil. The look on his face as he did so, his smoldering intensity, filled her with unexpected contentment . . . and routed all other concerns.

Silenced the raucous cheering behind them.

The wet, sniffing noises so close they could only come from Rhona, and even the droning voice of Father Tomas speaking the homily she'd heard so many times before.

Everything faded save the tenderness and pride on her champion's face . . . and the exhilarating knowledge that he was about to kiss her.

Now, while James yet recited all she brought to the union as her dowry.

Her heart thundering, she raised her chin as he smoothed back the shimmering silk of her borrowed veil, freely offering her lips in a gesture meant to publicly honor his gallantry.

And to speed the kiss she burned to receive.

A kiss the onlookers apparently wanted, too, for the din in the churchyard rose to a fevered pitch. Caterine blinked, fierce yearning scorching a path of twisting, breathless anticipation clear to her toes.

"I am going to kiss you," he said, beguiling her with six simple words.

*And once I have, I shall never let you go.*

Those words hovered between them, alive and pulsing, elusive as the frosty puffs of their breath. Truly spoken or heard with her heart, she'd never know because they'd no sooner touched her ear before he lifted his hand to her face.

Claimed her with one touch.

"My wife," he said, the depth of emotion in the two huskily spoken words pricking the back of her eyes. "May God have mercy on any who try to take you from me."

He wrapped his arms around her in a crushing embrace. A claiming so possessive, so demanding, the steel links of his hauberk pressed into her, branding her.

*Never let you go.* The words came again, lighter than a

sigh this time, sweeter than a caress, and pouring a floodtide of light and warmth into her heart.

For one interminably long moment, he looked deep into her eyes, that compelling intensity of his saying more than any ethereal words she may or may not have heard.

Cradling the back of her head with one firm hand, he splayed the other around her hip, urging her closer still, molding her to his strength.

She leaned into him, sliding her hands along the broad reach of his shoulders, staunchly ignoring the niggling whispers of doubt warning that with the giving of her kiss, she'd also lose her heart.

That danger paling beside the headiness of his embrace, she looped her arms around his neck and met his descending lips halfway, her boldness amply rewarded by the mastery of his kiss.

The seizing not just of her lips, but of her very essence. Wholly inappropriate for their sanctified surroundings, but so bone-meltingly right, its sheer glory stole her breath.

She swayed a bit and his arms tightened around her, drawing her higher, more *intimately,* against him. "You are mine," he affirmed, pulling back just enough to sear the claim against the satiny warmth of her lips.

"Now and henceforth," he breathed, slanting his mouth over hers for one last taking of her sweetness.

A gift she gave freely, parting her lips beneath his, boldly inviting the full sweep of his tongue and matching it with the heated glide of her own.

A sensual frenzy, a lascivious tangling far too rousing to indulge in on the church steps, before the final blessing, and in full view of all who'd braved the day's bluster to see them wed.

At last he tore his mouth from hers, but didn't ease completely away until he'd sealed their vows with a softer, gentler kiss.

The merest hush of his lips over hers, the slightest part-

ing touch of his tongue to the very tip of hers. Whisper-
sweet, but powerful enough to wrest a groan from the very
bottom of his soul when he finally set her from him.

A groan so glaringly loud in the utter silence surrounding
them, he couldn't even muster his field-of-battle stone-face.

Not even the muted thunder of de la Hogue's furious departure from the distant hillock helped abscure his wits.

His heart thumping, he shoved a hand through his hair,
the crushing quiet whirling around him, drawing all focus on
his passion, his total loss of control.

Even the wind seemed to have held its howling breath to
spy on his lusting.

The unaccustomed heat of a full-blown blush crept up his
neck and he turned his back on the gaping throng, more
shaken than he cared to admit. Braving the wide-eyed shock
of the priest, he grabbed his wife's hand and pulled her inside the church for the nuptial mass before the crowd's
jaunting could begin anew.

His men weren't so easily thwarted.

"Lord God, did you ever see the like?" Sir Gowan roared,
his deep voice cutting the stillness. "Would that Duncan
were here to witness the Sassunach's capitulation to a kiss!"

The Highlander's mirth unleashed a clamor of such unbridled jubilation, even the hushed solemnity of the fusty-
aired nave couldn't hinder its intrusion.

Blessedly, his men held their tongues once inside the
holy place, their knavery contained to impatient shuffling, a
few elbow jabs, and a smattering of over-exaggerated eye
rolls.

Determined to ignore them, Marmaduke held fast to
Caterine's hand as they knelt for Father Tomas's final blessing. And if it came with more of a quaver than there would
have been had he not just helped himself to a wild-slaking
kiss from his bride's tempting lips, he pretended not to notice.

If a worse fate than suffering his men's antics and testing

Father Tomas's sensibilities did not befall him before the dawn, he would deem himself a well-blessed man.

His head still bowed, he slid a glance at his new wife. Thick-fringed lashes, surprisingly black for one so fair, rested on her cheeks, and the golden coils of her braids gleamed in the candlelight.

Her lips moved in silent prayer . . . promptly recalling the sharp visceral thrill that had shot through him when they'd moved so sweetly beneath his in their first shared kiss.

The first of many, and all manner of them.

At the thought, elation swept through him.

A joy so tempestuous even his devils didn't dare question his right to revel in it.

Returning his gaze to the stone-flagged floor, he fought back a smile and finished the prayer.

He was indeed a well-blessed man.

⚜

Not long thereafter, in the hushed gloaming of a near-perfect day, the returning wedding party neared the rising bulk of Dunlaidir's gatehouse. Torches blazing just inside its tunnel-like entrance beckoned refuge, but the low-hanging clouds, the same pewter-gray as the sea, pleased Marmaduke more.

Their roiling masses almost touched the churning waters, blurring the horizon and blending with the fog to promise a fine, moonless night.

A blessing, if the small raiding party he would lead later that night wished to traverse the sleeping moorland, swiftly and unseen.

But the persistent throbbing in his temples had naught to do with blessings. His gaze trained ahead, he expelled a sigh of relief when the slow-moving column of revelers began passing beneath the raised portcullis.

He scanned the arched entrance for movement that

shouldn't be there, but the sputtering torchlight revealed nothing more ominous than wildly dancing shadows. Naught gave cause for undue alarm save the sharp-edged uneasiness flitting around his every nerve ending like a swarm of whirling midges.

An odd prickling in his nape that kept his hand not far from his sword-hilt.

His gaze, alert and wary.

Sir Ross fell in beside him, edging his shaggy-felled garron closer to Marmaduke's larger steed. "I mislike this more than if a horde of screaming Infidels poured from yon gatehouse," he bit out. "At least then we'd ken where to aim our blows."

"Think you we cannot—" Marmaduke broke off at a sudden commotion in the scrubby trees to their right.

Kneeing his horse in front of his wife's, he whipped out his blade with an ear-piercing *zing* just as an arrow whistled past his shoulder, missing him by inches before it cracked into a nearby boulder.

"Christ's disciples!" he roared, reining round to scan the little copse of stunted ash and bramble.

Swords drawn, his men spurred forward to form a protective cordon around Caterine and Rhona, and the metallic scrape of countless other weapons being wrenched free filled the air as burghers all along the cliff road took up fighting stances, fully prepared to test their new arms on any and all comers.

But none came.

Nothing else marred the stillness save the frantic baying of dogs somewhere in the distance and the frenzied clashing of arms coming from the copse of trees.

Cold fury washing over him, Marmaduke threw a quick look at his lady. Assured of her safety, he kicked spurs into his horse's flanks and tore off toward the skirmish.

A second arrow sped past him as he neared the copse, this time from a different direction. This arrow flew into the trees, a dull *thwack* and a sharply cut-off invective signaling it'd found a mark.

But only one . . . for the thrashing and cursing continued.

Urging his mount to greater speed, he pulled up before the trees just as a wild-eyed, hard-panting, bear of a man crashed out of the underbrush, a reddened battle-ax in his hand, a dead man slung over his shoulder.

A dead man with an arrow shaft protruding from his back.

The giant carrying the body lumbered forward, swaying a bit under the dead man's weight. Marmaduke recognized him as Black Dugie, Dunlaidir's newly returned smith.

A man he'd deemed trustworthy . . . if a mite simple-witted.

Leaping down, Marmaduke closed the distance between them with long strides. "Patron saints! What devil's work goes on here?"

The blacksmith dropped the felled man onto the ground and . . . spat on him. "I spotted him creeping through the trees and followed him," Black Dugie panted, glaring at the corpse.

He nudged the quiver of arrows at the man's belt with a worn-toed boot. "When he drew an arrow, I hurried to stop him but . . ." He trailed off when James and Sir John thundered up, their faces as dark as the fast-descending night.

They reined in so violently, their steeds reared high, the beasts' powerful forelegs flailing in midair before pounding back to earth mere inches from the slain man's body.

His temper clearly strained, James stilled his mount with surprising mastery. "*But what*?" he prompted the long-errant smithy. He leaned forward to eye the big man with rampant mistrust.

Black Dugie thrust out his bearded jaw. "But I wasn't fast enough to get to the Sassunach bastard on time, is what."

Marmaduke grabbed the man's arm. "He was English?"

The smithy nodded. "I heard him speak. He cursed me to

hell and back when I ruined his second shot. He was aiming for you again, or maybe Lady Caterine. I dunno, but I jumped hi—"

"How do we know you didn't loose the arrow that nearly struck Sir Marmaduke?" Sir John grated, suspicion blazing in his eyes.

Keeping his mount, he glanced from the body to the bloodied battle-ax still in Black Dugie's hand. "Mayhap you axed that poor soul so you could blame him for your own dark deed?"

Black Dugie flung down the ax and clenched meaty fists. "I'll own I hacked at him a few times but not so good as to kill him."

He turned to Marmaduke. "Word was not to kill anyone because you'd want to question any troublemakers," he said, somewhat calmer. "The second arrow did him in, not my ax."

"An arrow you could have shot." That from James.

"Nay, he couldn't have," Marmaduke said, grimacing at the implication. "The arrow came from yon woods."

Pushing up in his stirrups, he pointed his sword at a wooded knoll some distance away. "It exited from there."

*And whoever fired it, meant to silence that wretch's tongue before Black Dugie could haul him before me.*

Keeping that sentiment to himself, Marmaduke sheathed his steel, no longer concerned that a second assassin lurked in the surrounding woods.

His instincts—and the chill slithering down his spine— told him the danger lurked much closer.

So keenly aware of looming treachery he could taste its foulness on the frosty air, he clamped a hand on the smithy's blood-sullied shoulder. "I am indebted to you," he said simply, but meant every word.

"I'd like to see you tending Dunlaidir's forge, but if you so desire, you are welcome to accompany me to Balkenzie when I leave. I am in need of a good smith."

The big man inclined his head, clearly unaccustomed to praise.

James's face colored. Sir John began muttering beneath his breath about insolents and minions.

Marmaduke ignored them both. "Do something with the body, then hie yourself to Eoghann," he ordered Black Dugie, raising his voice to overtone Sir John's diatribe.

"I'll ensure he prepares a bath and fresh clothes for you. Then join us in the hall for the wedding feast." He let go of the smith's shoulder, but clapped him on the arm before he turned away. "You will be made welcome, I promise you."

Swinging up onto his saddle, he schooled his features into his best set-faced expression, then looked at the other two men.

James.

Sir John.

One, a traitor.

But why?

He burned to know, and would, but first, he'd bide his time. An enemy watched closely was a harmless one.

He also had other matters weighing on his mind.

"Come, my bride waits," he said, heeding the most pressing of them. "And we, my good men, have a long night ahead of us."

❖

A scant few hours later, but worlds away from the parish church steps and the exhilaration of a champion's kiss, Caterine stood in the shadowy cold of Dunlaidir's undercroft and tried not to show her trepidation as her new husband pulled his handsome blue surcoat over his head.

He tossed its resplendence onto the stone-flagged floor, then discarded his mailed hauberk as well. Wearing naught but leather hose, knee-high boots, and a linen undershirt, his magnificence stole her breath.

A bold air of confidence surrounded him, a calm and steely determination she hoped would see him through the coming raid unscathed.

Her own bravura faltered when he took a fine English-styled gambeson from Eoghann's outstretched hands, and donned it with the quiet assurance of a man who'd seen many battles . . . and didn't flinch at facing another.

*She* did flinch at the notion, and the well-padded leather shirt sent rivers of dread pouring through her.

Knights—the well-equipped Sassunach ones—wore such garments beneath their hauberks to absorb the shock of heavy blows.

Or lessen the penetration of a well-aimed bow shot.

Ne'er had she seen one donned for the clandestine lifting of a few head of Scottish cattle.

Alarm constricting her heart, she stepped from the shadows. "I would speak with you," she said. "Privily."

He arched a brow, the dangerous glint in his good eye warming to one of . . . tender amusement. "Lest you wish to discuss that which we shall attend to upon my return, there is naught you cannot address before my men."

Behind her, one of his not-so-gallant stalwarts sniggered.

The others followed quick suit.

Her cheeks flaming, Caterine slid a pointed look at Black Dugie.

The smithy guarded the archway out of the undercroft, blocking the stairs with the sheer mass of his bulk and a frown as dark as his name.

Fisting her hands against her hips, Caterine looked back at her husband. "All here are not your men."

"Mayhap not, but there is nary a man present whose heart I do not trust."

Caterine compressed her lips.

*He* folded his arms . . . but relented first.

With a shrug of his wide-set shoulders, he chucked her

under the chin. "I thought I married a plain-speaking woman?"

"You did."

His gaze not leaving her, he lifted her hand and kissed it. "Then please me here as you do abovestairs, and say your mind."

A new spat of chortles sounded from his men.

"Well?" He held fast to her hand and rubbed his thumb back and forth over the large ruby of his signet ring.

A ring now on her hand.

Wholly distracted, she glanced around the undercroft at his men . . . and quickly recalled the reason for her disquiet.

The Highlanders stood about in varying stages of undress, each one adorning himself with the trappings of war. All save Sir Lachlan, who'd been ordered to remain behind to help maintain the pretense Sir Marmaduke had vanished abovestairs to bed his new wife when, later, he and his small raiding party slipped from the hall.

"Well?" her husband asked again, smoothing his knuckles down her arm. "Are you still troubled by the incident on the road?"

"Naught privy 'bout that," Sir Gowan tossed between them, his words muffled by the boiled-leather jerkin he was drawing over his head. "We all ken what happened."

Sir Ross looked up from stuffing mail coifs, and the padded head-caps worn beneath them, into a leather pouch. "That blighted devil won't be darkening the road to Dunlaidir ever again."

He aimed a reassuring smile her way, but the sight of the steel-mesh headgear dangling from his fingers proved more disconcerting than comforting.

It was . . . *telling*.

And the reason for the ill-ease marching up and down her spine.

"I am not concerned about the dead man," she said. "He would only trouble me if his arrow had struck true."

"Indeed?" Sir Marmaduke cupped her chin and looked deep into her eyes.

"Aye, indeed," she spoke the truth, frustration writhing like a trapped serpent in her belly.

She jerked free and waved a hand at the panoply of knightly war-goods scattered all about them. "Since when is such metal needed to lift a few cattle?"

*Since I learned we'd be routing out a swine along with fetching a bit of fair eating for your table.*

"Since someone attempted to fire an arrow in your back or mine on our return from the parish church," Marmaduke said, and hoped the half-truth would appease her.

It didn't.

She squared her shoulders, a wealth of comprehension pooling in her sapphire eyes. "Sirrah, I believe you seek to calm me."

"And is that not what champions are meant to do?" He deliberately laid a note of easy gallantry on top of the words. "That, and slay dragons?"

Something indefinable, but disturbing enough to lance his heart, flashed across her face. "I doubt anyone can slay mine." The words came so softly he scarce heard them. "Not all of them."

"You err, my lady." Slipping his arm around her shoulders, he drew her aside, out of hearing range of his men. "You err greatly."

She'd removed her sister's veil and he touched his fingers to the sleekness of her coiled braids. The urge to undo them and bury his face in her unbound hair near unmanned him, but the clink of metal all around them kept his head cool.

He'd explore the glories of her golden hair later.

*All of her golden hair.*

"And how do I err?" she breathed, disarming him with one limpid blue gaze.

Gladly capitulating, Marmaduke gathered her close and

knew true peace when she slid her arms around him and pressed her cheek against his shoulder.

"You err, because I shall not only slay each and every one of your dragons, but scatter their remains on the four winds so they can never darken your heart again."

The promise made, he lifted her chin and kissed her.

Not the hot slaking kiss he'd given her in the church, but one of great tenderness. A smooth and gentle caressing, a mere grazing of his lips over hers, until he'd absorbed enough of her sweetness to hold him through the hours to come.

And, hopefully, until some of the doubt left her heart.

Easing away at last, he nuzzled his face against her cheek. "Every last dragon, my lady, and we shall begin hastening their demise as soon as I've returned."

⚜

*As soon as I've returned.*

The promise steadied her, shoring up her backbone with each blessed whirl across her heart. Embraced by the faith she put in his vow, Caterine sat beside her husband at the wedding feast, if the chaos reigning in the hall could still be called such, and struggled to ignore the swiftly passing hours.

Soon it'd be time for him to steal away.

The surety of it stood reflected in the drunken cries of the revelers, in the spit and hiss of the guttering torches, their flames nearly spent, and in the increasing number of heads slumped upon the trestle tables.

Snoring heads.

Carousers too deep in their cups to notice when her brave champion and his stalwarts took their leave.

Or, as evident in some of the hall's murkier corners, too lost in wanton pursuits to care.

Peering past the rows of tables, Caterine's gaze sought and found Rhona. Like many of the ale-headed celebrants, her friend and James had indulged in amorous tanglings most of the evening, but now the secluded alcove where they'd entertained their passion loomed empty.

Save for Rhona.

She leaned against the stone tracery of the lancet window, half-hidden in the shadows, strumming her lute and singing a love song. But when Caterine caught her eye, she set the lute on the window seat, a signal meant for Caterine alone.

Confirmation that James had left her side to tryst with Sir John in the darkest corner of the bailey where they'd wait with saddled horses until the other men joined them.

The time had come.

*Every last dragon.*

The words, and the dragon slayer's hand sliding over hers where it rested atop the table, gave her the strength to continue the game.

Pushing back the trencher they'd shared, she spoke the rehearsed words. "Faith, if I eat another bite of roasted seabird, I shall fly away."

Her husband's fingers, strong and warm, gave hers a reassuring squeeze.

His man, the bearded Gowan glanced sharply at her . . . and inclined his head. Then, pushing to his feet, he strode off through the smoke-hazed hall and . . . vanished.

Soon the others would rise as well and, one by one, disappear.

Playing their parts, as had she for the last hour or so, plying her new husband with all the dubious delicacies Dunlaidir's depleted stores could muster. Imbibing more braised sea-tangle and bannocks than her stomach could bear.

And smiling all the while.

She'd sipped hippocras from the same cup as her groom and indulged the onlookers' glee by letting him kiss droplets of the heady spiced wine from her lips. He'd even caught one or two from her chin with his tongue.

*That,* the watching throng had loved.

And so had she, boldly wondering how many dragons his wickedly rousing tongue could banish.

But for now, such delights spun unheeded on the farthest edges of her mind, banished there by the departure of another MacKenzie. Sir Ross, a large man of no particular grace, had slipped away as quietly as if he'd ne'er been there at all.

And he'd taken Sir Alec with him, for that veteran knight's place at the end of the high table raged vacant as well. One moment he'd been there. The next, he was gone.

Only Sir Lachlan remained . . . and would.

To staunchly declare Sir Marmaduke Strongbow had taken his bride to bed, should any possess the wits to notice their absence.

Or the daring to comment if they did.

"It is time for us to win away." The words, murmured just above her ear, startled her. Without realizing she'd moved, she was on her feet, the iron strength of his arm firm around her waist.

No one objected.

No one called out.

Only he hesitated, looking at her with such intensity it seared a path of heat clear to her heart. Taking her elbow, he began guiding her from the hall, but stopped short after just a few paces.

"*Hellfire and botheration,*" he muttered, catching her beneath the knees and sweeping her into his arms, holding her tight against his mail-clad chest as he carried her from the hall and up a winding stair.

Not the stair tower to her bedchamber, but a darker one, dank and cold.

A little-used turret, poorly lit and reeking of the sea, and accessing several lesser-used passages. Including the one he'd follow to his trysting place with the other men.

He paused on the first landing, easing her to her feet, but not releasing her. Seizing her to him, he slanted his mouth over hers in a thunderous kiss. She slid her arms around him, clinging fast to his shoulders when he broke the contact.

"My sorrow that I must leave you," he said, his hands caressing her back. "In especial here, but I haven't the belly to carry you to your chamber and not stay."

He pressed a kiss to her forehead, then pulled back to look at her. "I shall carry you to your bed as a proper bride upon my return. That I promise you."

Stepping away from her, he caught her hand, bringing it to his lips for one last kiss. "I will see you sometime on the morrow, and with fine Keith cattle in tow."

Caterine shook her head. "I know you seek more than beef for our table," she spoke plainly, letting her words and the lift of her chin dare him to deny it.

He didn't, and her stomach clenched at his honesty. She touched her fingers to the steel links of his hauberk, felt the thick layer of toughened leather beneath.

He rode out expecting battle.

Or another ambush.

And the knowledge sent her heart plummeting to her toes. "W-will you . . . return?"

To her surprise, a slow smile spread across his face.

*A confident smile.*

"I always return," he said, leaning down to kiss the tip of her nose. "The saints wouldn't allow otherwise."

Then he turned away and was gone.

Her man of steel, experienced and able-armed, vanished like a wraith into the darkness before she could question him further.

She waited until his footfalls faded before she turned and walked away. And with each step she took, she prayed.

For the successful execution of whate'er it was he truly purposed to do.

For the safe return of his men upon its completion.

But most of all that, once again, the saints would smile on Sir Marmaduke Strongbow.

## Chapter Sixteen

❖

Much later, in the windy dark of the still-moonless night, Sir Marmaduke, those men he most trusted, and one craven snake he didn't, drew rein on a steep hillside high above Sir John's English-held Kinraven Castle.

The stronghold's walls rose dark and proud above the far shore of a long and narrow loch, with an endless expanse of low, rolling hogbacks spreading out behind.

Smooth, grassy ridges.

Prime pastureland dotted with a large number of slow-ambling darkish *lumps*.

Keith cattle.

The finest beef to be had within a three-days ride.

"*Here*?" Sir John kneed his horse through a patch of thick-growing gorse-bushes to reach Marmaduke's side. "Did you mis-hear me? There—"

He broke off to thrust his arm toward the distant loch-head where Kinraven raged up through the mist. "There on yon grasslands is where the cattle graze."

Ignoring the other man's vexation, Marmaduke let his gaze follow Sir John's pointing finger across the night-blackened waters. Some lights still glimmered in Kinraven's narrow slit windows and shadowy forms could be seen moving about on the parapets.

"You are full mad if you think to find even one bullock roaming this hillside," Sir John persisted, hot-voiced.

"Some would say you are mad to speak thus." Sir Ross turned on the dispossessed Scottish lord. "There are those have lost their tongue for less," he added, drumming his fingers on the hilt of a dirk thrust beneath his belt.

The other two Highlanders rode closer, menace glittering in their narrowed eyes. James urged his horse between them, his own face tight with anger.

But not at Sir John. James stared past the lot of them to the black specks scattered the length and breadth of the distant shore.

Tension poured off him, thick and heated. "It galls me to ken how long my people have gone to bed with naught but fish and seaware in their bellies."

He blew out a hot breath. "They are all there, our entire herd," he seethed, glancing at Marmaduke. "Do not tell me we have come all this way to search for one bullock on a wooded hillside when so many are within reach?"

"One is all we need this night, though two would serve better," Marmaduke gave back with all the calm he'd learned in years of battling demons. "Be of patient heart, my friend, we will retrieve the others soon enough."

*And if we rode down to fetch them now, we'd find more waiting for us than bullocks and mist.*

Sir John gave a derisive snort. "You'll find naught but scrub and brush clinging to this precipitous ground."

"Think you?" Marmaduke met his haughty stare, then dismounted. Untying his rolled oxhide from the back of the saddle, he looked over at Sir Alec. "Tell Sir John where you were two nights ago."

"A-poking about this very ridge is where I was," Alec furnished, dropping to the ground and reaching for his own oxhide. "Looking for bullocks and swine."

Shaking out the somewhat tatty skin, he slung it round

his shoulders. "Saw more than enough cattle grazing through the gorse hereabouts, but no swine."

He gave Sir John a mirthless grin. "We're a-hoping to catch one tonight, though."

A flash of irritation crossed Sir John's face.

Irritation and . . . something else.

"Then let us have done with this foolery and begone from here," he snapped, dismounting as well. "Why you wished me to accompany you when you will not heed my advice about where to best employ such thievery—"

"Thievery?!" In one smooth motion, James leapt from his saddle, closing the short distance between them with heated grace.

And nary a stumble or hitch.

Marmaduke turned away to hide his smile.

The Highlanders did the same.

Behind them, James railed at his father's friend. "How can you dare utter such a word when Kinraven lies occupied before you? If we were to retake its walls this night, would you call that thievery, too?" he raged. "Where is the difference?"

Swinging back around, Marmaduke found James gripping Sir John's arm . . . and appearing a full head taller than just moments before.

Clearing his throat, he intervened. "My good men," he said, purposely using the word *men,* "your bellows will give warning to any lying about these hills in wait for us."

"Lord save us!" Sir John exploded, jerking his arm from James's grasp. He whirled on Marmaduke. "First you'd see us skulk about with oxhides on our backs, now we are to be set upon as well?"

"Mayhap I am of a mind to hear that from you," Marmaduke challenged him, swirling his own oxhide demonstratively about his shoulders. "Are de la Hogue's men about? Or was the ambuscade only planned for yon grazing ground?"

He indicated the nearest end of the loch, its night-bound waters visible at the base of the steep hillside. "Mayhap there, where the track narrows so severely it is scarce possible to ride two abreast?"

"You *are* mad." Sir John's hand flew to the hilt of his sword. "A baseborn son of—"

"And you are a dead man if my suspicions prove true." Marmaduke seized him by the neck of his hauberk, hefting him off the ground before he could draw the blade.

"Be glad I have enough honor to wait until I am certain," he added, releasing him.

Panting, Sir John rubbed his throat. He glowered at Marmaduke. "That shall cost you—"

A rustling in the gorse-bushes cut him off.

Thrashing noises . . . and the shriek of drawn steel as each man took his sword to hand. Each man save Sir John. Red-faced with anger, he stood glaring at the gorse and hawthorn thicket whence the noise came.

A disruption greeted with amazement and tension-cutting smiles when its source lumbered from the shadows.

A bullock, and as fine a one as they come.

"By the Rood!" Gowan lowered his blade and grinned at the great beast. "He is fat enough to feed every mouth at Dunlaidir and in the village, too."

But then the blustery wind carried other sounds to their ears. More rustlings, only this time accompanied by an ominous chorus: the jangle of bits and bridles, the *chinking* of armor, and the muted *clopping* of iron-shod hooves on damp ground.

"To horse!" Flinging the oxhide to the ground, Marmaduke vaulted into his saddle. "Swords!" he yelled, his own already aloft, its well-hewn blade gleaming in the darkness.

"*Cuidich' N' Righ!*" his men roared the MacKenzie battle cry, their bold shouts rising above the ever-louder rumble of drumming hooves.

At their cries, and the whinnying of the nervous, sidling horses, the bullock plunged wild-eyed into the underbrush. In the same instant, a host of mounted knights burst out of the trees and all chaos erupted.

The sword-wielding riders thundered into the clearing, circling Marmaduke and his men, their blades flashing silver against the pale gray of the fog.

With a calm control the hot-blooded Highlanders lacked, Marmaduke pushed up in his stirrups, his broadsword raised high above his head and waited as the knights surged forward in swift, furious attack.

The instant the first assailant came within striking range, he brought down his blade in a deadly arc, smiting his opponent with such shearing ferocity he near sliced the wretch in twain.

"Strongbow! To your left!" one his men warned, and he swung around to deflect a vicious blow from the side.

Undaunted, this new challenger hauled out for another slashing swipe. Their swords met with a loud, jarring *clank*, the sheer force of the clash shooting up Marmaduke's arm.

He blocked the next jabbing thrust with the flat of his own steel, sending the other to the ground with sheer brute strength.

Sir Alec appeared at his side, his great Highland brand already dripping red. "There are more," he shouted over the din of clashing steel. "A sea of the bastards streaming out of the woods."

Blinking to clear the stinging sweat from his good eye, Marmaduke shot a quick glance toward the edge of the clearing.

Alec hadn't exaggerated.

A veritable tide of steel-girt horsemen swarmed onto the hillside now. They barreled forward to hem Marmaduke and his men into the very middle of the hellish pandemonium by the sheer press of their greater number.

"In mercy's name," Marmaduke breathed, and hoped the saints looked on.

"Ho, lad—my ax!" Sir Gowan's cry rang out somewhere to his left, the urgency in the Highlander's voice chilling Marmaduke's blood.

He jerked round to see Gowan toss his battle-ax to James. His sword gone, James Keith grappled with a helmeted knight, valiantly attempting to fend off the man's slashing attack with his shield.

His breath rasping, Marmaduke stared across the chaos, his heart plummeting when the ax sailed past James's reaching fingers.

James himself let out a cry of savage rage at the miss and, his face a dark mask, he raised up and brought down the hard edge of his shield onto the sworder's extended forearm, striking with such smashing fury the man's arm-bone snapped with a sickening *crack.*

Letting loose of his blade, James's opponent toppled from his horse, his shrieks of pain swallowed by the unholy cacophony of clashing and clanging steel.

But he'd no sooner hit the ground before a second assailant hurtled toward James, his blade already drawn back for a killing blow.

"Mother of God!" Marmaduke dug in his spurs, but Sir Ross, much closer to James, tore through the slashing steel at a thunderous speed, his huge Highland sword extended before him like a lance.

"*Cuidich' N' Righ!*" he cried, reaching James first and skewering his attacker before the man could finish his deadly sweep.

Without pausing, he heaved the body off his crimson sword and pressed on to join Marmaduke and Alec at the center of the fray, James hot on his tail.

Drawing together in a tight phalanx, they fought on, the ear-splitting screech of blade sliding along blade, a deafening accompaniment. The stench of spilled blood fouled the air, filling their lungs with its metallic sweetness with each drawn breath.

A bit apart, Gowan stood tall in his stirrups, windmilling his Highland two-hander in such a wicked manner, hardly a challenger dared near him.

And when one did, the burly cateran felled each such fool with a single, viciously arcing swipe . . . and a smile on his bearded face.

A shrill cry rent the red-hazed air, louder and more agonized than all before. Marmaduke swung around to see Sir John, far from the apex of the fighting, crash to the ground . . . the whole left side of him, a sea of crimson.

As was the dripping blade of the English knight who'd slain him.

Too stunned to even blink, Marmaduke stared across the melee, wholly transfixed. He swiped the back of his arm across his brow and watched as Sir John's riderless horse bolted into the night.

Sir John's bloodied body, having gained momentum from the violence of its fall, rolled down the hillside, leaving a red-stained path in its wake.

"If that isn't beyond all," Ross panted beside him, his own heaving chest well splattered with blood.

But not his own. "So we erred—"

"God's mercy, don't speak it," Marmaduke cut him off, instinctively lifting his sword to repulse yet another attacker, hot bile rising so thick in his throat he could scarce breathe.

His suspicions about the older Scotsman lashed at him as furiously as the man-at-arms closing in on him. Swerving in his saddle, he avoided the man's swinging blade, but not the biting sting of his own shame.

All the rage of the night, and the greater swell of his guilt, flooding him with renewed strength, he swung back to face the sworder.

As if the man had glimpsed the very devil in Marmaduke's own face, he tried to wheel away, but, with a roar of outrage, his cool broken at last, Marmaduke drew back his sword-arm and slew him with one great, downward stroke.

*You are a dead man.*

*If my suspicions are true . . .*

*A dead man.*

For the rest of the long night, through all the blood-letting and cries, Marmaduke's own words rode his back.

A constant companion, a leaden weight on his honor.

And a greater foe than all de la Hogue's metal-bound henchmen combined.

❧

Above and all around the hillside, a cold wind blew, its own wail echoing the moans of the dying . . . souls it'd soon carry from the relentless fray. And though Marmaduke himself would've sworn the saints had deserted him at last, they'd simply sent an angel to watch over him in their stead.

Though he couldn't see her, a lone woman stood beside a hawthorn tree at the very edge of the fracas. Tall and dark as the moonless night, she made no sound.

Nor did she move.

Wrapped in cowled robes and the swirling mist, she followed his every move throughout the night, a world of pride in her shadowed eyes.

A wealth of love to keep him safe.

And if her own heart bore a trace of sadness, she didn't let it show.

He glanced her way once, and for a moment almost saw her, so she lifted her hand and forced a little smile. A reassuring one to let him know, this night, too, would pass. And though her time here was gone, he had many long years yet before him.

Bright days and bliss-filled nights.

Her smile fading, she stared across the silence at him,

lending him her comfort as best she could, marveling at his valor and strength.

As she always had.

After endless-seeming hours, the fury of the battle finally lessened, the outcome clear. With a deep sigh torn from all her yesterdays, she sent one last smile his way, then slipped into the shadows of her world once more.

One with the mist and darkness.

Until he needed her again.

✤

"So you do believe in the Laird's Stone?"

At Rhona's amused whisper behind her, Caterine gave a startled shriek and slammed down the lid of the iron-bound strongbox at the foot of her bed.

"Since when do you roam the halls in the middle of the night to go poking your nose where it doesn't belong?" Caterine said, straightening.

She put a hand to her breast. "And," she added, pausing for emphasis, "I was not peeking at that fool piece of granite."

Rhona folded her arms. "Then why aren't you abed?"

*Because it will soon be cockcrow and our men have yet to return.*

*Because I fear for him.*

"Mayhap I could not sleep," she owned, stating the utter truth, if not the reason.

Cold apprehension had churned in her belly all night and still roiled with unabated fury. Her heart slamming against her ribs, she slanted a glance into the darkness of the ante-room where, ignoring the comfort of his own bed, Leo lay curled atop the rough pallet.

Until just a short while ago, he, too, had roamed the bed-chamber, his short legs carrying him on endless treks between the ante-room, the window embrasure, and, always, the closed door where he'd drop onto his wee rump and turn pleading eyes on its oaken planks.

Waiting for a champion.

As the long, empty hours of the night had consigned her to do as well.

"Can it be you could not sleep for the same reason I, too, am restless?" Rhona peered at her, one finger tapping lightly against her chin.

Caterine drew her bed robe more securely about her shoulders against the frosty air seeping through the shutter slats. But mostly so Rhona wouldn't see the nervous rise and fall of her breasts.

"You've taken up a mistaken cause if you wish to pry admissions from me about things that do not exist," she said, sorely wishing Rhona would cease her finger tapping.

She did.

But the dark brow her friend arched proved equally vexing. "You care about him as I do James," Rhona said. "You worry because they haven't yet returned, and that fear is robbing you of sleep and sending you to examine the Laird's Stone."

"Aye, I care about him," Caterine admitted, running a hand through her unbound hair. "He is a gallant and noble-hearted man. But I was not examining the Laird's Stone. I was putting away his ring."

*"Putting away his ring?"*

Lifting her left hand, Caterine wiggled her bare fingers.

"But you admit you care for him?"

"I put away his ring *because* I care," Caterine said, opting for her best defense against Rhona's badgering: plain speech.

"I put away his ring because I honor him too much to wear it so long as I cannot give him my heart."

Rhona looked skeptical. "Something in the way you said that tells me you already have given him your heart."

"Nay, I have not." The denial sounded hollow even to Caterine's ears.

Her patience waning, she crossed to the darkened window embrasure and wrenched open the shutters. Needing, welcoming, the blast of icy air that streamed into the chamber the instant she did so.

Following her, Rhona made a snorting noise. "If you have not given him your heart, then I am a virgin."

"My heart is and shall remain my own," Caterine shot back, sinking onto the window seat. "I have told him so."

Hugging the bed robe tightly about her, she clung to the frankness that protected her from folly.

And pain.

"He shall have all else I can give him," she said, stunned by the pang of longing that ripped through her just thinking about him. A tight and breathless yearning for the fierce passion she'd only begun to catch glimpses of.

She wanted more, much more than the kisses and caresses they'd shared thus far.

"So what 'all else' do you mean to bestow on him?" Rhona persisted. "Admiration? Respect? Companionship?"

"So long as he is with us, aye. All those things and . . . my body."

Rhona's jaw dropped. "Your body?"

Caterine nodded. "I have told him I should like to explore desire."

"Explore desire?"

"You needn't look so shocked," Caterine fixed her friend with a reproachful stare. "If I mind a-right, 'twas you who claimed I am in dire need of such?"

"But, my lady, I never meant the one without the other." Rhona dropped to her knees, reaching for Caterine's hands in a strange mirroring of how *he'd* knelt before her in this very alcove.

How easily he'd made her want him.

Rhona squeezed her hands. "I'd hoped you'd find both love and desire with your champion."

"With an English champion?" Caterine amazed herself with how little that mattered now.

"I do not believe you are still troubled by his Englishry," Rhona pressed her.

"Nay, I am not," Caterine didn't deny. "It is the Englishry of other men that plagues me . . . as you aught know."

*Their ghosts and the stains they left behind.*

Digging her fingers into the satiny covered comfort of a pillow she'd drawn onto her lap, Caterine stared out at the thick sea mist drifting past her window.

A barrier as impenetrable as the gateway to her heart.

With surprisingly little effort, she concentrated on the wild physical yearnings her champion had stirred in her . . . and tried to banish the cold other Englishmen had put in her soul.

*That* proved a more difficult task.

"Have you told him?" Rhona tightened her grip on Caterine's hands, massaged her cold fingers. "Does he know how they used you before your first husband's eyes, then slew him before yours?"

Caterine kept her gaze on the swirling mist. "Not in so many words, but he is wise enough to have guessed. I told him I have not known much physical pleasure and would enjoy exploring such intimacies."

At her companion's silence, she straightened her spine. "I am not getting younger," she said, suddenly weary, the sleepless night bearing down on her. "Why should I not sample what other women claim to glory in?"

She met Rhona's tight-lipped stare. "He agreed, so you've no need to look so disapproving."

"Agreed to what? Pleasure you?"

Caterine answered with the merest nod.

Her companion's brow soared to lofty heights.

"Why shouldn't he?" Caterine didn't even try to hide her

pique. "He is a lusty natured man. I can tell that by his kisses. I vow he'd gladly indulge any woman desirous of experimenting with such urges."

"Nay, nay, nay, my lady," Rhona said, releasing Caterine's hands and pushing to her feet. "Not any woman. Have you not seen the way he looks at you?"

Caterine pressed her lips together and plucked at the folds of her bed-robe, not quite able to believe her braw champion would harbor such rampant passion for her.

"Oh, but he does, my lady," Rhona crooned as if she'd read Caterine's doubt. "That is why he will be pleased you fancy him in such a way. He is sore smitten with you. Only you."

"He agreed to more than . . . the pleasure part," Caterine said, and the deepest reaches of her heart quickened in fierce objection to the other half of what he'd agreed to.

"What other agreements?"

Caterine drew a breath. "That any intimacies we indulge in shall be just that . . . pure physical acts without emotional attachments."

"And you believed him?" Rhona's voice rose two notches. "That he will pleasure you senseless and not claim your heart?"

"And what is wrong with allowing him to pleasure me?"

"Nothing, except that if you deny him your heart, that is all it will be . . . simple pleasuring." Rhona fingered the ends of her braids, a slight flush creeping onto her cheeks. "That, my lady, is what I did with the garrison men. It brings swift pleasure, but fades as quickly."

"You keep your heart from James." Caterine sought to change the subject. "Are you merely 'taking swift pleasure' with him, too?"

"I do not keep my heart from him, he does," Rhona said hotly. "He can claim my full affections the day he chooses to, and it is my hope that will be soon."

Smoothing her skirts, she glanced heavenward and

sighed. "And, nay, we have not yet come fully together, though he knows I am experienced. That part of me, I am keeping from him." She looked back at Caterine, her gaze dreamy. "For now."

"But you want to . . . lie with him."

Rhona nodded, her brief discomfiture gone. "Oh, aye."

"I want that, too," Caterine sighed. "I am weary of feeling cold and empty. I want to know intense pleasure. Delicious and wicked pleasures."

"My lady!" Rhona's cheeks tinged pink again, but as quickly, a conspiratorial smile spread across her face. "What kind of wicked pleasures?"

Caterine stood to whisper her most secret desires into her friend's ear.

Rhona gasped. "That is beyond wicked." The tops of her ears glowed red. "A lascivious act."

"Rousing is what I believe it would be. *Incredibly* so." Languid heat and a tight, pulsing anticipation spooled through Caterine just thinking about such carnality.

She dropped back onto the cushioned seat. "I believe it could be done very well in this window embrasure."

Rhona cast a furtive glance toward the door, then leaned forward. "Do you think he would do such a thing?"

"If such acts are all we can share, he might." Caterine speculated, and hoped. "Mayhap if I tell him doing so would help accustom me to . . . such intimacies."

"Do you fear for him this night, my lady?" Rhona blurted then, finally voicing the unspoken reason they were both awake at this late hour. "Are you as worried for him as I am for James?"

Caterine blinked back her own trepidation. It sat too close to the backs of her eyes, hot and burning, its dark shadow the reason she'd clung to other, pleasurable and stirring, images the long night through.

Steeling herself against a dread she didn't want to ponder, she turned toward the sea. Still blanketed with fog, nothing but its ceaseless crash against the rocks hinted at its proximity.

That, and the chill, brine-laced air.

"We needn't worry," she said then, the words coming more from the swirling mist drifting past the windows than from her. "They will soon return, and unscathed."

A strange but welcome conviction she simply knew to be true.

As if an angel had whispered it into her heart.

# Chapter Seventeen

✦

$\mathcal{L}$ATE THE NEXT afternoon, strong winds drove sleety rain across Dunlaidir's bailey, the gloaming dark just beginning to set in, as Sir Marmaduke and his bone-weary companions finally clattered into the stronghold's deserted inner courtyard.

No trumpets sounded, no cheering acclaim rose to greet them. Not a single gasp of wonderment for the fat bullock and equally plump milk cow they led behind them.

Nary a soul stirred, and a deep quiet—almost a death pall—hung heavy in the chill air. An eerie place and moment, shrouded in silence, with no wish to be disturbed.

As if the whole castle slept.

Or mourned.

From the corner of his good eye, Marmaduke caught Sir Alec crossing himself. Sir Gowan, the most rough-hewn amongst his men, appeared ill at ease as well, his wary gaze flitting about the empty bailey.

"They will not know we are back," Marmaduke spoke at last, swinging down onto the rain-dark cobbles. Shoving back his mailed coif, he ran a tired hand through his damp hair.

A queer foreboding rode his back, too, but he quelled his own disquiet long enough to rake his friends with a stern look, daring them with his calm to reach inside themselves and recover their own.

"I thought they'd come flying down the stairs the moment we rode in," James said, his frowning gaze on the empty outer stairs.

Cold and wet, the stone steps rose to an equally unwelcoming landing where the hall's main door remained unmoving, its iron-studded solidness firmly closed against them.

"I would've sworn they would have waited by that door," James declared, dismounting.

Marmaduke clapped a hand on the young man's shoulder. "Think you I would not have relished a warmer welcome, too, my friend?" He forced a jovial tone. "Come, let us see to these beasts, wash the muck from our limbs, and then we shall see what keeps our ladies."

He broke off at the sound of pounding footsteps.

Black Dugie's.

The great bear of a man ran toward them, his eyes wild and staring, his massive chest heaving when at last he reached them.

"Great Caesar's ghost!" he panted, looking for all the world as if he'd just seen one.

Or, even now, stared at a whole host of departed souls.

"We thought you were dead! Every last one o' you," he cried, clearly dumbfounded.

"Dead?" Gowan snorted. "Dead weary and ready to drown ourselves in ale rather than this slashing rain, but not dead as you mean," he said, swiping the dripping wetness off his forehead with the back of a burly arm.

"It'd take more than a handful of sword-swinging Sassunachs to put MacKenzies to earth." Sir Alec strode up to them, his own bedraggled and blood-stained appearance making him look every inch a dead man.

"But . . ." Black Dugie gaped at them, his broad face still wreathed in doubt.

"We may look dead, but I assure you we are very much alive," James said, speaking to the smithy, but still staring at the hall's closed door. "Where are our ladies? Why aren't they here to greet us?"

"Because they will be preparing a fine reception for us in the hall." Marmaduke slung an arm about James's shoulders . . . and hoped he spoke the truth. "Be glad they—"

"Oh, nay, that isn't what they're about," Black Dugie said, something in his words drawing the rapt attention of all. "They're a-huddled at the high table trying to come up with a way to pay for perpetual prayers for the lot of you."

"*Perpetual prayers?*" Marmaduke's astonishment couldn't have been greater. "Did they have so little faith in our return?"

Black Dugie shuffled his feet. "My pardon, milord, but how could they think otherwise when Sir John told us you'd all been killed?"

"*Sir John?*" Marmaduke stared at the smithy, sheerest incredulity whirling through him.

It couldn't be.

They'd seen the older Scotsman slain.

"There must be some mistake." Ross put voice to Marmaduke's amazement. "Sir John cannot have told you aught. The man is dead."

He glanced at Marmaduke, then back at the smithy. "We saw him cut down."

"Then his wraith rode in here all a-fire to lie to us." Black Dugie pointed to the hall door. "He's up there now. Trying to console your womenfolk."

"By the Rood!" one of the Highlanders swore, the oath accompanied by the *zing* of metal as his sword left its scabbard.

"But . . ." Gowan puzzled, rubbing his rain-flecked beard. "We saw him killed."

"Nay, my friend," Marmaduke said, comprehending at last, "we saw him fall from his horse and roll down the hill."

"To ride back here and announce our demise," Ross embellished, and Marmaduke agreed.

"So it would seem," he said aloud, reaching for his own steel. "Come, men," he said, already striding for the keep. "Now we have certainty."

It was time to corner a swine.

⚜

The instant the hall's great oaken door crashed open, Caterine whirled around and choked back a sob. Her heart near bursting with relief, she stared in amazement at the men coming through the open door.

Icy wind swept in with them, its gusty draughts setting the nearest torch flames to dancing, the wildly flickering light casting weird shadows over their granite-hewn faces.

Reaching across the high table, Rhona closed her hand over Caterine's wrist. "Lady, they live," she breathed, her voice a tremulous whisper, the joy and wonder in her words matching Caterine's own.

Her throat too tight for words, Caterine wrapped an arm around the little dog on her lap, clasping him hard against her as she sent silent prayers of thanksgiving heavenward.

*He* towered over them all, contained anger pouring off him, its intensity palpable from clear across the hall. Every glorious inch of him very much alive . . . as were they all.

Their brows dark in the smoky torchlight, they came forward, advancing on the high table without a word of greeting. Jaws set and hard-faced, their outerwear caked with mud, the mail beneath, smeared with blood.

Black Dugie came with them, by no means as sorebattered-looking but equally wet and grim-faced. And with a long-bladed dirk clutched tight in his hand.

"God be praised!" Caterine found her voice at last, relief spiraling through her, the heat pricking her eyes, blinding her to the menace on their faces.

And the oddity of drawn steel in her hall.

"A miracle," Sir John said beside her. "By Lucifer, who would have—"

"Do not compound your treachery with still more lies," her husband cut him off, speaking loud enough for all to hear, his voice as cold and deadly as the gleam of his blade.

He fixed Sir John with a long, hard stare. "Come," he said, beckoning to him, "you mention Lucifer, let us hasten your journey to his side."

"Dear God, you are witless," Sir John scoffed, the words dripping scorn.

Ignoring the slur, Sir Marmaduke trained his gaze on her. "My regrets, lady, that I must blacken the name of a family friend, but this man is a traitor," he said, and Caterine believed him for the truth was writ on his face . . . and in her heart.

"He is Sir Hugh's man," her husband accused, his expression growing colder by the minute, darkening with the first scowl she'd seen him wear.

"Is that not so?" He turned to the men standing close beside him, and without hesitation, they nodded agreement.

Even James.

Black Dugie, too.

"Lies!" Sir John shot to his feet, his face scarlet. Glaring at Marmaduke, he lifted his hands. "A liar, and no true knight for you challenge an unarmed man."

Angry murmurs rose at that, growing louder as they sprang from one table to the next. "Unarmed?" one of the garrison men called out. "Sore straits easily remedied!" Coming forward, he slapped his own blade full-length on the high table.

Without so much as glancing at the weapon, Sir John snatched up his cloak. "I will not be party to rabid posturings," he said, swirling the mantle around his shoulders. "Mayhap once this foul night has passed, the good folk within these walls will have regained their senses."

His head high, he started forward, not looking left or right until he strode past Marmaduke. Then, with astonishing speed for a man of his years, he threw back his cloak and spun around to lunge at Marmaduke's back, a wicked-looking dagger flashing in his upraised hand.

Someone's scream—her own or Rhona's—filled Caterine's ears as, with even greater agility, her husband whirled to face Sir John, his fingers closing in a fierce-looking grip around the older man's wrist.

The dirk dropped to the rushes, but the forward momentum of Sir John's own spinning whirl plunged him against the well-honed edge of Marmaduke's sword. He cried out as a bold slash of crimson appeared across his middle—a true wound this time, and a fatal one.

His shriek of pain muting into a horrible gurgling sound, he stared at his own red-flowing death, utter astonishment in his bulging eyes, and sank to the floor.

Chaos and uproar filled the hall as men noisily thrust back from their places at the long tables, rising almost as one, to press forward and crowd around Marmaduke and the soon-to-be-dead Sir John.

Caterine and Rhona clung to each other, looking on in horror as Sir Marmaduke cast aside his sullied blade, then knelt beside Sir John's prone figure.

"A well deserved end," someone called out above the din.

"A black heart done in by his own false move," another agreed, the angrily spoken words, sharp, loud, and echoing off the weapon-hung walls.

In stark contrast, pathetic moans, scarcely audible, issued from Sir John's gray lips, his eyelids flickering as he tried to focus on the men peering down at him.

Biting back his own anger, Marmaduke cradled the man's head. "Unburden your soul before you breathe your last," he said, lifting his voice to cut through the whir of confusion, the growing swell of heated murmurs and darker slurs, the shrill yapping of his lady's little dog.

Glancing up at the men thronging near, he raised a hand to still their grumbles, then reached for Sir John's blood-drenched tunic and carefully lifted its hem.

The wound, an angry red slit just beneath Sir John's ribs, was his only one. Not even a bruise or scratch marred the whiteness of his flesh.

"But he was smeared with his own blood," Gowan's voice came close to Marmaduke's ear. "We saw—"

"Not his own blood." Ross spat onto the rushes. "The bastard sullied hisself a-purpose. To make us think he'd been cut down."

Glancing at the battle-hardened Highlander, Marmaduke signed for him to hold his tongue.

"My lord of Kinraven," Sir Marmaduke said, lowering the shirt, then leaning down to speak into the dying man's ear, "your treachery has cost you all. We would have helped you win back your home had you but asked."

Sir John's lips moved, but no words, no explanation of his duplicity poured forth.

Only a welter of pink-flecked froth.

"N-never lost Kinraven—" A mere rasp, pushed from his lips by death itself.

"Never lost Kinraven?" That from James. He stared at Sir John's waxen face, his own paling. "What foolery is that? All know—" He broke off at a warning glance from Marmaduke, and a sharp elbow in the ribs from Alec.

His eyelids flickering again, Sir John met James's astonishment as best he could. "'Twas Dunlaidir he wanted . . . all along . . . p-promised to leave Kinraven untouched if . . . if . . ."

"—If you'd help him gain Dunlaidir," James finished for him, pushing hotly to his feet when Sir John gave him a silent, anguished nod.

"By all the saints!" James shouted in a burst of temper. "To think I welcomed him, gave him sanctuary!" Whirling away, he exited the hall, his long-strided gait as straight as the fine red line stretching across Sir John's belly.

"M-my regrets . . . sorry . . ." Sir John whispered, his glassy eyed stare fixed on some distant point beyond Marmaduke's shoulder.

Mayhap beyond this world.

And then he was gone, his feeble peace offered, his troubled eyes rolling up, his last breath spent.

Equally troubled, Marmaduke lowered Sir John's head to the floor, then stood. His gaze seeking and finding his wife's, he shrugged off his cloak, and, after swirling it over the dead man's body, he went to her.

She came toward him, her arms extended as she pushed her way through the throng. He opened his arms as well . . . and waited. His courage, so bold on the field of battle, proved not quite stout enough for him to believe she'd fling herself so wholeheartedly into his embrace.

But she did, and in that precious moment, the very world tilted beneath Marmaduke's feet.

The glory of her acceptance, her unabashed joy at his safe return, felled him with a far greater blow than any English steel could ever deliver.

His heart swelling to a such degree he could scarce breathe, he wrapped his arms around, letting her cling to him, marveling that she did, blood-sullied and grimed as he stood before her.

"My lady, but I love you," he breathed the words against her temple, too overcome to care that she stiffened upon hearing them.

Setting her from him, he cradled her face with his hands and touched his forehead to hers. "Do not say it," he murmured into the warm silk of her hair, "just *be,* and let me revel in holding you."

He slipped an arm beneath her, lifting her to him before she could object . . . or ruin the moment.

The most precious he'd had in many long years.

"Yon wretch was not one of the dragons I meant to slay for you, my dear heart," he said, carrying her from the hall, "and I believe it is time for us to challenge the true ones."

She leaned back to peer at him, astonishment banking in her sapphire eyes. "Are you not—?"

"Aye, my love, I am too weary even for that fair bliss," he answered honestly, wishing it wasn't so.

*Wishing desperately it wasn't so.*

"But," he amended as he began the circuitous climb to her bedchamber, "I've brought a fine bullock for your table, and as soon as this *true* wedding feast is past us, I shall make good every one of my promises."

He paused to kiss her. Deeply, and with all the fierce exultation she stirred in his heart. He drew back only when the last vestiges of stiffness eased out of her and she went limp in his arms, the soft sigh escaping her, enough.

For the moment.

"This night, my heart, a bath and a warm bed will suffice," he said, pleased when she didn't balk at his deliberate use of the word *bed*.

Bed, not pallet.

"I ask only that you let me hold you," he said, resuming their climb up the turnpike stair. "Hold you, and savor your warmth."

⚜

Much later, in the stillest hour of the night, Caterine stood beside her bed and peered down at the man sleeping so soundly within its curtained depths. She clenched her hands against her mounting frustration.

She wanted more than simply being held.

She wanted to *feel*.

Her heart pounding slow and hard, she watched the fire glow steal across his exposed back, the silvery ridges of his scars twisting her heart; the wide set of his shoulders and the well-muscled arm he'd slung over a pillow, tempting her to be bold.

To heed the desire pulsing deep inside her.

A tight, winding, and breathless need as sweet and rare as the clear and lustrous night stretching beyond her bedchamber's arch-topped windows.

A glittering expanse, as broad and far-reaching as the sea.

A magical night.

For once swept clean of clouds and mist, and studded with countless twinkling stars. Cold and distant each one, but winking down at her with encouraging smiles.

Their silvery light assured her she could be daring enough to awaken her slumbering husband and tell him she desired more than mere sleep this night.

Need, expectant and sharp, twisted inside her. A fierce and demanding ache crying to be slaked. Slanting a glance over her shoulder at the shadowy window embrasure, she swallowed hard.

Could she be so bold?

The stars winked . . . yes.

Her blood quickening, and before her nerve left her, she cast one last look at her sleeping husband, then crossed the room and lowered herself onto one of the two bench-style seats carved into the walls of the window alcove.

"S-Sir . . ." A mere squeak.

Not loud enough for a mouse to hear and certainly not . . . bold.

She moistened her lips. "*Sir!*"

That, he heard.

Ne'er had Caterine seen anyone exit a bed so quickly.

Or recover his wits as swiftly.

"Thunder of heaven!" Chest heaving, he stared at her. "Saints, woman, I thought we were under siege."

*I am under siege,* her awakening womanhood affirmed.

She said nothing. The sight of his hard-muscled body, magnificent in nothing but his braies, swelled her tongue.

And sent delicious eddies of excitement whirling through her.

He came toward her, wholly at ease with his near-nakedness, fully unaware of her brazen intent. Stopping in front of her, he raked a hand through his sleep-mussed hair. "Do you not know it is unwise to awaken a man so abruptly? I could have hurt you when I leapt from the bed."

"I wanted you to see the night sky," she blurted, not looking at the stars at all, but at his groin . . . and the hard ridge of his phallus, still swollen from his deep slumber and pressing hard against the thin linen of his leggings.

"You are not looking at the stars, my lady," he said, his voice low and husky.

Meeting his gaze at once, Caterine began inching up the skirt of her camise. Slowly, casually, and as naturally as she could.

"Can we not sit here for a while?" she asked. "I could not sleep."

He cocked a brow, but came deeper into the window embrasure, settling himself on the opposite facing seat . . . just as she'd hoped he would.

"To admire the night sky, hmmmm?" His voice held a trace of amusement, but he turned dutifully toward the windows and, the instant he did, Caterine quickly curled her legs beneath her . . . and hitched her camise's skirt to her knees.

Just high enough so that if she shifted her position, and parted her thighs a bit when doing so, her raised hem would pull taut and give him an innocently exposed glimpse of the thick pelt of golden curls between her legs.

He twisted back around. "Did you truly wake me to sit here and peer at the—by the Rood!" He stared transfixed at her exposed womanhood.

"Lady, I am no monk and what I am staring at pushes me past restraint," he said, his heated gaze not budging. "Are—you—aware—of—what—I—can—see?"

"I am, sir," she said, her boldness sending streaks of white-hot excitement shooting through her. "I told you I wish to explore all manner of intimacies and I thought it might be wise to ... to get accustomed to one another through *looking* before ... before—"

*"You wish for us to sit here and stare at each other between the legs?"*

His blunt words enflamed the pulsing heat low by her thighs and weighted her belly. "It would help me overcome my hesitancy to ... to—in truth, sir, I think it would be titillating."

"Indeed." He still hadn't torn his gaze from her. "But I must warn you, if we do this, I will do more than look."

"Can we begin?" Caterine breathed, the anticipation of testing her daring, the pleasure already trickling through her, almost too exhilarating to bear. "I would see you as well."

"Woman, you may unman me this night." With all speed, he shoved down his braies and kicked them aside.

"So!" He perched on the edge of the seat. "There you have me, my lady. What is your will?"

"I just want to look at you," Caterine whispered, scarce able to breathe.

"At ease or fully charged?" He lowered his hand to his groin, his fingers just grazing his already-engorged manhood. "If you prefer the former, I cannot maintain such a state for long."

"I would like to see both ... *conditions*, please."

He lifted a brow. "First relaxed?"

She nodded, a rash of delicious tingles spreading across her woman's flesh as he curled his hand around his swollen shaft. He squeezed until his arousal ebbed. "As you wished," he said, opening his knees so his shaft, long and thick, hung fully exposed for her perusal.

"Mind you, it is against nature for a man to remain flaccid with a woman's heat pulsing so near," he said after a few minutes, his voice thick, his tarse already swelling anew. "I would pleasure you now . . . and look on you as I do so."

"Sir?" Her eyes flew wide, a bit of her bravura slipping now that he'd wrested control from her. "But . . ."

"Never you mind, sweeting," he murmured, dropping to his knees before her. "Just open your legs and relax."

*That* part of her pulsed with mounting urgency, cresting almost unbearably when he spread her knees wider and began lightly stroking the soft skin of her inner thighs. "Easy, sweet." He eased her legs even wider apart. "Breathe deep and simply feel what I am doing to you."

He toyed with her intimate curls, cupped the whole of her, massaging her with his palm, then trailed one finger along the cleft of her mound.

"Does this please you, Caterine?" He began stroking her cleft in earnest, tracing its pouty length with slow, lazy strokes. "Shall I keep touching you this way?"

"Aye," she gasped, her voice ragged. "*Please.*"

"Then open your legs as wide as you can," he encouraged her. "I want to see and touch all of you."

Another little gasp escaped her and she scooted forward until her bottom rested on the very edge of the seat, her hips rocking in a silent plea more eloquent than any spoken words.

"Be still," he said, pressing his palm flush against her heat. "You will enjoy this more if you remain perfectly still . . . and open."

She moaned this time and shut her eyes, finally letting herself completely relax. Holding his swollen shaft with one hand, he used the other to pleasure her. He still traced her cleft, but now explored each pouty fold, gently rubbing, plucking, and toying with her until she cried out her need.

His own release surging near, he breathed deep of her arousal, sating himself on her musky, woman's scent, and tightening his hold on his shaft. He began pulling on its thickness, discreetly easing his own need, even as he toyed ever more deliberately with her damp nether curls and heated sleekness. His own ease breaking, he circled one finger over the tight, swollen bud of her sex, his focused rubbing sending her the same shattering fulfillment.

"Oh, dear saints," she breathed, and fell back, completely limp, against the seat cushions.

His own body spent, Marmaduke slid his arms around her hips, resting his head against the soft warmth of her inner thigh. Her intimate curls teased his cheek, and her pulsing heat, sweet and musky, proved such a temptation, he nestled closer until he could not only inhale deeply of her scent, but caress her very cleft with each exhaled breath.

Aroused anew, he touched his tongue to her.

The merest lapping at her sweetness.

Not licks, but simple touches of the very tip of his tongue to her tender flesh, and so light he doubted she noticed, but sheer intoxicating to him. For truth, the lady slept. As would he . . . soon.

But first he wanted to hold tight to the bliss he'd found a while longer. A sated smile, wondrous in the peace and contentment it brought, tugged at the corners of his mouth.

And all because she'd wanted to show him the night sky.

Instead, he'd taken her to the stars . . . which is exactly where she'd wanted to go.

And what a glorious journey it'd been for them both.

⚜

Many leagues away, on the other side of Scotland, a new day dawned bright and crisp. Nary a ripple marred the glassy surface of Loch Duich, and a fine dusting of frost coated the mountains hugging its shores. Even Eilean Creag's stout walls gave themselves quiet and unthreatening in the clear, blue-white light of the icy cold morn.

But inside those walls, the stronghold's master shook

with fury, and prepared himself to threaten any fool, man or beast, who dared to happen across his ire.

His hands clenched at his sides, Duncan MacKenzie stood in his empty hall, frowning blackly at the sweetly scented layer of newly-strewn floor rushes, sheer roiling murder in his heart.

"*Fergus!*" he bellowed, full aware none but the scrawny shouldered, impertinent seneschal bore responsibility for the hall's tidy appearance.

For his bed had disappeared from the raised dais, and his fair lady wife was glaringly absent.

"Hie yourself in here, you old bandy-legged old goat, lest I—"

"Lest you what, laddie?" The object of his wrath bristled from the concealing shadows of the screened passage.

One of his favored hidey-holes.

And where he'd no doubt been lurking simply for the pleasure of spying on Duncan's distress.

Taking his time, the old man shuffled forward, his scraggly-bearded chin thrust out in brazen defiance. "Lest you shout down these walls with your bluster?"

"*Where is my wife?*" Duncan put all the dread in his heart into the shouted words.

His concern for her, his *fear,* working him into fine, fuming rage, he aimed a pointing finger at the raised dais which, once again, held the innocently mute high table.

"What have you done with my bed?" he roared, not even trying to contain his fury.

The seneschal folded scrawny arms and glowered back at him.

And said not a word.

Duncan glanced up at the hall's vaulted ceiling and began counting.

At length, and in somewhat better control of himself, he turned his attention back to his grizzle-headed seneschal.

"The bed—and my lady—were here before I left to make my rounds not an hour ago," he said, his deep voice calmer.

A little bit calmer.

But not enough to pry answers from Fergus's ancient tongue.

Duncan heaved a great sigh. "Sooo, Fergus, you've restored notable order to the hall," he said, trying to imitate a certain one-eyed lout's winning manner with servitors by spouting praise and resting a hand on the seneschal's knobby shoulder.

"And I see you've had the last of Strongbow's frippery hauled down to the boat for our last trek to Bal—"

Breaking off, Duncan narrowed his eyes at the recently emptied front section of the hall.

Not a single stick of furniture or stack of prized gewgaws blocked the entrance.

Everything was gone ... piled high in Eilean Creag's largest galley to await transport.

A sick feeling in the pit of Duncan's belly joined the heated tightness banding around his ribs, comprehension washing over him in cold and hot waves.

Tearing his gaze from the spotlessly tidy entrance vestibule, he looked back at Fergus.

The slight quivering of a muscle in the old man's jaw told Duncan the truth: His bed *and* his lady were, even now, happily ensconced on the galley, jammed in amidst the remainder of Strongbow's household wares and nonsense.

Awaiting the journey to Balkenzie Castle.

In blatant defiance of his orders.

"By—all—the—saints—and—apostles!" Duncan released all his savage wrath in one ear-splitting bellow.

"'Twas her own doing," Fergus dared to extract himself from the dark deed. "You ken how persuasive she can be, and she swore it was time—"

"*Time*?" The very word curdled Duncan's blood. "Time

for the bairn? And her planting herself and our wee one in a boat?"

Fergus shook his head. "Nay, time for the Sassunach to return."

"And she thinks to await this glorious day at Balkenzie?" Duncan shoved a hand through his hair. "And you assisted her in this foolery?"

"She said if I didn't, she'd find some other way to get there."

With great effort, Duncan fought back his temper. "And the bairn?"

For the first time that morn, the old seneschal smiled.

A fearsome sight . . . his gap-toothed grin not for the faint-hearted.

"The bairn, a fine and healthy what-she-told-me-but-made-me-promise-not-to-tell-you, will be born at Balkenzie," Fergus declared, his thin chest swelling at being the bearer of such privy news.

"She saw the whole of the birthing with her gift," he added, the moist gleam in his eyes revealing how pleased he was that Linnet MacKenzie had trusted *him* with her secrets. "You will soon have a braw new bairn, laddie."

Duncan's shoulders sagged even as his heart swelled with joy. A braw and strapping babe, lad or lassie, was well worth the short boat ride across Loch Duich.

And certainly worth looking a fool for ignoring his own orders.

"Then, come, you old buzzard," Duncan conceded defeat, "let us not keep the lady waiting."

And then Duncan MacKenzie, dread laird of Eilean Creag, and his fool-grinning seneschal, made their way down to the stronghold's little jetty for the passage across Loch Duich to Sir Marmaduke's Balkenzie Castle.

But not before Duncan wiped his own silly grin from his handsome face . . . and replaced it with a dark frown worthy of his formidable reputation.

# Chapter Eighteen

✦

SOMETIME IN THE hushed stillness before dawn, Marmaduke woke to find a slender thigh, sleek, warm, and smooth, draped over his legs. His new wife's head rested on his shoulder, her unbound hair spilling free in glorious disarray, its silken warmth caressing his chin . . . its scent, of fine summer days, delicate and light, a gift to stir his senses.

And set his pulse to racing.

Other parts of him stirred as well. Darker, more beastly urges, for still another warmth pressed against him. Unashamedly close, infinitely soft, and deliciously hot.

His wife's feminine heat.

Remembrances of their encounter in the night, of stroking and petting her, swept through him like a blaze of liquid fire.

Whatever vestiges of sleep still clung to him, took instant flight, scattered with startling ease by the searing sleekness of her woman's flesh, the lush tangle of curls crushed so intimately against him.

Raw, pounding need poured straight into his groin. Shockingly urgent waves of sheer, rampant sensual awareness.

Unbridled want.

But even as his blood roared, he took equal bliss in the simple stirring of her breath against his shoulder.

Both pleasures, the carnal and the tender bonding, blended to weave an inescapable cordon around his heart. Silken chains of passion and promise, tying his very soul to her, and filling him with untold contentment.

A precious and rare joy he wasn't quite ready to relinquish.

He slanted a sidelong glance through the half-opened bed curtains, the corners of his lips lifting in satisfaction. The coming morn hadn't yet spread beyond the deep alcove of the window embrasure.

The rest of the chamber still lay in cold and silent darkness. Ample time remained of the early hour's calm for him to relish the intimacy of Caterine's soft warmth wrapped so sweetly around him.

A comfort he'd well savored throughout the small hours after he'd gathered her into his arms and carried her, sleeping, from the window seat.

And somewhere in the splendor of the night, something magical had happened. The wonder of it firmly closed a door on all the hurts and regrets of other days, and banished the emptiness of countless lonely nights.

A moment, a touch skin-to-skin . . . her supple length stretched languidly beside him . . . and all his demons had fled.

Or so he could almost believe.

*Hope.*

A wild and giddy joy he'd never thought to find again, but he had, and the miracle of his good fortune filled him with awe. He drew a deep breath of the chill morning air, and let his mouth curve in a slow smile.

A smile that glowed bright and true deep inside him and warmed him clear to his toes.

He loved her.

The words spoken in passion on the turnpike stair hadn't been frivolous, born of the moment . . . he'd truly given her his heart.

He, Sir Marmaduke Strongbow, Duncan MacKenzie's man, friend and mentor to many men, staunch defender of women and small children, and soon-to-be lord of Balkenzie Castle, had fallen irrevocably, maddeningly, wondrously in love again.

With every fiber of his being, every face he had: the handsome one wrested from him so long ago, the scarred one now blighting all his waking hours, and the as-yet-unknown one he'd wear in years to come.

Aye, he loved her, and the enormity of his discovery made him want to leap from the bed, run to the windows, and shout his jubilation clear to the distant horizon.

That she yet lay beside him, beckoning with the satiny warmth of her skin and the shining glory of her golden hair, opened up horizons of a wholly different nature.

Ones he burned to savor to the fullest degree.

And now was as good a time as any to continue what they'd begun in the star-studded magic of the night.

With all the finesse he'd mastered, he smoothed his hand along her side in a light, barely there caress. Her blue eyes flew wide just as he splayed his fingers over the curve of her hip to urge the silken heat of her woman's flesh tighter against him.

She gasped, the sweetness of her sleepy-eyed confusion going straight to his heart. "W-what are you—"

"Slaying more of your dragons," he lied.

*Slaking his lust was what he was about.*

"Last night we only tossed out our first challenge to them," he said, caressing her alluringly rounded bottom in a manner designed to put her at ease . . . and to enflame her blood to the same degree as his own.

"Beginning this morn, we shall launch a full assault," he promised, nuzzling his cheek against her unbound hair, pressing kisses into its glossy length. "But you must will their demise, too, my lady."

He grazed his lips along the smooth line of her neck. "Do you?"

"Did I not prove last night that I am desirous of having . . . certain dragons addressed?" she gave back, now fully awake.

Wholly unabashed—even angling her head to give him better access to her skin.

"And have you not already begun? Slaying them?" Her words came on a soft, sensual sigh. "Your touch pleased me well, sir. You—"

"Pleasuring you with my fingers is not what I meant, my sweet, and I believe you know it."

The deep smoothness of his voice sank into her, flowed around her . . . seductive as the tip of his tongue flicking at a sensitive spot just beneath her ear . . . tantalizing as his fingers moving so wickedly over the rounds of her bottom.

Faith, he even trailed a bold finger along its crease, that dark intimacy sending a bolt of hot, licking desire streaking through her.

"All of your dragons will be dealt with soon, my lady. That I assure you," he breathed, nipping at the lobe of her ear.

"And it is the dragon that dwells here—" He slipped his hand between her thighs and, very slowly, traced the tip of one finger along the center of her heat. "—that I burn to address this moment."

Caterine sighed, writhing, his intimate touch as breath-stealing in its intensity as she remembered from the night. His caress ignited a pulsing ache in the deepest part of her belly. A weighted tension potent enough to send undulating waves of delicious tingles rolling across her woman's flesh, and into her very core.

The shrill, twisting birth of true desire.

And the wonder of it ripped through her, wild, insistent, and glorious.

Heady and sublime.

"Those are the dragons I *want* you to slay," she spoke at last, parting her thighs without encouragement in a silent plea for him to keep touching her.

Assuring he did by capturing his hand and pressing his fingers to her ache. There, where she burned to be touched. He obliged at once. Stroking, plucking, *rubbing* her in ways that sent her spiraling toward exquisite, shattering bliss.

Excruciatingly pleasurable, his fingers lighted over her pulsing flesh, tugged playfully on her intimate hair, the magic of his touch intoxicating her.

Boldly, she spread her thighs a bit wider . . . welcoming, encouraging his caress. "You stir me greatly," she breathed, her voice thick with banking passion, her eyes going a deeper shade of blue.

She looked at him, her lids half-lowered and heavy with arousal. "I have never known such abandon, such pure visceral bliss. *This* dragon you have already slain, my lord," she said, arching her hips into his touch. "I wish to continue exploring these pleasures with you . . . for so long as you remain with us."

Her last words sliced clean through his roused state. Somewhere deep inside him, a tiny shard of uneasiness splintered away from the tight, spinning joy he'd taken in touching her so intimately.

At giving her these first tastes of carnal passion, and at her free and willing behest.

He started to object, to warn her he would leave very soon . . . and her with him, but she'd begun sliding her hands over his chest and abdomen, and before he could form a protest, she plunged her fingers lower. Thrusting them straight into the thick nest of his own nether hair, the backs of her burrowing fingers brushing repeatedly against the hot ridge of his aroused shaft.

Lightning quick touches, mayhap unintentional, but rousing enough to send a less-controlled man shooting off the bed.

He sat bolt upright, his heart pounding near as fiercely as his throbbing tarse. He circled her wrist and eased her fingers from the thicket of dark hair at his groin to the safer zone of his stomach. He flattened her palm over his taut flesh, pushing down, against his skin, with gentle, staying pressure before he released her.

A silent warning not to let her hand wander lower again.

Not this moment.

That greater intimacy would come later—when he was certain she'd welcome all of him and not just his well-skilled fingers.

Her fingers slipped boldly over the slabbed muscles of his abdomen, examining each tightly tensed ridge, and pushing him closer and closer to the edge of his endurance.

He looked down at his belly, followed her caresses. "Do you truly think I will leave without you, Caterine? I am not a halfling whose affections—and passion—can be trifled with. I am a man—a man who loves you, and it is too late. . . ."

Trailing off, he stared at her hand, the nakedness of one particular finger sluicing icy water all over his hopes, his belief, she'd come to care for him.

Chilling the fire in his blood in a thorough dousing.

He seized her hand, staring at her bare ring finger, cold bands of doubt sliding round his heart, and throwing open its gates so his demons could march right back in.

*Did you truly think she wanted you for more than a diddle, you blighted beast?* they taunted.

*'Tis the size of your tarse and your skill in pleasuring she desires, not your fool heart . . . or your ring!* they shouted with glee, laughing even harder as their jeering deflated his ardor.

Closing his ears to them, Marmaduke tugged the bedcovers more securely over the evidence of his dismay, schooled his features into his best mask of casual indifference, then met her guileless blue gaze full on.

"I knew the ring would not fit," he said, his voice rougher, more agitated than he would have wished.

Secretly hoping the heirloom's large size was indeed the reason she'd removed it.

"I've brought you a fine gold chain so you can wear the ring around your neck until we return to Balkenzie," he rushed on, not giving her a chance to deny his explanation.

Silently praying she wouldn't.

"Once we are home, I will have the ring altered for you. I meant to give you the chain after the second wedding feast . . . but I shall fetch it now."

She grabbed his wrist when he made to stand, the regret on her lovely face, unsettling him as little else could.

"I do not want a gold chain," she said, and his heart almost stopped. "I removed the ring because I do not wish to wear it." Her honesty dropped a heavier weight on his crushed hope with each word she spoke.

"I honor you greatly, sir," she declared, her straightforwardness prancing hot foot all over his soul. "But my own honor will not allow me to wear your ring. Not on my finger, not on a chain around my neck."

Marmaduke swallowed past his dignity. "And why not?" he managed in a voice scarce his own. He had to know.

"Because I care too much about you to do so," she replied, a whole troupe of demons leering at him over her shoulder.

Without a word, Marmaduke stood.

Heedless of his nakedness, and fully uncaring that, even now, his shaft still raged half-roused against his groin.

Uncaring if she and all the sons of Beelzebub laughed at his weakness. He looked down at her, saw her eyes widen when she glimpsed his pitiful condition.

"You care for me too much to wear my ring?" He forced himself to push her, the gruffness in his voice a paltry shield for his vulnerability. "Fair lady, I fear I do not comprehend your logic."

"Upon my word, sir, I do care. Far too much." She pushed to her feet as well . . . flush naked before him, her lush thatch of golden curls, so lusciously thick, still mussed from his own fool explorations.

He caught a faint whiff of her arousal, and his shaft filled anew, jerked and leapt with its own lewd agenda.

"Well?" he snapped, his valor sorely dented, his shame now complete . . . his tone dark enough to rival Duncan MacKenzie at the very best of his bellowing.

Amazingly unruffled, she slipped past him, trailing her beguiling scent and more carnal promise than a man in his state should have to bear. She stopped before an iron-bound strongbox at the foot of her bed.

"Your ring rests here," she said, indicating the large chest. "I put it there because I will not do you the injustice of claiming it so long as I cannot give you my heart as freely as I'd share my body with you."

Lifting her chin, she stared right at him. Not from coyly lowered lids as a more coquettish maid would have done, but with the level-eyed look of a woman who never lied.

"You are too worthy a man for anything less," she said . . . or so Marmaduke thought.

He could barely hear her for the hoots and howling of his demons. They'd returned en masse and from the racket they made, it sounded like they'd brought a whole regiment of reinforcements with them.

❧

*Too worthy a man for anything less.*

The words sat heavy in his heart as, a good while later, Marmaduke stood high on Dunlaidir's ramparts. Gripped by freezing winds, he gazed out across the open sea. Slate-gray and cold, its endless expanse stared back at him.

Uncaring of his woes, or those of any man, its ceaseless

roar muffled by pale, low-hanging clouds . . . and the first
snowfall of the winter.

Too worthy, she'd said.

*Too blighted,* his own doubts amended, for they, too, had
ridden roughshod back to torment him.

Clenching his jaw against the biting wind, and the bitter
irony of his life, Sir Marmaduke Strongbow, once the
sought-after ladies' man, dashingly handsome, his mere
kisses coveted, suffered the injustice of having hands skilled
enough to make an angel sigh, passion that never failed to
please, yet a face too marred to win a woman's heart.

To win his own lady wife's heart.

Turning into the gusty wind, he let the swirling whiteness
cool the frustration searing his cheeks. His left cheek—the
blighted one—still sticky with Linnet MacKenzie's ragwort
salve.

Her *beauty treatment.*

A fool's delusion, he'd recently discovered.

He hadn't even known he'd smeared on as much as he
had until Ross had commented on it, blessedly mistaking its
yellow coloring for a smudge of grime.

His lips twisted in a bitter smile.

The only smudge on his face was anything but grime, and
couldn't be removed as easily.

Couldn't be removed at all.

Drawing his fur-lined cloak tighter about him, he peered
down at the little golden-brown dog that, for a reason he
couldn't fathom, had tagged along with him to the ramparts.
The wee creature, pressed its small body firmly against his
boots, and met his stare with round, unblinking eyes.

Eyes as frank and assessing as his mistress's.

"Well?" Marmaduke spoke above the whipping wind.
"There is nary a spot of beauty in this ravaged face is there,
my little friend?"

To his amazement, Leo cocked his head to one side and

he would've sworn the dog's brown eyes held a wealth of understanding.

No, not understanding.

*Pity.*

"That is not the answer I'd hoped for," Marmaduke said, bending to scoop the dog into his arms.

He nestled the shivering creature inside the warmth of his cloak, taking some small comfort when the animal stretched up to lick his chin. "Not bothered by my scar, little man?" he pushed past the burning tightness in his throat.

He didn't want pity.

Nor canine adoration.

Though the latter proved decidedly more palatable than the dog's usual fare of snaps, growls, and piddles.

Squirming in his arms, Leo wiggled himself ever deeper into the folds of Marmaduke's fur-lined great cloak, his little-dog-groan of satisfaction once he settled himself, a clear indication of the true reason for his sudden show of affection.

The wee beastie was merely cold and sought Marmaduke's warmth.

His mantle's protection from the swirling, wind-driven snow.

Much as his lady sought comfort from him as well, albeit comfort of an entirely different nature.

A dark scowl settling round his heart, and his wife's clever pet clutched tight in his arms, Marmaduke turned away from the sea to face toward Kintail and Eilean Creag.

Toward home . . . Balkenzie.

Too distant to be seen even by fair weather, but there nonetheless. And tugging on his heart more fiercely in this moment than in all the long weeks since his departure.

Waiting for him, and his bride . . . whether she chose to go or not.

He would make her love him.

*Accept him.*

Even if he had to employ every sensual trick, every art-ful touch and kiss, he'd ever learned. Secrets taught him by court harlots at an early age. Base acts performed on, and by him, with the light-skirts he'd tumbled in recent years.

Dark and lascivious measures, to be sure, but bold and rousing enough to melt any woman's bones and to break the strongest resistance.

For the first time since he'd left her bed, a tiny spark of hope glimmered in Marmaduke's breast, for in his lady's quest to explore desire, she'd innocently given him the means to seize that which she meant to keep from him.

An ignoble path to a lady's affections, but the only course she'd left him.

And she'd need never know that, with each sweet, carnal sigh he wrested from her, each tumultuous release, he'd be stealing back a piece of her heart.

⚜

Several nights later, the brightly burning flames of count-less resinous pine torches lit Dunlaidir's crowded great hall. Their flickering light cast a cheery glow over the wedding feast revelers, though several discreet alcoves and corners remained murky enough for those desirous of more amorous entertainments than gorging, guzzling, and the singing of bawdy songs.

The rich smells of wood-smoke, heavily spiced wine, and roasting meats lent a festive air to a hall long filled with naught but shadows and the too-familiar reek of braised seaware, roasted gannet.

Amidst this tumult and din, Caterine sat ramrod straight at the high table. She hoped the throng of celebrants, all in high good humor and sating themselves on fine Keith beef and rivers of cool, frothy ale, found themselves too occupied to pay heed to her flaming cheeks.

Or if they did notice, she hoped they'd credit her flush to

the overcrowded hall's smoky warmth and wouldn't peer close enough at her—or her husband—to glean the real reason for her discomfiture, for the heat searing her cheeks couldn't compare to the raging burn spinning low in her belly.

A fire put there by her husband's stroking fingers . . . a casual toying with her beneath the fall of the table linens, through the folds of her skirts, and executed with such expertise only sheer force of will kept her from squirming all over her chair.

But, while hidden from general view, *he* knew of her edginess, and its reason . . . and clearly reveled in tormenting her.

Tremors of exquisite sensation, highly inappropriate for the moment, spooled through her over and over again. She slanted a sidelong look at him. An agitated look that left him wholly unfazed.

Confident and proud, he sat calmly beside her, conversing with his men, offering her prime morsels of roasted beef from their shared trencher or sipping hippocras with clear appreciation . . . all the while rubbing slow, lazy circles across her pulsing woman's flesh.

Snatching the wine cup they shared, Caterine took a healthy sip. She let the warmed, spiced wine flow down her throat . . . and thanked the heavens his questing fingers couldn't breach the cloth of her skirts.

He glanced at her then, a devilish light in his good eye, and, for just an instant, flicked the tip of his middle finger over the throbbing nub at the very core of her womanhood.

Caterine jerked, her thighs tensing in immediate reaction to the blinding jolt of pleasure ripping through her at the single, fleeting touch.

He gave her a slow, knowing smile, then turned back to his men. And, wanton that he was making her, she parted her thighs in a shameful admission she craved his lewd ministrations, and wanted more.

Even here, in her seat of honor at the very high table itself.

Comprehending at once, he nodded imperceptibly and immediately implemented more simple flickings to his slow, sensual rubbing of her beneath the table linens.

And she let him.

For truth, she would have cried out if he ceased, for over the past few nights, she'd learned the meaning of *nub of pleasure*.

Her champion had proven himself well-versed in extracting pleasure from the mysterious spot that seemed to be the very apex of all carnal bliss.

Leaning toward her suddenly, he brushed his lips against her temple, using the kiss to whisper in her ear. "When we've retired to your chamber, I shall kiss you there," he said, just as he pressed one fingertip hard against the throbbing nub.

Very deliberately, he began rotating the finger . . . only to lift it away before her building pleasure could shatter in the fierce release she now knew came swift on the heels of such concentrated toyings.

*Kiss me there?* She almost gasped the words aloud, the very thought almost pushing her over the edge.

Surely she'd misunderstood.

"Nay, you did not mis-hear me," he murmured, his breath warming her neck, the flick of his tongue over her heated flesh firing her blood. "I mean to *lick* at you all the night through and do not even think to try and stop me."

Caterine disguised her sharply indrawn breath with a generous gulp of hippocras, swallowing the potent wine so quickly, her eyes teared.

She struggled not to cough as she dabbed at her cheeks with the corner of her linen napkin and scanned the faces of those crowded round the high table. Relief filled her when no reproachful glances stared back at her.

No one seemed to have seen or cared.

At this late hour, many of the carousers were already sleeping off the heavy meal, their heads resting on folded arms, their snores blending with the general ruckus.

Others, including the young knight, Lachlan, and even James, had taken themselves off to join the hardiest of the celebrants dancing with great vigor at the far end of the hall.

And some, her husband's hard-bitten Highlanders mostly, held earnest discourse over the matter of Sir Hugh and what to do about Kinraven.

"—and after he's confessed himself besieged, we return to Kintail?"

*Return to Kintail.*

The words, spoken by one of the Highlanders, ripped through Caterine's sensual haze with the ease of heavy hands rending silk. She listened as the other caterans echoed the first's concerns . . . all wanted to know when they'd be home again.

Her heart hammering, Caterine glanced at her husband. Seemingly unaware of her concerns, he lifted wide shoulders and greeted his men's query with a jovial smile.

"By Yuletide, my good fellows," he assured them, lifting his wine cup to underscore the promise. Not that any such firmly spoken words needed embellishment. The utter conviction behind them slid down Caterine's spine like little chips of ice.

As if sensing her disquiet, he withdrew his hand from between her thighs, and, touching the backs of his fingers to her face, gently smoothed a few strands of hair from her brow.

But for all his tenderness, something in the set of his jaw told her his planned return to Kintail was an issue he would not bend on . . . despite the breath-stealing intimacies he lavished on her behind her closed chamber door.

The knowledge—that he meant to leave—sluiced through her with a cold certainty as physical as his touch.

She looked away before he could see her own steely resolve, her determination to keep him at her side.

At Dunlaidir.

She peered across the smoke-hazed hall, her gaze reaching the circle of whirling, energetic dancers just in time to see James stumble. Unable to keep up with the dance's strenuous pace, he tripped and fell face-long to the floor.

Barks of laughter accompanied his plight as dancers leapt over or sidestepped his sprawled form. Her heart twisting, Caterine looked on as he pushed to his knees in the thick layer of newly spread rushes, his face dark, the cruel taunts of a few ale-headed revelers reminding her why she must convince her husband to stay.

Across the table, unaware of James's embarrassment, Father Tomas coughed discreetly. "And how will you persuade Sir Hugh to concede himself besieged?" he wanted to know. "His arm is long and his treachery great."

"Sir John's was the blackest treachery," James ground out, limping up to the table. He drew back his laird's chair with a painfully loud scrape, and sank heavily into its oaken embrace.

"I've no doubt it was he who fired an arrow into the back of the miscreant who took aim at Strongbow and Lady Caterine the afternoon of the wedding," he said, nodding stiff thanks to Eoghann as he plunked another steaming platter of roasted meat onto the table. "He no doubt sought to still the blackguard's tongue before Black Dugie could haul him before us."

Murmurs of agreement and hearty nods circled the high table.

James dabbed at his moist brow, his fury at Sir John's duplicity clearly vexing him more than losing his footing in the dance. "The man broke every rule of hospitality long held sacred in this land, and all the while he consorted with the devil behind our backs."

"And he now sups at the horned one's own table," Sir

Ross commented, helping himself to a long draught of ale. "His friend Sir Hugh will be joining him there anon lest he is wise enough to ride south on a very swift steed."

"Hugh de la Hogue has learned we are not a pack of halfling laddies he can whisk aside like a swarm of pesky midges," her husband said, placing his hand over hers on the table, idly kneading the tops of her fingers as he spoke, her heart quickening at his touch.

He glanced sharply at her, a knowing gleam sparking in his good eye, before he turned back to his men.

"Either he has made a retiral to England by the time we return to Kinraven to fetch the remaining cattle or he can prepare himself to make peace with his God," he said pouring himself a generous portion of hippocras. "A sad prospect, for I doubt the good Lord will greet him fair."

"And Kinraven?" That from James.

Her husband took a sip of his wine, exchanged telling glances with his men. "Kinraven will be no more," he said. "Naught shall remain but soot and ash. Allowing it to stand will only invite another of the same ilk to take Sir Hugh's place."

"And how shall you turn as well-watched a stronghold as Kinraven into a burning pyre?" Caterine masked her concern with a note of pique.

*What shall I do if—this time—you fail to return?* her heart demanded.

"I mislike seeing worry on your brow," he said, looking right past her lifted chin and straight into her heart. "You've no need to fret yourself for I shall return without the merest scratch. We all shall."

"But . . ."

"Never you worry, my sweet." He brought her hand to his lips and placed a bold kiss in the center of her palm. "We shall take Kinraven as we've taken other such occupied holdings in the most turbulent times of the past."

Releasing her hand, he chucked her under the chin. "With stealth."

"Stealth, a dark night, and well-sharpened blades," the bearded Sir Gowan tossed out, sitting a bit forward and looking as if he'd relish the moment. "That, and enough good men to scale the walls and turn the whole to a burnt, blackened shell before they ken—"

"Nay, my men," her husband's objection came swift. He gave them each a long and level look. A warning look. "We shall not sully ourselves by adopting their methods of villainy."

He raised a silencing hand at their protestations, the ground-swell of grumblings rising from the nearest long tables.

"The garrison men are no different from ours. They merely fight under de la Hogue's banner," he said, speaking loud enough to be heard by all. A calming, authoritative voice in the chaos.

He looked from one to the other, waiting for them, and those at the other tables, to still their tongues before he continued. "They will be given a choice: return to England and their families on their knightly honor never to cross the border again . . . or remain and die with Sir Hugh."

Silence greeted that . . . silence and creased brows.

"And de la Hogue?" Father Tomas's quavering voice came over-loud in the heavy, listening quiet. "What of him?"

"I shall challenge him," Sir Marmaduke returned. "He can die by the sword, and on his feet, as a man of worth should hope to do . . . or within the burning walls of Kinraven as a coward."

His lips set in a taut line, he stood, drawing Caterine up with him. "That, good sirs, shall be his choice." He wrapped his arm about Caterine's waist. "The man has made his fate."

"And from the looks of it, you're about to make yours!"

an ale-slurred voice rose from a nearby table, the ribald call breaking the thick tension in the dais end of the hall.

Darkness slid from his men's faces as well, as, at once, all manner of well-meant jesting and bawdish hollers rose to the smoke-blackened rafters.

"Ale and wine will flow freely late into the night," Sir Marmaduke called out, his commanding voice lifting above the ribaldry. "Partake and enjoy."

Lacing his fingers with hers, he raised their linked hands for all to see. "My lady and I have . . . other plans, and bid you a good night!"

Caterine stood motionless beside him, her heart pounding wildly, gladful when he lowered their hands and swept her high into his arms.

Gladful, and freely giving herself over to the little flickers of heated excitement licking through her now that the long evening was about to come to an end.

Or, better said, begin.

*I shall kiss you there,* her champion had said.

Her worries momentarily forgotten, a tiny smile curved her lips as he carried her from the hall.

Kiss her *there.*

*Lick at her.*

A delicious tremor rippled through her at the very thought. And he'd voiced concern she wouldn't let him.

Pulsing with need even now, Caterine sighed and began counting each step of their circuitous climb up the winding turnpike stair.

Let him, indeed.

She could scarce wait.

# *Chapter Nineteen*

❧

"*W*ILL YOU TRULY?*"

The three words, whisper-soft but smoldering with the smooth, dark heat of a woman on the verge of passion, ripped into Marmaduke with all the force of a howling winter wind descended upon him in full gale.

Blasting not cold, but pure, molten heat straight into his loins.

Halfway down the dimly lit passage to her bedchamber, he halted at once, angling her in his arms so the flickering light of a nearby wall torch could better illuminate her face.

Not that he didn't already know what she meant.

Nor what a tempting sweetmeat she was—he'd already tasted her once, if fleetingly.

This time he meant to sate himself on her.

Oh, aye, he knew what she wanted with every fiber of his body, every beat of his smitten heart. It was writ all over her.

She met his gaze full on, her keen-edged excitement almost shimmering in the air between them, the lush swell of her breasts rising and falling with a rapidity that didn't lie.

"Will I what?" Marmaduke spoke at last, amazed he could push the words past the tightness in his throat—the *want* coursing through him.

He caressed her face, traced the line of her jaw with his

thumb . . . and waited, silently willing her to voice her desire.

She blinked, clearly delving for courage. "Will you truly kiss me . . . *there*?" she finally blurted.

"Where, my love?" devils made him ask as he set off again, this time great-strided . . . eager to reach her chamber and the bliss awaiting him there.

She held her tongue, her lower lip caught between her teeth, as he neared her door. Some far-thinking soul had cracked it, and a gentle urging with his boot was all it took to send the door swinging inward.

"Will I kiss you where?" he prodded, crossing the chamber with swift strides. Needing, wanting to hear her speak the words.

"Where do you want to be kissed?" He grazed his lips across her temple. "Here? Or somewhere else?"

A great tremor tore through her—he could feel it ripple down her back and flow through her thighs. "Between my legs," she blurted, two spots of bright pink appearing on her cheeks. "I want you to kiss and lick me between my legs . . . as you said you would."

A shudder of his own tore through Marmaduke at her plain speech, his shaft swelling, lengthening, to a painful degree. "Lady," he said, his voice husky with need, "I shall lave you, and till the breaking of dawn if it pleases you."

Flinging back the heavy bed curtains with one hand, he eased her onto the edge of the great four-poster.

A bed already occupied by a four-legged contender for her affections.

"Be gone with you, little man, for your lady is mine this night," he said, then snapped his brows together in his most intimidating scowl when his words had no effect.

The scowl worked.

With a little grunt of displeasure, Leo hopped from the bed and toddled off to seek his own.

Some kind soul had stoked the fire and it threw off a fine

reddish glow that, together with the wall torches flooded the room with so much light and warmth his lady would be able to lie fully unclothed before him and not shiver.

He cleared his throat. "Caterine, I mean to love you thoroughly this night." He locked his gaze on hers. "I wish to absorb your very essence, and give you all of mine."

*A union of our bodies to meld your soul—your heart—irrevocably to my own.*

"But first I must tell you something." He placed his hands on her shoulders, kneading them.

She nodded, her eyes earnest, accepting.

He touched the coiled plaits at her ears. "Shall I unravel your hair as we speak?" he asked, and she inclined her head again.

"When a man kisses a woman intimately," he began, slipping the pins from her hair, "when he touches his tongue to her, or opens his mouth over her as I shall do to you, he becomes so enflamed, he may no longer be able to withhold himself."

Her eyes widened, but she held his gaze. Keen interest, not revulsion, on her face, and for that, Marmaduke knew true relief.

"Are you asking if I am ready to take you fully?"

Marmaduke nodded. "Until now I have only pleasured you with my hands and my lips," he said, placing a handful of hairpins on the table beside the bed. "Once I've kissed you as I intend to this night, I shall want you in every way."

He lifted her chin. "I want you to know that before we proceed."

"I will welcome you," she said, and the heat simmering in her eyes assured him she would. "I imagine I shall be more than willing if you truly mean to put your mouth—"

"Oh, I shall, my sweet. Do not doubt it."

He pulled the remaining pins from her hair, allowing it to spill free in silken waves clear to her hips. Its beauty stole his breath. Fully enchanted, he twined his hand in the golden mass, let its silk stream through his fingers.

Thoroughly besotting him.

He lifted brimming handfuls to his face, nuzzled his cheek against the cool, satiny skeins. "A man could lose his soul in your hair, but, this night, you have other charms I would explore."

*And a heart I mean to capture.*

*How do you mean to do that, you fool?* One of his demons taunted from somewhere in the shadows.

*By loving her,* a softer voice gave back . . . beautiful and precious, but barely there. A mere whisper on the wind racing through the cold night beyond the shuttered windows.

*He is very good at loving . . . at winning and holding a woman's heart.*

*Better yet at giving his own.*

Marmaduke wheeled toward the row of night-battened windows, his nape prickling. He strained his ears, listening hard, but heard naught save the muffled wash of the sea and the wind's keening echo.

And then the wind sped on to harry some other corner of the night . . . taking its echo and, as *she'd* meant to do, some of Marmaduke's doubts along with it.

A chill swept down his back, but he shook it off . . . and with surprising ease, for, of a sudden, a wondrous warmth spilled through him and he simply knew he could win his new lady's heart.

Knew he could make her love him.

And for far more than his renowned skill at diddling.

He slanted that barb into the dark shadows of a particularly menacing corner . . . one that seemed needy of a firmly spoken reprimand.

Then, before his doubts could mass force against him again, he dropped to one knee and began removing his new wife's slippers. "Are you ready to be loved, Caterine?" he asked, meaning anything but the physical act he was about to perform on her.

"I am ready to be . . . *kissed,* aye," came the wrong reply.

Refusing to face defeat, Marmaduke tossed aside her plain leather brogans. "And how would you like to be kissed? Shall I draw deep and fully on you?"

*And how shall I win your love?* his heart echoed. *Shall I batter down your defenses with a passion so fierce every resistance will be futile?*

Lifting her skirts, he began untying the garters at her knees. "Or would you prefer barely there little licks across your sweetness? Feather-light kisses to drive you wild with bliss until you can stand no more?"

*Or shall I win you with a tender wooing? Ply your heart with the lightest of touches until it melts into my waiting hands?*

"What would you prefer?" she asked, her heart tripping at the odd way he looked at her.

As if he meant so very much more than the mere words.

And as if the unspoken ones already worked some strange and heady magic on her.

"I prefer a little of both," he said, his only falsehood being that he preferred a great deal of both.

His course thus laid, his determination unflagging, he lifted her hips and slid her under-hose to her ankles.

Holding her gaze, he drew her to her feet. "Take off the rest of your clothes, Caterine," he said. "I would see all of you."

Ripples of exquisite anticipation eddying through her, she untied the lacings of her bodice, eased her arms out of the sleeves, then let the gown shimmy to the floor where it pooled around her feet.

Her camise quickly followed.

At ease with her nakedness, she stood proud before him, her arms at her sides. "And now?"

He reached out and trailed his fingers over her breasts.

"Much as I'd like to, I shall not toy much with your breasts this night," he said, his heated gaze making the place between her thighs throb with a heavy, warm pulsing.

Sliding his hands beneath her breasts, he cupped them, lifting and weighing them. He rubbed slow circles around her nipples . . . his thumbs circling round and round the puckered flesh of her areolas, taking great care not to touch the hardened, distended peaks.

"Prolonging one's release can heighten sensual pleasure and, much as your breasts enthrall me, I want to kiss you, *lave* you elsewhere tonight," he said, his words, his touch, sending hot streaks of tingling pleasure rippling across her tender parts. "I burn to lick you senseless."

Grasping the swollen peaks of her nipples at last, he rubbed them, pulling on them a bit, before he eased her onto the edge of the bed.

"You have very large nipples," he said, smoothing one hand down her side, across her belly, and into the nest of her intimate hair . . . tugging gently on the curls.

"Your areolas are especially large and I find that maddeningly rousing. But it is the hidden flesh *here*"—he slid one finger deep between her legs, traced its tip along her cleft—"that stirs me this moment."

Caterine wet her lips, scarce able to breathe for the pounding need consuming her. A hot, tight spinning deep inside her that would surely burst any moment.

"Open for me, Caterine. Show me your sweetness again as you did on the windowseat. Let me gaze upon you."

Biting back the ragged gasp of pure, unbridled passion rising in her throat, Caterine bit hard into her lower lip and spread her knees.

Fully, unashamedly, and as wide as she could open them.

"*Lick me.*" A half-choked voice rasped the plea. "I—cannot—stand—it. . . ." She squirmed on the bedsheets, the mind-numbing, base glory of sitting so fully open, so *exposed,* pushing her beyond all modesty.

"Hold what you are feeling." His deep voice came as if from a great distance, and she glanced up to find him staring at her, his face dark with passion.

Keeping her gaze, he knelt between her thighs. "I shall touch my mouth to you—*lick you*—very soon, my sweet. Just keep your legs spread like this."

He began caressing her. Toying at her with his fingers, light, almost playful touches . . . soft *pluckings,* gentle tugs on her feminine hair and quick, barely-touching-her strokes along her center.

"Do you enjoy having me touch you thus?" he asked, probing her hidden flesh, massaging each pulsing fold. "Having me play with you? There, between your legs? Does what I am doing make you feel good, Caterine?"

She nodded, unable to speak for the torturously sweet pleasure winding so hotly through her.

"I am going to tell you what I'll be doing to you before I do it, Caterine, so listen carefully, for speaking such things aloud is stirring, too."

He glanced at her, smoothed her hair behind her ear. "You may find you enjoy such love talk as well, so voice anything you wish to. There is no shame between us, only what gives us both pleasure."

*Only my love for you and my desire to win yours.*

She blinked, almost asking him to repeat what she thought he'd just said, but the headiness of his sensual ministrations weighted her tongue.

Her heart pounded slower, harder, with each new caress, each lasciviously turned phrase. Digging her fingers into the tender flesh of her lower thighs, she held them wide for him.

"I am going to rub my face against you now," he was saying, palming her as he spoke the words . . . slow, rough circlings every bit as bliss-spending as the lighter pluckings and tugs. "Just a moment or two to savor the softness of your intimate hair, and then we shall move on to more . . . serious pursuits."

Hollow tension, tight, pulsing, and exquisite, coiled low in her belly as he came ever closer until hardly a heartbeat stood between his mouth and her heat. His very breath caressed her, warm and soft, the feel of it whispering across her, melting her.

"Your beauty unmans me." He slid his hands along the inside of her thighs. "The scent of your arousal fires my blood."

Leaning closer, he drew several deep breaths, holding them long moments before he exhaled, and only after the second or third time, did she realize he was inhaling her.

*Her scent.*

"I could sate myself on you," he said, nuzzling his cheek, his face, into the thick tangle of golden curls crowning her woman's mound, the sheer intimacy of the act he performed on her shattering the tight coil of heat spinning inside her. It melted into a slow, trickling warmth, infinitely sweet.

"Do you know you have more hair here than most women?" He grazed his lips back and forth across her softness. "Such a luxurious fleece is worth a king's ransom to many men . . . especially a golden one such as yours. I could spend hours simply threading my fingers through its lushness, but. . . ."

He pushed to his feet, discarding the knight's belt slung low around his hips. "I would lick you now," he said. "*That,* my love, is what I am about to do . . . flick my tongue over your sweetness."

"Barely there little licks?"

"So I have said." He yanked his tunic over his head, let it drop to the floor. "Would you enjoy that?"

She nodded, watching him tug off his boots, shed his hose and braies, her breath catching at the size of him, his magnificence.

Confident in his nakedness, he planted his hands on his hips and looked down at her . . . at *that* part of her.

"Do you know how beautiful you are? Lying there with

your knees apart . . . so very wide apart," he said, his voice
thick, dark. "I could take my ease just by looking my fill on
you."

He knelt before her. "I will show you lascivious now,
Caterine," he promised, the heat in his voice making the
heavy pulsing between her legs throb even more. "Lie back,
my dear one, and be *licked*."

Leaning forward, he traced her cleft with his tongue,
licked at her. "Do you like this, Caterine?"

She twisted, bucking beneath him, her moans throaty and
primal.

"Easy, sweet," he soothed her. "Just feel. I am going to
lap at you now. I shall lave you, with long, leisurely strokes
and you will best enjoy them if you are fully relaxed."

Trembling, she did as he bade, lying perfectly still as he
lapped at her with slow, wide-tongued strokes. "Do not
move, Caterine," he cautioned her when her hips began
rocking in a slow, rhythmic motion. "Simply enjoy what I
am doing to you."

Pounding need firing his own blood, he drew back to
look on her, his gaze devouring her lush beauty . . . the sheer
bounty of her. She was so well-haired he could barely make
out the pouty folds of her cleft. Never had he seen a more
luxurious thatch, one so lush, so golden.

"I am going to lick you more thoroughly this time," he
told her, parting her thick curls with his thumbs until he had
a tantalizing view of the pulsing flesh at her very core.

Her thighs tensed, almost clenching as her hips lifted off
the bed. "Nay, my sweet, no moving . . . just keep your legs
spread wide," he urged, then swept his tongue the length of
her.

Once.

"Each time you move, Caterine, I will stop," he warned,
caressing the insides of her thighs, toying with her damp
curls, *plucking* at them. "Can you be still? If you can, I shall
continue licking you. But you must lie perfectly still."

A little cry escaped her and she wound her hands deeper into the bed coverings, her thighs clenching, but still beautifully open . . . the scent of her arousal, sharp and musky, rising up to intoxicate him.

Savoring it, he inhaled deeply of her tang and cupped her, the flat of his palm rubbing slow circles over her silken heat. "You are lovely in your passion. Keep your legs opened for me . . . as wide as you can. Only so can I lave you fully."

And he did.

He opened his mouth over her, wide and hungry, spending bliss with slow, wide-tongued licks. Again and again, he tongued her, sometimes probing her pouty, throbbing folds, most times simply licking her.

Long, *slow* and thorough licks meant to wrest every sigh, every sweet shudder from her . . . and lay bold siege to every barrier she'd raise against him until he'd won through to her heart.

On and on, he laved her, *drew* on her, swirled his tongue over and around the tiny, hardened nub at the very crux of her sweetness.

He claimed her with all the passion he had, branding her with the desire she craved, until with a great, shuddering cry, she seized her release, her sensual ecstasy ripping through her.

She went utterly limp, the way to her soul, at last, laid as wide open to him as the golden expanse of her dampened intimate curls and the hidden flesh beneath.

Or so he hoped.

His own pulse hammering in his ears, Marmaduke stood, relief flooding him that he'd pleased her so. Watching her eddy down from her bliss, hearing her gasping breaths, proved a sweet enough victory to keep his demons silent for a good long while.

But not his heart.

It thumped hard against his ribs, irrevocably lost.

And wanting so much more than sated sighs and passions spent.

Indulging himself in a tilting, roguish smile, content with what they'd shared, he looked down at her and savored the depth of his triumph mirrored in her passion-clouded eyes.

*Sated eyes.*

Never had he seen a woman more beautiful in her release, and never had his own need pounded with such urgency.

"So," he said, trailing his fingers back and forth over her damp curls. "Are you pleased, my sweet?"

She reached for his hand, laced her fingers with his. "I am well pleased," she said, her voice still thick with her passion, her honest admission of her pleasure warming his heart.

Her brow knitted. "But you, my lord . . ."

Marmaduke followed her troubled gaze. Not that he needed to look down to know his manhood still rode hard against his abdomen.

He drew a long breath. "See you, I have waited many years for such a night as this," he said, catching her hand to his lips for a kiss. "A bit longer will not be my death. It would please me to give you a special gift now . . . something your sister and her husband sent along for you."

Releasing her hand, he trailed a finger down the side of her face. "Someone left us a ewer of hippocras." He indicated a moisture-beaded jug on the nearby table. "Why don't you draw on your bed robe so you won't chill, and we can enjoy the wine while you admire Linnet's gift."

Turning away, Marmaduke sought the shadow-cast shelter of the little ante-room . . . but not merely to fetch the bejeweled chalices Linnet had sent along as a wedding gift for her sister.

With a weary sigh, he dragged his large, leather satchel beneath the bluish-silver light slanting through the two narrow window slits, then rummaged through the bag until he found the goblets.

But rather than hasten back to his sweet wife's side, he stood unmoving in the pale bands of moonlight . . . and willed his passion to ebb.

Clenching his hands, he thought hard on all the shriveled faces of every crone he'd happened across on his long journey across Scotland, recalled with a shudder the odious task of securing the latrine chute, and other sundry unpleasantries, until, at last, the fire left his blood.

When it did, he snatched his fur-lined cloak off its peg, swirled it around his shoulders, and cursed himself for, once again, bowing to his dark side.

The beast in him he couldn't seem to tame.

Frowning into the shadows, he rained a parade of invectives on the foolhardiness of trusting his skilled hands and practiced lips to bestow the sheerest of bliss upon his lady, but being too much of a coward to risk seeing revulsion cloud her lovely eyes in the instant he plunged his need into her.

But, practiced champion that he was, he ran a hand down over his face to smooth the cares from his brow, retrieved the two chalices, then left the ante-room's darkness.

And his own.

Confident he'd face down his most grievous dragon on the morrow . . . and be bold enough—next time—to see the battle through to the very end.

⚜

*She'd seen the chalices before.*

Caterine peered at the magnificently jeweled chalice in her hand. The multi-colored gemstones adorning the elaborately worked wine goblet gleamed in the soft light of the hanging cresset lamp, winking at her . . . teasing her with the chalice's familiarity.

She glanced at her husband, but found no answers. He sat in the heavy oaken chair near the hearth, one powerfully muscled leg resting casually over the side of the chair, his fur-lined cloak gaping just enough to reveal a tantalizing glimpse of the hard-muscled planes of his chest and abdomen.

And a titillating hint of his bold masculinity, now fully relaxed and resting against his thigh. Though only partly visible, its length and thickness, even at ease, quickened her blood.

Very conscious of the proximity of his maleness, she smoothed her dampening palms on her bed-robe, a fine liquid heat winding steadily through her . . . and pulsing hotly across her womanhood.

*Again.*

And simply from stealing a wee peek at his dark virility through a shadowed gap in his cloak.

Lifting her gaze at once, her heart near stilled, for his casual expression had fled, and he now watched her with a look of infinite adoration.

A look of love.

Shining, pure, and true.

The same look she'd seen him wear the day she'd imagined him sprawled in Niall's chair so many weeks ago . . . holding the very same jeweled chalice in his hand.

Only that time, she hadn't known who he'd been looking at.

Now she did.

And the meaning of that look sent her heart climbing clear to her throat, set her pulse to racing.

"You are pleased, my lady?" his sonorous voice flowed around her, tightening his hold on her as soundly as if he'd reached out, grasped her arms beneath her bed-robe and pulled her into a hard embrace.

"P-pleased?" Caterine blinked, her gaze dropping to where a fold of his mantle had slipped a bit to reveal even more of his proud manhood. She could now see not only the entirety of his impressive length, but also his sizable ballocks.

Languid warmth pooled deep in her most womanly place. "You pleased me well, milord, as I thought you—"

He held up Linnet's gift, toasting her—just as he'd done the day she'd imagined him in Niall's solar. "I meant are you pleased with the goblets?" he supplied, his smoldering gaze assuring her he knew full well *he'd* pleased her.

"Linnet has a complete set waiting for you at Balkenzie," he added, his words dousing the sensual heat curling in her belly. His firm conviction that she, too, would soon be at Balkenzie, squeezed her heart.

She didn't want to go to Balkenzie . . . nor did she want to lose her champion.

Or the fragile stirrings of *her* convictions: that she'd finally discovered not just desire, but love, too.

Pulling her bed robe more securely around her shoulders, Caterine lifted the finely wrought chalice to her lips and took a sip of hippocras.

A sip of determination.

Steely determination.

She moved closer to his chair, rested a hand on his broad shoulder. Its muscled strength, *his warmth,* reached her even through the thickness of his cloak. "I would rather Linnet and her husband visit us here," she said, forcing a light tone. "They can bring the other goblets with them."

"Your sister will not be venturing anywhere for some while," he said, his words carefully measured, his demeanor guarded enough to make her forget her own cares for a moment.

She looked sharply at him. "Is she ill?"

Marmaduke hesitated, weighing the concern on his wife's face against the depth of his honor . . . the value of a promise given.

If Caterine knew her sister would soon birth her first

child, she'd be certain to accompany him to Balkenzie, and even if she planned to stay only long enough to see the child born. And once he had her at Balkenzie, he knew he could persuade her to stay.

But he wanted her by his side because she *wanted* to be there.

Because she loved him.

"Linnet is well," he said at last, leveling his wife with the most neutral gaze he could summon . . . and silently praying he spoke the truth. "Eilean Creag is a large and busy holding, her duties as laird's wife do not allow her to travel far."

Not a lie, but not the entire truth.

And half-truth or nay, enough to make his wife press her sweet lips into a firm line.

To his amazement, she set down the jeweled chalice and, with the artfulness of a well-skilled lady-of-pleasure, leaned against the table's edge in such a way that the front edges of her robe parted to expose one full half of each of her areolas.

The peaks of her nipples remained hidden, but enough of the largish rounds peeked at him to heat his blood anew and shoot jolts of fiery desire straight into his filling shaft.

"And when will you retrieve those other chalices, my lord?" she asked, her voice soft, the slight tremble revealing she knew exactly what she was about, knew full well the sight of her generous areolas, even just the halves of them, would stir him beyond restraint.

She meant to use her charms to keep him from leaving.

Marmaduke drew a deep breath . . . and willed the pull at his loins to recede. "I shall not be retrieving them," he said, forcing himself to keep his gaze above her shoulders. "In a few days, after Sir Hugh has been dealt with, my men and I—and you—shall depart for Kintail. The goblets will await us, and remain, at Balkenzie."

"I see." With one smooth movement, she unfastened her bed robe's clasp and let the voluminous robe billow to the floor. She bent to snatch it off the rushes, purposely choosing an angle that would give him the most stirring view of her golden fleece as she did so.

"I shall retire now, my lord. I would welcome your . . . embrace, if you choose to join me."

*Nay, my lady, you shall join me . . . at Balkenzie,* Marmaduke's heart amended.

His arousal roared at him to follow her, but before he could push to his feet, a small, cold nose bumped against his shin.

As if unsure of his welcome, Leo pushed up on his back legs and pawed Marmaduke's knee, the accompanying little-dog-whimper assuring Marmaduke's attention.

And the instant he gave it, the wee creature dropped back down on his rump, turned pleading brown eyes on him, and began to shiver.

A ploy if Marmaduke ever saw one.

He cast a wistful glance toward the great four-poster across the room. His lady had pulled the bed curtains and the saints knew what sultry pleasures awaited him behind their drawn folds.

But another whimper reached his ears just then and this one sounded decidedly pitiful.

Heaving a great sigh of defeat, Marmaduke pinched the bridge of his nose, and sent up a silent prayer that if he and his lady were ever blessed with a son, the lad would be spared his father's soft heart.

Then, his decision made, or, better said, made for him, he leaned down and scooped the furry little bugger onto his lap.

All pretense of his oh-woe-is-me demeanor vanishing from his button-round eyes, Leo promptly nosed aside the edge of Marmaduke's cloak and swiftly disappeared beneath its warm folds.

The little dog settled himself without a single glance or grunt of gratitude. And, soft-hearted fool that he was, Marmaduke settled back for a long night, too.

And consigned himself to kneading the wee beastie's still-shivering shoulder rather than plying the lush bounty of his lady's irrefutable charms.

Charms he meant to claim in full very soon.

Her charms and her heart.

Resting his head against the chair back, he listened to her tossing and turning behind the bed curtains. All the night through, the rustlings and her frustrated sighs continued. They hung sweet in the air . . . fair music to his ears.

Burgeoning hope to a heart besieged.

For even one as blighted as he recognized what lurked behind her inability to sleep.

A slow smile curving his lips, Marmaduke stared into the darkness, for the hearth fire had all but burned itself out, and the torches had long since flickered their last.

Slipping a hand inside his cloak, he rubbed gently behind Leo's floppy ears and savored each and every soft *swishing* noise to leak past the bed curtains, relished each breathy little burst of impatience to escape her sleep-deprived lips.

Utterly feminine sounds, pointed and recognizable, their meaning well-known to any man capable of satisfying a woman.

Even more so to a man accustomed to winning a lady's heart.

His own heart quickening in response, Marmaduke pulled his cloak closer about his little friend and settled back in the chair to await the coming dawn.

And revel in the knowledge that his lady wife wanted more than just his prowess . . . she wanted his love.

And mayhap, if he was very, very lucky, she'd want it enough to give him her own as well.

*She already has, my dear heart,* the keening wind whispered somewhere out across the night-blackened waters.

*She already has.*

# Chapter Twenty

❧

A SENNIGHT LATER, in the small hours of a silent, moonless night, Sir Marmaduke, James, Black Dugie, and a few carefully selected garrison men reined up on a low, tree-dotted knoll at the head of a shallow valley. Cloaks as black as the cold heavens hid the gleam of their armor as they stared across the winter-brown gorse to where Kinraven's towers rose dark against the night sky.

Faint light shone in but a few of the stronghold's narrow slit windows and the blustery wind carried only deep quiet and the gentle slapping of water on the nearby lochshore.

One of the garrison men edged his mount forward. "Should we mount a sham attack on one of the towers before we move in?" he asked, his low-spoken words overloud in the quiet.

Marmaduke shook his head. "If my men scale the walls as swiftly as they've climbed others, and those with them spread enough tinder in the right places, Kinraven will be a blackened waste by first light whether we draw our swords or leave them sheathed."

He glanced round at the lot of them. "Nay, my friend, we have no need of such a ruse. Dark of night, surprise, and our own good sword arms will suffice."

Murmurs of agreement rose from the gathered men.

"James." Marmaduke addressed the younger man. "You have the best vision amongst us. Can you tell if our men have breached the parapets?"

James narrowed his eyes to stare across the valley. "The ladders are in place and the two men I can see are nearing the topmost rungs."

"Any sentries in sight?" A second Keith man-at-arms wanted to know.

James shook his head just as another of the garrison men emerged from the thicket. The man kneed his winded horse closer. "All is in readiness," he said, shoving back his mailed coif.

"Our men are in place," he said. "Every last twig of dried gorse and broom we've collected over the last days has been put about. We even plundered the stables of straw."

Marmaduke looked toward Kinraven, could just make out the stream of men moving up the rope scaling ladders. They appeared to be slipping unhindered over the parapet walls. Satisfied, he returned his attention to the man-at-arms. "And those entering the keep have enough tinder to set the inside ablaze?"

The other nodded. "We pulled the thatch from a few out-buildings."

"The cattle?" James tore his gaze from the distant stronghold. "Are they out of harm's way?"

"The herdsmen are gathering them now," the man-at-arms answered, rubbing his spume-flecked horse behind its ears. "They'll have them past the loch-head and on the way back to Dunlaidir before the first flames—"

"By God, they've started!" Black Dugie thrust out an arm, his finger pointing to where shooting flames, orange and bright, punctuated the inky darkness. Already, great, pluming clouds of smoke rose above Kinraven's walls.

The wind carried the noise of distant shouting, shrill cries and curses, and an eerie reddish glow began spreading across the night sky. The stronghold and its surrounds, no longer dark and sleeping, erupted in hellish chaos.

Wheeling his horse around, Marmaduke raised his mailed arm. "Come, men, it is time to show yon blackguards the road to England," he called out. "God's mercy on those who choose not to follow it."

Then, digging gold spurs deep into his horse's flanks, he sent the beast plunging down the scrub-covered slope, the others spurring after him. Together, they thundered across the valley floor toward the flaming pyre that had once been Kinraven Castle.

⚜

Within the sheltering walls of Dunlaidir Castle, in a tower chamber high above the tossing sea, Caterine passed the night pacing the magnificent arch-topped windows curving the length of her stepson's lairdly quarters, chased there by the emptiness in her own bedchamber.

A void she hoped to assuage with at the dubious comfort of Rhona's chatty presence. But this night even Rhona gave herself subdued. She reclined on James's bed, contenting herself with petting Leo.

Ignoring her, Caterine prowled at the windows, her gaze repeatedly flickering to the cliff road. She tried willing her husband and the others to appear, but the mainland cliff-head, stretching as far into the darkness as the curving bank of windows allowed her to see, remained deserted.

She glanced at Rhona. "Shouldn't they have returned by now?"

"Nay, my lady. I doubt we will see them before cock-crow. Mayhap not even until Vespers."

"*Vespers*?" Caterine's heart dipped. "It will be gloaming by then."

Rhona peered at her. "Think you it will be an easy task to turn a holding the size of Kinraven into soot and ash?"

"If I thought such a feat could be accomplished without risk, I would be asleep in my bed this moment," Caterine said, staring out at the night-darkened waters as she paced past the bank of windows.

"You are wearing a track in the floor rushes," Rhona said, and Caterine glanced sharply at her.

"James is very particular about such things," Rhona explained with a shrug.

Caterine stared hard at her, striving to see if some spark of distress hid behind her friend's dark eyes. "Are you not at all concerned for them?"

She *had* to be, for the depth of her feelings for James permeated the chamber . . . in the array of her trinkets and clutter scattered about, through the number of her clothes hanging on the wall pegs.

"Oh, lady, have you so little faith?" Rhona stroked Leo's back. "Your precious champion swings a mighty blade," she said. "If I am not worried for *my* love's safety, then surely you should have no concerns for—"

"He is not my love," Caterine denied, stepping closer to the nearest window and resting her forehead against the cold, grainy stone of the elaborately carved tracery.

She welcomed its cooling relief on her heated brow.

"I enjoy his attentions," she said, squaring her shoulders lest Rhona attempt to pry deeper. "He is . . . well-skilled in such arts."

"Truth tell?"

Trailing her fingers along the window's molded edge, Caterine stared out at the thin white mist rising slowly from the sea . . . determined to drop the subject.

Rhona rattled on regardless. "He is a fine, braw man, my lady," she claimed. "A gallant knight, a *champion* of men. How could he not steal your heart?"

"You are not going to press a declaration of passionate devotion out of me," Caterine broke her silence. "The only thing he has stolen from me is my aversion to his English blood and my . . . my desire to live an abstemious life."

"So you enjoy lying with him."

Caterine could feel her friend's I-told-you-so smile clear across the chamber. "That does not mean he has stolen my heart. One pleasure can be savored without the other, as you of all people aught know."

She whirled around and immediately wished she hadn't for Rhona was tapping a finger against her chin. And whatever gem of wisdom she was about to let fall had to do with *him*. And thus far, all her pronouncements and predictions had come true.

"I have it!" Rhona cried suddenly. "You are full right. He has not stolen your heart at all . . . you've given it to him."

Caterine drew a strangled breath . . . of cold, briny air and bitter denial.

"You are in love with him," Rhona declared, and Caterine's heart agreed.

"Nay, I am not," *she* returned.

Rhona snorted.

And Caterine wondered.

But before she could look too deep into places she might not want to go, she swung back to the windows. Far out to sea, billowing white fog blotted out the horizon, smudging it from view much as her champion's smooth gallantry and fiery passion had blurred and knocked down every barrier she'd thought to raise against him.

Until not a one remained.

None save her determination not to let him go.

A tiny smile curved her lips.

She possessed one remaining *allure* he hadn't yet partaken of, and she knew instinctively that once he had, he'd never leave her side.

Her smile deepened.

Upon his return, as soon as he'd refreshed himself and bathed, she would love him.

*Fully.*

❧

Chaos and confusion greeted Sir Marmaduke and those with him as they thundered up to Kinraven's burning gatehouse. Sleep-dazed men, most half-clothed, some naked, poured from its ruined, smoking entrance to scatter in the turmoil of the red-glowing night.

A brave few souls clashed furious swords with Marmaduke's Highlanders, and the clanging ring of steel on steel made a hellish echo against the pandemonium of running, shouting men and the neighings of wild-eyed, prancing horseflesh.

Other Keith guardsmen rounded up the English soldiers seeking to flee, while those already subdued, stood under guard in a tight cluster, stamping their feet against the cold, their faces dark and unsmiling.

Pressing into the middle of the fray, Marmaduke pushed up in his stirrups, his blade raised high. "Cease!" His deep voice rang out above the fracas. "Hear you, my own good men and the rest of you. This is between de la Hogue and myself. All others, put back your steel."

"A pig's arse, I will!" someone called back.

*Sir Gowan.*

The rest of his men obeyed at once, expectant, knowing grins spreading across their faces. Others followed suit more slowly, until gradually, the worst of the tumult died down. The Keith men exchanged dubious glances, but kept their blades lowered . . . so long as their opponents complied as well.

The remainder of the shirt-clad English soldiery, divested of any arms they may have wielded and encircled by grim-faced Keith guardsmen, looked on with a mixture of wariness and grudging respect.

Considering them, Marmaduke drew a long breath of the biting, acrid air. Without the resplendent trappings of their knightly station, wild-haired and half-clothed as they stood shivering before the burning gatehouse, they made a pitiful sight.

With their bared limbs and torn night-shirts streaked with soot, some with blood, they appeared more frightful-looking than his caterans at their worst.

And they looked . . . young.

Too young to die for an ill-chased cause.

Too *English* to deserve the leniency Marmaduke meant to spend them.

Swallowing the great oath rising in his throat, he swung down from his saddle and tossed his reins to James. "Men of de la Hogue," he addressed them, raising his voice above the roar of the flames, "I, Marmaduke Strongbow of Balkenzie, greet you."

Tight-lipped silence greeted him.

Unfazed, he swept them with a measuring stare. "Where is your lord? I would challenge him to single combat . . . if he is man enough to accept."

"I am man enough, Strongbow, but I see you are some-what . . . *lacking* since last we met."

The voice came from behind him and Marmaduke spun around to see Hugh de la Hogue emerge from the billowing cloud of smoke pouring from the gatehouse's arched entrance. Ruddy-faced and full-armed, he strode forward, a handful of bedraggled, choking men stumbling out behind him.

"I'd heard the rumors, but now I see your renowned handsomeness is indeed but an ill memory," he taunted, his voice amazingly unaffected by the shroud of thick smoke he'd just pressed through. "I scarce recognize you."

"You, son of a sow," Sir Gowan rushed him, his two-handed Highland blade raised for a smiting blow.

Sir Hugh sidestepped the vicious downward swing with surprising agility. He blocked Gowan's second slashing arc with equal skill, their blades meeting with an ear-splitting *clank.*

"Enough, MacKenzie!" Marmaduke stayed his friend, even as Sir Ross and Sir Alec pushed forward to strong-arm him back into the growing circle of onlookers.

"You've taken up with a wild pack, Strongbow," de la Hogue sought to provoke him. "A heathenish lot."

Ignoring the slur, Marmaduke raked the other's steel-girt form with disdain. "Heathen?" He lifted a brow. "And what do you call a man who, under siege, dallies behind to array himself in metal while leaving his men to face their challengers in naught but naked skin?"

Grumbles of terse comment arose from the ranks of Sir Hugh's soot-blackened men, some underscoring their agreement with nods and accusatory glares aimed not at Marmaduke, but at their red-faced liege.

"Do not heed him," Sir Hugh spluttered, his heavily beringed fingers clenching and unclenching on the hilt of his sword. "The fool was ever blessed with a silver tongue and high looks."

Raising his blade, he pointed its tip at Marmaduke. "A pity you've lost the latter," he drawled. "Persist in harassing me and you shall lose your life as well."

The Highlanders snorted in chorus at that and, at the sounds, Sir Hugh's face suffused purple.

He waved his sword at the teeth-chattering group of bare-bottomed men huddled some distance away. "Think you they are my only guards?" he cried. "Sniveling women! They ran at the first sign of trouble. But I have other guards . . . better-skilled ones."

He threw a quick but significant glance at the smoke-clogged gatehouse. "They are yet inside, arming themselves as we speak. You are out-manned in more ways than one, Strongbow."

"Think you?" Before the words were fully past his lips,

Marmaduke arced his steel in a flashing, sideways sweep that knocked the other's blade from his hand.

The sword hit the cobbles with a resounding clatter even as Marmaduke pressed the tip of his own into de la Hogue's mail-covered paunch. "You, sir, could not out-man a lowly earthworm," he said, jerking his head toward the Highlanders and Keith men-at-arms who'd been inside the keep. "Show him your steel, men."

And they did.

Not a blade was raised that didn't gleam red . . . and not from the licking flames raging all around them.

Marmaduke waited for comprehension to dawn on de la Hogue's face before he continued. "Any men not yet amongst us perished in the fire . . . or forfeited their life for a mistaken cause when they rose against yon men as they poured over the ramparts."

Sir Hugh wet his lips. "There are more . . ." He cast a nervous glance toward the cold, windy dark of the nearby lochshore. "—on patrol. They will—"

"James," Marmaduke called over his shoulder, "do you see any of de la Hogue's guard moving about?"

"Nay, sir," James returned after a moment. "I see naught but the starry night and the flames of hell waiting for the bastard."

"*We* came across a patrol," Ross's deep voice came from the sidelines. "But they are no more," the Highlander finished, the glee in his voice earning chortles of a dark sort from the other caterans gathered round him.

"Those sorry souls met their Maker when they tried to keep us from taking a bit o' thatch off the outbuildings," Alec explained.

"All dead?" Marmaduke kept his gaze on Sir Hugh.

"Every last one." That from young Sir Lachlan.

"Lies!" de la Hogue denied, hostility flashing across his face. "They were too many to be felled by a handful."

Marmaduke only arched a brow. "That would depend on

the handful, I'd say. It would seem, good sir, that *you* are out-manned and in more ways than the obvious."

Withdrawing his sword-point from de la Hogue's belly, he used it to gesture to the other's fallen blade. "You'd be wise to commend yourself to God's care, for very shortly you shall face Him," he advised. "Now retrieve your blade and fight nobly so you may leave this world with more honor than you peopled it."

Sir Hugh slid another uneasy glance at the cluster of pathetic, freezing souls who'd made up his guard. It'd begun to snow, and their bared heads were dusted with white, making them appear more like a band of dottering graybeards than an assembly of England's best.

His jaw working in anger, Sir Hugh snatched up his sword . . . and tossed one, last desperate look at his men. "Think you they will stand by and—"

"They will do what is wise and return to their homes," Marmaduke finished for him, his tone deceptively mild. "They'd no doubt fetch a fine ransom, but I believe this land is better served if they take themselves from it this very hour . . . on their knightly honor never to return."

"Have a care," de la Hogue sneered, lifting his blade, "each time you've harped on honor in the past, you've paid a high price."

Controlling his anger as expertly as he wielded steel, Marmaduke advanced on Sir Hugh. He circled him with measured steps, as keenly aware of the snow-and-soot-slicked cobbles beneath his feet as he was of de la Hogue's every move.

Driven by rage, Sir Hugh lunged and stabbed, swinging furiously, his every hacking thrust falling short or blocked until he began shouting his fury with each clumsy, slashing arc.

An eerie silence fell over the watching throng, the baited hush emphasizing the roaring crackle of burning timber.

And always, Marmaduke advanced, pushing his opponent ever farther toward the burning gatehouse.

Sir Hugh shrieked when a shower of sparks and falling, burning debris rained down on him. Cursing, he dragged his free arm over his eyes and raised his blade for a wild, downward strike.

A blind strike, the fury of which would've lopped off the arm of a less-skilled sworder, but Marmaduke avoided the blow with ease and dealt one of his own.

A wide sideways slash, lightning quick, and slicing across the exposed area beneath Sir Hugh's arm, the earl's shrill cry and the shooting spray of bright red blood giving unmistakable voice to the depth of the cut.

"You bastard!" he screeched, grabbing beneath his arm, his sword clattering to the cobbles. His face purple with rage, he flung himself at Marmaduke, his feet slip-sliding on the slick cobbles.

His arms wheeling, he almost righted himself just as a large section of the gatehouse door behind them burst into an inferno of leaping flames, then crashed down in a great plume of sparks . . . directly on top of him.

"'Fore God!" One of Marmaduke's men cried, running forward, the others quick on his heels.

de la Hogue's death screams ringing in his ears, Marmaduke stood frozen as his men beat their hands on his head and shoulders, knocking off the burning bits of wood and sparks before they could catch flame.

"Saints a-mercy!" James dashed the sparks from Marmaduke's eyebrows with the pads of his thumbs.

And when at last they stepped back from him, he did thank the saints.

Once more they'd stood by him.

"It's over," he said, squeezing shut his good eye for a moment.

His breath still burning his lungs, he looked to where de la Hogue lay buried beneath the burning rubble. Only his boots could be seen. Already smoking, they poked out from a mound of splintered and smoldering wood.

"A fitting end for the dastard." Gowan scratched his bearded chin. "A foretaste o' where he's at now."

"And the others?" One of the Keith garrison men nodded to de la Hogue's men, still huddled in a tight knot some distance away. "What do we do with them?"

Marmaduke followed the man's gaze, then heaved a great sigh. Glancing heavenward, he remembered his own zeal and pride when he, too, at their young age had made the mistake of following the wrong man.

After a long moment, he ran a hand through his singed hair and sighed again. "See them home, my friend, see them home," he said, once more, as so often in his life, following his heart rather than prudence.

"Gather what raiments the lot of you can spare them, then escort them to the border," he added, capping his own men's welling disapproval with a stern, warning glance.

Then, before prudence could seize him after all, he gave the guardsman a light shove toward the waiting captives. "Go now," he said. "Off with you, off with them."

"And I say, off with us!" Sir Alec declared as he vaulted into his saddle.

The other Highlanders chorused hearty agreement. As one, they mounted their steeds and reined round, putting the burning pyre of Kinraven swiftly behind them.

Only Marmaduke hesitated.

With a heavy heart and a disturbing tightness in his throat, he watched the young English knights swallow their pride and don whatever articles of clothing the Keith men tossed to them.

Then, before the Keith guardsmen could begin herding them south, Marmaduke turned his back on the ragtag group, on his own long-ago past, and swung up onto his saddle.

"Aye, Alec," he agreed, the moment he caught up with

the Highlanders. "The good Lord willing, it is time to go home."

And not a man who heard him had to guess which home he meant.

⚜

Caterine came awake the instant Leo hopped from her lap and streaked to the door. His mistress forgotten, he plopped onto his rump, his golden-brown head cocked to the side, his floppy ears lifted in rapt attention.

Even from behind, from the cushioned confines of the window embrasure where she sat, Caterine knew his round eyes stared unblinking at the door's heavy oaken panels.

Knew they brimmed with abject adoration.

*Expectancy.*

As did hers, no doubt, for Leo's behavior could only indicate one thing: *he* had returned at last and would soon stride through her door.

Blinking the gritty weariness from her eyes, she strained her ears but heard only the deafening crush of silence. Even the ceaseless pounding of the sea against the rocks below seemed hushed.

Her heart hammering nonetheless, she pushed to her feet and scanned the dimly lit bedchamber. Blue-violet shadows stretched across the rushes, darkening the corners and proving she'd slept long and deep.

Even the wall torches and the hanging cresset lamp had extinguished themselves, leaving only the orange-glowing hearth embers to illuminate the silent chamber.

The interminable night and the endless hours of the day had slipped irrevocably behind her. Vanishing without her notice, whisked away as if by some enchantment during her exhausted slumber.

And something, some great and mysterious secret that had hovered so near as she'd dozed, escaped her as well. A slight frown knitted her forehead as she grasped for whatever it was, and failed.

Conceding defeat, she pressed her hands to the small of her back and stretched. Sleeping in the relatively small area of the narrow window seat, had taken its toll.

Just as the palpable quiet unraveled her calm.

Tilting her head to the side, she listened hard, but again, heard only silence. No familiar footfalls, confident and proud, approached her door. No muffled stirrings sounded from the great hall below.

A sidelong glance at the unshuttered windows as well as the bite of the icy air pouring through them, revealed the reason for the eerie stillness: sometime during her fitful rest, it'd begun to snow.

Whirling curtains of fast-falling snow slanted past the arch-topped windows, and a fair dusting of the white-glistening crystals already mounded along the outer stone ledge.

Then a noise *did* intrude on the silence.

Just the creak of a floorboard, and a distant one from the sound of it, but loud enough to set her pulse racing and persuade Leo to give up his patient vigil.

With a shrill yap of joy, he launched himself at the closed door, his tail wagging, his button nose sniffing at its seam . . . as high up as the limitations of his size allowed.

Trembling, her fingers shaking nearly as furiously as Leo's wagging tail, she looked about for something to do. Anything to occupy herself so, if the approaching footfalls *were* his, he wouldn't immediately see she'd fretted through every minute of his absence.

How fervently she'd prayed for his safe return, *dreamed* of him as she'd dozed.

Vivid dreams of passion and . . . love.

*Love?*

At once she remembered. Everything. And with the realization, she almost burned her fingers on the candle flame she'd been holding to the wicks of the extinguished cresset lamp.

"*Ouch!*" She set down the offending candlestick and thrust the tip of her smarting finger into her mouth just as the door swung wide.

"Ouch?" He stepped inside with his usual lordly grace, pausing only to drop the drawbar in place before bending down to scoop Leo into his arms.

Leo wriggled with glee, squirming wildly as he welcomed Sir Marmaduke with enthusiastic little dog kisses. And all the while he regarded her with a look that could only be called . . . smoldering.

Smoldering in a sensual *and* practical sense, for patches of his hair appeared singed, as did one eyebrow. Setting Leo on the floor, he crossed the room with great strides, the little dog running exuberant circles around him.

He gathered her in his arms, crushing her to him. "It is over," he murmured against her hair, his voice tired but thick with some emotion she hadn't heard before. "Kinraven is no more and Sir Hugh has breathed his last."

Caterine pulled back to look at him, an odd mixture of relief and dread coursing through her. Relief that he'd returned, dread at knowing he'd now see his purpose here fulfilled.

"I thank you," she managed, her gratitude sincere even if the words sounded frightfully hollow.

He shook his head. "Nay, my lady. It is your companion and your sister we must thank," he said, clearly meaning something entirely different from Sir Hugh's demise.

"Those fair ladies and mayhap one handsome devil of a Highland laird," he added, his good eye crinkling in amusement.

Caterine's gaze flickered to his singed hair. "You have been burned," she said, skimming her fingers across his right eyebrow.

He gave her a lopsided smile. "The saints only protect me

from sword cuts. Swords and other sundry arms of evil."
The mirth in his voice assured her he bore no more serious
injury than patches of frizzled hair. "They never promised to
keep me safe from flying embers and sparks."

He quirked his blackened brow at her. "I'd hoped if I
bathed and washed my hair before I came abovestairs, you'd
not notice."

Marmaduke cringed inwardly at the grave understate-
ment.

He'd taken greatest pains to comb his unmarred hair over
the singed patches, had even rubbed some of Linnet's *beauty
treatment* on the crinkled spots, all in the hope of disguising
the damage.

Apparently in vain.

But to his vast relief, a tiny smile curved his lady's lips
and she pushed up on her toes to brush a kiss against his ruined eyebrow. "It doesn't matter, my lord," she said, reaching for his hand.

"Come, and let me give you a proper welcome home,"
she added, leading him to the bed.

And Marmaduke gladly followed.

The morrow would be time enough to tell her it was indeed time to go home.

Home to Balkenzie.

## Chapter Twenty-one

❧

$\mathscr{A}$ GOOD WHILE later, as the dark night wrapped itself around Dunlaidir and the rest of the world slept, Sir Marmaduke tossed in a tangled whirl of satiny bedcoverings and his lady's silken thighs, and . . . dreamed.

Of dark, smoldering passion and throaty, sated sighs.

Of sensual ecstasy, tight and winding, the shattering glory of his lady's release.

The thundering spill of his own.

The lingering bliss of her so sweet upon his lips. Her musky female scent, warm, roused, and fanning the flames inside him, its heady tang flooding his senses with each drawn breath.

He came awake at once . . . and found his wife's sleek, golden heat poised mere inches from his mouth. She straddled him, holding him pinion between her supple thighs, her lush thatch of curls tangled and glistening . . . *saturated*.

Desire, hot and thick as molten steel, shot into his shaft, stretching and swelling him as great waves of hunger and longing swept away all but his pounding need.

"Christ and all his saints!" Blooded lust hammering through his loins, he inhaled deeply of the sleek temptation hovering so near. He touched his tongue to her, swirling its tip over the tiny, swollen nub at the very heart of her passion.

She cried out, collapsing against him, limp and sweet, the whole length of her quivering with the fierce breaking of her swift release.

Smoothing his hands over the satiny warmth of her back, Marmaduke soothed her . . . *loved* her.

"I didn't think you'd ever awaken," she breathed at last, the whispered words thick and ragged. She slid a trembling hand along his muscled shoulder, down his hard-slabbed chest. "I've been . . . touching you for hours."

Marmaduke swallowed . . . thanked the saints he'd awakened, and that her touch, the *love* brimming in her passion-glazed eyes hadn't been a dream.

Raging need consuming him, he pushed up on his elbows and watched her hot gaze caress the hard length of his arousal. Her hand teased across his abdomen, and he willed her to explore *lower,* his heart almost stopping when she plunged her fingers deep into the thicket of dark, springy hair at his groin. He almost spilled when her fingers brushed against his swollen shaft. Near to bursting, his arousal bucked and strained, urgently seeking relief.

A husky groan swelled in his throat and he released it on a ragged breath. "Would you see me run mad?"

"I would pleasure you." She curled her fingers around him, sliding her hand up and down his rigid length.

"You pleasure me my every waking hour," he vowed. "Watching you *breathe* pleasures me."

He caught her to him, kissing her deeply, but she pulled away, straightening her back so the full thrust of her breasts pushed through her streaming, unbound hair.

"You have not yet taken full ease with me," she said, her hand still gripped tight around his shaft, caressing him. "I would give you that release now."

*And she almost did.*

Simply by stating her intent.

His passion surging, raw, wild, and set free at last, he

looked at her, studied her face for any sign of wariness or hesitation . . . and saw none.

Nothing marked her save her beauty and willingness.

Her acceptance and desire to please him.

*That* wonder swirled around him, caressing his very soul. Embracing him as surely as her stroking hands drove him toward the bursting release of all the tight hunger and need roaring through him.

"I shall never let you go," he vowed, the shackles of his doubt finally falling away . . . spinning into the shadows.

Dissolving as if they'd never been.

*And I shall not let you go,* he thought he heard her say, though, in truth, she'd only sighed.

*I want you to stay.*

That, he heard . . . with his heart.

Truly spoken or nay, the words hovered between them, a challenge tossed, but not accepted. And not menacing enough to dim the blazing need raging inside him.

Her golden hair spilling around her in wild abandon, she held his gaze and parted her streaming tresses so the distended tips of her full breasts could peek through.

"I know you enjoy looking at them." Very deliberately, she eased away every last strand of hair until her nipples were fully displayed. "I want this night to be filled with everything that brings *you* pleasure," she said, the over-large rounds of her areolas tightening beautifully beneath his gaze.

Marmaduke clenched his hands, another ragged groan rising deep in his throat.

Still sliding her hand up and down his hard arousal, she began caressing his inner thighs with the other and he caught another delicate whiff of her scent . . . and knew.

His lady was sore aroused.

Sheerest want consumed her, and seeing it near broke his last restraint.

She wanted him.

As fully as he burned for her.

And this time, he would assuage that burning.

He lowered his head to her breast, licked her large, swollen nipples, drew one deeply into his mouth, sucking on her . . . *hard.*

Reaching between her legs, he caressed her, testing her dampness. "Shall I kiss you first?" He gave her the choice, full aware of the pleasure she took in his intimate kisses, intoxicated by his own need to taste her.

"Or shall I stroke you a bit instead?" he probed at her, his skilled fingers already working their magic.

Unable *not* to.

Acute sensual need ripping through him, he slid his fingers into her golden fleece, massaging her, stroking her cleft. Up and down, and up and down . . . luxuriously slow strokes . . . a lanquid gliding along her most tender flesh.

A worshipping of the wetness he found there.

"If you wish me to kiss you, then settle yourself above me so I can lick you until you are ready," he offered, his finger circling, *rubbing,* her most sensitive spot, the tiny nub at the very crux of her dampened curls.

Something—passion?—darkened her eyes and she slipped off him to stretch back against the pillows. "Did you mis-hear me, my lord?" she asked, and parted her thighs, spreading them wide. "I *am* ready. I want you to take me. Fully, and with all of you."

"You are certain?" he had to ask, his doubts and demons not quite ready to clear the field, their insistent voices warning that revulsion would flash across her face the instant he mounted her.

But the desire in her eyes, the rocking of her hips, and her opened arms called louder.

And he capitulated.

"I love you, Caterine," he said, at last moving over her.

"Then have me," she said, reaching for him again.

Not the answer he'd hoped for, but her touch, her fingers

moving so sweetly on his swollen phallus, blinded him to all else.

Wholly besieged, he positioned himself over her, taking his weight on his arms and letting her guide him to her sweetness.

Touching him to her silken cleft, she cupped his cheek with her free hand, traced his scar. "You are a true champion," she said, "and I care deeply for you."

*Care deeply?*

Alarm bells clanged loud in Marmaduke's ears, and a bone-chilling cold iced his heart in the very moment the tip of his shaft slipped inside her.

And then he was lost.

Too consumed by her velvety tightness, the pulsing heat clenching around him, to heed the frost of a poorly turned phrase.

With the last thread of his restraint, he paused, holding himself above her with just the head of his shaft inside her ... waiting only long enough to slide his hand between them to rub at her little nub of pleasure, and thus ease his taking of her.

Verging dangerously on the edge of his own release, he plied the swollen nub with slow, circling strokes ... and *very slowly* began inching his length ever deeper into her silken heat.

Only when her breathing became shallow, little gasps and the rocking of her hips grew frantic, did he draw back and plunge fully inside her, making her his with one smooth, claiming stroke.

The sheer pleasure of possessing her near milked him at first glide. She arched her hips, pressing against him, and he lowered his head to draw one of her nipples into his mouth. He swirled his tongue round and round, *pulled* on the swollen peak as he glided in and out of her with long, languid strokes. And all the while he kept his hand wedged between them, and *rubbed* her.

*No . . . please . . .*

Marmaduke stilled at once, cold dread plunging icy talons deep into his gut, into his pride, but then she moaned . . . a sweet sigh of bliss, and his doubts withdrew.

With another, deeper cry—a throaty, full-passioned one—she dug her fingers into his shoulders, clinging to him, her body trembling and tensing beneath him, her wild abandon thrilling him, and assuring him as nothing else could, that he'd imagined the barely audible protest.

One last taunt thrown at him by his devils.

Ignoring them, he lifted his head to capture her mouth, catching her cries and giving her his, their very breaths melding as he claimed her lips in a deep, slaking kiss, and made her his with his lips and his passion.

Her thighs clenching around him, she drew him closer, the tremors of her release ripping through her in splendid rhythm with the thunderous pull of his own.

And then a brilliant whiteness seized him, a spinning whirlwind of sensual ecstasy so powerful, so intense, he could scarce breathe.

He moaned with the glory of it and even thought he heard her cry his name, but his blood pounded so fiercely in his ears, he couldn't be sure.

So he simply held her . . . and hoped she'd called out his name.

He *knew* she'd found release.

And he'd found the veriest of heavens.

⚜

*Hold her legs wide. . . .*
*Whore.*

The words . . . the taunts and jeers . . . began even before her champion slipped back into the deep sleep she'd pulled him from. They came at her from the shadows, long-suppressed images crashing onto the wildest shores of her heart, haunting her even as the triumph of their tumultuous passion still washed over her.

Ghosts of the past to damn her.

And steal the freedom she'd thought she'd seized at last.

Lying perfectly still, Caterine tried to close her ears to long-faded slurs, the brutal visitations of memories best forgotten. She closed her eyes, hoping to cling to the bliss of being wrapped so protectively, so lovingly, in her champion's arms, but the images followed her.

Cold and relentless, inescapable as the incoming tide, her darkest hour rose to claim her, sneaking into her very bedchamber, stealing round her curtained bed, and even pulling back the bed hangings to leer at her.

An assemblage of jeering apparitions gathered in the predawn gloom to gleefully declare their hold on her. To superimpose their lust-crazed faces over her husband's beloved one, and remind her that the arms now holding her, were *English* arms.

Would always remind her of *their* English arms.

And to assure her they would never leave her.

Never allow her to fully love him.

Not as he deserved to be loved.

And Sir Marmaduke Strongbow deserved to be loved with a full and glad heart. Not one he'd have to share with the shadows and shame of a past she couldn't flee.

As carefully as she could, Caterine pushed up on her elbow to peer down at him, willed herself to see only *his* face and, blessedly, she did.

His face was relaxed and beautiful in sleep, his scar not marring, but highlighting his handsomeness—the shining glory of a truly noble heart.

A champion's heart.

She smoothed her fingers over his hair, her heart welling as her fingertips skimmed over the singed parts . . . another badge of honor, another reason he needed a woman who could love him fully, with all of her heart and not just her passion.

Her own heart wrenching, Caterine slipped from the bed. Deep in an exhausted sleep, he didn't notice her leave. Or mayhap he did, for he rolled onto his side and thrust out an arm, moving his hand over the bed sheets as if he sought her warmth.

*And have you decided, my lady?*

She started, hearing the words as surely as if he stood before her, hands on her shoulders and looking down at her with his special smile.

The rare one that brought out his dimples.

"Have I decided what, my lord?" she whispered into the quiet, her voice soft and tremulous, so tight was the burning constriction in her throat.

"Have I decided what?" she asked again, reaching for him, almost touching her hand to his pitifully singed hair.

*If I am a charmer of women?*

*A spell-caster?*

Her heart heard his query . . . and answered him as well.

*Aye, you are, my dearest.*

And he was . . . in the most wondrous of ways.

For a long moment, she stood gazing at him before she gave him a wistful smile and eased the covers over his shoulders. Fine, wide-set shoulders, powerful and braw, but not quite sturdy enough to carry the weight of the ghosts plaguing her.

Her very worst dragons.

And it was those beasts she had to flee, not him, for their presence in her bedchamber, even in the inky shadows of the corners, proved more than she could bear.

As quickly and quietly as she could, Caterine dressed, eager to escape before the stinging heat at the backs of her eyes could turn to tears.

At the door, she cast one last glance toward her sleeping husband, then wished she hadn't, for the accursed shadows in the corners had shifted . . . their darkness stretching across the room to encompass the bulk of her bed.

Lifting her chin, she turned her back on them and raised the drawbar. "You will not besiege me," she whispered as she opened the door. "Nor will you make me cry."

Squaring her shoulders, she waited for Leo to join her, then, together, they slipped from the room. And all the way down the dimly lit passage, she struggled against her tears.

But she needn't have, for someone else shed them for her.

A darker, more solid shadow than her dragons.

And not nearly as ominous.

Only . . . sad.

Standing vigil in the corner, her cowled robes drawn tight against a cold more chilling than any icy wind to ever lash at Dunlaidir's stout walls, the woman waited patiently until the other shadows faded.

Until their menace moved away from *him*.

And when at last they did, she gave a little sigh he would have credited to the wind, and, wiping the dampness from her cheeks, she, too, faded away.

⚜

*She was gone.*

Sir Marmaduke knew it even before he came fully awake.

Blessed—or ill-wished, depending—with an uncanny knack for simply knowing things at times, this proved an occasion when his gut instinct sent his heart plummeting.

His blood pumping in his veins, not hot and thick as only hours before, but icy cold and thin with dread, he snaked the flat of his palm across the bed sheets . . . and knew true alarm at the cold that met his fingers.

Nary a hand-span of lingering warmth remained of where she'd lain so sweetly beside him.

Of where they'd loved.

And she hadn't simply slipped away to tend certain early morning necessities. His fair lady wife, *his heart,* had vanished in the small hours of the night.

All his doubts and regrets massed together and sat on his heart. A cold and heavy weight even one as hard-muscled as he couldn't shoulder away.

So he frowned.

Scowled up at the heavily carved ceiling of her great four-poster bed and wondered if he *had* dreamed the glories of the night they'd shared.

Had she truly writhed and moaned beneath him?

*Invited* him to take her?

Aye, she had, for the scent of their loving, their spent passion, still clung heavily to the bed sheets, even permeating the very air within the silken confines of the curtained bed.

Aye, they'd loved and with the greatest of passion.

And in the darkest hour of the night, when all the world slept and shadows hid what one didn't want to see.

Like the ravaged face of a man who'd once, in a long-ago life, been amongst the most dashing of men.

Heaving a weary sigh, Marmaduke shoved back the bed coverings and pushed to his feet, prepared, if not eager to face the cold-cast new day.

The saints knew he'd had ample practice in rising above himself in trying times.

Thus steeled, he ignored the frantic thudding of a heart undone, and strode straight into the little ante-room to dress. And the moment he had, he dropped to his knees beside his leather satchel and rummaged for two things: his finely-wrought bronze mirror and Linnet MacKenzie's ragwort *beauty salve.*

The latter seemed to have gone missing so he upended his traveling pouch, letting its contents spill onto the piddle stained pallet he'd called his own in the nights before his lady had allowed him entry to her bed.

Marmaduke at last spied the round earthen jar—his *won-*

*der* treatment. The last of his supply until his return to Kintail, for he'd used the salve with a heavy hand of late, all in the hopes of making himself more appealing.

Not handsome again, for, though a romantic, Marmaduke Strongbow was anything but a fool.

Nay, simply more appealing, though now, this foul and black morn, even *acceptable* would suffice.

Then, before he lost his courage, he pulled the handsome, loop-handled mirror from beneath a mound of recently washed chainsil braies, snatched up the jar of false hope and shattered dreams, and went long-strided to the window embrasure in his lady's bedchamber.

Still scowling, he dropped both items onto one of the windowseats, then yanked open the shutters. A cold, white world greeted him . . . chill and icy, its stinging bite as numbing as the ache settling round his heart.

He stared out at the pewter sea, at the white haze hovering low above its gray swells, and at whirling curtains of snow undulating clear to the horizon. The brooding early morning sky, heavy with pale, dense clouds foretold more of the same.

Time of the essence now, he picked up the mirror and peered hard at his likeness. Thanks to his black frown and his singed hair, a more frightful beast than he'd ever glimpsed in the mirror's depths looked back at him.

A visage so grim, so fierce, he could not blame his lady for slipping from his side.

His mind made up, Marmaduke set down the mirror and retrieved the jar of *beauty treatment*. Closing his fingers around its familiar shape, he clung to his hopes and dreams for just a moment, then sent the little jar sailing through the opened window and into the sea.

Taking grim satisfaction at having freed himself of all illusions, he turned away from the windows.

It was time to find his wife.

# *Chapter Twenty-two*

❖

*L*ATER THAT MORNING, in Dunlaidir's great hall, Rhona plunked a large wooden bowl onto the scarred surface of the high table and, with a flourish, whipped away the bowl's cloth covering.

The Laird's Stone wept.

Utter astonishment washed over Caterine as she watched the impossible.

Rhona could scarce contain her glee. "See you, my lady, I told you the stone cries."

Her amazement too great for her to confront her friend about having lifted the stone from its strongbox, Caterine looked on in awe as crystal-clear beads of moisture appeared on the quartz-speckled Laird's Stone.

The glistening droplets leaked from the stone's very heart to trickle down its rounded sides, swiftly filling its smooth wooden bowl.

The stone wept copiously . . . just as the legend claimed.

A sniffle beside her proved Rhona was on the verge of weeping, too. "James!" she cried, turning to him. "The Laird's Stone is recognizing you."

"Or we're about to see his death," someone in the crowded hall declared. "Last time the stone wept, the old Master passed on."

The jostling and low-voiced murmurs around the high table stilled at once. James, lacking in elation from the onset of the miracle, blanched.

"From what I have heard of the legend, the stone cannot herald his passing before he has been accepted as Master of Dunlaidir," a deep voice said behind Caterine, and her heart tilted.

Sir Marmaduke drew up beside her, something raw-edged and indefinable simmering beneath his calm. "The tears we see are celebratory tears for the valor he's shown of late." He touched his hand to her shoulder, glanced down at her. "Is that not so?"

Caterine nodded, too unsettled by his proximity to give him a more eloquent reply.

Eoghann suffered no such difficulty. A broad smile spreading across his weather-lined face, he snatched an empty drinking mug off the table, filled it with frothy heather ale, then thrust the brimming cup into James's hand. "Lighten your heart, my lord, for the stone is saluting you."

"Come, then, and let me commend you as well," Sir Marmaduke said to James. Stepping away from Caterine, he slid out his sword.

"Oh!" Rhona's hands flew to her cheeks. "He is going to knight you." Joy lit her pretty face and was quickly taken up by the onlookers thronging the dais.

Only Caterine forced her smile, for her skin prickled with an eerie foreboding of the announcement her husband would next make. Clasping cold hands before her, she watched him place a hand on James's shoulder. "Kneel, my friend, and accept the stroke of honor."

Hot color flooded James's cheeks, but he dropped to his knees and bowed his head. A solemn quiet descended over the hall as Sir Marmaduke raised his silver-gleaming blade.

"Be valiant, James of Dunlaidir. Honor your fellow knights. Love God and keep your soul stainless at all times."

His commanding voice rang out as he struck the flat of his steel first to one of James's shoulders, then the other.

"I, Marmaduke Strongbow of Balkenzie, dub thee knight," he finished the brief adubbement. "Now rise, Sir James, and be ever proud."

"I shall, good sir, and I thank you," James gave the proper response, and stood.

Marmaduke sheathed his blade. "Be worthy and always stand tall," he advised, giving James a comradely *thwack* on the arm. "I know you shall."

"Hail Sir James!" a shout rose from the crowd. Similar cries and comment issued from others, respectful if not exuberant.

Leo seemed most pleased of all, dashing away from Caterine to streak circles about the hall, his excited barks leaving no doubt that he, at least, believed something extraordinary had happened.

"I crave your ear, my lady," her champion said the instant he returned to her side, the summons she'd expected, cushioned by a gallant offering of his mailed arm.

Their gazes met and held for a long moment before she slipped her hand through his proffered arm. "You wish to inform me you are leaving?"

He nodded, as she'd known he would, and led her to a fairly quiet corner of the hall. "It is time. I wish to celebrate the Yule at my own hearthside." He placed his hands on her shoulders as he so often did, but a new chill coated his words and his expression, though calm, held no warmth. "I do not care to winter here, my lady."

Caterine took a deep breath. "The winter is already upon us and will worsen by the day."

"More reason to depart with all haste," he said, weighing his words. "The road home may be fraught with some hazard, but my men will be used to worse . . . as am I."

His wife glanced back to the dais end of the hall where James engaged Lachlan and a few of the younger Keith guards in animated conversation. He'd slung an arm around the lady Rhona's waist, clearly holding her in his thrall.

Marmaduke watched them, taking some small comfort in the young lord's newfound pride and grace. But a trace of concern marred his lady's brow, and he smoothed it away with the side of his thumb.

"The older garrison men will flock to him, too," he promised. "Especially after my men and I are gone."

"And Rhona will make him a fine and able consort." The thickness in her voice alarmed him, for he knew instinctively it had little to do with her companion and James.

"A fine and able consort is the wish of all men." He smoothed a tendril of hair back from her face. "A rare and precious bliss."

She paled at that, and the gravity of her demeanor swiftly squashed what hope still flickered in his breast.

"You are my bliss," he said, damning his pride. "Will you deny the pleasure we shared this past night?"

"Nay, I will not." She lifted her chin. "It was bliss."

His hope surging anew, Marmaduke cleared his throat. "Lady, are you man enough to stomach a bit of . . . roughness on the journey?"

*Can you look past my grim visage and love the man beneath?*

Before she could answer, he wrapped his arms around her, drawing her close. He wanted to savor the feel of her soft warmth crushed against him for the twisting in his gut warned it might be the last time he'd hold her.

"I am not going on a journey," she said, and the finality of the words sank his heart. "But I am *woman* enough to tell you, you are better off making the journey without me."

Pulling back, she pressed her fingers against his lips when he made to protest. "You deserve a woman who can love you with a full and open heart. I am not that woman."

Marmaduke released her, let his arms hang at his sides. "I

will ask you once and never again," he said, stamping on his pride one final time. "Will you ride with me?"

"Nay, sir, I will not."

Five simply spoken words.

Utter honesty.

And then she was gone.

Vanished into the milling throng, leaving him alone in the smoke-hazed corner, the shattered remnants of his heart winking at him from a glittering, mocking pile at his feet.

⚜

The next day, in the frozen quiet of near-dawn, Sir Marmaduke and his MacKenzie Highlanders rode through the arched pend of Dunlaidir's gatehouse, putting that once-more great stronghold behind them as they set off on the long journey home to Kintail.

A blustery wind, icy and black, accompanied them and nary a soul who dwelled within Dunlaidir's stout walls hadn't braved the frigid morn to pay their respects.

Scores of chilled, red-nosed well-wishers had waited for them in the bailey, some having stood vigil since before first light. And they tagged along now, on foot or mounted, keeping pace with Marmaduke and his men as their steeds clattered across the precipitous neck of land to the mainland.

His lady rode at his side as well, but only in a parting gesture of respect.

James, Rhona, Black Dugie, and others accompanied her, and even Leo trotted along. The little dog frolicked in the snow, weaving in and out of the legs of those trudging beside them, clearly unaware the slow-moving procession was anything but a gay excursion.

Marmaduke knew and that was enough.

They'd all stay with him until he and his men reached the outskirts of the village. Then they'd return to Dunlaidir . . . and their lives.

As he would, too, and with all speed, for he burned to pass through the village, spur his steed, and return to Balkenzie never to leave again . . . no matter how many pressing requests his liege's sweet lady wife plied him with.

No matter how many pointed stares Duncan MacKenzie aimed his way.

He'd steel himself against them all and remain where he belonged—a wounded beast sheltered deep in his lair, free to lick his wounds in peace.

Squaring his shoulders, he nodded to the villagers lining the road, his heart wrenching at the smiles they wore, the sincerity in their shouted well-wishes.

Peace and prosperity had returned to the region, and if the prattle-mongers were to be believed, the proud new Master of Dunlaidir would soon take a wife.

A fine and good lass, well-loved by all. Able and big-hearted. And if some suspected her of being a mite meddle-some at times, no one really cared.

Aye, the good people of Dunlaidir and its surrounds had ample reason to rejoice.

Only their lady appeared solemn, her expression as grim-cast as his very best field-of-battle stone face.

She rode quietly beside him, taking little heed of the crowd, even ignoring the sleet-laced wind tearing at them in great blasts and buffets.

Her guard only began to slip as they neared the end of the village road and the dark edge of the woods suddenly loomed ahead of them.

But it wasn't toward that boundary that she stared. "Leo!" she cried then, yanking her mount's head around, then plowing straight through the crowd of tag-alongs to spur down a gorse and boulder-studded slope to a tiny loch some distance off the road.

Her little dog and another dashed about on the loch's thin crusting of ice. And even as she barreled near, calling his name, the ice cracked. The second dog leaped to safety, but Leo disappeared beneath the loch's smooth, gray surface.

"Holy Christ!" His own woes forgotten, Marmaduke kicked his horse in the sides and sent the beast hurtling across the frozen ground.

Reaching the lochside before his lady and those chasing after him, he leapt from his saddle, cast away his sword, and dived beneath the icy water.

Caterine reined in only seconds later . . . just as Leo scrambled to safety. Jumping down, she raced to the water's edge. "Oh, Leo!" she cried, relief coursing through her.

Wet, shivering, and not at all contrite-looking, the little dog shook himself, dousing her with a great spray of freezing water. Grabbing him, she thrust him beneath the warm folds of her cloak, then glanced around for her champion.

And the moment she did, cold dread more punishing than the biting winter wind clamped down on her heart, for unlike Leo, Sir Marmaduke hadn't yet left the loch . . . her braw champion was still beneath the water's ice-littered surface.

Panic whirling through her, she pressed a fisted hand against her lips and stared at the place where he'd vanished into the water. Frozen with fear, she willed him to reappear.

But he didn't.

Only his words flew at her . . . borne on the icy wind.

. . . *they only protect me from sword cuts and other-sundry arms of evil* . . .

*They never promised to keep me safe from flying embers and sparks.*

Nor had they vowed to keep him safe from drowning.

Caterine shuddered, sheerest dread churning through her. Fear squeezed her chest in a vise-like grip as she stared in horror at the silent waters of the loch.

His men ran past her and plunged into the frigid water . . . only to surface and re-surface without him, her heart sinking deeper each time they failed.

And through it all, she looked on as if from a great, disbelieving distance.

Young Lachlan clambered out first. Trembling with cold, and dripping wet, he raced at James. Grabbing his arm, he dragged her stepson to the water's edge. "You have the best eyes," he cried. "We can see nothing. The water is too dark. You must look for him."

James blanched. His panicked gaze darted to Caterine and then to the loch, to the men thrashing about in the water.

"Go!" Lachlan shoved him forward, toward the loch.

"I am . . . I cannot . . ." he began, and then, to Caterine's amazement and relief, a look of steely determination settled over his face, and, whipping out his blade, he flung it aside, and plunged into the icy water.

Once, twice, over and over, he re-surfaced, spluttering with the cold, his own fear of water etched sharply onto his face, but each time he broke the surface, he drew a long breath and dived anew.

Then, just as the coldest anguish began to seize her, when she no longer cared if her shoulders shook and tears streamed, a great cheer rose from those gathered on the lochshore.

James had re-appeared, and this time, he'd found him. He held one arm slung about her champion's neck, but his head lolled at an odd angle and—as the crowd's ominous hush indicated—it appeared the saints had abandoned Sir Marmaduke Strongbow at last.

They'd turned their winged backs on him in his darkest hour, and left him to drown in a pitifully small, ice-crusted loch on the wrong side of Scotland.

⚜

"Lady, you must rest."

Caterine ignored her friend's admonishment—the hundredth such plea Rhona had made to her that morning alone—and continued to massage her champion's fingers.

A desperate attempt to force her own warmth into his hands as they rested, cold and limp between hers.

A vain endeavor, but one she'd repeated with grim patience ever since his men had carried his unconscious form above-stairs and gently settled him in her bed.

"Lady, please," Rhona wheedled again.

Caterine shot her friend a look of sharp reproach. "Later," she said. "I shall rest after I am certain he will not . . . after I am sure he will . . ." She trailed off, another hot rush of tears scalding the backs of her eyes, another searing lump swelling her throat.

"For truth!" Rhona yanked back the bed hangings to peer at Sir Marmaduke's still form. "He *sleeps* . . . he is not dead and everyone beneath this roof has assured you he is nowise near dying."

Caterine pressed her lips together.

Rhona blew out a breath. "If James hadn't been able to find him, and free his cloak from the underwater branch it'd caught on, mayhap he would have died," she owned, "but he did not and isn't going to."

Placing her husband's hands atop the covers, Caterine gave Rhona another arch look, intending to send her away with some peppered comment, but the retort froze on her tongue when she noted the dark shadows under her friend's eyes.

Rhona's face appeared as haunted as she knew hers must be.

"For one so confident, you appear mightily distressed," she said, hoping Rhona would deny it.

Not disappointing her, Rhona seized her hand and pulled her off the three-legged stool where she'd spent the last two days—and nights—tending her husband as he'd drifted in and out of a fitful rest.

A deep slumber the leech insisted he needed.

"It serves no purpose for you to exhaust yourself, bending over him like an angel of death," Rhona chided, dragging her from the chamber. "I vow he senses your fretting and cannot rest fully for worrying about *you*."

Holding her arm in an iron grip, Rhona herded her into the dimly lit passage outside her bedchamber. "Were you not so blinded by guilt or whate'er fool notions are plaguing you, you'd see by his steady breathing and fine color that he will be up and about before long."

Caterine wasn't so certain.

No one had directly told her, but from snippets of conversation floating about, and dire murmurings she suspected she wasn't meant to hear, she knew the Laird's Stone still cried.

And some amongst the castlefolk believed its doing so meant her husband's death, and not James's acceptance as new lord.

But she let Rhona usher her along the corridor, and guide her down the winding turnpike stair to the hall. She was exhausted, and hadn't eaten in days.

Sensing her capitulation, Rhona flashed her a smile.

"It will do you good to spend some time below," she crooned. "Everyone is praising James for rescuing your husband." Pausing, she lowered her voice to a conspiratorial whisper. "My lady, I vow this means they have accepted him."

Caterine nodded, too weary to speak.

"After you've eaten, you can rest in my . . . in *James's* chamber, sleep away the whole of the day if you desire," Rhona rushed on.

*Desire.*

The word brought another fresh rush of tears to Caterine's eyes, but she blinked them away and walked with Rhona to the high table, the turmoil whirling inside her keeping her from paying too much heed to the notable absence of the Highlanders.

"All will be well," Rhona promised as she pulled back Caterine's chair, "you will see, my lady."

But all wasn't well.

And the overly loud hush that greeted her when, hours later, she finally returned to her bedchamber, only underscored how very *un*-well things were.

Her great four-poster loomed accusingly quiet, its mound of silk and furred coverings flung back to reveal . . . nothing.

Her champion was gone.

About the same time, in the frost-gleaming uplands a goodly distance from Dunlaidir, Sir Marmaduke Strongbow drew rein so violently, his horse near reared up on his hind legs.

The beast *did* neigh shrill protest.

Marmamduke's *men* laughed.

Great choking bouts of glee.

The purest of know-it-all vaunting.

"Holy saints, but that took you a while," Ross egged him, already turning his mount.

The others followed suit, all swiveling their heads toward him. And not a one looked shocked.

Or even surprised.

Truth tell, they all grinned.

Well warned, Marmaduke kneed his horse before they could bedevil him anew. Digging in his spurs, he urged his mount into a thundering gallop and tore off in the direction whence they'd come, his horse's drumming hooves mirroring the hammering rhythm of his heart.

"By the Rood!" Sir Ross called out a short while later, pointing. "Looks like you charmed that one, but good."

Following Ross's outstretched arm, Marmaduke spotted

her—a lone female figure, bent low over her mount's neck, and swiftly closing the distance between them.

" 'Fore God," he breathed, his heart near to bursting, scalding heat blurring the vision in his good eye.

Leaving his men to stare after him, he spurred across the winter-stubbled ground, meeting her halfway. He swung down from his saddle before she'd even reined in. His men reached them just moments later, their wild shouts and hoots bringing a furious blush to his lady's face.

The little dog peeking at him from a leather pouch affixed to the back of her saddle, made his heart pound even faster. Leo's presence had to be a good sign.

Striving for a semblance of dignity—lest indeed she'd only come to tender her farewell—Marmaduke ran a shaking hand over his singed, wind-blown hair and strode up to her.

"Lady," he addressed her, damning himself for a sentimental fool when a tear leaked from the corner of his good eye. "What brings you this way?" he managed, his throat almost too thick for him to speak. "Did you come to bid us farewell?"

Sliding down from her horse's back, she came toward him, the smile on her face *almost* banishing his demons. "And you, my lord," she countered, an odd tightness to her voice, "are you not riding in the wrong direction?"

Something in her damp-shimmering eyes, and the catch in her throat, allowed Marmaduke's hope to soar.

Even his men's bawdy jaunting ceased as, gathering near, the leering bastards followed the exchange with unabashed nosiness. Wheeling around, Marmaduke swept them with his most wicked glare, but they only laughed.

To a man, they threw back their ugly heads and guffawed to the heavens.

And at the sound, the utter *joy* behind it—their undeniable belief that she'd chased after them for the one reason Marmaduke himself was too afraid to believe she had—

something deep inside him cracked open and his demons, every last one of them, took flight.

With a great flutter of black wings and all the doubts that had e'er plagued him, the whole host of them were caught up by a sudden, peculiarly strong gust of cold, wintry air and whisked away.

*Be gone and harry him no more,* the wind seemed to call after them, but then the chill gusts slackened and his men's chortles and hoots began to sound suspiciously wet and sloppy.

When Gowan blew his nose and dashed a meaty hand across his bearded face, Marmaduke knew he'd won the day . . . and his lady.

For his men were rough-hewn but no fools.

Drawing back his broad shoulders in best champion fashion, Marmaduke turned to his wife. "I was not riding in the wrong direction, I was returning for you," he admitted. "I told you I always do."

"And I was coming to join you on the journey," she gave back.

"It is a rough journey, my lady."

"A lady who loves never fears a spot or two of roughness, my lord."

Marmaduke blinked. "What are you saying, Caterine?"

She smiled. "Do you not know?"

"I would hear the words," he said, his heart swelling, already flooding with joy.

She glanced at his men, then apparently uncaring that they gawked, she gave a little cry and flung her arms around his neck, clung to him.

"I love you," she said, her words strong and loud enough for his ear-straining friends to catch every privy word. "I believe I have since the day you rode into Dunlaidir and kissed my hand so gallantly," she confessed, running her fingers through his less-than-perfect hair, pressing so sweetly against him, he feared he'd melt at her feet.

He'd consigned himself to never seeing her again, never again feeling her supple curves crushed against him.

The soft fullness of her breasts, and something very small and decidedly . . . hard.

Hard, and jabbing ever deeper into his own chest, the closer she pressed herself to him.

Pulling back, he glanced down, the hot tears he'd tried so valiantly to hide, spilling free the instant he spied the small, hard object.

*His ruby signet ring.*

The heirloom hung about her neck on the fine, golden chain he'd meant to give her for it.

The ring she'd claimed she wouldn't wear until she was able to give him her heart.

*His* heart slammed against his ribs and his throat went completely, utterly tight. His men, for once, had the decency to turn away.

His lady, her own cheeks wet with tears, spoke her mind. "I found the chain in the ante-room, half-buried in the floor rushes," she explained, cradling his face as she did so, pushing up on her toes to kiss his scar.

Smiling through her tears, she turned her blue gaze on him—the open gaze of a woman who never lied. "And, yes, my lord, I wear the ring because you hold my heart," she told him. "Fully, irrevocably, for all our days and beyond."

And Sir Marmaduke believed her.

But later, after they'd all re-mounted and resumed their homeward journey, traveling once more in the *right* direction, he cast a grateful glance heavenward and thanked the saints all the same.

*Epilogue*

# BALKENZIE CASTLE,
# WESTERN HIGHLANDS AT YULETIDE

✦

A FIERCE WINTER gale tore across Loch Duich, whipping its slate-gray surface and lashing at Balkenzie's stout walls with a ferocity seldom seen even in these wilder reaches of the Highlands.

But the night's fury couldn't dampen Sir Marmaduke's high spirits as he surveyed the castle's gaily festooned great hall. Many revelers had come to celebrate Yule.

And welcome him back to Kintail.

*Home.*

His own, and his sweet lady wife's.

At last.

Nay, the black night raging outside Balkenzie's snug walls did not bother him a whit, nor steal a teensy bit of the joy from his heart.

And neither would the dark-frowning countenance of his best friend and liege. Pointedly ignoring the festivities, the handsome Highland laird glowered at the Yule log rather than joining Marmaduke and the other carousers in spreading good cheer.

"How much longer do you think she will need?" he asked Marmaduke for the hundredth time.

Lounging against the edge of a nearby trestle table, Marmaduke shrugged. "However long the good Lord wills she must, I'd wager," he said, and lifted his cup of spiced wine in calm salute.

His cheek earned him another sizzling glower. "You can wipe that smirk off your ugly face," Duncan MacKenzie groused. "I have every right to be concerned."

"No one doubts your rights, my friend," Marmaduke conceded, sipping his hippocras, "though I sometimes wonder how the lady tolerates your bluster."

He slid an eloquent glance at the empty four-poster bed still crowding the middle of his hall. "I do commend you for allowing her to birth the child above-stairs rather than . . . *there*."

To Marmaduke's amazement, his old friend had the decency to look contrite.

But only for a moment.

"She disregarded all good sense and persisted in traipsing about despite her frail state," he argued. "I had no choice but to keep her where she could be watched over at all times."

"And her old nurse and my own good wife watch over her now, so you've no cause to stare holes of wrath into the hapless Yule log."

Duncan's brows snapped together. "I am not *staring* at anything, you great lout, I am straining my ears for the cry of a bairn."

He made a great sweeping gesture with his arm. "A near impossibility with all the buffoonery going on around us."

"It *is* Yule," Marmaduke reminded him, filling a mug with the warmed, spiced wine and handing it to Duncan. "Even one of your sour disposition should be able to tolerate a bit of revelry."

"And a *bit* would have been enough." Duncan snatched the hippocras and downed it in one great gulp. "Ne'er have I seen a more gaudy display."

As if to prove his point, he strode to the nearest table and, with two fingers, lifted a long, winding garland of twined holly and ivy a few inches above the tabletop. "Whoever heard of draping every table in the hall with greenery? Is it not enough to hang the stuff on the walls? And all the mistletoe—"

"A blessed custom and one that pleases me. And my wife. I vow we would be taking full advantage of the tradition this very minute were she not needed above-stairs," Marmaduke said, glancing at a window alcove across the hall where young Lachlan laid bold siege to his lady love beneath one of the hanging clusters of pale-berried mistletoe.

Closer still, beneath yet another of the kissing boughs, Sir Gowan took sore advantage of a toothsome serving wench, the buxom maid's squeals of delight underscoring *her* joy in the holiday tradition.

And even young Robbie, just eleven, and Duncan's son from his first marriage, had been seen earlier using that very clump of mistletoe to sneak chaste kisses from the bonniest young lassies.

The image bringing a smile to Marmaduke's heart, he refilled his friend's wine cup. "Surely one so lusty-natured as yourself would not deny others a spot of amorous adventure?"

"I do not care how many lasses are ravished this night, how loud the trumpets are blasted, how much roast boar is imbibed, how often every blithering fool in your hall shouts 'Wassail!' . . . nor if they all dance so hard they fall flat on their faces," Duncan declared, folding his arms when Marmaduke tried to offer him the hippocras.

"Tsk, tsk." Marmaduke shrugged and set down the wine cup. "And I'd thought your fair lady wife had mellowed your temper."

"And it is that fair lady who is on my mind, you dolt!" Running a hand through his dark hair, Duncan glanced for the hundredth time at the vaulted ceiling. "She is up there, mind you, and—"

A babe's cry, faint but undeniable, sounded from above, fine and lusty enough to be heard over the din, its portent instantly wiping the dark from Duncan MacKenzie's handsome face.

A grin spreading across his own face, Marmaduke drew back his hand to give his friend a hearty clap on the shoulder, but his liege was already sprinting across the hall toward the turnpike stair. Marmaduke ran after him, and, together, they took the winding stairs three at a time.

The bairn's wails grew louder the closer they came to Marmaduke's and Caterine's bedchamber, and the door burst open as they neared. "You have a fine bairn, my lord," Caterine beamed upon seeing the MacKenzie laird. She held wide the door. "A wee lassie with your dark hair and deep blue eyes."

"A maid?" Duncan's eyes widened, his heart laid bare and smiling. "A wee lassie?"

Caterine nodded, dashing away a tear. "And such a fine one. She is perfect . . . *beautiful.*"

But Duncan had already pushed past her into the room.

"She looks just like him," she said, smiling up at Marmaduke, her eyes brimming with unshed tears. "Raven-black hair, and lots of it, a sweet rosebud mouth, and the deepest blue eyes."

Pausing, she swiped the back of her hand across her cheek. "Ne'er have I seen a more lovely babe."

His good eye watering as fiercely, Sir Marmaduke slung an arm around her and led her into the bedchamber, purposely hanging back in the shadows to allow his liege a few private moments with his wife and their new child.

As private as one could be with old Elspeth, the midwife, bustling about, hovering over the bed and clucking like a mother hen.

Worse, every fool from below now gathered in the corridor, straining their necks to catch a glimpse of the MacKenzies' new bairn . . . *some* cheeky souls even pressing straight into the birthing room.

"I told you, you had naught to fret about, laddie," Fergus

declared, his scrawny chest puffed with pride. The cheekiest of the lot, he marched right up to the bed.

Leaning forward, the aged seneschal examined the child for an indecently long moment, then turned to the knot of merrymakers crowding the door. "A bonnier lass ne'er graced these hills," he pronounced, and, with even more cheek, smoothed his gnarled hand down the side of the mother's face. "As we knew she'd be, eh, lass?"

"... *as we knew*..." Duncan mimicked beneath his breath, but even he couldn't sound very fierce with a quavering voice and over-bright eyes.

Joining them at the bedside, Caterine smiled down at her sister as Elspeth smoothed a damp, scented cloth over Linnet's brow.

Pale and shadow-eyed, Linnet MacKenzie lay back against the pillows, her new daughter cradled in her arms.

"She is beautiful." Caterine touched a finger to the babe's teensy, pink hand, her heart swelling.

"And *you* are beautiful, my sister. I am so pleased to have you back." Linnet reached for her hand. "You are not angry at me for ... for ..."

"For sending my champion?" Caterine glanced at him, her free hand straying to the large ruby ring hanging about her neck. "Nay, my dear, I only wish you had sent him sooner."

Linnet nodded, clearly pleased. "And neither because I—"

"Because you kept a sweet secret from me?" Caterine reached out to stroke the black down crowning the babe's head. "Nay, that, too, I understand," she said, sending another sidelong look at her love, her heart swelling when he wrapped an arm around her, drew her close.

"And you were right ... had I known, I would have come at once, and then a certain champion would ne'er have known if I'd truly given him my heart."

"And have you?" Linnet asked. "Do you love him as—"

breaking off, she shot a quick glance at her own husband, "as we'd hoped you would?"

"Nay." Caterine shook her head. "I love him more. Much more," she assured her sister, and anyone else who cared to hear.

An audible sigh, or mayhap just the restless night wind, issued from somewhere close by, but when Caterine glanced around she didn't see anyone standing near enough to have made the sound.

Rubbing at the odd tingling along her nape, she gave her sister a tremulous smile. "You've created a fine and beautiful new life."

"*You* have a fine, new life, too," Linnet said, her voice thick with emotion.

"Aye, I do," Caterine agreed, reaching for her husband's hand. "A new and *good* life."

"And what shall we call *this* new life?" Duncan wanted to know, his dark blue eyes gleaming a tad too bright. He touched his wife's cheek. "Have you thought of a name for our fair daughter?"

"What do you think of calling her Arabella?" Caterine suggested, the name popping into her mind just then, but somehow seeming so very right.

Her husband glanced sharply at her, but when she squeezed his hand and smiled, the look he gave her warmed her clear to her toes.

"Well?" Caterine glanced back at her sister, at the wee girl-child.

"Aye, Arabella is a fine name," Linnet agreed, glancing at her husband. "And you, my lord?"

Duncan peered hard at Sir Marmaduke, then, apparently satisfied by what he saw, a bold smile spread across his handsome face. "Arabella, it shall be."

And the moment the words were spoken, somewhere in the dark of the cold, blustery night, a raven-haired angel smiled.

# About the Author

❖

SUE-ELLEN WELFONDER is dedicated medievalist of Scottish descent who spent fifteen years living abroad, and still makes annual research trips to Great Britain. She is an active member of Romance Writers of America and her own clan, the MacFie Society of North America. Her first novel, *Devil in a Kilt*, was one of *Romantic Times's* Top Picks. Sue-Ellen Welfonder is married and lives with her husband, Manfred, and their Jack Russell Terrier, Em, in Florida. Visit Sue-Ellen's website at *www.welfonder.com*.

# THE EDITOR'S DIARY

*Dear Reader,*

Prepare to enter a world of romance that will offer you a lifetime of pleasure reading . . . Welcome to Warner Forever! This January, Warner Books launches an exciting new imprint that spotlights a variety of passionate, powerful tales of romantic fiction. From historical to contemporary, dramatic to lighthearted, these sensual stories are sure to captivate your imagination . . . and your heart. Two exhilarating romance novels will be published each month—that's *double* your pleasure. So indulge yourself and pick up these delightful treats today!

*New York Times* bestseller **Carly Phillips**, author of the "Reading with Ripa" book club selection THE BACHELOR (7/01), returns with **THE PLAYBOY**. This enticing novel is the second in a series of lighthearted romances about the irresistible Chandler brothers and their matchmaking mother who will go to almost any lengths—even feign illness—to get her sons married so she can have grandchildren. In **THE PLAYBOY**, Rick Chandler is a sexy cop and ladies man who falls for a real-life runaway bride. Will the town's most popular playboy discover his own "happily ever after" with a woman who is through with weddings?

Hold onto your kilts, because **Sue-Ellen Welfonder** has penned another sensual tale set in medieval Scotland! **BRIDE OF THE BEAST** is a sumptuous feast full of valiant knights and fiesty ladies. Lady Caterine Keith of Dunlaidir Castle is a young widow beset by contenders for her hand due to her valuable estate. Another husband is the last thing she wants. What she needs is a champion, or so she is told. Her matchmaking sister sends for Sir Marmaduke Strongbow, a loyal Highlander with a face scarred by battle. Being a man of honor, Marmaduke agrees to protect Caterine from unwanted suitors—but only if she will marry him. She warily agrees in order to keep her land . . . yet she soon realizes she may lose her heart to her warrior husband.

Be sure to enter our Warner Forever contest and also visit us at www.warnerforever.com. Enjoy!

With warmest wishes,

Karen Kosztolnyik, Senior Editor

P.S. Be sure to watch for Valentine-worthy heroes coming to your local bookstores next month! In February, Warner Forever will deliver a first-time father in **Joan Wolf's** wonderful women's fiction novel **HIGH MEADOW**. And keep an eye out for the Zorro-like bandit hero in **Amanda Scott's THE SECRET CLAN: HIGHLAND BRIDE**.

# Official Contest Rules

### PURCHASING DOES NOT IMPROVE YOUR CHANCES OF WINNING